Dragon Prophecy

Novels by Melanie Nilles
Published by Mundania Press

The Legend of the White Dragon Series

Dragon Prophecy
Dragon Legends
Dragon Legacy
Dragon Child

Dragon Prophecy

Legend of the White Dragon Book One

Melanie Nilles

Mundania Press

Dragon Prophecy Copyright © 2008 by Melanie Nilles

All rights reserved under the International and Pan-American Copyright Conventions. No part of this book may be reproduced or transmitted in any form or by any means, electronic or mechanical including photocopying, recording, or by any information storage and retrieval system, without permission in writing from the publisher.

The scanning, uploading and distribution of this book via the Internet or via any other means without the permission of the publisher is illegal, and punishable by law. Please purchase only authorized electronic editions, and do not participate in or encourage the electronic piracy of copyrighted materials. Your support of the author's rights is appreciated.

This is a work of fiction. Names, characters, places and incidents either are the product of the author's imagination or are used fictitiously, and any resemblance to any actual persons, living or dead, events, or locales is entirely coincidental.

A Mundania Press Production
Mundania Press LLC
6470A Glenway Avenue, #109
Cincinnati, Ohio 45211-5222

To order additional copies of this book, contact:
books@mundania.com
www.mundania.com

Cover Art © 2008 by SkyeWolf
SkyeWolf Images (http://www.skyewolfimages.com)
Interior Map design by Brian Sevart, used with permission.
Book Design, Production, and Layout by Daniel J. Reitz, Sr.
Marketing and Promotion by Bob Sanders
Edited by Kent R. Miller

Trade Paperback ISBN: 978-1-59426-206-7
eBook ISBN: 978-1-59426-207-4

First Edition • April 2008

Production by Mundania Press LLC
Printed in the United States of America
10 9 8 7 6 5 4 3 2 1

Warning: The unauthorized reproduction or distribution of this copyrighted work is illegal. Criminal copyright infringement, including infringement without monetary gain, is investigated by the FBI and is punishable by up to 5 years in federal prison and a fine of $250,000.

Dedication

I would like to thank everyone who made this book a reality, from those who supported my writing obsession all the way through each step of the process to the staff of Mundania Press. Most of all, I wish to thank you, the readers.

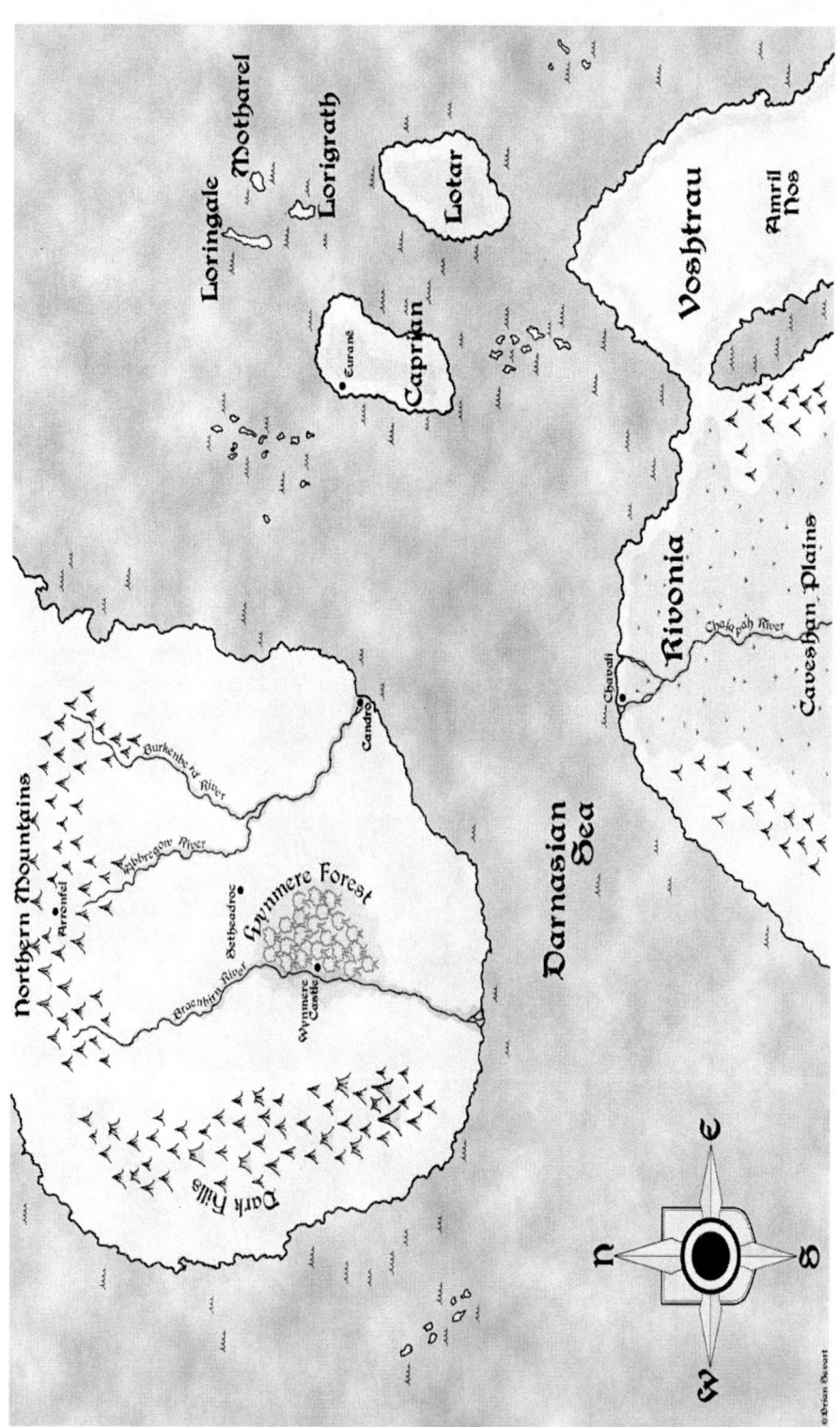

Prelude

15.3 pc 936

I write this for those who find my translations. My waiting is almost done. This curse of immortality will soon be lifted. My soul will find rest from my crimes.

After aiding the death of the white dragon while under Lusiradrol's spell, I have made my penance. I have done as has been requested of me to guide the outcome.

Our Mother, Jahronen, bid me stay with Tyrkam, a foolish mortal, but one who has intentions on Gilthiel's power. He shall not have it.

It will come his way, quite sure, though not as he expects. He has made plans for the chosen one. I am loathe to watch in silence his cruel methods, but perhaps it will work for the best. Her fate awaits in the forest of Wynmere, which lies at the doorstep of this castle. The spirit of Gilthiel knows this.

I have left the tale of the white dragon and my righted wrongs in the library of Cavatar for all to read. All children of the Light must understand the past to be ready for the war that will come. In the tome I have described events from three thousand years ago as I saw them. My memories have not faded; my guilt would not allow it.

I pray you take my words to heart.

Though the events in the stories of the Second Race are said to be mere legends and myths, they are real.

I wish you to understand. You must believe, or our world, our hope is lost.

You must be ready to battle the darkness, if you have not already. Not warlords like Tyrkam, but true darkness. The corruption of the Darklord when he touched the hearts of the Second Race is in every one of us.

I would tell you his name, this Lord of Darkness, that you might recognize him; but to do so would hasten his return to power much sooner than we can afford. He cannot remember who he is since he tried to flee his destruction once, in another time. To hear his true name would break the enchantment that binds him. We are not ready for that. Every passing moment gives us a greater chance of final victory.

But that is another story, one I included in the tome in the library. (Though not his name)

Know that I have bound his vile Red Clan under a spell of sleep. There they will remain as long as the secret is never uttered. I have also spent my years battling his demons. Some I destroyed, others my power could only subdue into a dormancy that will not last. I did these things to provide some time to coordinate all forces of Light.

The descendants of the Ancients must also join the fight as their ancestors did, were created to do. The Majera know this. The First Race guard their secrets and themselves, but you must find them. There is one I know among you, perhaps a second, who can guide you to them.

Yes, two, a rare treasure. Look to the flame.

I can say no more, as I have sworn to them, to the lovers who came to Ayrule and died in their quest for answers.

With Gilthiel's return, no more shadows will fall.

Walk in the Light.

Makleor, last of the Great Maji

Prologue
12.6 pc 936

(twelfth day of the sixth moon cycle in the 936th year post confederation of the kingdom of Cavatar)

In the dark of the quiet chamber, the steady drip of moisture echoed. The cool of night rose from the cut stones to fill the void of the high-walled ruins.

Lusiradrol stood in the center of a circle of candles, her hair blacker than ebony and her hooded mantle a close match. Her thoughts had created the darkness surrounding her, twisted by thousands of years trapped within a human body. The emptiness of her soul absorbed all light, leaving only the stain of her malevolence.

In equal spacing in a circle on the floor, nine candles flickered. Their light barely penetrated the gloom.

Within the circle, Lusiradrol had placed nine dragon scales, the only ones she could gather in her quest. The scales represented nine of more than a hundred of her clan that had lived at one time. Dragon scales were almost eternal, but long ago men of the First Race had gathered all they could find and ground them up as ingredients in the metal of their weapons. The shadow of magic within them imbued the objects with far greater durability and strength than they would otherwise possess. Luckily, with the First Race went those secrets.

In the void of her dragon heart, Lusiradrol resented the humans for all they had done. Her Red Clan should have wiped the world clean when they had the chance.

If only the others had not stopped them.

She desired revenge.

Tonight she would have it. The alignment of stars in the heavens fell into place, after thousands of years of waiting for this moment.

The time had come. A faint smile gleamed on black-red lips. *Soon, we will be reunited. Soon, my clan.*

She began the spell to resurrect the proud and terrifying red dragons. Focusing her mind on the always twisting, almost tangible threads of magic, she sat within her candle formation and spoke her intents. Using the scales, she could focus on those individuals who had shed them.

Not long after the white dragon had cursed her to human form, she realized that hearing her intentions spoken aided the process of working complex magic. As a dragon, she had no voice, except through the mindspeech of magic.

"Come to me," she whispered. Her voice sliced through the silence, sending the air quaking as if she spoke in a tongue of thunder. "Send your spirits to me. Rise from your graves. Together we will destroy this world and take our vengeance upon the others and their magi. Come forth and live again!"

A sudden gust of wind whipped the candle flames. Two blew out while the others beat angrily at the air.

Lusiradrol smiled in satisfaction. *I await your arrival,* she thought and concentrated deeper. The magic swirled about her in a torrent, chasing the target of her desires. She reached out for the spirits of her dead clan—

Emptiness.

Her smile dropped into a frown. What was this?

Again, she called for the spirits. If they were dead, they should have arrived ready for the next turn of magic—giving them solid bodies.

"Come to me!"

When the wind of touching the spirit realm died down, she rose from her place. *Why do you not come when summoned?*

Only one answer satisfied her question—they were not dead as she had thought.

"Where are you? What trickery has he pulled?"

In the battle between her clan and the other clans, she had realized at the last moment the true power held by the old mage, an *athêrred rî Lûmea* of great power. In his hand he carried a staff topped by dragon's tooth, which held a special crystal. Though she knew not what mastery he possessed, the confidence of his manner and the intensity of magic that emanated from him had warned her. She had fled before he completed his spell.

"What less than deception can hide you from me?"

Anger simmered inside her. Had the wizard not destroyed her clan as she had thought? Had she waited an eternity for this night when she might have revived her clan sooner?

How could this be? *How dare he do this to me!*

Lusiradrol looked up. In the old ruins, the ceiling had rotted away and many of the stones had toppled, but she had made a few repairs. She made it her home, a place of solitude that satisfied her cold heart and her human needs.

"Damn them all!" Her words crackled in the confines of the ruins. If the other dragon clans had not killed her clan as she thought three thousand years ago, where were they?

She would find them, starting with the old man who had stolen her clan and hidden the secret of the white dragon.

When she found her clan, she would have her revenge, on the white dragon and the mage. None of her enemies would realize the prophecy of the white dragon's return.

Chapter 1
5.2 pc 937

Calli's eyes fixed on the veiled princess as they had the last two days since leaving the security of Setheadroc, which surrounded the palace, their home. Deep in her heart she mourned. Istaria Isolder had been betrothed to the son of the governor of Cavatar's far northeastern province.

As her friend and personal attendant, Calli swore not to leave her side. However, she mourned for the palace. She could never hope for Phelan Isolder to see her as more than her younger sister's servant.

Istaria's cheek twitched in her sleep, disturbing her veil.

A faint tingling touched Calli.

Istaria's white hair almost glowed with an inner light. The princess twitched again and whimpered.

Calli leaned forward with the intent of calming her friend, but decided against it and sat back. She had never seen beneath the veil. The queen forbade it, and her friend had never offered to show her face. After eleven years, Calli had learned to ignore her curiosity out of respect for her friend.

Nevertheless, the sensation of someone watching her increased with the faint halo around Istaria. It had to be Calli's imagination.

Istaria jerked and sat up, the halo fading. Sniffles from beneath the veil tugged at Calli's pity. The princess put a hand to her throat and straightened on her carriage seat.

Calli leaned forward from her seat and touched her friend on the leg. Although she could only imagine what Istaria had dreamt, she had a fair idea. Istaria didn't want to marry. "I'm here."

Istaria lifted her hands to her face beneath the veil and leaned forward, her shoulders trembling.

Upset by her friend's distress, Calli made the quick jump to Istaria's side and pulled her close. Istaria pressed her veiled face to Calli's chest, her body shaking with sobs.

Istaria had been a friend since their childhoods. When Calli's father,

Kaillen, had been awarded the status of training the palace guard, he moved Calli and her mother with him to Setheadroc. While her mother had taken over cooking duties, Calli, at only six years old, had been made the personal attendant of the then five-year old princess. Though Calli knew nothing of her mistress's affliction nor had seen her without the veil, she had accepted Istaria without question. A childhood of friendship bonded them as sisters of uncommon spirit, a relationship stronger than blood.

"It'll be alright. I'll not leave you." She paused. "I hear Derek is a good man."

Silent tears choked her friend. In all the time they had known each other, Istaria had never said a word. The queen, Damaera Isolder, had said she lost her voice a year before Calli arrived. Istaria had hidden in the cavern on the palace grounds sealed since that incident, which had also turned her hair white.

Despite her words to soothe Istaria, a foreboding sense darkened around them. Never in her life had Calli experienced such a chilling sensation.

Istaria sat up and reached beneath her veil to wipe her eyes.

"Something's not right."

Calli pulled back the curtain from the nearest window and peered out. The squeaks and groans of the carriage drowned out any animal noises. Nevertheless, the trees around them with their branches barren of all but new leaf buds hid a secret.

The soldiers accompanying them rode in closer. They must have sensed it too.

Calli turned back to Istaria, but her friend had pulled the nearest curtain aside.

Before she could warn the princess to sit back, something thumped into the side of the carriage. Outside, a horse squealed.

"Milady!" Calli pulled Istaria to the floor of the carriage, which lurched to a stop.

A second later, an arrow ripped through the curtain of the opposite window and implanted itself in the door. A man chastised another for risking their reward.

Istaria gripped Calli tight.

The fighter inside Calli desired to join the soldiers, whose voices rose to a raucous level with the shouts and hollers of their attackers. Her father had been the best warrior, perhaps because he had come from another culture with better martial training. He had trained her in his ways, until his death three years ago.

Unfortunately, he had taught her to use the moves for defense, not attack.

Calli would do best to stay with Istaria and protect her.

The clash of metal on metal rose outside.

Calli risked lifting her head and peeked out the window.

A group of bandits engaged the royal guard. However, rather than bumbling through their attack, they coordinated. Already half the soldiers lay dead or mortally wounded.

"Driver!" Calli sat up and pounded her fist on the side of the carriage.

No response.

One of the gruff men outside fixed his eyes on her.

Calli ducked back inside and hunched with the princess.

Istaria clutched to Calli's gown.

"I'll not leave you."

The door of the carriage burst open, and the gray light of a spring day poured in.

The man standing in the open door leered at them. "What have we here?"

Before he could enter, he slammed against the carriage and fell to the ground. One of the guards gave them a look and closed the door.

Calli swallowed her relief and took a deep breath to calm her heart.

The fighting subsided, but by the voices outside, she feared they had lost.

When the door opened, a man with the cunning look of a warrior in his eyes grinned. "My ladies," he said with exaggerated politeness.

Calli scowled, realizing the reason for the satisfaction in his grin. "You'll not have us."

"Pardon me, girl, but you're not the one I want."

The cool of his voice sparked her temper. Calli peeled Istaria's hands off her.

The brute watched her closely and leaned in towards them.

Calli kicked at his hairy face with all the force she could amid the fabric of her dress.

It gave her only a moment, not long enough. He snarled and grabbed her.

Calli fought with him, intent on keeping him from touching her friend. However, in the confines of the carriage interior, she had no room to maneuver.

When he slammed her against the side of the carriage, her head rang. Spots danced in her vision and the distant sound of voices jumbled into darkness.

Chapter 2
5.2 pc 937

The torches flickering about the chamber lit up the map on the wall. Eerie shadows crept across the painted skin like armies marching across the land.

A stake jutted out of the center of the largest section on the map. It stabbed the word "Cavatar" at its core.

To the west lied the second largest, labeled "Hadeon," formed by Tyrkam's conquests.

Tyrkam stared hard at the map; his dark eyes fixed on scorching the kingdom to the east with his gaze. He clenched his fists and clamped his jaw.

He had sent a group of his best men away from battle to carry out a mission of high importance; a mission he expected them to accomplish. The rest of his men gathered deep inside Cavatar for the moment he had prepared for many years. This year would see the end of Cavatar and his rise to power over the entire continent of Ayrule.

He hoped the young princess would satisfy the legend and open the magic of the white dragon to him, but that would come after Setheadroc Palace fell to his siege. Rumors of her purity hidden by the veil had reached him. While others feared what lay hidden, he hoped to use it to his advantage. By the end of summer he would know whether his decision to capture her and keep her out of the fighting gave him what he desired.

The magic of the white dragon would make him immortal and all-powerful. The world would bow to him. Sovereign Farolkavin of Rivonia would have no power before him.

The idea wove its appeal through his thoughts, and a thin smile touched his lips.

It retreated at the advance of a sudden coldness slithering down his spine. He straightened and clamped his jaw on the anger before it spewed forth. "Lusiradrol."

Tyrkam turned to face her.

The woman's black-red lips curled up seductively. She leaned against the long table, one leg crossed over the other beneath the fabric of her gown. No mortal alive would have guessed her true origins, although many perceived her as one of the demons of the Darklord of ancient times.

Dark eyes fixed on him. "You disappoint me, Tyrkam." She chastised him in a clear, haunting voice.

Tyrkam crossed his arms, muscles tight with the struggle to control his simmering temper, and his fear.

"Come now." Lusiradrol glided away from the table with a faint rustle of her dress. "Surely your army can defeat Cavatar. Or do they lack the heart to fight?"

She traced the lines of his steeled arms with her black-tipped fingernails. "Surely you've not forgotten our bargain."

Tyrkam narrowed his eyes. The sooner she left, the better off he would be. "I've done my part. What of you? Of no aid have you been but to feast off the hardship of my men."

"Your part? *My* part?" Her voice radiated innocence as she traced a line to his cheek. A rueful smile gleamed from her lips.

Tyrkam refused to acknowledge her. She had toyed with him for the last time.

Danger flickered in her eyes.

"My part," she repeated. "This is my thanks? I've no less than handed these lands to you on a platter. So little time you've had to gain all this, yet still no rewards are you to appreciate. Have you no thanks for my gifts?"

Lusiradrol let out a forlorn sigh. "If that is what you wish, I'll leave now; not to return."

Tyrkam relaxed and eased out the breath he held. Perhaps breaking their pact would prove less risky than he had expected. She gave no hint whether she deceived him or played with him. His lips twitched with a question, but he held his tongue.

"But first—" Her voice carried an undercurrent of menace. "You dare try to conquer me than remain content to serve me! You think me a fool? I know you seek his magic for yourself."

Lusiradrol's eyes glowed red with a menacing power. With deceptive strength on such a delicate frame, she clutched his neck, choking him. From deep in her throat, she growled. "Do not defy me, Lord Tyrkam! With a thought, I'd reduce your army to ash. You *will* find my clan."

Fighting the spots blurring his vision, Tyrkam gasped for air and tried to pry her fingers loose. An evil, mocking laugh echoed somewhere in the growing distance and darkening surroundings. "Poor Tyrkam." The chiding melted into a sinister snarl. "You should never try to deceive a dragon."

"Evil creature!" Old but powerful, the voice cut through the fog closing on his mind. The distraction granted Tyrkam a few breaths and clearer vision as she loosened her grip.

Lusiradrol turned to the disturbance and hissed.

Tyrkam blinked away the spots and looked to the source of the voice. A hooded figure entered the room, leaning on a tall staff. A dragon carved from dragon's tooth topped his staff, clinging to a clear crystal.

Makleor.

"Leave him!" Makleor reached her threshold and Lusiradrol retreated, snarling at his advance. "Be gone, Lusiradrol!" His voice thundered in the chamber.

She turned to Tyrkam. "I'll not forget your betrayal." In a swirl of fire, the sorceress vanished from the room. The evil of her being lingered, coating the air with a chilling threat long after her departure.

Tyrkam rubbed his throat and turned back to his study of the map without a word. As she wished, she might do, though he doubted she would destroy him.

Not so. Manipulation and subterfuge were more her style, a weapon he had long since learned from her; a weapon he carried with as much skill. The ancient evil she proclaimed herself would not defeat him, and she knew it. Though she had come to him offering power in exchange for his men finding her lost dragon clan, no single victory had been of her influence. He would do better without her.

"Absolute power destroys its bearer."

The words grated on Tyrkam's patience. The tap of a staff on stone announced the wizard's movements.

"Heed your loose tongue, Makleor, or it will hang by the noose with your head."

Makleor's hand went to his throat. "A head that I'm most fond. Perhaps another to try yet?"

"Speak sense or be gone!" Tyrkam stepped to the nearest window to watch the dawn awakening of his castle. He neither liked the wizard nor hated him, but he proved useful. Without Makleor, he had no hope of capturing the power of the white dragon.

More important, he needed the old man to restrain the power of Lusiradrol. He realized she feared Makleor when he first saw the two face to face.

Neither wished to tell him why.

"Sense?" Makleor smirked. "Good sense? Or perhaps reason you ask?"

Tyrkam clamped his jaw on the rage boiling within him. He crossed his arms and watched from the corners of his eyes.

"No, no, no." The wizard chuckled and stopped beside him. "No sense." Makleor studied the wooden stake in the map. "Wisdom, but no sense, but neither wisdom for fools."

Growling, Tyrkam turned his head. The old man had better start talking plain or he would not see the next day.

"No." Makleor traced his finger along a line on the map from the castle within Cavatar's territory, toward Tyrkam's castle. "Hmm..." He shook his head and hobbled to the window. The awakening sun peeked over the distant hills. "Today you think about the princess. Is this not true?"

The old man annoyed Tyrkam by reminding him often that he, Makleor, had suggested abducting the princess and bringing her to Wynmere. This close to bringing his goals to life, Tyrkam could afford no mistakes. Cavatar would soon crumble and he would claim the heart of the white dragon and the magic within it. Nothing could stop him but ignorance.

He was not ignorant.

Nor was he stupid. He would not seek the red dragons that had nearly destroyed the world and mankind thousands of years ago. The legends spoke of black earth and skies of fire. Only the other dragon clans had been able to stop them, along with the magi of that time. He doubted they would feel as generous a second time around.

With one hand, Tyrkam reached into the collar of his tunic. His bare fingertips scratched at his neck for the chain and the amulet hanging on its length. When he found the round edges of the palm-sized carving, he pulled it out to examine in the dawn's rays.

The silver, flying dragon spat flame from its mouth. Its eye glittered with the sapphire set on the head of a body curved into an "S" with wings unfolded from its back. An ancient symbol of cooperation between humans and dragons, its legend claimed that the fires of the white dragon had forged it. It allowed Tyrkam to resist the magic Lusiradrol tried to use on him.

Makleor backed away. "Beware the power of such craft. Not anyone can touch the magic of the white dragon."

Tyrkam whirled in anger. "You've said enough! No more words from you! Be gone, old man." He had familiarized himself with the necessities of claiming the mystical powers; the wizard's warnings were neither needed nor wanted.

The Flying Dragon would protect him from Lusiradrol's magic; although she had proven she could do as much harm without it. Lusiradrol knew it too.

Damn her!

Makleor stared out the window next to him, silent for a change. A brief smile flashed across Tyrkam's lips. He tucked the amulet into his tunic and left the old man alone.

He had an alliance to build. Graelyn Cathmor had thrown him a peace offering he could not refuse. The baron had promised his cooperation in the final defeat of Cavatar.

~ ~

When the warlord had gone, Makleor limped to the window to watch the activity outside. A satisfied smile curved beneath the long beard.

He knew the prophecies and legends. He knew the limitless powers of the white dragon. He knew too well how greed for that power would carry a man to claim it.

Tyrkam sought to make it his. He never stopped to consider the consequences of his actions, nor that the spirit of Gilthiel guarded that power. The spirit would never allow any ordinary person to claim it. The magic of the white dragon was not to be stirred by men, for any reason. It would choose its time.

That time had come. It had claimed Istaria Isolder. Soon she would be within reach of those who could best guide her to fulfill the prophecy.

Makleor's core burned with the certainty of the approaching moment when they would all praise the resurrected dragon.

He had waited more than three thousand years, time passed as his punishment. He had watched the world reshape itself and fall as men tried to prove their superiority and failed.

The corruption of the Darklord ran deep in the Second Race, and the descendants of the Ancients grew fewer in each generation. Now the ages of men had come full circle. He was ready.

Every day he had spent in patient anticipation, praying for the moment of his release from the threads of time holding him to life. Had he not himself sought the powers of the white dragon, the centuries would have followed a different course.

Like a puppet, life followed prophecy. When it was written that they would fear the dragon's power, it was also written that he would be awakened within another. Many a greedy lord and general had searched the texts over the centuries for clues and watched for signs of the dragon's resting place. Just as many had failed.

Until recently.

A year ago, Makleor had guided Tyrkam to a reference that sparked his interest. Buried within hidden caverns not far from the forest of Wynmere was the amulet of the Flying Dragon. Next to it, etched by the claw of a dragon, was a rock with the single greatest clue to the mystery—a map. Immediately, Tyrkan had pinpointed Setheadroc Palace, unaware that the mage who cast spells to the advantage of his army knew the exact location already.

The name of the city had been a clue that Tyrkam overlooked. In the language of the First Race, it was known as *senthir rī afdroc*, the hill of the dragon, since they knew of the resting place of the white dragon's body. The men of the Second Race abbreviated the name to Setheadroc when they drove out the original inhabitants who guarded the hill. Over time the legend was forgotten but the hill remained important in their minds and became the Place of Kings.

Makleor had been there in the end. He, the last child of Tahronen, whose mistake had set the cycle in motion.

He had lived the last three millennia with the knowledge that he had led the warrior to slay the benevolent dragon because of the spell the jealous Lusiradrol had cast.

For his crime, he had been cursed with immortality. He could not die until the chosen one came to release him from the spell. Death crept up his bones, thrilling his soul in anticipation of eternal rest.

He feared only one threat—that Lusiradrol would discover the truth about her clan, the red wyverns. Though magic could not kill a dragon, it could entrap it. When she escaped the battle in which she believed her clan destroyed, he—with the help of the other dragons—cast a sleeping spell on all but her. For almost four thousand years her clan slept in a secret vault guarded by an order of vigilant and deadly guards known as the Sh'lahmar. No creature passed the threshold without facing death.

Led by one of the three Majera, the Sh'lahmar swore to absolute secrecy and enshrouded the vault with magic.

However, as long as the terrible clan lived, the risk remained. No one dared slay all in their sleep for fear they would awaken. They had wrought destruction and terror upon men long ago. Only the dragons, the First Race, and the *m'athêrred rî Lûmea* had the power to defeat the abominations of the Darklord, which included the Red Clan. The Majera would not interfere; their purpose was to face the Darklord when the time came.

When Lusiradrol discovered the truth and awoke her clan to follow her, their curse would cast the world in a darkness from which it could not escape.

The white dragon had promised his return to prepare mortals for the next war. When that day came, he, Makleor, would find rest.

Chapter 3
6.2 pc 937

Calli woke up to the sound of voices and a crackling fire. When she tried to move, her head throbbed. A chill made her shiver, which brought more pounding in her head. She tried to move but the pain made her groan.

"Easy, milady."

She opened her eyes to dark, blurry images. "Where am I?" At the hoarseness of her voice, she made an effort to clear it.

"Yeh had a bit of a hit."

Calli blinked and rubbed her eyes. When she opened them, she recognized the smudged face as one of the younger guards who had accompanied them. From his chest shone the royal crest, a rearing white horse with five stars arched over it. Immediately, her thoughts jumped to Istaria.

"Where is she? Where's the princess?"

He dropped his eyes a moment and shook his head.

Despite the pain in her head, Calli sat up. "We have to follow them. We cannot leave her—"

"They're long gone."

"But—" She winced at the throbbing in her head.

The man leaned forward and pressed her back to the hard ground. "We can do nothing. Come the morn, we'll return to Setheadroc."

"No! We have to find her! I'll not leave her." The grief poured out through her tears. She had failed to save her best friend.

Calli pinched her eyes shut and struggled against the overflow of emotions. "Istaria." When she had lost her father, the princess had been there for her. Now, she had lost her best friend. The pain of the losses compounded.

Nevertheless, Calli fought the tears. She sniffed away the grief in a struggle that left a lump in her throat.

"Rest now. You'll have to ride back if you wish to hurry."

The four shadowed faces watched her from the fire. They had started out with over twenty guards. How had this happened?

Calli tossed and turned throughout the night, but the pain in her head subsided as long as she remained laying on the hard ground. The soldiers had stripped the carriage and what belongings remained for material to keep them warm. They had taken turns through the night watching, but no more raiders attacked.

Who would have wanted the princess?

Calli could think of one person who might find her a valuable asset in this time of war. Tyrkam could use her as leverage against the king and queen. Calli could think of no other reason for him to take Istaria.

But if anyone dared defile her, Calli swore she would avenge her friend.

She should have been able to protect her.

She had failed.

That pain stung worse than the throbbing in her head.

Calli nibbled at her food when the soldiers offered her something from their supplies.

They said little to her or to each other about the incident. Instead, they saddled horses for each of them, and her. The one whose face she had awakened to last night offered a hand up.

Already dirty and undignified in her unkempt state, Calli ignored his hands and mounted as any of them. She had ridden her father's horse many times, against her mother's wishes.

The young soldier's surprise curved into a sheepish grin as she gathered the reins of the bay.

The soldier said nothing and mounted his horse.

They rode hard that day to reach Setheadroc after sunset. Travel went much faster without the carriage and the rests they had allowed in setting out on the long journey to Marmath.

At the closed city gates, the guards in the towers on either side questioned them.

The guards around her answered their questions with short tempers. Hers mirrored what she heard in their voices and the grumbles under their breaths.

The gate guards finally opened the gates. Calli kicked her mount forward. The horse raced through the city streets, past darkened shops and houses to the palace gates.

She reined the horse to a clattering stop on the stones before the arched gateway with its elaborate guard towers on either side.

"Let me pass!"

"We let no one pass after sunset!"

"For the love of Goddess, Lester!" Calli knew all their names. And they knew her, and the wrath of her temper, although she imagined they found it more amusing than threatening.

"Lady Calli?"

"Yes!"

"But, you left—" His words cut off and he called to someone behind him, "Open the gates! Let them pass! Let them pass!"

A commotion rose behind the tall wooden doors. Chains clinked and wheels ground. The outer doors swung open to an arched passage and a set of inner doors that also opened.

Calli rushed through.

The quiet courtyard came alive with the clamor of familiar voices. She ignored them and rode to the elaborate structure of the palace with its three levels of windows and balconies. The horse skidded to a halt. She jumped from the saddle and landed on shaky legs. It had been too long since she straddled a horse for any length of time.

The tromp of steps rushed toward her. Calli regained her strength after a few seconds. Holding the hem of her dress out of her way, she rushed up the steps to the front doors.

Even at night, two men stood guard. One of them reached forward and pushed one of the two doors ajar for her.

The Grand Hall stood full of guests. Minstrels played what seemed to her to be a mournful melody. It threatened to pull tears from her eyes at the news she bore. She had to find the queen and king and tell them before her grief overtook her sense of purpose.

She searched the faces around her, ignoring the grimaces directed at her. She knew she looked pitiful. Had they endured what she had, they would fare no better.

When she saw no sign of the queen, Calli caught the arm of one of the serving maids.

"Gretchen, tell me where I can find Lady Damaera."

The girl looked up the stairway to the upper level with its columns overlooking the Grand Hall. "Her quarters, I believe."

"Thanks." Calli jogged through the crowds and flew up the steps.

At the top, her steps pattered through the corridor, past the Grand Hall, through two more sections of the palace, and into the royal quarters. There, she slowed her feet and leaned against one of the wide, round columns of the upper balcony while she caught her breath.

The thick columns started at the lower floor to support the balcony and continued up to the ceiling.

The hall beyond rose high to a glass dome through which the moon shone. Moonlight spilled down onto the shallow pool in the reading hall below, which reflected it around in shimmering streaks.

Istaria loved sitting by the pool, Calli remembered. Her favorite time had always been the full moon. If it shined right, the pale light reflected from the water up to the walls and ceiling. Candles worked too, but the effect was muted. The two of them would dip their fingers into the still water to send ripples of light around the hall.

Calli shook the thought away. It twisted the knife of failure in her heart. After she told the queen, she would find a quiet place to mourn and rest.

She rushed past Istaria's empty room to the tall doors at the end of the corridor. The dark lacquered wooden doors towered high and met at a point. The figures of a man and woman holding hands along a sunlit path loomed above her at the entrance. The guards at either side looked her way.

When Samuel's eyes met hers from beneath his gleaming helm, he gave a nod.

Calli pushed the doors aside.

"Calli!"

She blushed at her rudeness and bowed her head a moment before rushing up to the lady. Damaera stood still while her servant finished tying her golden hair back.

Calli stopped before the queen, her eyes dropped. "Beggin' your pardon, milady, but I must speak with you."

When the girl finished her hair, Damaera waved her out.

Calli waited for the girl to leave, watching until the door closed. "Forgive me, highness, but I bear ill news."

"What is it?"

Calli looked up at the queen's face, unable to say the unthinkable.

"Why are you back? What happened?"

The horror that grew on Damaera's face told Calli the queen understood.

Damaera looked aside, her eyes fixing on nothing but what horrors only she saw. "The king must know." Her voice, though strong, uttered the words barely above a whisper.

"The king must do more than know. He must send his army!"

Watery blue eyes met Calli's, Damaera's face a mixture of emotions. "I fear any touch on Istaria," the queen said. "An unclean spirit must not spoil her innocence."

❧❦

Lost in her tears, Calli pressed against Istaria's heavy door. It opened with a faint creak. Never had she cried as much as that evening. Neither she nor the queen had joined the festivities, but held each other until the king had come. The guards had told him. When he took Damaera into his arms, Calli left.

She had been left alone, her emotions catching up to her unbidden. At least in her friend's room, she found some solace.

In the glimmer of night from the window across the room, she found the familiar lines of the canopy and tied back curtains of the bed. Those velvet curtains hid the princess while she slept. The queen had forbidden anyone from seeing her face.

With a sigh, Calli scanned the far distance where the starry sky met the rolling hills. Istaria was gone. Calli prayed she was not mistreated, but she doubted the men could not resist using her to their pleasure. The thought sickened her into sobs.

Her memories of their lives growing up almost as sisters flashed by in succession.

She had been the last to see Istaria. She had failed to stop them.

Chapter 4
15.2 pc 937

After nine days of mourning the loss of her friend, Calli had to escape from the crowded grand hall and residential areas. The stable had become her lonely refuge.

She sat in the straw of one of the empty stalls with thoughts of how best to end her suffering. She could not restrain the quiver of her lips with tears threatening to spill.

She should have been able to protect her friend. Ever since the abduction she had considered a million times what she should have done. The only outcome had been blame. Had she continued her father's teachings, she could have better served the princess and protected her properly.

The king had sent out a small group, but they returned with no news. Since then, no others had been sent.

She would not accept defeat. She had to search for the princess. How? What horrors lay in wait along the road between here and Tyrkam's castle?

Calli shuddered. She had to go; no one else dared. What had she retained of her father's teachings? He had trained her with battle skills, but she had not practiced since his death. Surely she was no match for even a modest swordsman, not to mention she knew how to handle few other weapons.

A faint rolling thunder reached her, the thunder of running hooves. An army rode towards the stables.

With unfocused eyes, Calli rose to her feet and shuffled to the door. A distraction from her regrets might help her.

From the shadows of the stable doorway, she made out the clump of men and horses. The banners and trumpet announced their arrival. The yard ignited with calls of Phelan's return.

The mention of his name made her heart pound against her chest. She retreated deeper into the shadows of the stable and focused her eyes on the figure that burst into the courtyard. The symbol of the land spread over his purple cloak trimmed with gold. The mail hood had fallen off his head, exposing a shag of brown-gold hair she recognized.

She swallowed her regrets and fixed her eyes on the prince as he managed to keep Baron under tight control. The dapple gray stallion pranced beneath him.

Phelan's entrance brought a faint smile to her lips. The prince of Cavatar returned, but his diplomatic errands had increased and stolen him from his home far too often.

And from her sight.

Wiping her eyes with her fingers, Calli sniffed away her tears and returned to her corner. With luck, he would fail to notice her absence from the ritual gathering that formed for his return. Her heart forbade her from seeing him any time soon. He could not know of her failure. None of them could, but Phelan would most certainly ask the questions that would lead to the revelation spewing from her lips.

⚘

At the terrace of the main entrance, Phelan reined in Baron and swung out of the saddle. He looked up with a smile at the elaborate stonework of Cavatar's and Rivonia's finest artisans.

How glorious was his home! His heart had yearned to behold her magnificence once more.

At some points he had doubted he would. Graelyn Cathmor had put up quite a protest to Lord Almont's support. Phelan wondered if the old baron had plans of his own.

He took a deep breath and pushed the thoughts from his mind. The troubles could wait until later. Right now, he wanted only to enjoy the warmth and peace of his home.

The whole palace radiated the wealth of the land he would inherit. With the sturdiness of a mountain, each stone had been laid as several large buildings with the main hall and dining halls in one, the residence for nobility connected to that and servants quarters opposite, the living area for the guards, bakehouse and pantry, and more all encompassed in a sturdy shield wall. The magnificent scope of the palace reflected the wealth of the land. The beauty of Setheadroc never withered, never faded. Nor did the loveliness within.

Without looking to see if anyone came, Phelan called, "Jamison!"

The boy skidded to a halt, surprising him by his swiftness. Other stable hands also rushed to take the reins from the dismounting soldiers.

The lanky Jamison stood at attention with Baron's reins in his hands. "M'lord!"

"See that Baron gets all the hay he wants. We've traveled far and he's rather thin. And give him a thorough grooming." Phelan patted the sweaty, dappled neck. The horse had saved his life a few times. Not the usual heavy type the warriors preferred, but a lighter muscled and slightly smaller animal they often ridiculed at first impression.

Baron's speed blew them away; he had outrun all the highwaymen and rogues who tried to rob them. Phelan had treasured every moment since the colt took his first breath from the mare that had been a gift. He felt a connection with Baron that no other horse could replace, a special bond that could not be broken.

"Aye, your grace!" Jamison said and led the horse away.

With his friend cared for, Phelan jumped the steps two at a time. His three best soldiers accompanied him, slower in climbing the few steps than he had in his twenty-one year old exuberance. They also wore more mail than his simple, hooded piece. He despised the full raiment of armor, which restricted his movements. The Rivon, like others he had observed in his travels, succeeded without plate and mail by being lighter and quicker.

His eagerness to tell the king of his successful negotiations lifted each step higher. All had gone as well as they had hoped. Cavatar would have her support for an offensive against Hadeon.

Once again, he had accomplished the goals of the king, yet he tired of the travel that kept him from his home. Many arcs of the sun had passed with his mind tossing around the notion that they had kept him away from the heat of battle for a purpose.

Putting the thoughts to rest, Phelan strode past the servants who stepped aside. They bowed their heads, but he paid them no mind and continued through the corridors of the palace. At that time of day, he knew where he would find his family and other important individuals.

He proved himself correct. Voices murmured through the corridor as he neared the dining hall. He entered the open door, silencing all circles of conversation.

From the head table, Damaera's expression froze for an instant. "Phelan!" A hint of relief hung on the surprise in her voice. It dropped to reveal itself in a smile that warmed her delicate features.

He passed the long tables of guests, ignoring their curious stares and stopped before the head table where the king and queen sat. He bowed before his parents and frowned upon sight of the empty seat next to the queen.

"You were successful?" the king asked, wiping his mouth with a cloth. "Almont accepted the offer?"

Putting the absence of his sister aside for the moment, Phelan turned to his father. "Doncran shall provide their support."

A spark lit in his confidence at the king's smile. Damaera watched her husband with suspicion frosting her gaze. Isolder glanced once at her, avoiding her critical glare, and looked back to Phelan. "And what of my other request?"

Phelan dropped his eyes for a moment and inhaled. He had hated negotiating for this portion. Neither the queen nor he had approved, yet the king had insisted on ensuring a solid treaty.

In the middle of the meal, however, was not the time to regurgitate their previous argument. Visitors watched.

The king expected encouraging news. "With reservation the lord of Doncran has agreed." He met the eyes of his father, squaring his shoulders under the scrutiny. Never could he hide his disdain for his father's arrangements, nor could he hide the fire of challenge rising in him against the king's authority.

Phelan glanced at the queen for support, but she gazed back with accusing eyes and sat away from her full plate. Her expression softened to something regretful. He might have sworn a shimmer of a tear glinted from her fair cheek.

King Isolder nodded. "Very good."

He bit his bottom lip a moment before looking up again. "But for one piece... No matter. We'll speak later of this. Leave us. Conduct what business you must while we finish our meal."

Phelan bowed. "Yes, my lord."

He spun on his heel, his cape waving out behind him in a flourish as he marched out. Indeed he had other business, particularly seeking out the elusive beauty who haunted the palace.

Chapter 5
26.2 PC 937

They traveled for days, more days than Istaria had expected.

Thain and his group took Istaria deeper and deeper into Hadeon's borders. She realized that little hope remained of escaping from her fate, unless she was willing to use the magic that she feared.

Thain's repugnant body caged her in the saddle. The filth and grime of their travels clung to her. He had allowed her no chance to cleanse herself. She hated the stench of her own body. She longed for a bath and clean clothes, to change from the tattered and mud-stained dress, to reclaim her dignity.

She stared at the road ahead. Her eyes blurred with silent tears.

Almost a full moon cycle must have passed. Had no one been sent to rescue her? She might have saved herself, but for the unfamiliar territory and her fear of the untrained magic flowing wildly within her. At least the men had not exercised the horrors she had overheard from the generals visiting the court.

Istaria yawned, her eyelids creeping down. The steady swaying of the horse rocked her to sleep.

Later in the night, she awoke to the splashing of water. They crossed a stream. With all the noise of the horse's steps, she could have sworn an army accompanied them.

When they rode into a clearing, she gasped at the shadows moving with them. From behind her veil, she made out countless others on horseback in the shadows of their torches and the full moon. The small group had multiplied several times.

They rode on through the night. Dawn crept its lighter hues up the eastern sky behind them. The fires of torches lit up a castle of immense proportions before them. The fortress ranged high above.

The mass of riders halted outside the gates. "Hail, there!" the lead soldier's husky voice bellowed.

"Who comes?" asked a guard from one of the towers above.

From behind her, Thain's middle expanded with his breath. Every movement he made disgusted her. "I return with a prize for his lordship. I have fulfilled his instructions."

"What name have you?"

"He is the warrior Thain!" The lead soldier's tone scolded the men above.

They waited for the guard to respond. When he replied to them, his voice hinted of a modest level of respect. "He awaits you."

The heavy wooden gate parted for them and the portcullis ground open. The army surrounding them formed precise rows before and behind. From inside, a buzzing inquiry hushed into silence. The clop of hooves rang through the quiet but failed to cut the fix of awe that overtook the small crowd of servants.

Istaria held her head aloft with pride, despite her destitution. The soldiers took her to the steps climbing to the main entrance.

At the base of those steps, Thain stopped his horse and swung off. He reached for her.

Istaria clung to the horse. She twined her fingers in its mane further up on its neck than the bare place she had grabbed many times throughout the journey. Nevertheless, he managed to drag her off and stand her on her feet. Clumps of coarse, black horsehair stuck out between her fists.

"Come now, *girl*."

Offended, she balked at his insulting form of address. However, it gave her no surprise. The days of interminable riding and enduring his presence next to her had taught her that he cared little. She had come to expect such insults from the men.

Thain grabbed her bound wrists and dragged her forward.

Istaria gasped.

The others snickered and whispered behind them. Two guards jumped ahead and pushed the heavy doors open. The groan of objections from the hinges echoed from within.

Despite her struggles, Thain led her into the dim hall. Torches lit the faces of the group of three who stood on the raised section at the far end of the hall.

When the doors slammed shut behind her, Istaria caught her breath with a start. They had sealed her within the gloom of this place that made Setheadroc Palace look like a city of gold.

In sharp contrast, this place could have been the legendary lair of the Darklord. Her steps echoed in the emptiness lit by half the candelabra lining the hall. The brightest place lay ahead, where several torches encircled the raised dais on which the throne sat.

A nagging shadow within her darkened her confidence as overheard conversations about her father's enemy whispered from memories. All the reports of scouts and the battle-hardened generals had mentioned the ruthlessness of Tyrkam's men and described the warlord as a demon in human skin, a warrior of no virtue. Thain's treatment of her had been proof of the truth in rumors.

She had hoped from the security of the palace that in all her life she would never encounter the man.

The aloof man who stood foremost of the group looking down on them could be none other. His broad shoulders and stern gaze commanded obedience. Contrary to what she expected, he had dark-toned skin and charcoal black hair, similar to that of the Rivon emissary, Lord Faramus. A broad, muscular chest stuck up in brute arrogance, unlike the slender and graceful Rivon visitors she had met at Setheadroc.

The boy standing behind him had the same darker complexion and powerful build. Both stood out from the pale Ayrulean guards standing near the side entrance.

Thain shoved her toward the dais where the trio's feet stood at the level of her knees. She stumbled but kept her balance, dropping her eyes from the face of her doom. What would he do with her? She risked a glance up.

Tyrkam's scowl fixed on the man beside her. "Pay your respects, Thain! One so delicate and of noble blood deserves a degree of care. Unbind her hands."

Istaria looked from one to the other, curious about the strange accent in Tyrkam's voice and this small act of mercy. He was the same as Lord Faramus. Had he come from Rivonia? How had he come to power here?

"Yes, m'lord." Thain fought with the tightened leather he had strapped on her wrists to keep her from escaping. He jerked on it, pulling her off balance.

"You are untouched, my lady?"

Istaria looked up at that dark-complexioned face and shuddered at what he meant.

Thain yanked and pulled her attention with her balance.

"Gently, Thain."

He pulled less on her and loosened the leather strap, which had bound her wrists for most of their trip.

"Did any man defile this woman?"

"None, m'lord."

"I should hope not." The cold threat in Tyrkam's voice chilled her. "Is this true, my lady?"

She gave a nod.

"Very good."

When Thain finally moved away, she touched the red, raw skin of her wrists. It stung. She grabbed below her right wrist, the sorest one, and held it next to her.

Tyrkam stepped down to her level. "My apologies, your grace, for his behavior."

Istaria scowled behind her veil. When he reached for her hand, she pulled away.

However, he was quick. He caught her hand and pulled it close, to examine her wrists. The roughness of his hands belittled the respect of his words. In spite of his initial show of concern, he could not hide his insincerity.

"Had I known of this, I would have sent another." He released her hand and studied her, his eyes on her veil. "He is ill prepared in the manners of royalty. But here you are. We may not undo what we have done."

Tyrkam's face relaxed and he looked up at the young man not much older than Istaria.

She followed his gaze in curiosity. The younger man's face showed only a hint of the years of carnage displayed in the harsh lines of Tyrkam's. But his dark eyes bore a ferocity that sent a chill down her spine.

Istaria looked away from them both.

"The servants will attend to your sores." Tyrkam raised a hand. "And your...condition."

Istaria glowered beneath her veil. Condition! Let him think that.

A girl who could not have been older than her rushed up from nowhere, her steps pattering across the hall. Not even Calli at her worst presented as rugged an appearance. This girl looked as if she had worked nonstop all night and the day before. Her dress was patched and dirty; her brown hair tangled and her face grim.

The girl stopped next to Istaria, bowed her head, and glanced at her before returning her attention to Tyrkam. "You called, m'lord?"

"Take her to her room, and treat her sores. As our guest, she must be tended with the greatest care."

Istaria hated his sickening grin. Guest? They had abducted her. Had they asked, she would have refused. She was no guest here. She was a prisoner, like the servant beside her.

The girl reached for Istaria's hands. With a gentle touch, she lifted them closer. Istaria winced at the pain of her broken skin but let the girl bend her hand back to see what they had done to her.

The other girl shook her head and released Istaria's hand. "A dreadful welt has she, m'lord. Many days will pass before she heals."

"Much as I expected. I fear the travel has also weakened her. Tend to her needs."

The servant curtsied awkwardly and grabbed Istaria's upper arm to lead her away. "Come, m'lady. We'll care for you."

Anxious to part from the warlord's company, Istaria followed. She could have objected to the girl's manners but let the servant lead her. At least she would not stand in Tyrkam's presence.

Nevertheless, bitter thoughts continued to taint her mind. She knew he would press his advantage in a matter of time.

The servant led Istaria through the dismal passages of the castle. Never had she visited Wynmere when the duke controlled it, but she could imagine it in much better condition than now. Plaster chipped, paint cracked and faded, and metal rusted.

"We'll fill a bath for you, Princess, and Gena's salve works miracles. Your sores will heal before you know. Lord Tyrkam will be pleased when next he sees you."

Istaria winced. She dreaded pleasing any of the men here, afraid of what that might entail. If only she could be home!

"I am Lwyn." Her voice echoed through the long hall and returned as if ghosts whispered back at them. "If you wish anything, call on me."

Istaria dropped her head, wishing she could call anyone. Years ago she might have, but the fright of her youth had taken that from her.

They continued through the halls, passing other servants, few of whom appeared anything but somber.

From an arched doorway, something stirred in the shadows. The forces within her caught it before her eyes. Like ripples in a pond, the presence of magic washed against her with its approach.

A hooded figure hobbled into view. It leaned on a staff topped by an engraved ivory dragon curled around a crystal. The dragon's eyes glittered at her. A gray beard hung down his chest from under the hood.

She froze and stared into the shadow of the dark blue hood. Gentle ripples increased with each step he took. Two arm-lengths away he stopped. No menace radiated from him that she could detect, though he showed a great curiosity.

He granted her a small bow, something that pained him by his stiff motions. "Your secret is safe with me."

"Be gone, old one! Yeh be not wanted."

Istaria allowed Lwyn to pull her away but peered back at the old man. She frowned at the stranger's words. What had he meant by her secret being safe? Did he know of the dragon that haunted her?

As her angle shifted, she caught a glimpse under his hood of one glimmering blue eye staring back at her. She shuddered, but sensed no hatred or dishonesty from him. Instead, she pitied his feeble condition. Who was he?

She had plenty of time to find out, and someday she would. As sure as the change of seasons she would seek him for answers.

Lwyn rushed Istaria up a spiraled tower. "He be nothing more than horse fodder. Pay him no mind. Harmless, albeit strange. Why our lord bothers to keep him around, none of us understands." She shook her head and said no more.

At the third floor, they parted from the staircase.

When they arrived at the third door down, Lwyn pushed it open. "Your room, m'lady. If y'll stay here, I will return with what we need."

Istaria peered around the door, expecting a dismal room of the same harsh manner that characterized the warlord, barren and cold in its entirety.

Instead, the opposite greeted her. Fine white linens covered the large bed, while the curtains around it billowed in a gentle breeze like the curtains over the window. Several candelabra warmed the room with their soft glow and illuminated the dancing patterns of several tapestries hanging about the walls. Hardly a shadow fell in the room. Here was an island of peace in this otherwise dreary place. It chased away the brutality of the journey she had endured.

Istaria entered the room, her eyes on the intricate designs of the tapestries. She forgot for a moment that she missed her home and allowed herself the briefest instant of solace.

"I'll return quickly, m'lady." Lwyn pulled the door shut behind her.

The heavy grind of the door shattered the illusion of peace that had formed. Istaria let her breath out and the grief flooded in. She hurried to the open window and gazed out, the tears already blurring her vision. Somewhere in the distance was her home, and her family and friends. Somewhere out there were the people she loved.

She was here, away from them and a prisoner of their enemy.

Chapter 6
8.3 pc 937

When she and her parents first arrived at the palace on an autumn day eleven years ago, Calli had gazed in stunned silence. Cavatar's richest home had been grand and from a dream. It sparkled in her eyes, radiating power and an almost ethereal peace that awed her as a child. She had come from a hut in comparison in a lowly village to the east.

At that time, her father had been alive. Despite his duties, he had always made time for her.

Word of his bravery and skill had reached the highest echelons. Alric Isolder sent a personal invitation for him to reside in the palace and train the palace guards.

What a day that had been! Her mother had packed all their belongings onto the carriage sent for them. It had been both a tragic and a joyous day. Calli missed her old home, but she also claimed a new one so magnificent it might have been laid by the hands of the Creators.

Now the palace was a prison of her emotions.

Calli stared in the tall mirror with its fancy, gold frame and sighed. She had changed, as had the others. Istaria had opened up and accepted her friendship, while Phelan had grown from a nuisance into a gentleman.

Three years ago her father had been slain, brutally and without honor. Someone had slipped a poisonous snake into his bed. She missed him every day, although the pain numbed with time.

In that time, she had grown older and was able to care for herself and think for herself.

Her thoughts focused on Istaria and the friendship they shared. After all, what was friendship without someone to share it? Honor without the courage to stand for one's beliefs? Bound by an unspoken promise of loyalty, she had become the last hope of her only true friend. She valued nothing more than that.

If all others lacked those qualities to rescue the princess, she would do it herself. None, not even Phelan, could stop her. Had it not been her failure, she would yet take on the challenge.

Before she left, she would complete her duties. She would rest and leave at the first hint of dawn. Despite the slim chance she would survive, she wanted someone to make a sincere effort to rescue her best friend. Better to do it herself.

With the fire of her determination blazing inside her, Calli gave a nod to her dressed reflection, who agreed with her. "We shall return triumphant together, milady."

Now, however, she should attend to her duties as if nothing was amiss.

She exited the princess's bedroom, which the queen had insisted she take, and padded softly through the corridor to the end. The tall figures in the scene on the closed doors held hands on a road stretching into a distant horizon. A guard stood aside from each door, stiff in his uniform but vigilant in his poise.

Ignoring the men she knew by name, she knocked.

"Enter!" Something in Damaera's muffled voice brought out a frown on Calli's face.

She pushed one door aside and slipped into the room. With the curtains tied away from the two tall, arching windows, the light spilled onto the two beds on the opposite side.

The queen stood before her dressing mirror with her undergarment covering her. The white, sleeveless gown revealed all the queen's elegant beauty in the simplest form. Her lush golden-brown hair hung loose in waves, flowing to her slim waist. Just as Calli remembered when she first saw the queen, Damaera's beauty had not diminished.

Damaera looked up, her eyes full of the grief not displayed in public; red and swollen with tears. Her lips twitched to a smile.

"What do you wish, milady?" Calli spoke with hesitation, her eyes taking in what little of Damaera she saw. Every day the queen shrank away.

"Only that which you cannot give." Damaera's voice softened into depression. She straightened her posture to its usual regal state and added, "But now I request advice of which to wear. My favorite is drying in the sun."

Calli opened the long closet set into a shadowed corner of the room. After digging through a few dresses, she found what she liked best on the queen. She held up the plain, short-sleeved dress.

"Of course." Damaera smiled. "It's right for today." She stretched her arms forward and Calli held the bottom open for her. Together they fit the dress on her, which had grown loose since the last time Damaera had worn it.

Calli stood before the queen and fastened the sash with a silver clip bearing an intricate design of knots and flowers carved into it. "Why do you weep this day?" This day, she thought, that she had decided to do something useful rather than wait for others to do nothing.

Damaera sat on her stool, facing the windows and the bright, glaring sun. It sparkled with the promise of bringing life to the world for another season. Despite the brightness and the hope it promised, she shook her head. Her shoulders drooped. "Not this day, but every day and morning and night."

Calli grabbed a hairbrush and the ties she needed. She loved this part of her duties, but rarely had she the option of practicing on the queen's soft trusses.

"Darkness walks over my heart, Calli. It stabs me, bleeding me of all feeling, that every waking moment I am but a shell of myself."

Damaera caught her breath. In the silence, Calli thought she heard her swallow.

"Never have I felt such torment. That my daughter is gone does not bother me, but that she was taken to Hadeon tears at my spirit."

Damaera dropped her head. "You were dear to her. You were her only friend and still are a friend."

Calli grimaced. Such words tore her soul from her flesh with the ferocity of a wild beast in a feeding frenzy.

Like a second daughter, that you place me in her stead? The queen had assigned her to Istaria's room, and her place at the dining table. Despite the woman's attempts to keep her as another daughter, Calli would never replace Istaria.

Calli continued brushing the lush stream of hair in an attempt to distract her mind from what bothered her. "No hardship is it to aid one's friend, milady. But as I needed company, so she was of near age. Playing together as children came natural."

"But Lord Phelan was another matter." Calli brought up the name to change the subject.

"Ah, my son," Damaera said with a hint of reminisce. "Much like his father. Most boys older thought him a pest—"

"He was."

"Always. While not caring for the small boys, he found ways to bother you. Much of my husband in him, yet grown separately..." She dropped into silence.

Calli frowned, halting her progress. After an eternal minute of silence, she brushed again, wondering about the queen's thoughts. She deserved not to interrupt the mind's wanderings, but would provide an ear if Damaera chose to share those ideas.

"So long ago." Damaera's shoulders rose and fell with a deep breath. "Long ago we changed to what we are now. I was young and full of dreams of finding a true love, but it was not to be. When my foster mother came to me with news of finding a husband, I cried. I had not met him, feared what he might do. But of most worry to me, I did not love him. Nor did he love me." She inhaled a deep breath and paused for several long seconds.

"A convenience is marriage to some, not to forever unite two people in love but to ensure peace or use their children for their means.

"I was of the same age as Istaria. He was a decade's years older and heir to a great kingdom. That to Tahronen and my foster family granted the highest importance to their arrangement."

Damaera sighed and closed her eyes. "I grasped my dignity throughout the first year and struggled with my fear of what he might ask. He found other ways to busy himself. I tried to ignore him and avoided him when granted the freedom."

After a pause, she whispered. "Phelan was not my idea, but his advisors saying he needed an heir. I so feared his approach; every night I laid in my bed praying he stayed in his."

Calli separated the queen's fine hair to twist it. This story she had never heard, nor, she expected, had anyone else. That Damaera would open to her of this touched her inside with a chill of guilt.

"Then it happened." Damaera inhaled a shaky breath. "As I sat on my bed with the intention of sleep, he came to me. I knew his purpose.

"But I knew none of his hesitation, Calli. He knew my feelings, and did not touch me when he sat. Rather, a question he posed; a question of my cooperation. I thought no other choice could be.

"I realized others since, but not until the birth of our son. By then, none mattered but for what he had given me. Though I could never love him, I learned to respect him, enough to want another when our son had grown out of that delicate age."

"Why do you tell me this?" Calli tied one twist and paused. Her insides twisted in torment. To learn so much of someone all at once seemed an invasion of their soul that no one deserved.

Damaera turned to her. "Our past was generous, but not so oft is it. She was to be married to Lord Tarcott's son. Though damned be his majesty's soul for it, my heart would rest better to have her with him than with Tyrkam.

"And I would not see you make a mistake." Damaera reached to take Calli's hand, a determined fire in her eyes. Calli leaned down, caught by the queen's gaze.

"Calli, never deny your heart. We are granted but one life, not to be wasted."

"I shall forever follow the calling of my heart. Fear not for me." Calli squeezed the queen's hand, smiling gently. When Damaera gave a nod, Calli continued her task.

"I see what my daughter had that I missed. I knew you were right for her. But never had I foreseen my need for you. Your spirit uplifts me with hope. A fine daughter has Beadu raised."

Calli swallowed the lump that materialized in her throat. "Thank you, milady."

In silence she finished her work, while the queen continued to praise her qualities. She completed tying the double spirals into a long twist, but the guilt threatened to suffocate her.

Damaera stood and walked to the mirror. A pleasant smile graced her face in admiration of the results. "Lovely, Calli. What would I do without you?"

Calli grimaced, averting her eyes. Why had she not considered this when she made her plans? Why had she not realized how needed she was here? Most important, why did she yet feel the need to leave but want to reveal her plan that they would no longer be secret? Did she want the queen to convince her to stay, or was she trying to make her disappearance easier?

She knew none of her reasons, only that the guilt of leaving without notice after all the queen had suffered choked her conscience.

"You must learn to." Calli faltered a moment before finding her voice again. "You have been more of a mother than she who claims it. I thank you for that, but I cannot stay."

Damaera frowned. "What are you saying? What is this nonsense?"

"No nonsense, or maybe. I know only that for a friend I would risk my life." Calli carried a greater degree of confidence in her voice than she felt. "More than a moon's cycle has passed and my lady, my friend, still has not returned. His majesty has done nothing; therefore, I must."

She steeled herself for an vocal objection, but Damaera fixed her with a look she had seen before—the disapproving frown she had used many times to discourage prankish behavior.

Calli's confidence cracked under that look, but she held tight to the pieces. "No others have tried."

"All others know the fate that awaits them." Damaera's scolding tone made Calli shrink back. "The lands Tyrkam holds may once have been those of the noble Duke of Wynmere, but since he slew the duke, Tyrkam now holds it with other conquered lands as his kingdom. He is clever and bold. Without an army, one shall never withstand his men; less than that to retrieve our beloved Istaria. Let the king do as he will. He is skilled in strategy and his army is strong."

"But they do nothing! I refuse to sit here praying for her return when I am capable. I *must* do something!"

"You are a lady, and most vulnerable to his savage manners."

"I'll take that risk." Calli locked eyes with the queen, fierce in her determination.

When the queen said nothing, Calli curtsied and hastened away. After opening the door, she hesitated and peered back at the room's lone occupant. "I may not return, but I must try." Before Damaera could say anything, Calli rushed out.

"Calli!"

Calli raced through the corridor to the nearest stairway and hurried down, nearly stumbling. Her plans to leave would have to be changed from dawn to immediately, before anyone could stop her. Damn her conscience!

Chapter 7
8.3 pc 937

Damaera hurried after Calli, but when she pulled the door open the girl vanished into the shadows at the end of the corridor.

As Damaera raced after Calli, a welcome figure emerged from around the corner. Startled from her panic, she halted and sought to catch her breath.

"Phelan!" Relief poured into her. "My son."

His brow furrowed. "Mother? Why the hurry?"

She grabbed his shoulders and held him facing her. "Find Calli. She must not be allowed to leave."

"Leave? Where would she go?" His hands on her arms steadied her, and she dropped her hands to his.

"Madness drives her to Hadeon."

"Hadeon?" He stiffened. "Istaria."

Damaera nodded. She knew his affinity for the girl would drive him.

Without a word, he tore away from her and ran off.

※

Calli raced across the courtyard full of soldiers and the normal assortment of servants and caretakers. She dodged their slow shuffle, squeezing between bodies where they stood close. When she reached the stable door, she hesitated and scanned left and right for the help she now needed.

"Jamison!"

No one answered. Rushing into the stable, she searched the aisle of horses. "Jamison!"

"Here."

Startled, Calli spun on her heel. She scowled at the nuisance holding the pitchfork. "Damn you!" He had a nasty sense of prankishness to materialize from nowhere.

"Then I be leavin' you." He started to turn.

"Come back! Saddle the fastest horse."

"Ah, that be Baron, m'lady. I'd rather not, what with his grace's orders and all."

"Then the next fastest." Calli fumed at his nonchalance. He took far too much pleasure at her expense.

He arched one eyebrow in curiosity.

She would dare not take Phelan's stallion. Jamison could think enough for himself to suggest another. "Now!"

He set his fork against the wall and shrugged, then walked down the aisle and untied a bright chestnut. A jagged patch of white streaked along the side of the horse's belly. "Will Lightenin' do?"

"If he's fast."

"Oh, *she* runs. She be called Lightenin' not by only that mark." He pointed to the white on the mare's side.

Calli marched down the aisle to the tack area. High-pommeled saddles hung on thick poles sticking out from the three walls of the end of the stable. Bridles hung on various scattered hooks amongst the saddles.

She snatched a bridle and saddle from the wall. With the heavy equipment clinking in her hands, she started back to the horse. One step out of the corner, she tripped and lost her balance from the weight she carried.

The saddle was lifted from her. It permitted her to keep her balance. At least Jamison was good for something—

"Planning a ride?"

She knew that voice, but it was not the one she expected. How dare he! "Unless you intend it yourself."

She reached for the saddle.

Phelan held it, despite her fight to reclaim it. Firm in his stance, he risked a glance over his shoulder. "Jamison!"

"M'lord."

"Leave us."

Calli's eyes fixed on Phelan in defiance. Behind him, Jamison tied the horse in its stall and rushed out. His hasty steps on the stone vanished with his presence.

She tried again to yank the saddle from Phelan's grasp, but to no effect. "Am I now a prisoner, unable to enjoy a warm day?"

He pushed past her to replace the saddle in its corner. "A horse thief has no rights."

"I've stolen no horse." She crossed her arms and glared at him. She would no more steal a horse than she would stay, but she would borrow a mount for her purpose. Was it not legal for cavalry soldiers to use other horses for duty? Did not the rescue of the king's daughter matter as important enough? Apparently not. "I only intended to borrow one."

"For what purpose, might I inquire?"

"My purposes." If he would just leave! But she knew that was as likely as Tyrkam returning the princess.

"What purpose?"

Calli flashed a nasty look at him. His stiff-lipped frown told her all she needed. His hand outstretched to block her clarified any questions. He knew her purpose. He could not be there by chance. In a manner unknown, the queen had managed to find him in much less time than she had ever imagined possible.

Phelan stood in the middle of the aisle and crossed his arms. "Perhaps a desperate madness. A horrible folly, then, that beckons you to your death."

"Not death I seek but my friend." She burned him with her glare, unwilling to play his game. "Since others refuse to help, the duty rests upon *me*, coward."

Calli would have thought his expression unable to darken. However, the nasty gleam in his eyes sent her back a step. Her taunt had aroused his anger, maybe enough to do something.

She could only hope.

When he failed to respond further, Calli straightened. Perhaps he was a coward after all. "Then we've no argument." She moved around him with the intention of bringing the horse to the saddle.

His arm shot out into her path, not quite reaching the side of the aisle. He left her more than enough room to move around his barricade. As she swerved around his arm, the rest of him followed. He blocked her path.

"You're not leaving."

Calli swiped a loose strand of red hair from her face and tried to push past him. "I will if I choose."

He continued to block her path. She dodged left and right, but his impenetrable stance moved with her. Frustrated, she pushed against him. Her father's teachings about attacking someone for no reason restrained her. "Don't make me hurt you!"

Before she could get away, he grabbed her wrists and held firm.

"Let go!" She pulled with all her strength but his grip never budged.

"So you can die?"

Calli paused in her struggles and looked up at the blue eyes she knew too well. She expected a hard, cold stare. Instead, a deep sadness shone from his gaze. She knew not how to react.

"Will you ever listen to the voice of reason? This is madness, Calli!"

Despite his pleading tugging at her emotions, she had to leave. She refused to let him convince her to stay.

Only one option remained to get away from him. She hated to do it but he gave her no choice. She released her knee in a sudden blow between his legs. It connected with a solid jab, and he released her wrists.

"Why'd you do that?" Phelan squeaked, hunching over.

"Never preach to me!" Calli pushed past him with a clear shot to the door.

However, something stopped her and she turned. Was it the need to justify her reasons, or something else?

Slowly lifting his body to stand upright, Phelan caught his breath and said, "I alone could not hope to rescue her. What hope have you? Unless you've something we've not?"

"My strength."

Recovering sooner than she expected, Phelan clamped his mouth on a smirk betrayed by a glint in his eyes.

"What strength is that?"

Calli scowled but could not meet his eyes. His statement made her hesitate. "Strength enough."

"And what fighting skills have you?" Moving with care, he leaned against the wall of one of the many stalls. "Certainly not more than chasing strays from the bakehouse."

Calli muttered a curse under her breath that she had not practiced the skills her father taught her since his death. The memories of their secret time together had been too painful, and she hadn't needed the skills until now. Now, she needed retraining, but not even Phelan knew of her previous skills. She would prove herself without exposing what she had learned, just as her father had asked, since girls in this land were not taught as the women in his homeland.

She grabbed the pitchfork Jamison had left leaning against the nearest doorframe and marched back to Phelan. With a determined scowl, she aimed the middle prong at his throat.

"I've banished more than my share of your likes from the bakehouse." She pressed closer with her weapon.

Phelan stood unmoved, showing no fear. "And what tactics as this are proven?"

Calli stared hard at him, her confidence in her decision shaken by his persuading words. What tactics indeed had serving him granted? Already too long had it been since her father had lived to teach her. Of what use was she if she could not defend herself, as when she had failed her friend?

One course of action shone clear, the answer she sought.

She pressed the middle prong into his throat. "Teach me to fight."

"You?" He grinned in amusement. When he attempted to swipe the prongs away, she pushed harder. She forced him to back away.

"Yes!" A new fire sparked within her from the idea. "To fight as any of the men who guard the palace, that I might defend myself."

Phelan batted the fork aside, a frown on his face. "I'll teach no woman to fight."

"Teach me." She thrust the fork at him. "If you will not, I'll go it alone. If you wish me to have a chance, you will teach me."

He shook his head and sighed. When he met her eyes, a mischievous smile played across his face. "Give me a day or two. Then we'll get you out of that dress."

Calli pressed the fork closer, fixing a cold glare on him. His reputation had reached even her ears.

He chuckled. "Not like that. I'll find you some breeches and a shirt." When she lowered the fork, he let his breath out and shook his head. "A fiery one you are, Calli."

"I'll not let you forget." One corner of her mouth hooked up with a new confidence. She set the fork against the wall, and with a decisive nod, marched out.

His voice reached her from behind when he replied. "Of that I'm sure."

Chapter 8
10.3 PC 937

"Furthermore, you *will* pay attention!" Tyrkam scowled.

Vahrik reined his horse to stand or at least dance in place. He had fallen because, as he battled the warrior opposite him in this practice, his horse had jumped out from him sideways.

The boy needed the lesson in patience, and the lesson in humility.

"Then saddle a trained horse. I cannot tolerate this colt."

"You'll learn on whatever is available."

Tyrkam stroked the sweaty brown hide of the horse chewing its bit. Foamy spit dropped from its mouth. "This colt is as fine a creature as you will see. He must be taught to respond in battle, as you must learn to ride better."

"It will not happen again." Vahrik's voice echoed with a defiance that made Tyrkam clench his teeth. The boy would never learn.

When the horse jumped away from him, Tyrkam cursed and stumbled backward. He caught himself against a large stone to keep his balance. Vahrik might be his son, but he was brash and impetuous, and growing into a problem.

He scowled at the boy, who recklessly attacked his trusted Lieutenant Dorjan.

The dark-haired youth of some nineteen years was far too young to inherit a kingdom yet too old to control. Like a wild horse, he simply reacted on instinct without any thought. When he stretched the moment into moments, and moments into years he might be ready. Until then, his falls would be harder because he did not see them coming.

Dorjan unseated the boy again. Vahrik landed on the hard spring ground. What excuse would he use this time?

Tyrkam growled in dissatisfaction and marched over while another mounted warrior caught the flighty colt.

Dorjan pinned Vahrik with a blunted lance pressed against his mail-protected throat. "You're dead, boy."

Vahrik fixed a burning glare on Dorjan as if to spear the man with a look.

At Tyrkam's approach, Dorjan removed the lance and rode aside. Untamed red hairs poked out from beneath his helm. "He's worthless," Dorjan said.

Vahrik rolled over and rose to his feet.

"What have I taught you?"

Vahrik stiffened. "The bloody horse threw me! He's no more trained than a wild beast."

Tyrkam suppressed a smirk. "Only twice before was he saddled."

"Twice!" Vahrik yanked his helm off and threw it to the ground with a loud clunk.

Dorjan shook his head.

Vahrik flashed a dirty look at him and returned his fury to Tyrkam, who found the whole situation enlightening if not amusing. "You put me on a damned colt with no training."

"To train you."

"Darkness take your training!" Vahrik looked to a young foot soldier leading the heavily muscled colt. "Bring him in."

When he turned back to Tyrkam, fire smoldered in Vahrik's eyes, blazing out of control. "Once I rid myself of this armor, I'll train that horse."

Vahrik marched back to the residence quarters and disappeared inside. Tyrkam took a deep, contemplative breath as the soldier followed and stopped outside with the colt's reins in his hand. Had he raised the boy in his homeland, Vahrik would have grown up on the back of a horse so that none could have thrown him.

But Tyrkam could not stay after his dishonor. He would do it again if it meant Sovereign Farolkavin suffered for his atrocities. One day the plains peoples would be free of the Rivon. He vowed that he would defeat them with every fiber of his being. Before he could, he needed the power to defeat the armies of the sovereign. Defeating Rivonia's strongest ally was only the first step.

"Vahrik fights with passion and skill," Dorjan said. "Had the colt not jumped, he may have been a match."

"But he is as wild as that colt."

Dorjan shifted in his saddle, by the squeak of leather behind Tyrkam. "But for the fighting, I'd swear other purposes behind your choice of mounts."

"You might." Still watching the horse, Tyrkam straightened when the princess and her servant appeared, wearing cloaks. The servant carried a basket.

"And what of your intentions for that one?"

Istaria approached the horse, reaching her delicate hand to the black muzzle. The colt quit his nervous dancing; his ears pointed forward. When she laid her hand on his long dark face, he lowered his head to her. Istaria moved beside him. She stroked his neck and moved to his shoulder, laying her veiled head against him for several long seconds.

"See how he calms for her."

A surge of confidence rushed through Tyrkam. "She will give me power. The heart will respond to her."

"Has she accepted this?"

"She will. That will come in time, and time will pass before Cavatar is taken."

The girls moved away from the horse and altered their course toward Tyrkam and Dorjan. Lwyn carried the basket on her arm. She stopped first and curtsied. "M'lord, we request permission for a walk in the forest."

Tyrkam stepped forward and lifted the cloth cover on the basket. A loaf of bread and cakes?

He looked at the pair, suspicious of a plot to help Istaria run away. Although he doubted she could survive on her own or even with the servant helping her, he would not risk losing her. She possessed the gentle, "innocent" quality he hoped would appeal to the white dragon to help him claim its power. He also needed her to convince Isolder to give up.

Lwyn's throat flashed with a nervous swallow. Her dark eyes stared hard at his chest with only the briefest glance up. The princess hid her face, but from the faint outline behind the veil she might have watched him.

"And this involves a picnic?"

Lwyn bit her bottom lip and faltered. "We...planned a time in the woods to enjoy the good day. Istaria has seen only the inside o' th- *your* castle and none o' the wonders o' Hadeon."

He silently chewed on the request, tasting each outcome of flavor, not all of them pleasant. The princess had stayed within the castle since arriving. She had given no indication of disobeying. Nevertheless, the bitterness persisted in his mouth until the colt neighed in their direction. The reaction added a new sweetness. Granting a simple request could work to his favor, but he would take precautions.

"Wait for Vahrik. I'll not have the wolves, or the woodsman, bring harm to my guest." He smiled at the frown creasing the young servant's face. At least they would not have reason to run, or escape far if they tried. And, he would learn of her intentions.

Lwyn grimaced. "Thank you, m'lord." In silence, they waited for Vahrik.

When the boy emerged from the keep without his battle raiment, he snatched the reins of the colt and mounted. With a scowl, he raced to the gate.

As he bore down on the two women, they stood their ground. He jerked against the colt's mouth. The horse shook his head in irritation but stopped. "What's this?"

Tyrkam fixed a warning look on the arrogant boy. "You will accompany the princess and her servant to the forest for an outing."

Still fighting the flighty colt, Vahrik snarled his frustration. He loosened the reins and jabbed the horse in the ribs with his spurs. "Follow me, ladies."

The women exchanged looks but followed behind the dark horse and his rider.

When they had moved out of earshot, Dorjan leaned over to Tyrkam. "Is that wise?"

"It will build trust with her. And it will teach him patience." He never took his eyes off the trio until they vanished within the trees.

⁂

Istaria frowned beneath her veil. Vahrik fought with the colt a step ahead of them. She had hoped that getting outside the dismal castle would be her chance at freedom, though she hated to trick Lwyn into helping. Now, she knew Tyrkam had considered the possibility. He would not permit her to run. On horseback, Vahrik could easily overtake her.

Vahrik would not grant her a moment of peace.

After a near blow-up that ended in the colt rearing, he dismounted and led the animal. Unfortunately, he walked beside Istaria. Somewhere behind them, others followed; soldiers more than likely.

The intangible menace of Vahrik's presence darkened the colors of magic.

"Eager to reach the forest?"

Ignoring his sarcasm, she continued her march into the trees. When she stepped beneath the branches bearing unfurling leaf buds, a sense of comfort fell over her like a warm blanket. She relaxed, realizing that this forest was different than any other place she had been. Magic lay within its bounds. It enveloped her within its embrace, pushing aside any darkness to lighten her heart. She wondered why she had not noticed it when she arrived but remembered that she had been tired and despondent about her situation at the time.

Istaria peered into the woods spattered with sundrops. Within her stirred the power she had suppressed. She squeezed her eyes shut and forced it down. The magic faded and fell dormant again. She took a deep breath and continued forward, eager to explore this new realm.

"You're at home in Wynmere Woods?"

With a grimace, Istaria nodded. She hesitated at an embankment, but gathered her dress and climbed. In a few steps, she reached the top. The others followed behind.

She continued through the trees, around boulders, and over the growing carpet of grass. Vahrik stayed close with Lwyn dragging her feet behind him.

"M'lady." The servant gasped for a breath. "Can we not stop and enjoy our picnic?"

A faint laughter tinkled like little bells somewhere ahead.

All three stopped, but the sound hushed.

"My lady," Vahrik said as he came up on her side, "Let us go no further into the forest. Strange creatures call it home."

What else could she do but give in? She wished not to arouse Vahrik's temper as she had witnessed on occasion.

When she found a boulder on which to sit, Istaria halted her journey into the woods. Vahrik tied the colt to a sturdy tree and took a place near her, his presence in the magic nauseating.

Lwyn opened the basket and handed each of them a cake. "Eat well, m'lady."

A hint of laughter tinkled from the trees above. It called to her, to the forces within her. In a voice unheard and undefined, it promised freedom and guidance away from Vahrik, Tyrkam, and the men who served them.

Istaria turned her eyes skyward as the others did. Who or what had it been?

Who are you, she wondered. Had the others heard the same as she?

Vahrik stood up, listening, the arrogance gone from his face. "We should return to the castle. It is not wise to intrude upon the creatures of the forest."

Had she imagined the touch of fear in his voice?

After a few seconds of silence broken only by the rush of the wind through the treetops, he sat next to her. While enjoying his snack, Vahrik opened up by bragging about his accomplishments in battle.

Istaria heard little of what he said, listening for the almost-voice that had spoken to her. At the fringe of her awareness, she caught the disturbance in the magic of the forest. It returned and danced around, unbound by the world in which she lived. The joy and fun radiating from multiple sources shone like stars through the gloom. Welcoming the good feelings, she lifted her hold on the magic a fraction. It permitted her to narrow the locations of these unseen beings.

They surrounded Istaria and the others in air, tree, and ground.

Join us, they said.

Istaria turned her head slowly to study her surroundings but nothing stood out of the ordinary that she could see. Join who?

You are welcome here, Lady of the Dragon.

Who are you? she asked.

The laughter tinkled again. This time, however, the colt squealed and pulled back on the reins.

Vahrik jumped to his feet and ran to the horse pulling against the tree.

Come. Now!

Eager to escape from Vahrik, Istaria followed the voice into the trees. Her heart pounded with the impulse to run. She glanced back but the voices urged her forward.

"Get back here!" Vahrik's heavy steps followed for a short distance before fading amid the tall trees and low brush.

Chapter 9
10.3 pc 937

Hurry! The voice commanded.

In the distance, Vahrik shouted her name as a curse. "Istaria Isolder!" The crack of a branch followed by his curses rang out from behind her.

She ducked between trees, watching her footing.

With a glance back, Istaria saw only tall trees reaching to the sky. They all looked the same. Where was she?

Rarely had she ever set foot outside the palace, and this, the first time outside the fortress created from Wynmere Castle, she ran into strange territory. Where would she go?

This way, the voice whispered. She turned in the direction the magic guided her and stepped carefully over the flotsam littering the forest floor.

As she calmed, her head cleared and she focused deeper in the magic surrounding her. She found them, tens, perhaps hundreds of tiny points like candles in the dark. Some zipped about her while others remained stationary. She saw nothing, however.

Uncertain where to go from there, she followed them with the hopes that they would lead her someplace where she could find help. So far they had helped her escape from Vahrik.

Lost amid the trees, Istaria wondered if the voices had guided her the wrong way. Why had she trusted them?

In answer, darkness rose through the magic behind her. She turned, holding her breath. Who or what followed?

In the silence, she caught the distant baying of hounds.

Her heart pounded in her chest. She ran the opposite direction, forgetting the voices that had called to her. Her pursuers would find her through the skills of Tyrkam's hounds. No wolf made as much noise stalking its prey that she had ever heard in stories; but she worried about them too.

Istaria glanced back at the increasing noise. In her haste, she tripped on a root and fell.

After a moment to catch her breath, she pushed herself to her feet. When she did, pain shot like a knife through her ankle. Istaria hobbled forward in spite of the pain, desperate to stay ahead of the dogs.

However, she could not travel far. After a few minutes, she stopped and leaned against a tree to take the weight off her ankle. She allowed only a minute to catch her breath before continuing forward. Pain wracked her leg with each step and increased each time she put her weight on it.

Where were those who surrounded her? Why did they not help? Had she imagined them?

She searched for them, opening herself to the magic of the forest and always looking around her for a sign of them. When she allowed the magic to wash through her, she found a familiar sensation. Like the ripples created by the old mage, it disturbed the flow.

When she turned right, a man appeared from nowhere. Istaria gasped and halted.

"Fear not, lady." He spoke in a soft voice. His clothes spoke of labor, with sweat stains prominent beneath his arms. A full beard covered his jaw, matching the disheveled brown hair on his head.

The barking of the dogs resounded through the trees, close enough to spring on her any moment.

Istaria turned but saw nothing.

"This way if you wish to avoid them."

She looked to the man, who waved her forward. With no reason to distrust him, she followed.

In a few steps, she stumbled on a moss-covered log. The stranger rushed to her aid with a frown. His blue eyes studied her swollen ankle. "You're injured. I'd not realized."

When he offered his arm, Istaria accepted the help.

"Please, come with me."

For the first time, she noticed the faint, unfamiliar accent. She had never heard anything like it before, a hint of a musical quality.

The stranger studied her, a gentle smile on his lips. Meanwhile, the baying of Tyrkam's hounds grew louder.

He glanced in the direction from which the noise came. "We must move quickly if you wish to escape."

She watched him, not sure what he had in mind or whether she could fully trust him. His eyes bore a sadness she could not comprehend and a secret that whispered in the magic.

Before she could take in any more, he gathered her in his arms. Istaria gasped with the sudden motion of his sweeping up her legs from beneath her. She clasped her arms around his neck.

"It's the only way, if you cannot walk." He rushed with her through the trees, his strides covering at least twice the ground she had with her injury. For that she was grateful, but where would he take her?

The baying and barking now sounded too close for comfort. Istaria buried her face in his warm chest and prayed he found a safe place to avoid the devil chasing her. She hung on, until he stopped running. Why did he stop?

She looked up to his face, but he shook his head, his eyes elsewhere.

A dark shadow within the magic sent Istaria's stomach turning. So close was the presence that she thought he must have seen her.

The stranger had stopped in a patch of brush. Although his chest rose and fell with each heavy breath, he showed no signs of weakness, nor of worry. Instead he closed his eyes. His lips moved but no sound issued from them.

The intensity of magic around her spiked. It blasted away the sickening darkness, cutting her off from all but the sounds of the riders and their hounds. She peered over the stranger's shoulder and watched the dogs sniffing the ground in circles while half a dozen riders led by Vahrik waited.

The arrogant prince shouted orders to the others while their horses fidgeted. Metal clinked on metal. Leather squeaked with movement. They showed no sense of quiet, but let urgency master them.

The scowl on Vahrik's face cursed all within sight.

When the hounds picked up something and ran off in the opposite direction, Istaria relaxed. The riders galloped after them and vanished within the forest. In minutes, silence reigned.

The stranger opened his eyes and lowered his arms to set her upright. "They're gone now."

Standing on her good leg, Istaria let out a sigh. She wished she could thank him but feared revealing herself. At least he had not betrayed her.

"My lady, if you would permit me, I have supplies within my cabin to tend your ankle."

Caution blew through her, but she knew not what other options she had. She wanted to trust him and accepted the arm he extended around her to support her weight.

"Strange creatures live in these woods." He peered through the trees, his steps crunching over dried leaves of the year past. "They— You may not believe me. They led me to you. I know not why, but I've lived with them long enough to know not to ignore them."

She looked up with a smile. Of course. She should have realized that it had been too much of a coincidence. Whatever, or whoever, had told her to run had known this man would be here. She hoped his intentions were honest.

"If you wonder, I am called Woodsman, though Darius is my preference."

When he smiled, a strange feeling warmed her cheeks.

"Have you a name, my lady?"

She lifted her head and patted her throat.

"Forgive me. I had not realized." He looked ahead along their path through the trees.

Darius, she thought, wishing she could trust him enough to make him hear her. *You need not ask forgiveness for lack of knowledge.*

In a short while, they came to a large black horse with feet like large stones beneath it. A thick forelock covered its long face, hiding its eyes. It stood quiet, hitched to a wagon piled high with wood. Before she thought them within sight, the horse lifted his head, small ears pricked toward them.

When they reached the wagon, Darius lifted her up to the driver's seat. From the top, she looked down at the massive back of the black gelding and the indentation of its spine halving it. Here was an animal capable of doing its job. She had never seen such a large horse up close.

The seat shifted as Darius took a place next to her. He gathered the reins and released the break. "Ready?" Without waiting for her answer, he slapped the reins on the horse's back.

When the horse started forward, the wagon lurched in response. Istaria grabbed the seat for balance. Never had she ridden on a wagon like this! Only a couple times had she ridden in a coach, which traveled much smoother.

At least she could rest her foot on the way to wherever he took her, which was away from the dreaded castle.

At the easy pace set by the horse, the sun shifted a little more in the sky before they neared a small cabin among the trees.

"There it is. My little bit of peace."

His home? Istaria made out a small paddock on the far side, notable for the wood fence that surrounded the enclosure. At the back of the cabin, an overhang covered a stack of cut logs next to a pile of hay.

The word quaint sprang to mind; not what she was accustomed to.

What else could she do? She could not hobble off into the woods alone.

Her stomach grumbled. Perhaps he would feed her. She knew nothing about cooking. Her every need had been filled for her by servants and hired help all her life.

"Though it seems not much, it is sufficient." Darius wore a gentle smile that settled her questions.

Any shelter would be better than returning to Tyrkam and Vahrik.

At the front door, Darius stopped the wagon. He jumped to the ground with ease and reached up for her.

Understanding what he intended, Istaria slid to the edge of the seat. She let her legs hang in the air and leaned forward to balance her hands on his shoulders. His roughened hands held her waist and pulled her down before him.

When she landed gently with his support, a wave of heat rose to her face. Istaria looked up and caught his smile before ducking her eyes in shyness. She knew not how to react to the warmth that he showed her.

"Please, come inside, my lady." His soft voice and steady arm invited her to lean on him for support. She accepted his assistance to hobble forward.

When he opened the door, Istaria squinted in the light that filtered through the single window. The cabin contained only a small table with two chairs, one bed, a fireplace, and shelves stacked to the ceiling with various trinkets and tools.

The carvings on the middle shelves caught her eyes. She limped away from him to the shelves, her hand on the wall for balance.

"My evening hobby."

One in particular caught her eyes out of the many imaginary creatures presented—a girl with a flower in her tiny hands. The most innocent of moments, it seemed to her, and full of joy. A smile crept to her lips in response to the child's expression.

"You may keep it if you like. I have no use for them other than the peddlers who visit to buy them to sell in other villages."

Holding the precious child to her, Istaria turned around. She smiled, wishing he could see her appreciation but not daring to show her face.

A hint of pride gleamed within his eyes and he guided her to the bed to sit. "Now, shall we see to your ankle?"

Darius helped her sit without falling and knelt at her feet. Using only a light touch, he lifted her injured ankle into the sunlight slanting across the room and removed her shoe. "Not a pretty sight, my lady, this I mean."

When she looked at her ankle, she gasped at what she saw. It had expanded to twice its normal width while purple blotches discolored her skin. Istaria winced and looked away.

"No need to worry." Darius lowered her foot with care. He stood and turned away to search for something. "Only a matter of proper care. With a little rest and perhaps a wrapping, it will heal, but you'll not be getting far on it."

She could have told him that last part. It had been the reason he helped her. In no way could she have escaped those hounds alone.

How *had* they escaped?

He turned around with a smile on his face and a rolled cloth in his hands. "Always prepared for the worst when it comes to handling wood. *You* I was not prepared for, but this will do. Now then…"

Darius knelt again at her feet and proceeded to wrap the ugly ankle with delicate care, asking questions she dared not answer. She marveled at the lightness of his touch. He wrapped the cloth around her ankle and foot several times, pulling it snug but not too tight, and talking all the while. She could have listened to him talk all night.

When he finished, Darius lifted her foot out for her inspection. "There now. You'll not be seeing it until it's better." He lifted her legs to the bed and helped her lie down. "I suggest you rest now and keep your foot up."

She nodded and watched him in curiosity. He hesitated on a thought, his eyes distant a moment. After several seconds he looked on her with a puzzled face. "Have you a name, or shall I call you the Lady of the Woods?"

Chapter 10
10.3 pc 937

The human intelligence of the hawk watched the forest with grave concern. What would the dragons think of this? The faeries had lured the princess away, but they had led the woodsman to her. What plans had they?

The dragons would wish to know.

She spread her wings and flapped into the air. The land raced wild and free below. In the distance a pillar of smoke rose from the battlegrounds. She turned away, towards the haze of a valley as far from the mountains as the dragons dared, the place they hid outside their sanctuary realm.

When Gaispar arrived, she dove from the currents below the clouds into the haze. She hovered a few feet above the land for a moment and took a new shape.

In seconds, a tall, robed figure grew from the bird, a hood over her blonde head while the cloak hid her slender form beneath. She waited patiently for her masters, as she had in three hundred years of immortal life as a twenty-three year old woman.

A subtle shift in the forces around her whispered her name in her mind: *Gaispar.*

She stood unmoved by the richness of the power emanating from the fog. That power lapped against her and washed through her, joining her in its endless connection.

Soon, the haze parted before her. A blue-scaled head poked through, smooth and slender but twice as long as she was tall, with two spiraling horns projecting towards the back. A proud neck arched high above as dark eyes fixed on her. The rest of the serpentine body emerged from the gray, towering above her as the dragon came into full view.

This was Jêrafînas, one of the three matriarchs.

The dragon set her head on the ground next to Gaispar, a wisp of smoke trailing up from each nostril. The dragon's hot breath blew over her.

What of word or order do you seek? Jêrafînas asked.

Gaispar bowed. *Mistress, the faeries play their pranks on me. In the forest have I seen the chosen one, led away from Tyrkam to the waiting woodsman.*

Ah... The dragon sighed. Her sides expanded and contracted with a deep breath.

This one of prophetic intentions sought,
though Tyrkam knows of anything naught.

A sense of awe washed through Gaispar as she considered the matriarch's statement. *His magic I sense from her, a power greater than any other but the immortal ones. She is safe now with the Sh'lahmar, I suppose.*

A low rumble rose from the depths of the dragon's throat, passing through her body in a thoughtful "Hmm" of displeasure.

Of this that is and may yet come,
shall all lead the chosen one.
In good hands, I doubt not,
but far from harm and danger fraught.
We must her steps to that day guide,
when his spirit will abide.

Gaispar nodded, wishing the time of the return of the white dragon would come soon. Though the faeries had granted her immortality to serve the dragon's return, they had done so to save her from death. At the time she had wished to live, but now she longed for a rest. She understood Makleor's discomfort.

When?

A deep sigh rumbled from Jêrafînas. Wisps of smoke curled from her nostrils.

Your question is at best quite bold
but never in the future told.
The lives of men have past and gone,
their futures lost and sometimes won.
Patience is the truest test.
He will choose his time, which time is best.

She should have realized they would not reveal the future. Gaispar straightened her shoulders, setting her mind on the work yet to come.

A large slit eye swiveled away from her for a second before fixing on her with a knowing look.

Gaispar waited. All the time in the world availed itself to immortals and she could wait another three hundred years if need be, but the princess could not.

Go now, the dragon said.
Take to Tahronen of the light
that prophecy has taken flight.

*Though she will not interfere
but tend the sisters of the Lumathir.
Take the news of Tyrkam's loss
along the mage's path to cross.*

Gaispar nodded and threw up the length of her hooded cloak. It shrank into the wings that carried her from the valley to return to the lowlands.

Chapter 11
10.3 pc 937

Tyrkam slammed his fist on the table, sending a thunderous boom echoing through the chamber.

In spite of his stoic poise, Vahrik flinched. He had not wished to lose the princess. The faeries had helped her, first by distracting him in scaring the colt and then by tripping him when he tried to follow. Somehow they had fooled his hounds following her scent.

"You lost her." The icy tone of Tyrkam's voice caught all sound captive within the room.

Vahrik swallowed.

"I trusted you to prevent her escape."

"It was them."

Tyrkam's glare froze Vahrik in his seat. Like anyone who had lived in Wynmere long enough, he also knew of the faeries that inhabited the forest. They were mischievous creatures. "*They* do not concern me. You failed a simple assignment."

"It happened so fast."

Vahrik had sworn Tyrkam could not show more anger. He was wrong. Before he could react to the sudden rage that flared over Tyrkam's face, the warlord grabbed him by the collar and pulled him to his feet.

The chair clattered to the floor behind them, and Tyrkam swung him around and slammed him to the wall.

Vahrik grunted at the sharp pain that knocked the air from his lungs. The hold of his collar choked out the breath he struggled to catch.

Tyrkam's hot breath blew on his face. "This is the last time, Vahrik. Find the princess! If you come back without her, your head will stick on a pike to demonstrate the price of failure!"

Tyrkam shoved him aside. Vahrik fought to keep his feet. He scowled, hiding his fear.

"Go now. Bring her back alive."

Vahrik rushed out of the chamber. Argument would be useless. If the princess was so important, why could Tyrkam not search himself?

If she was so valuable, any price on her would attract attention.

As he strode through the corridors of the decaying castle, a thin smile curled up his lips. The idea lifted his mood. He could post a reward for the capture of the princess. It would require less work, although he would rather find Istaria himself than leave it to others to fail while he suffered the consequences.

"One step at a time." He knew a few contacts in the villages who might help.

Chapter 12
12.3 pc 937

Istaria awoke to the crackle of a fire and the burble of water boiling. As the grogginess lifted further, the scent of stew sent her stomach into fits of hunger.

With a grimace, she sat up from the hard bed she lay upon and opened her eyes. In a glance, she recognized the small cabin.

"Had a nice nap?"

She blinked at the unexpected voice, but soon recognized the cabin's owner. Darius turned from the fire, a knife in one hand and a block of notched wood in the other. A pile of shavings accumulated on the floor beneath his feet.

The memories poured back.

A gentle smile curved up his lips. "You slept well, I trust?"

Istaria nodded and motioned to her chin with her hand outside the veil.

Darius rubbed his clean-shaven chin. "Feels strange." He shrugged and dropped his hand. "I had let it go so long, but it was time for a change."

Though she suspected other reasons, Istaria made no further inquiries. Instead, she swung her legs over the edge of the bed. She had rested the last two days, giving her ankle time to heal. The swelling had decreased some but still puffed her ankle.

It throbbed with pain when she put her weight on it. She winced and stiffened, sitting back down on the bed's edge.

Darius jumped to her aid and knelt before her. "Easy now. I told you it would take a while to heal. You need more time." He lifted her foot for examination but froze in his tracks.

Istaria shivered at the coldness that blew through her core. Someone approached; someone familiar with an icy heart.

Darius lifted her legs to the bed and stood up. In a hushed voice, he said, "Make no move, my lady."

Before she could protest, he murmured in words she had never heard. A surge of power surrounded her as if he had dunked her in a pool of colors that formed a pattern. She frowned but did as he commanded, realizing he used magic, as in the forest when they had escaped Vahrik.

Darius returned to his chair and picked up his knife and wood to resume his carving. When he looked up to check on her, she swore she heard his voice in her mind.

Before she could focus on the magic, the crunch of steps rose outside the door. Gruff voices and the clinking of metal accompanied the sound.

One of them made her gasp. *Vahrik!* She cowered near the wall at the edge of the bed and lay still.

The harsh pounding on the door echoed within the room a second before it slammed aside.

In the firelight, shadows danced over the hated face. "Woodsman!"

Darius sprang to his feet as if stung. The heir of Hadeon fixed dark eyes on him.

Istaria winced. Never had she seen such a look of malice.

"My lord." Belatedly, Darius bowed. "To what do I owe this honor?"

Vahrik sneered and scanned the small one-room cabin. "I am looking for someone."

She tensed, uncertain of how either would react and surprised that Vahrik had not noticed her.

"Have you found a young girl in the forest recently?"

"No, my lord. I've seen no one in the forest. None dare for the rumors that abound." He glanced to where Istaria lay on the bed but in the same motion swept his eyes across the room.

Vahrik followed his gaze.

Istaria was sure he had seen her, although his eyes grabbed no focus. Should she run?

Fear not, my lady.

Istaria blinked and looked to Darius, but he watched Vahrik.

After a few seconds of silence, Vahrik glanced outside at the noisy soldiers. "Unfortunate." When he returned his gaze to the woodsman, Darius swallowed. "Should you happen to find her, notify me at once. I've a great interest in her."

"As you wish."

Istaria held her breath. So far Darius had helped her and had not turned her over to the young brute.

Vahrik took one step out the door and turned, his eyes studying the room one more time before fixing on Darius. "You will speak only to me if you find her."

With that, he slammed the door shut behind him. His heavy steps faded outside.

Darius let out a deep sigh and relaxed his shoulders. *Be still yet.*

His voice reached her through the magic, though his lips had not moved.

How had he such power? She thought no one else capable of mindspeech.

He is searching the area. He suspects a lie, Darius warned her.

Istaria nodded and laid her head down. Darius picked up where he left off in his whittling.

After many long minutes, he rose from his chair. He came to her and whispered a word. In an instant, the colors of magic resumed their normal flow. Istaria sat up, a puzzled frown on her face.

"Be not afraid, Lady of the Forest. Though I serve Hadeon as a lowly woodsman, I do not aid the tyrant that rules it."

He took a seat on the bed next to her, the lines of a frown dragging his face down. "But I will be watched. You cannot stay here."

What? Istaria searched his blue eyes for hope, but only sadness remained. How could he kick her out after she had come to trust him?

Panic rose up within her. She wanted to stay, not to leave on her own. Despite the meager conditions, the last two days had been the happiest she had known since her last days at home. Where would she go? How would she survive?

She grabbed his arm and clung to it in desperation.

"Please, my lady."

Istaria buried her face in his shoulder and refused to let go. She would not go on alone.

He sighed and relaxed. "Rest here tonight. The stew will be ready soon, and night has come."

Lines of guilt shadowed his face. He must have known that he sent her into peril on her own.

The burbling of the kettle over the fire drew his eyes away.

When he pulled his arm away, she released her hold. Darius left her to stir the pot. "It will not be as hard as you think." Gingerly he lifted the steaming spoon with a bite of potato to his lips and tested it. "Almost done."

Istaria watched as he settled back to his whittling. He said little, and nothing about the magic he had used. She wanted to ask how, but the warnings of her mother not to reveal her power stopped her.

She did her best to ignore her curiosity until the food was ready.

When Darius offered it, she took a bowl of stew. Although the bland taste gave less than her tongue would have liked, she appreciated his care.

After eating, she laid down while he leaned back in his chair and closed his eyes.

Although she knew little about him, she wished that morning would not come so she would not have to leave.

≈≈

Images materialized from the clouded backdrop of the dreamscape.

Surreal and dark, the cave surroundings clarified. The cave ceiling curved above, following long white columns that arched to meet overhead in a thick, segmented trunk running along the ceiling towards either end.

From the distance, a light shone. Power radiated like waves rippling from a boulder tossed into a pond. It crashed against her, familiar and dreaded.

Recognition swept over her with a chill. Not again!

Unlike every other nightmare, Istaria watched as an observer. She watched a girl—herself as an innocent child—exploring the dark cave into which she had crawled to hide from her brother. He would never find her there. She would win the game.

A strange light drew the girl closer. Panicked, Istaria raced towards her. If only she could stop her; to keep her from the dismal error of her curiosity.

When she reached out, she could not grab the child. Her arms passed through. *No! I'll not let it go on like this.* Every attempt to restrain the girl failed as her arms swept through air.

"Mama?" The girl's voice echoed in the silent passage with the slightest tremble. "Phelan? I like this game no more. Find me now."

The light brightened and the girl approached it. Istaria's stomach knotted. The irrevocable act repeated itself once more. She watched in horror as the whole incident replayed before her, and she could do nothing to stop it.

The child neared a shimmering crystal pulsing with a steady rhythm. Where the ceiling slanted down, the light projected from its pedestal of rock raised from the ground.

The Light blinded Istaria. The cave spun with unmerciful dizziness. What was this? Never before had the magic affected her in her dreams.

Gradually, the dizziness subsided. Istaria wished she could shout to the girl to run before she committed an error she would live with the rest of her life.

She was too late and could do nothing.

The crystal pulled the child into its depths, where colors swirled like rainbow snakes twisting themselves around each other.

"Phelan should see this." The child's eyes grew wide with awe. She reached for the inviting surface. Small hands set on the sides that expanded and contracted like living flesh, like a heart beating.

In a burst of light, the forces exploded outward. The girl stumbled back with a shriek. She scrambled to her feet and backed away, her eyes wide with terror as the light surrounded her. Out of the haze a monstrous, ghostly form materialized.

The girl screamed and fled.

Istaria screamed in silent sympathy. She raced after the dragon chasing the child. However, it overtook the girl in just a few steps. The stream of its magic knocked the girl down into stillness.

The dragon stopped. It waited.

Istaria ran to the girl. The magic absorbed into the small body, leaving the cave dark. The child's brown braids turned a sparkling white.

Why? Istaria spun on the beast. *Why did you do this?*

The dragon's blue eyes blinked at her with warm patience, like a parent to a confused child. The translucent haze smiled in its reptilian gaze. Istaria clamped her jaw. *Release her! She did nothing wrong to you.*

A whisper echoed through the cave in response, washing against her with the gentle push of a wave. A great sadness invaded her emotions; it quickly shifted into something of hope and purpose.

Before it could say anything more, familiar voices rose from the other end of the cave.

Istaria started awake, sitting up from the hard bed. However, her heart beat normal and her breathing was calm. The usual nightmare had not ended at her panicked flight. Instead, she had seen it through, as an observer rather than the victim.

The dragon had seemed to attempt contact this time. Never before had that happened. She had taken control and stood up to it, faced her fear.

After a quick scan of the dark cabin, Istaria spied Darius, who had slid down in his chair with his chin to his chest. She sighed and laid her head down on the pillow again. What would come with the morning?

Although she closed her eyes, sleep eluded her. Instead, she tossed and turned with worries chasing through her mind. Gradually the light in the cabin grew and she realized that morning approached.

When Darius stirred from his slumber, he groaned in discomfort and stretched. The chair beneath him creaked in protest.

Istaria pretended to sleep while he moved about. When her side ached, she rolled over to relieve it.

"Morning, my lady." His soft voice broke the stillness of the dawn like the light that would soon peek through the window. "I must apologize that you had a restless sleep." He turned to face her, a hint of a smile on his lips. "This is not befitting the beds you normally sleep on."

Istaria dropped her eyes, her cheeks warm in embarrassment. How had he known?

His lips curved further into a clear smile. "How is your ankle?"

Blinking, she realized she had forgotten about her ankle. It had not bothered her when she slept or rolled within the bed. Slowly she sat up and brought her legs over the edge of the bed. Carefully she eased her weight onto it.

So far, so good.

When Darius reached down for her hands, she accepted his offer and let him pull her to her feet. The moment she put her full weight on her foot, pain gripped her ankle, though not like the night before. She leaned on Darius, who frowned while helping her balance to avoid standing on the foot.

"I was afraid this might be." He lowered her to the bed again. "Rest here."

Istaria frowned. His tone indicated he had other ideas. If so, he never explained his reasons but set to work gathering items from various places within the cabin. He handed her a bowl of dried fruit.

She gladly took it and ate.

After filling a small bag with a few supplies, he slung it over his broad shoulders and opened the door. The early morning breeze blowing in chilled Istaria. She pulled the blanket around her and curled up beneath its warmth.

I'll return quickly. He exited, closing the door behind him.

She stared after him. Could she trust him enough to ask how he used the mindspeech that came easily to her? It meant exposing her magic abilities.

The desire to know gnawed at her with an increasing appetite for answers.

As desire and caution debated within her, time passed in a blink. He entered without the bag but wore a grim expression. "The only way to aid your escape is to accompany you myself, though I am not certain which path is safe. We must hurry, however. If Vahrik follows his suspicions, he'll have scouts watching me. I hope to pass them without notice."

Istaria slipped out from under the covers. She slid her feet into her shoes and stood with his help.

Darius helped her hobble out the door. On the way out, he grabbed an old cloak and threw it over her. In the frame of the door he paused, gazing into the room.

After a long hesitation, he closed the door without turning back. He helped her to the saddled horse standing patiently with the bag of supplies stashed behind the cantle.

When she stood next to the gentle giant, Rowen turned his head. Before she could stop to think, Darius threw her up to straddle the wide horse. She gasped and caught the pommel to keep herself from falling off the other side. Never had she ridden a horse alone.

When she found her balance, Darius mounted behind her. The saddle shifted with his weight but Istaria held on to the pommel. Memories of her horrible abduction by Thain and his party returned.

This was not the same, she told herself.

Once settled, Darius clucked to the gelding. Rowen pricked his ears and started off at a lively walk.

Where they headed, Istaria could only imagine. Surely it could not match the dangers around them or the one that chased her. At least this ride would promise escape, unlike Thain's harsh manners when he had taken her from her home.

Chapter 13
13.3 pc 937

For a change, Calli tolerated helping her mother. To escape the queen's overbearing presence she busied herself in the bakehouse, something she usually avoided. With her sleeves rolled up and her hair back from her face, she found ways to stay out of the dining hall; away from the queen. In one of her old, patched dresses, she blended in with the other servants, noisily chatting or shouting orders.

Her mother knew nothing of her plan, that she would leave when the food trays returned empty. At that time, she would run off and change into the breeches and tunic Phelan had found. They fit as near perfect as not but they would allow her freedom of movement. Better than tangling herself in her dress while learning the fighting skills she would need to carry out her plan.

"My, your a buzzin' today," Ilde said with a coyness in her tone that put Calli on edge.

"I've not been kept busy enough lately." Calli fixed her eyes on the cooking pot she scrubbed, unwilling to entertain the loose tongue of the other woman.

"Sure, an y've not been exactly available." Her mother, Beadu, or Cook to most others, would never understand.

"I've been too available."

"Never too available to serve the queen." Beadu forced another pot into the basin as Calli finished the first. Grimy water splashed out. "'Bout time yeh did your chores."

"I'm needed there, too."

"Then why be yeh not with them?"

Calli shrugged. "I suppose I've needed time with my real mother."

"Y'd not be tellin' this mother the whole truth."

"I'm telling you enough. That were I needed, I'd hear her summons."

"Yeh best not upset her grace none, what with the princess gone. No daughter o' mine—"

"Oh, mother!" Calli slammed the scrubbing brush against the pan and turned to face the woman. "If that stubborn pride would drop for a moment, y'd see that not a burden am I but the poor queen's refuge. She sees me as her friend."

Beadu raised her eyebrows. "Told yeh herself, she did?"

Ilde waddled nearer, her impending childbirth clear. "What does she say?"

Calli glanced at her, at her swollen belly, and the curiosity within her eyes. If ever she became such a gossip as Ilde, she wished someone to shut her up.

She turned back to her mother. "What she says is of *my* concern. But she told me she needed me."

Her mother's eyes narrowed in a close examination for any hint of a lie. How her father ever could have tolerated such a woman was beyond her measure. "Mind your manners, child, and mind yeh stay far from that boy. Nothing but a cheatin' heart, he is."

Calli let out a sharp breath. Was it not enough to deride her about her duty to the queen that she had to reign in her fondness for the prince? "Mother!" She stormed out before either could comment.

"Callisara!" Cook's bellow reached her. "Calli, return at once! I've not finished with you!"

"Forget it, mother!" If not for Ilde, Beadu might not have spoken to her. Her mother never showed the same respect as the queen, but blamed her for any slight fault.

The further she marched from the bakehouse the less Calli fumed.

By the time she reached Istaria's quarters, she calmed enough to laugh at the incident. Her mother could be so stubborn and annoying.

Shoving the door open relieved the remaining tension. The door slammed against the wall and bounced back. Calli shoved it again and whirled to stand out of its way when it rebounded. A new excitement sparked at beating the door with the anticipation of what was to come. Phelan had been too busy yesterday to begin her training but he had promised this day.

She jumped in a burst of excitement and ran to the chest where she had stored the precious clothes dug up two days ago.

"What would mother say to this?" Calli opened the carved wooden lid. The tunic, belt, breeches, and boots lay neatly on top. For all their worth to her, the clothes could have been the most valuable gems.

Without any servants assisting her, she changed her clothes. The tunic hung loose on her but she belted the middle and fastened the leather bracers her father had once made for her to keep the sleeves out of the way and protect her wrists. They still fit.

After fitting the boots, she checked her reflection. The breeches were a bit large, but she had grown out of the ones her father had given her. They would do.

Still, one thing was missing.

Long red locks on an otherwise boyish image were out of place.

With her brush and ties in hand, she sat on the bed to braid her hair. She refused to cut it, but would not tolerate it hanging in her face.

While she worked on her hair, her thoughts drifted to her friend. What was Istaria doing? What conditions did she endure?

Calli shuddered at the atrocities that came to mind. Her fingers worked fast, as if every second would bring her closer to the princess she served. She would work hard to learn what she could, but she could not wait long.

Calli tied up one braid before a knock on the door interrupted her thoughts. If her mother had come to harass her, she refused to answer.

"Calli?"

The low pitch of the voice could mean only one person.

"In here!" She fumbled with the second braid.

"Are you dressed?"

"Yes."

"That's disappointing." The door opened to reveal a tall, handsome figure. The dapper clothes of a soldier hid none of the air of nobility. He stood proud and tall, too true to his birthright for anyone to mistake him for anything less.

Phelan's eyes watched her fingers within her hair while the door thudded closed behind him.

Her fingers worked with mechanical accuracy. All those years of braiding Istaria's hair had served her well.

"You'll be as any awkward recruit."

She snorted her defiance. "Y'll see otherwise."

"So will you. Hurry now. We've limited daylight to work." He leaned back against the door. "A lady no more are you."

Calli tied the end of the braid and fastened both around her head under Phelan's scrutiny. "No less a lady, but more a warrior in training."

She rose from the bed and wandered to the mirror. While standing before her boyish reflection, she glanced aside at Phelan. A broad smile stretched across his lips. He took a deep breath that swelled his chest.

He acted almost like the boy she remembered. Not too many years ago, he wore a similar posture when talking about winning races with the colt he had raised and trained from the Rivon mare.

What prompted the prideful smile now, she held a fair guess. In spite of her desire to stay with him, she refused to succumb to his charms. Istaria needed her.

"Very good." Phelan stepped away from the door. Before she walked through, he grabbed her arm. "You're almost a soldier."

Calli frowned up at him, then at his hand on her arm.

Phelan ignored her and dragged her to the door with a firm hold. In the empty corridor, she shook herself free and marched ahead of him. Phelan jogged to catch up to her. "A little eager? Stay with me, unless you want to attract curiosity."

With a scowl, she slowed her pace. He led her by way of the long corridor that arched around the rear. They passed no one in the corridor, and the library door stood closed to peering eyes. At least he avoided the most trafficked corridors of the palace.

She knew where he led her—the most deserted place within the protective wall of the palace grounds.

The orchard.

The idea both insulted and relieved her. Insulted because of his lack of faith in her; relieved her that he spared her making a fool of herself before others, if it came to that.

Despite his earlier amusement of teasing her, he either by habit or on purpose held the door open for her exit.

Or, as it proved, a grand entrance before a pair of toughened, war-hardened soldiers.

"*Lady* Calli—"

She swore to wipe the grin off his face. However, she clamped her jaw on a retort and stepped outside.

"Your instructors, Donaghy and Morain."

Calli faltered. Her instructors? She looked at the two men, looked back to Phelan, and took a step forward. They wore mail and armor with swords belted at their waists. The one on her left grinned slyly, his dark eyes gleaming with challenge. The man on her right stood with a face of stone, his arms crossed. Both displayed scars of battle made grizzly by their beards.

"Milord, I understand none o' this."

She spoke too soon. A moment after the words left her lips, she caught on. He would not teach her alone, but would humiliate her before two of the best soldiers in the king's army.

She whirled on him with a snarl. "Damn, you!"

Phelan jumped away, his hands before him in defense. "I think you misunderstand. While I have the skills to fight, I've not the skills, nor the time, in teaching what you require."

The darkness take him! He could have his fun at her expense. She would learn to fight, whether from him or them.

Calli regained her composure and turned to the two men, refusing to give in to his pranks. "Then it shall be," she said with a confidence not truly felt.

Glancing aside, she caught the surprised look on his face before he recovered with a smile. "She's all yours, gentlemen."

"So, the lady wishes to fight?" the man on the left said. He turned to the other, who nodded.

Something happened in that moment that she missed. It left an uneasy feeling in her gut.

The man on her left stepped forward, studying her with a critical eye. "Not big, but not small either. The child o' Kaillen, be yeh? We'll see if yeh live up to the name."

Calli squared her shoulders. Her father had been the best and had taught her. She swore to extinguish their doubts. Her father would be proud. "By honor I'll earn that name."

They glanced at each other, the one near her raising his black eyebrows. The other shrugged and said, "As you will, Donaghy."

Donaghy circled her like a hawk preparing to strike. "By no means less than the fullest at that."

The intensity of his gaze left her feeling as if he stared into her soul. She stared back at the challenge he posed, daring him to back off with her growing annoyance.

After a long minute, Donaghy backed away to his companion. His eyes focused on Phelan next to her. "Not an easy task to make a warrior o' this one, but that yeh wish it, I'll take your challenge."

Morain stood with his arms crossed. "She's not worth it."

Calli stepped forward and started to object.

Before she could open her mouth, Phelan stretched his arm before her. "Calm, Calli. You match none of his skills."

She scowled at him. "Y'll see in time your mistake."

"He's only trying to stir you." Phelan turned to the men. "For your service to this land and to the princess, I thank you."

For a moment, no one said anything. Then Morain dropped his arms to his sides and let out a breath. "A long task it'll be. We do nothing standing here. This way to begin—" He extended his arm and pointed into the woods.

Calli took a deep breath and started past him in the direction indicated. Finally, after all her frustrations, she would act on her guilt. She would become a warrior, like her father. She would prove she could best them all.

She would fight. What would they start with first—swords, maces, axes, or one of the myriad other wicked weapons she had once handled?

They led her through the orchard to the small clearing at the far wall.

Phelan followed behind her, his presence mocking her intentions. Did he not realize how much more she refused to back down before this challenge? After all the years, all the quarrels, surely he knew her enough to foresee that she would continue in spite of this humiliation.

The soldiers continued to the far edge of the orchard and down the slope to the wall. A pile of stones awaited them with a small two-wheeled wagon balancing on its shafts nearby.

"Ah!" Donaghy stepped up to the pile. "Here we've made ready to begin."

Calli looked to the pile of stones he patted and then at him. "What training is this?"

"To build strength." He crossed his arms, matching her stubbornness and proving his point by the thickness of his arms. "If not for strength, y'd never hope to t'fight; not least one such as yourself."

She scowled but strode to the pile. There she stopped and turned.

Phelan lounged on the root of a tree jutting out of the slope. "Well? Have at it. Never did a man...or woman...reach his or her destination if not taking a first step."

Unfortunately, he made sense—they all did. She loathed them for it.

"You load this here wagon and haul these rocks to the shed, then—" Donaghy paused.

Then you teach me to fight, Calli silently finished.

"Dump them and reload them and bring them back here, five times today."

She blinked. "What?" What sense had left him?

He grinned and nodded.

Calli turned to Morain and around to Phelan behind her. They also nodded. All in agreement that this was her training. "This cannot be."

She twisted back to face Donaghy. "What good is it to load the rocks and dump them? No less than madness."

He shrugged. "We'd be glad t'make more use of our time."

Calli growled but held her ground. "This is what I wish, what nonsense you feel." The last part came out muttered as she bent over for the top stone. Her arms strained with the weight of lifting and carrying it to the small wagon.

"You wanted to train," Phelan said.

She scowled at the rock rather than granting the men the satisfaction of seeing her hatred and humiliation. They could have their fun. She would do this and any other task they dreamed, but she wouldn't give up.

They wanted her to fail. She would prove them wrong, and she would conquer their tests.

In two steps her arms quivered and ached from carrying the immense weight. She stumbled, but regained her balance dropped the stone inside the wagon. One there.

When she turned and beheld the mountain of stones, her shoulders sagged. This would be a long day.

Chapter 14
14.3 pc 937

Skies burned, though not with fire. Blinding light filled the air and her soul, cleansing her spirit. She smiled and let it flow through her.

In a flash, the light vanished, extinguished by a shadow.

Tahronen shivered at the darkness that fell over her as one form after another blotted out the light. The Red Clan. She nearly choked on the realization.

Still, the vision played. Flames consumed the land while the clash of magic sparked overhead.

In the midst of it all, a small shape appeared, lost in the glory of its power. It gestured and all the earth and sky and sea obeyed. Dragons and magi froze.

The prophecy is upon us! Tahronen blinked away the blinding vision. Whether literal or symbolic, she could not say.

She stretched her slender legs toward the sheer drapes separating her from the entrance to her chambers and brushed her golden hair behind her shoulders. The cluster of candles to her left pushed aside the night with their soft glow.

How long had she waited? How long had she prepared for the fulfillment of the white dragon's prophecy?

She had done as necessary, preparing the *m'athêrred rî Lûmea* for thousands of years. How many children had she sent out? Through the formation of the Lumathir, the children of the Light and the most powerful army against the darkness, she had aided in preparing mankind for the destruction that Lusiradrol would unleash.

As only one part of the Majera, she had not the full ability to see through time in any direction. Now, it seemed fate had played its hands, and would soon reveal its intentions to all.

A smile crept to Tahronen's lips. The three would be one; whole once more to carry out the work. Too long had it been since the one had been split into three. The Majera knew neither death nor hardship but were creatures of the universe.

However, first she must attend to the children who followed her. She was needed by them, and she wanted more information about the white dragon's resurrection.

She no sooner rose to stand than a hawk entered her quarters through the open window. The gentle waves of magic emanating from it identified the bird as the messenger.

Tahronen stepped from behind the drapes and studied the magnificent bird clutching to the frame of her open window.

"What news do you bring this evening, Gaispar?"

In a second, the bird formed into the young woman who served the dragons. The shapeshifter stood within the room and peered from beneath her hood. "Forgive my intrusion, mistress. The dragons sent me."

"To say the time draws near."

Gaispar blinked.

Tahronen smiled. "I know his plan is in process, that he will soon make himself known to the world again." Her smile dropped to a frown with the memory of the rest of the vision. "But he may not arrive in time to stop her."

"Lusiradrol."

"Yes." Tahronen suppressed a shudder at the name. "She will resurrect her clan from their sleep, I fear."

"How?"

Tahronen shook her head. "That has not been revealed to me." She fixed a sad look on the young woman. "Watch over the princess. She must accept her fate, or all is lost. Go now. Warn the mage that waits."

With a nod, Gaispar lifted her arms, transforming into the hawk. She circled the room and flew out the window.

Tahronen watched her go. Too much was at stake. Although she could not interfere, she could guide the others.

Chapter 15
19.3 pc 937

They had spent the last few days wandering the forest, avoiding the soldiers, whose numbers had multiplied since her escape. Istaria wished for a place to rest.

Darius had taken her to a place where she could find further help. However, when he told them she ran from Tyrkam, the husband and wife feared for their family too much to agree to the risk.

With their food running low, Darius expressed his concern.

On the morning of the sixth day since they ran, they circled back to his cabin.

Or what had been his cabin.

Rowen pricked his ears and stopped. Istaria stared, dumbfounded.

Darius said nothing, but his hands clenched the reins until his knuckles drained of color.

A pile of charred wood remained of what had been the cabin and corral.

Istaria placed her hand over his, wishing she could comfort him. This was her fault for displeasing the warlord.

"I'll be fine."

Istaria recognized the tension in his voice, despite his attempt to make light of the situation. She rubbed his hands, but he simply patted her hand and urged Rowen forward. The horse's large hooves crunched over twigs and grass.

At what had been the cabin, Darius halted and sat in contemplative silence. From high above on the back of the horse, Istaria could clearly see footprints in the soft ground around the charred remains.

"Vahrik did this. He now knows that I've betrayed him." Darius sighed and lowered his voice. "I know not where to go now, but we must leave this land to find safety."

He turned Rowen from the ruins and never looked back. "Better that I followed my instincts and left before he returned. I am homeless once again, but—" His voice lightened. "I'm in good company."

From behind her veil, Istaria smiled. Her guilt fell to the background of her worries, behind the question of what they would do now. She trusted Darius.

"I know where we can find some food."

They rode through the trees in a winding path, taking half a day to reach their destination. However, in the end they came to the edge of a town. By then, Istaria's stomach grumbled with hunger.

They stopped within the shelter of the trees and watched the activity in the flats below. The town consisted of various buildings around a central well. Most of the buildings were made of wood, though some of the poorer dwellings at the outskirts used sod.

At the sight of Tyrkam's soldiers mingling amid the commoners and buildings, Darius stiffened behind her. They watched in silence for several minutes before Darius dismounted. "We'll have to wait and go in at dusk."

Istaria put a hand to her stomach as it churned.

"I know. We've enough for a small meal. It will have to do." He led Rowen away from the town into the trees of the forest.

The afternoon passed slowly, but Istaria entertained her mind with the stream running through the forest. The chill of the water soothed her ankle, which had healed well by staying off it. Darius rested against a tree, though she wondered if he slept after the loss of his home and all that he owned.

Only Rowen seemed unconcerned.

By dusk, Darius grew restless. While tacking up Rowen, he stopped several times and froze to listen.

Istaria took his cue and reached out with the magic. She detected nothing. That concerned her more, since Darius obviously had noticed something and he also was a magic-user, or at least as near as she could tell he was.

When he finished, he lifted her into the saddle and led Rowen to the town. With twilight falling over it, almost no one walked about the streets. Lights from the windows provided patches to see by but no more.

An eerie quiet settled on the town.

Istaria took Darius's cue when he pulled his hood lower over his head and she pulled hers low also.

He nodded his approval to her and led her to the road that entered the town. Darius hunched with the posture of a laborer and allowed Rowen to lower his head to the ground. Istaria had to force back a smile at the sullen image they must have presented.

When they entered the town, no one greeted them or made any attempt to stop them. A couple of uniformed soldiers stood chatting on a side street nearby and paused to watch them pass. Istaria felt their eyes burn through her and tried not to watch them. She hid behind the hood of the cloak.

She and Darius wound through a couple streets until they came to an inn. From inside, the raucous noise of inebriation and good cheer rose up.

Darius ignored the commotion and led Rowen to a large double-door at the side. He pushed it aside and led both into the stable. Once they were safely inside, he shut the door.

The odor hit her first. Istaria put her sleeve to her face to block the stench of the animals. She had been in the stable at home many times to feed treats to her brother's stallion but it had never smelled so foul of animals.

Rowen's ears pricked up.

Two cows shuffled their hay in the back corner while three horses poked their heads into the light from the single lantern hanging near a door.

Darius stopped Rowen and helped Istaria dismount. She waited for him to tie the reins around the gelding's neck. Once turned loose, Rowen trotted into an open stall.

He knows this place well, Darius said and latched the stall door.

Before she could react, he led her to the door connecting the inn. Without a sound, he pushed it open and slipped through.

She followed into a well-stocked pantry.

He went no farther. Instead, he pulled the hood from his head and motioned for her to sit on a chest. "Rest, my lady. The innkeeper's wife will find us soon."

Istaria obeyed, hoping this person could be trusted with their security.

While they waited, Darius bent down to examine her foot. He unwrapped the ankle and smiled. "Much better." His whisper rang clear in the small room.

Leaving her foot unwrapped, he slipped it into her shoe. In the gloom of the small room, she could not see it but knew that he smiled in approval of the healing.

"You heal fast."

She shrugged away the compliment. When a chill from the night air touched her, she shivered and pulled the cloak tight.

Darius took a seat next to her and pulled her close to his warmth. She welcomed the closeness.

Not long in his company, she had come to trust him. Not once in the days she had spent with him had he mistreated her in any way. He had worked with a purpose meant to help her, not harm her as she had endured amid Tyrkam's men. She wondered why he had risked so much for her. Perhaps one day she would dare to ask, but not today.

They sat in silence for a long while before a woman's voice rose outside.

"Watch your load there!"

When a slit of light outlined the door, Istaria stiffened. Darius jumped to his feet.

The door opened, spraying them in the glow from a handheld lantern that added to the light from the room beyond.

A step into the pantry and the woman gasped. "Good heavens! Whence came yeh, Darius?"

"Shut the door, Hlynn."

She obeyed his gentle command, studying him in the light of her lantern with a look of concern. "Darius. Am I glad to see yeh! Those fools o' Tyrkam's been askin' questions about town. Nobody seen yeh in some days, so I thought yeh left us. Am I happy you're alive! What's this about?"

He turned his head to indicate Istaria. Her cheeks warmed at the sudden attention as Hlynn's eyes widened.

"What be this girl but the cause o' all the trouble?" Her eyes peered into the veil. "Cover yer face, eh?"

Ignoring her question, Darius said, "We need supplies."

"If yeh were not as family, I'd toss yeh out the door. We've not the means to be feedin' every mouth free, but for you... For *you* I'll make an exception. Were not the husband o' my sister long—Goddess give her peace—but yeh be family to us. We never turn away family."

Istaria let out a breath she had not realized she held. The woman smiled at her in the glow of her lantern. "Yeh need a cleanin' and to put a little flesh on them bones o' yours, miss."

What Istaria would do for a simple bath!

"I wish we had the time, but the soldiers are everywhere."

"Aye! I'd not be gettin' yeh past the brutes outside this door."

"Hlynn! Did ya lose your way in there?" The muffled voice rose loudly outside the door.

"Just checked the cows. Thought I heard them bellerin' and come check to see if it's that milk thief again!" she called.

The other voice came through clear, as if the person stood not far from the pantry door. "Make it fast. They're not good tempered on empty stomachs."

Hlynn hmmphed away the last and muttered under her breath, "None's good in that bunch no more."

"Trouble?"

"Jus' yeh mind your cares, Darius. I lost a sister and nephew to chance. I'll not lose yeh too, when she thought the world o' yeh."

Darius dropped his eyes and said nothing for a moment before regaining his composure. "Forgive me, Hlynn." He looked up and met her eyes.

"Though we need food, we've no time for idle chatter."

A new commotion rose outside the pantry door. "I heard voices."

At the sharp tone, all three turned.

"Outta my way!"

Before she could react, Darius wrapped his cloak about Istaria and muttered the same strange words he had used before.

In the flash before the cloak covered her face, Istaria caught sight of Hlynn reaching for a jar on one of the many shelves.

The door creaked open.

"All right, already!" Hlynn huffed. "Have yeh no manners to wait for a meal? I'm comin'."

She stepped out the door as another voice snapped at the intruder. "See? No one but my wife. Yeh had too much mead, if yeh not mind me sayin'."

"Yeh can have what you want," Hlynn said before the door closed behind her. The voices faded away, although the accusations had turned into teasing about hearing strange voices.

The magic faded and Darius lowered his cloak. *Hurry, my lady. We've no time to linger further.*

They took dried fruits and old vegetables that had kept through the winter in the pantry, and some fresh bread. When they returned to Rowen, the food supplies filled the bags on his saddle.

Darius lifted Istaria into the saddle and led Rowen to the door. He opened it and peered out cautiously. Istaria guessed the streets were clear since he led her out and closed the stable doors behind them. They ground on their hinges, stealing her breath with the fear that someone would come running.

Darius hurried through the twilight, his head moving constantly back and forth. They made it to the nearest edge of the town and into the forest without trouble, despite the rhythmic thuds of Rowen's hooves. Not until the town disappeared behind them did she take a breath.

However, Darius searched about them as if he distrusted their surroundings. The forest sounds came from a distance, not anywhere near them.

Istaria reached out through the magic and caught the disturbances around them. At least eight men caused ripples in the magic, and closed in fast.

They're here.

No sooner had Darius sent the words to her than the soldiers attacked. Three of them jumped Darius while two more took the reins of the horse. At least one more pulled Istaria from the saddle.

She struggled against the arms that grabbed her and dragged her down, but failed against the strength of the men.

Once they had her on the ground, one of the attackers pulled her hood back. In the wan moonlight, he paused. "What have we here, boys?"

Before she knew what happened, she looked through the moonlight at their faces without the veil to shadow them. Her heart pounded a race to flee but at least two of the brutes held her secure no matter how hard she struggled.

"Now, now, my dear. That's not ladylike." He smiled and slid his filthy hand along her cheek.

She turned away, disgusted with the slimy caress.

When he grabbed her jaw, his fingers pinched her. She winced in pain. "Have some manners now, or Lord Vahrik will be quite displeased."

Istaria froze at the name. Soldiers that answered to Vahrik?

"Let her go."

All eyes turned to Darius, who struggled against the three men holding him.

"Get rid of this traitor." The leader turned back to Istaria. "Thought you could escape so easily?"

Istaria jerked her head away, but the back of his hand slapped her face. The impact stung her into tears.

"No!" Darius fought the last man off him, leaving him groaning on the ground with the other two who had held him a moment ago. "Leave her alone!"

The leader signaled two more men to attack.

Magic burned inside Istaria. She recognized its build up and fought to keep it contained. *Not now,* she begged.

With her emotions scattered from the attack, she lost control of the power. It burst forth from her, sending the men holding her thudding into the nearest trees.

The others gasped, not daring a step toward her. Their eyes widened, their faces illuminated in a faint light.

She stood trembling from the surge of power and looked up to the ghostly figure looming over her.

Darius took the opportunity to act, subduing the soldiers before they could flee.

Alone and staring into the eyes of a monstrous white dragon, the leader of the group ran off into the woods.

Istaria's legs weakened with the fading of the power inside her.

Darius reached her before her knees buckled. "My lady!"

She looked up to the blue eyes of the dragon gazing down on her and could have sworn he smiled. The flow of emotions from the dragon spirit warmed her.

Weak from the immense use of magic and the fatigue of traveling all day, she allowed herself to fall into Darius's embrace. In that moment, she realized that he had not run like the soldiers but had stayed with her. She looked up at the smile on his face, confused by the events and his reaction.

He looked up to the spirit and bowed his head. *"Nâlasa fer enthander."*

Through heavy eyelids, Istaria made out what seemed to be a nod from the spirit before it dissipated. It faded from her vision, along with the rest of her surroundings. From a distance, a familiar voice said, "I know who you are."

⁂

A surge of power ripped through the realm of magic. Like a tidal wave of energy it radiated out from the source.

Lusiradrol gasped at the strength of the blast that passed through her. Though it was not enough to harm anything in its path, the crest of magic hinted of the full potential of the one who had released it.

She had to find them, and destroy them before they ruined her plans.

Chapter 16
9.4 pc 937

Weary and tired, Calli set the wooden sword within the weapons shed. She lost herself in the shuffle of evening activity on her way to her room for rest.

Donaghy had defeated her time and again. The clothes she wore told the tales of his strikes in her multiple patches and mending. Despite the constant repair of her training clothes, the work invigorated her and inspired her. The strangest part of all this was that she enjoyed it as much as she had with her father, because it challenged her.

Phelan had insisted Donaghy and Morain make the training dull and difficult.

However, Phelan had to leave. She expected him gone for at least a full moon cycle. She planned a surprise for the prince upon his return from this trip. His attempts to dissuade her had failed.

After a quarter moon cycle since Phelan had left, Donaghy and Morain had given in to her demands, more out of curiosity than her will. They promised to teach her to fight with several weapons.

After a week of intense sword practice, the years spent under her father's training returned to her. She learned the subtleties of their behaviors, reading the body language and flicks of eye movement that indicated the next move. However, the first few days had left her with a few cuts and bruises now healing. The sores encouraged her to learn to avoid them. The wooden practice swords had proven themselves just as destructive as sharpened metal swords.

Her father's lessons returned more each day.

In her shuffle to the servant door of the palace's tallest inner building, she avoided the crowds of visitors. If anyone on the back terrace caught a glimpse of her disheveled appearance she might panic, fearing they'd discover her there. No one knew of her training.

In the shadows of the growing twilight, Calli found the rear servant door. It whispered on its hinges as she crept inside. Once in the corridor, her mind grew alert. She stayed to the quiet corridors, taking her time to reach the princess's chambers.

After navigating around other servants in the corridors, she reached the solace of the chamber. The heavy door groaned in protest. She grimaced and glanced down the hall toward the royal bedchambers.

The guards made no move. She had made them promise to say nothing. Samuel had had a good chuckle the first time he had seen her and warned her to watch out for Donaghy's tricks. She had learned for herself the biting wit and the cunning of the man who had trained him.

After rushing inside the dark room, she breathed relief. The servants had not yet lit the lamps, but she quickly fixed that with the flint on the bedstand.

Through the window, the first star flickered. She stood breathless, watching others spark into existence. Those same stars looked down over her friend, wherever she was.

With a sigh of regret, Calli resigned herself to undressing before any disturbances came that might steal her secret. She packed the boy's clothes into her trunk and locked it, while shivering in the supportive undergarments she had trimmed to stay hidden beneath her training clothes. Later she would scrub all the garments and repair them, again.

The servants came in minutes, while she examined a new red spot on her side that immediately warranted concern. It was no use to hide it. If the men were rough when she took after them, so be it. What lie would that be?

Two servants helped her. Calli knew their faces but had never spoken much to them, as they normally attended palace guests.

The younger servants gasped at her disheveled braids and streaks of dirt across her forehead and arms. She held few doubts that the greatest of their fascination generated from the splotch of crusty red at her side.

She failed to quiet their worries with a quick word about the hunting dogs in the bakehouse fighting over scraps.

When she undressed fully, they saw only a small cut for the amount of blood. That allayed their fears. They cleaned the small scratch with the boiled water steaming from the cloth they used to scrub her.

After the washing, she dressed in a robe and sat with her head back while they cleaned her mangled red locks. With gossip amongst themselves about the recent guests, they scrubbed the grimy coating from her hair and left her feeling renewed.

The treatment emphasized even more the gap between her and the real princess. The need to rescue her friend, the only princess who deserved this treatment, called to her.

She excused the girls when they finished, anxious for time alone.

Her muscles aching from a hard day of training, Calli sat on the bed and gazed out the window.

The stars twinkled in the sky above. Istaria probably sought the same freedom of that sky. Calli vowed to bring her friend home.

But first to rest. The two men had beaten her into exhaustion. Tired and alone, Calli stretched out over the bed and closed her eyes.

"Impressive."

Calli's eyes shot open.

The woman standing over her smiled. Dark eyes bored into Calli's soul, enveloping her in an air of sinister intent.

Calli sat up and pulled her robe across her chest. "Who are you? How did you enter? I heard no door."

"I am a friend who can help you reach your true potential." The stranger stepped fully into view.

Calli beheld a simple woman in a red dress whose shimmering black hair fell loose about her shoulders. A face of cold, unblemished beauty made her shiver.

"Forgive me, my lady. I'm but a servant to those of a special kind. I can help you become what you wish most and, thus, accomplish that which drives you in your training."

Calli leaned away. Caution stirred within her. Obviously this woman had watched her, though how she had passed unnoticed through the castle baffled her. Never before had Calli seen this woman and of all servants, she knew their faces. This one was not of the household. Had she accompanied one of the guests?

"What means of such—of this—have you? I've not seen your kind before."

"My kind hides beyond the realm of mortals."

"Realm of mortals?" This woman either had a high opinion of herself or came from somewhere beyond reality. Calli frowned. "You are...immortal?" She loosened her white-knuckled grip of her robe and rose from the bed.

The woman gave a nod, a movement as controlled as the smooth current of her voice.

"What creature are you to say this—that none are known but for those forces beyond this world which demons come. Are you that—a servant of the dark world?" Calli swallowed her fear of the answer. Without the means to prove or disprove anything the stranger said, she suspected and feared the worst.

A light chuckle responded to her challenge. The woman smiled with coy grace. "None of that which you fear, lady. Of magic was I borne."

"Magic-borne. You claim to be a witch? They are heresy, stories to frighten children." Only legends spoke of such individuals. How could such a woman exist? How could someone of mad visions possibly make her a better fighter?

Still, she played along as her curiosity won the internal struggle against her sense of caution. "What can you teach me that I've not already learned?"

"First lesson of combat, lady—use appearance to your advantage. Never are you to reveal your true abilities but as a last resort."

Calli nodded. A good lesson. Perhaps this woman knew something worth hearing. "I'll listen to your words, stranger; but at what cost?"

"No cost, but a penance to another I ask as retribution for his crimes against me."

A true price then, Calli thought, leaning against the post of the bed. Still, if this woman knew something useful, she could not ignore it. "Who do you speak?"

"A man known throughout the lands as a demon. A tyrant." Her tone darkened. "Whose greed has stolen the one you seek."

"Tyrkam!"

The woman smiled, the shadows of the lamps twisting it into menace.

"What crimes has he done to you?" A common thread with this woman wove into the blanket of Calli's caution.

"He took advantage of me for his dark purpose. I'll not forgive him so easily."

Calli eyed the woman with caution. How had this woman escaped, or had she not been a prisoner? Or did she lie to get attention?

"Why seek me for this task?"

"To share such a pleasure with another of similar goals and determination. I've no intention of granting him any satisfaction of seeing my face as life passes from him. He may wonder forever the true force behind his demise. And I would not deny *you* the honor of revenge."

The vindictiveness of her tone rocked Calli back.

She stepped away to the closet with her dresses and opened the doors. Trying not to show interest but curious, nevertheless, she glanced back once to the woman where she had left her, now plucking at the curtain with her black fingernail.

To hide the conflict of emotions struggling inside her, Calli shuffled through her dresses for one suitable for this evening.

How had this woman known she sought revenge? She must have waited for the right time, perhaps calculating when Calli was most ready and most determined to defeat Tyrkam. Was it not her goal of learning to fight? What, if not to defeat Tyrkam, was her purpose? Donaghy and Morain could teach her the skills of their experience, but perhaps someone who knew Tyrkam might provide the advantage she needed.

Calli pulled out a dress and closed the doors. With no intention of saving her friend to destroy herself in the process, she could see no other choice. She could not take this woman's offer. However, her desire to save her friend proved a strong foe against her sense of caution.

While fingering the soft material, she stared past the dress on the possibilities; alternative routes this chance might take her. In one she saw herself tortured for such a pact. In another all rejoiced with the warlord defeated and Wynmere glorious once more, though she doubted that image would ever happen through her efforts.

Why make such a choice without time to consider? That was what she needed—a chance to think about this strange woman and her words. That was the right choice.

After a deep breath to calm herself, Calli turned.

The stranger watched her with a smile edged in threat.

"May I have time to consider your offer?" Calli winced minutely, afraid of a rebuke.

It never came. Instead, the woman glided forward a couple small steps. "Take what you need, Calli. But be forewarned—even now Tyrkam prepares to end the feud."

With such mild reproach to her voice, Calli never noticed her name. The woman's willingness to give her time lifted some of her suspicions.

The strange woman turned to go.

"Ah... Thank you, whoever you are." Calli hugged the dress like a security blanket. "Where can I find you, if I agree to this?"

"Call me by name and I shall appear."

"What do I call you?"

"Lusiradrol."

Calli watched her exit through the door. "Lusiradrol." Her curiosity strung itself tight as a bow.

Chapter 17
13.4 pc 937

Darius glanced back at the woman on the horse and marveled again at her connection to the legendary white dragon. Many times since that night its spirit had appeared he considered it. The dragon had not appeared before or since that fateful night, but they had avoided trouble since then.

A mystery of any other sort he would not consider unusual, but this caught his attention. The prophecy was on its way. Gilthiel would return soon, in his time. Had he, Darius Clennan, also been chosen to aid its fulfillment?

He had puzzled over the question since the apparition but came up with only one answer—the Sh'lahmar. Although he was an outcast, sworn to never speak of the secret order, only they could provide the answers he sought.

He had to return, even if it meant his death.

Something stirred at the fringe of his awareness, the same something that had followed them since the dragon appeared. The ripple of magic touched him for a second and vanished again. Had he not been trained to be aware of the flow of magic, he might not have caught the tiny fluctuation.

A slow grin spread across his face.

Of course they would have observed him, lest he break his oath as a former guard. He could only guess the individual was at least as skilled as he; perhaps an assassin to protect the secret of the Sh'lahmar. None of the guards had been told, but he had suspected since leaving that they would ensure their secret using some method. Why else would they allow him and a rare few others to live outside the hidden lands bearing their secrets?

Who was this person trained to kill if he broke his vow of silence about his former life? He would likely never know until his last breath. How had he not noticed their presence sooner?

The answer came to him immediately. He had never had reason to use much magic until the woman limped into his life, and the man following them was skilled in hiding his presence. No doubt a trick taught to a select few.

Darius traveled under cover of the trees, always aware of the creatures that inhabited the forest. Their magic would be useful if anyone attacked them again. If this individual had seen the white dragon, they would not bring any harm to the princess.

Darius glanced back to check on the woman who had been sent to him for help. No longer wearing her veil since the soldiers had attacked outside of Thealon, she caught his eyes and smiled. He was glad the veil had been pulled.

Never would he have guessed the extent of her beauty, a product of the finest ancestry and upbringing. Part of him suspected the Lumathir had played a part in bringing such a wonder to the world. No other women displayed the perfection of the women of the Light.

It would also explain her propensity to harbor the dragon spirit. The legends about the strength of its power stated that the power of the white dragon was so great that none could contain it. Such raw, overwhelming power would drive a person mad from the inability to carry out even the most mundane task. Only a person of strong magical lineage would have the ability to harness that power.

Through his awareness of magic, a cloud invaded his mind and grew more ominous each second. Like a void where all light disappeared, it darkened the magic.

It, or she, approached fast. They could not escape.

Darius looked back, concerned for the woman. She wore a pained expression, her eyes pinched shut and her arms wrapped around herself. "My lady—"

She opened her eyes, revealing the same blue glow that had accompanied the appearance of the dragon spirit days ago. *Help me,* she begged.

She spoke to him! Fighting his surprise, Darius sprang to her side and helped her from the saddle.

Make it stop. She curled into a tight ball on the ground.

Darius sat and held her within his arms. Magic poured from her, tingling in his senses. She whimpered and pressed her face into his chest. He rubbed her back and soothed her with his voice, but she clutched his shirt tight. The tension in her body increased.

The darkness closed in on them. Rowen pinned his ears, standing over the humans as loyal as a guard. Enchanted almost unnecessarily with a spell placed by Darius years ago, the horse could not desert them.

Darius searched around them through the quiet forest, but saw nothing.

Istaria pushed away from him, moving like a puppet on a string.

He stood up next to her, able to do nothing but watch as her arms made a sweeping motion. Magic swirled about her in a familiar pattern.

When the dark woman materialized before them, they were ready. Lusiradrol's black robes matched the void she caused.

"Who dares wake my enemy?" Lusiradrol asked.

"Lusiradrol."

At the name, she snarled and let loose a blast of magic. It had no effect on the shield Istaria had raised. The power of the white dragon held firm.

"You will die for this treachery!" Lusiradrol continued her onslaught. The ground trembled, undulated, and cracked around the shield maintained by Istaria.

After what seemed an eternity defending against the attack, Istaria faltered. The shield hissed and sizzled, weakening with each spell Lusiradrol attempted. Darius put his hand to her shoulder and focused on transferring his energy. She straightened again, but would not last long on his limited abilities.

The Sh'lahmar guards could protect against magic, but it was in their combined strength that they worked best.

Through the continuing attacks, sweat formed on Darius's brow. He realized through the haze from the maelstrom that the white lady also began to tire; she breathed hard, her body hot beneath his palm. With her strength and experience Lusiradrol would outlast both of them.

The stirrings of magic he had sensed earlier burst open. Darius searched around them, but his eyes found nothing. Only when he allowed his attention to drift with his hold on the magic did he find the man. Somewhere on the other side of the void of Lusiradrol's presence he lingered.

From out of his hiding, the other man cast a spell over the black-dragon-lady.

Lusiradrol ceased her attack and whirled on her new adversary.

The forest grew quiet.

For the first time, Darius saw his watcher, a moderately sized man with shoulder-length black hair and a few days of growth on his jaw. He recognized the face but the name escaped him at the moment.

"Uh-oh." The other's voice broke the silence a moment before he blocked a blast from Lusiradrol.

She screeched an ear-piercing shriek but stumbled. Whatever he had done had weakened her and distracted her attention.

Keep it up, Darius said to the other. The man nodded and focused another spell.

Lusiradrol deflected his attack but the continued rampage brought her to her knees. She turned to Darius and Istaria, a menacing shadow over her. "I will return to destroy you!" Before the other man attacked again, she vanished in a plume of fire.

A moment later Istaria collapsed. Darius caught her before her head hit the ground. Relieved, he laid down next to her, overcome with a fatigue he had never known. The strain of defending against the attacks had drained him.

He checked on Istaria, but she had fallen into a deep slumber. His eyelids closed but he struggled to stay awake. The fog in his mind stole his senses, closing out the rest of the world. However, at the crunch of steps, he forced his eyes open. The stranger leaned over him.

"I'll see you later," the man said.

Overwhelmed and trusting a face he recognized from his former life, Darius fell into a deep sleep.

⁂

Gaispar watched from a distance, observing the battle between ancient forces. The black dragon had discovered the reawakening of her enemy. She would prove more of a threat now than ever. Tahronen had been right.

Hidden by the brush, Gaispar sniffed the charged currents with the sensitivity of a wolf's nose. Magic crackled like lightening and left its tangible mark on the earth. She watched until Lusiradrol vanished, before changing to a hawk to cover more distance.

They would need more than the guiding force of the dragon spirit to defeat Lusiradrol. The princess would need to learn for herself how to use her powers.

Makleor would wish to know.

Chapter 18
14.4 pc 937

Istaria roused at the sound of voices, one of them the comforting tone of Darius and the other unfamiliar. Their words caught her attention. She pretended to sleep, despite the roughness of the ground bruising her shoulder and hip.

The more she listened, the more memories floated back of the battle. She had watched as if from a distance as someone else took control of her body and channeled the magic. She knew the dragon spirit had guided her to protect against the woman who attacked. It had saved her life.

The stranger had appeared as she weakened. Who was he? Why did Darius now speak to him as if they knew each other?

"All these years?" Darius asked.

"Since you left the order."

For a few seconds no one said a word. Istaria reached out with the magic to touch them, each bright with power, but the stranger's presence outshined Darius.

When she realized that Darius sat within arm's reach, her cheeks warmed. He sat between her and the stranger. The other man spoke with the same accent.

"You were one of the most worthy of guards."

"I disobeyed codes."

"You followed your moral code, Darius. That is why you were allowed to live."

Darius sighed. "Could you have done it?"

"My training is to kill when necessary, but that means not that I've no heart, only that I can more easily ignore it when it comes to obeying the codes."

"What about this? Were you sworn to secrecy?"

"I'll not allow you to have all the fun." The stranger sounded almost put off, but Istaria suspected he pretended.

Darius chuckled. "Is that what you call it?"

"That you have been selected by fate to guard the chosen one of the white dragon, I'm jealous."

"You always did have a strange sense of humor, Jayson."

"Now you flatter me!"

The hard ground pressed into Istaria's shoulder and hip until she could bear no more. She rolled over to a more comfortable position.

In an instant, Darius knelt beside her. "Good evening, my lady."

When she looked up, the light of a nearby fire shadowed his smile. She accepted his aid to sit up and turned to the stranger. He looked familiar.

She remembered seeing him through a fog on the other side of the woman who had attacked. He now stood and bowed before her.

"A pleasure to meet you, my lady, though I would wish for better circumstances."

She gave a nod of approval, and he sat down again. When Darius sat next to her, Jayson smiled, although she thought the flicker of the fire cast a sad look to his face.

"This is Jayson, an old friend," Darius said. "He saved us from Lusiradrol."

Istaria smiled her gratitude, a gesture Jayson returned. "You're welcome."

"He will be joining us for...a while?"

"As long as I can." Jayson's gaze fixed on Darius. "I must report to the others this news."

What news? What others? She turned to Darius, puzzled by Jayson's words.

He pursed his lips, his eyes down as if thinking.

What news?

Darius's head snapped up, his eyes wide with surprise. "What?"

What news must he report? He had heard her; that much she knew to be true. Since he had seen her curse, he might as well know she could speak as he could, using magic.

"What is it?"

Darius raised a hand to silence Jayson, his eyes fixed on Istaria. "He means the dragon spirit that protects you.

"Long ago, the white dragon lived. By the power of the Majera, he was gifted with magic far greater than any dragon. He became the most powerful creature alive for the purpose of tipping the scales to defeat the Darklord. For this he was the most hunted of the dragons, by both the humans who feared him and Lusiradrol, for helping defeat her clan.

"Before he was killed, he predicted he would rise again. Because of the greed surrounding the legends of his power, he swore that only the most innocent heart would be gifted with that power."

Darius paused and swallowed. "He chose you, my lady. Since meeting you, I have seen why. He will guard you and guide you to those who'll help him return to corporeal form, but you must learn how to use his magic. Lusiradrol will forever be after you to destroy the white dragon, because he cursed her to human form."

When Darius ended, Jayson said, "Tell her the rest."

Darius looked to the other man, who nodded confirmation. He took a deep breath before continuing. "Lusiradrol was a black dragon, a creature feared above all others because she is part of the Chaos that once ruled. She seeks her clan, the worldly half of her being, to complete the work of her creator. With them, she can extinguish the light from the world."

All of this Istaria had never expected. The news of her curse that was not a curse but a blessing swirled through her head in a storm of confusion. Some of what they had said had been told in bedtime stories by her mother. Most was new, but difficult to fully comprehend. It overwhelmed her.

"My lady..."

She turned to Jayson.

"As long as you live, as long as the dragon spirit that resides within you remains attached to this world, we have a chance to destroy her and send her back to the void."

How could she destroy a woman as evil as this Lusiradrol? She had fallen once when the dragon drained her in battle with this woman. The thought of failing chilled her to the core. How could she be responsible for the fate of the world?

They regarded her with hopes she could never fulfill. Her eyes burned, cooled only by the tears of defeat. *I cannot.*

Darius's arm around her shoulders pulled her near. She buried her face in his chest, and her fears drained away with his touch.

"You can. We're here to help. I'll not let her defeat you."

"If it means anything, we weakened her at least as much as she drained you."

Istaria peeked out at Jayson and the smile he offered. The thought of having weakened the dragon woman cheered her some, but offered little to comfort her new fears of failing. Why had she been chosen? Why did the dragon spirit not choose someone else?

"You will grow stronger." Darius's arms, strong from years of cutting wood, blocked out the forest and its dangers. Istaria was safe with him. After traveling together for so long, she had come to feel comfortable with his presence. He knew exactly what she needed to soothe her troubled mind.

They spoke no more of the dragons, but about people and places she had never seen. Istaria stayed next to Darius, listening to some of their conversation while reaching out to her surroundings.

Somewhere behind her Rowen grazed. The creatures of the night shuffled in the trees around them, too afraid of the fire to pose a threat.

When her mind calmed, she let out a sigh. Since discovering the heart in the cave, she had feared the dragon spirit and its appearance in her dreams. Now, she wished more that she had never found it, that none of this had happened, except for meeting Darius.

She could do nothing, however, to change the past. The only option was to learn to control the magic so she could defend against Lusiradrol. At least Darius and Jayson were there to help her.

But how long would it take Lusiradrol to recover?

Chapter 19
15.4 pc 937

"Milord!" The nearest soldier's voice rose above the clang of metal on metal.

Free of trouble for the moment, Phelan risked a glance.

Nathan spurred his horse from the cluster of raiders, striking down the one who had grasped his reins. Cleared of the bunch for an instant, he claimed his advantage by meeting up with the prince. He joined Phelan and fought off another who had nearly succeeded in his quest of slaughtering Phelan from behind.

Baron reared. Phelan sliced down with his sword as his horse dropped into the melee. He felled several more of the raiders before freeing himself with his guards.

With most of his entourage trailing him, he fled from the scene.

Once clear of the fighting, Phelan risked a furtive glance over his shoulder. The few of the raiders still on horseback pursued them. A passing regret slipped through him for his guards who had fallen.

However, immediate concerns fixed on escaping this group with as many men as possible.

With their horses tiring, he led his men through a maze of trees. In the trees, they lost all sight of those who dared pursuit.

Phelan slowed his group to a walk and waited for all his men to catch him. They listened for signs of pursuit.

"M'lord—"

"Hush!" Phelan raised a hand. Only the heavy breathing of their horses reached his ears.

Satisfied with their safety, he relaxed and counted heads. Thirteen of eighteen guards had survived to join him; not the numbers he hoped for but better than none.

"M'lord, we've but a small gain on them. We should keep our pace."

Phelan fixed a contemplative look on the rugged face outlined in brown hair asunder. Dark eyes gazed intently from beneath a heavy brow, waiting for an answer. The wisdom of experience shone from his face.

"Certainly a wise choice, but I've to wonder if they yet follow. A group such as they would rather find easier prey."

"We've a greater problem now," Nathan said.

"I agree." Phelan checked around at the land. He recognized none of the landmarks. "A greater problem such as a guide from here, my friends."

They were lost.

A few men whispered, but most watched him for a decision. "Have I no volunteers?" Phelan received no replies other than stares. He had hoped one of the older guards would step forward to lead them. "Very well."

He directed Baron to continue in the direction they fled through the silent forest. His soldiers did little to add to it, perhaps sensing the eerie silence themselves.

Only after some time, when his stomach gurgled, he realized that hunting would be slim. No animal sounds emanated from the tall trees or the brush around them. Opting out of a rest, he led the group forward.

After half a day, they found a road and followed it around a hill—

To a tragic sight.

They stopped a distance away. Phelan grimaced at the gruesome scene and from the twisting of his stomach.

What had been a four-wheeled wagon lay on its side, the wheels splintered. The horses that had pulled the wagon had vanished, undoubtedly taken for their worth in the market. Bloody corpses scattered about, their faces forever fixed in final, muted screams of agony or the serenity of giving in to death.

The bodies lay at odd angles as if scattered by the wind. They counted six men, four women, and two small children. One infant lay naked and lifeless in the dirt. His mother lay face-down in the wheel ruts with her hand reaching for her child. Stripped from her was anything but rags, like the others. A red stain spread from the wound in her back.

"They were thorough," one of the guards said. Nothing of value remained, including the infant's swaddling blanket.

Gerick and another dismounted, leaving their horses to approach the macabre display on foot.

"They deserve a decent burial."

The group uttered a few words of agreement, but none dared to volunteer. Silence consumed them as if a great somber blanket had fallen and smothered all joy.

A whiff of the rancid odor of decay carried on the breeze. Phelan wrinkled his nose and lifted his hand to his face.

"They've a small vindication." Gerick squatted near a man wearing the hilt of a sword from his chest. Eyeing the design on the hilt, he gave a brief nod. "Done by our same band of outlaws, this was; and we've culled their numbers by half."

Phelan swung down from his saddle and left Baron to stand. He strode forward to study the evidence for himself. On closer examination, he recognized the handle as that of their earlier attackers. Phelan grabbed the rounded pommel and pulled the blade from its victim. The sickening crunch of bones against metal brought a lump of disgust to his throat.

He held the bloodied blade before him and checked the sword for a sign of its maker, any hint of the source of these raider bands.

The obvious slapped him with reality as cold as these murders. The crossguard. His eyes narrowed at the carved serpent with wings outstretched toward the blade.

The dragon crossguard used by the favored of only one army, which meant it hadn't been left here by accident but likely as a blatant threat.

His fingers tightened on the simple proof. None could deny the evidence to present to his father; a reason to attack Tyrkam sooner.

How true Calli's honor! No more would he restrain her outrage when his anger now flared.

He clamped his jaw on the madness burning inside him and handed the sword to the nearest guard. "Take this. A gift for the king." The revulsion of the crime might stir Isolder to act. Phelan had argued with his father countless times about the atrocities he had seen in his travels and the raiding bands sent by Tyrkam. No more would he sit idly by while the king allowed these murders to happen.

The other man took it back to the horses, where more of their group dismounted.

With his jaw clenched on the erupting rage within, Phelan rose to his feet. He scanned the carnage around him, trying not to notice the odor from the rotting corpses.

Working together, his guards would have little difficulty finishing the task before nightfall. Eight of them together managed to carry off what remained of the wagon.

A funeral pyre would dispose of the mess with greater consideration to their haste and the awful stench from the carcasses. It went against their beliefs of burying bodies to return them to the earth which had supported them, but they had nothing to use as shovels.

The others agreed. They righted the wagon, piling the bodies on a bed of kindling inside it. Most of the guards had busied themselves gathering wood, a few with securing their horses.

When he gained the resolve to help with the final few bodies, Phelan wrinkled his nose in disgust. If he had any push or pull, Calli would never leave the security of the palace.

With her, however, he would expect nothing less than vengeance for this crime. He could never tell her of this.

At least he could give her a means to protect herself. He hoped his gift was delivered to Setheadroc. The swordsmith had promised to finish by the summer solstice. When he returned, he would present it to her with the hope that she would never have to use it.

Chapter 20
17.4 pc 937

Istaria felt it, like a refreshing splash of water during the heat of the afternoon. She inhaled sharply and stopped to keep her balance.

Darius stopped next to her with a steadying hand on her shoulder. He waited, scanning the trees with his eyes.

From the shadows walked a hooded figure leaning on a staff, a figure Istaria recognized. The old man from Tyrkam's castle hobbled into their path. Istaria gazed in surprise.

From behind him, Jayson stood prepared.

A knowing smile touched the old man's lips. "Tell your friend I mean no harm."

Jayson blinked, and relaxed his stance with a wry smile.

Makleor nodded. "Very good. Now, my lady, we must talk."

When she turned to him, Darius met her eyes. "It's your decision."

Istaria squeezed his hand and removed it from her shoulder. She turned to the old mage. *I am ready.*

Makleor looked to each in turn and moved toward a boulder. At his approach, it molded itself into the shape of a chair for him to sit.

Istaria hesitated nearing him when she realized what he had done. When she met him in the old castle of Wynmere, she had never expected this of him.

"Fear not, Lady," Makleor said. He let out his breath in a grunt as he sat down. "Had I wished harm to you, only the dragon could stop me."

With Darius leading Rowen behind her, Istaria stepped carefully over the dead branches scattered on the ground. The breeches Jayson had brought from a village for her provided greater freedom over such obstacles. She found a place near the mage and sat. Darius joined her, while Jayson stood watch nearby.

"A friend described your battle to me. Quite the sly one, she is, much as a fox. Sometimes that is more truth than not." He chuckled and looked away.

Istaria followed his eyes to the fox that approached with unwavering confidence. To her amazement, the animal grew into a hooded figure. Slender, feminine hands pulled back a dark cowl from long, blonde hair.

"Good day, my lady." The woman curtsied with more grace than Istaria possessed of herself.

"Istaria Isolder, meet Gaispar, messenger of the dragons."

She stared in awe. The dragons? They were real? How evil they must have been to command this woman to their will. Her face dropped into a disapproving frown.

Gaispar smiled faintly. "Messenger only. None but fate I serve. That is my price for immortality."

"For three hundred years she has prepared to serve you, princess. It is your place. It is your destiny."

What destiny?

"As the emissary of the only creature who can banish Lusiradrol forever. You have a long journey ahead, however."

He waved Gaispar away. She smiled and bowed to Istaria, and joined Jayson.

Like Istaria, Darius ignored the low conversation between the two and fixed his attention on the old man. "Why have you come?"

Makleor fixed his good eye on the woodsman and sighed, the weight of his years hunching his shoulders. "I am old, guardian, but may not rest until the curse is lifted. You must see her to Eyr Droc, where she will be well cared for and protected until the dragon is ready to return to this world. In the while, she must grow in her ability to use the powers he granted. It is the only way to defend against Lusiradrol. You know this."

"Why not take us if you can make a portal?"

Makleor let out a heavy sigh. "It is not my place to interfere."

"Are you not interfering already?" Darius's accusatory tone had no effect on the old man.

You worked for Tyrkam. Why did you not help me escape, if you intended I should do this? Istaria asked.

"So many questions...questions..." His voice trailed off and he paused for a moment. "I intend nothing, my lady. I only guide. I do what I must to direct the forces of fate to what lies prepared for you. I am no one, but a servant, like Gaispar. I am not a fighter. That is your training, guardian." His good eye fixed on Darius.

When the comforting warmth of Darius's hands set on her shoulders, Istaria relaxed. She had not realized the tension building from the burden placed on her. First Darius and Jayson, now the old man.

Makleor smiled, his good eye sparkling with approval.

What must I do? Istaria asked and caught a movement from the corner of her eye. She glanced aside and caught the nod from Gaispar before the woman threw up her arms and took to the air as a hawk. The taut lines of Jayson's face worried Istaria.

A worry that built when the steadfast support of Darius left her to join Jayson. He must have seen it too.

"I will teach you enough to understand the power you control, Lady," Makleor said, drawing her attention from the conversation between Darius and Jayson. "But I cannot stay long. Tyrkam will not take well to finding me gone. He must not suspect anything."

What good was this old man who continued to serve the hated war monger? How could she trust him?

Amusement sparkled in his good eye. "I see by your face you disapprove. My purpose bears no ill-respect, nor do I approve. Nevertheless, it must be played."

Istaria crossed her arms and looked aside at the two men speaking together in hushed voices. Darius frowned but nodded to Jayson. Something bothered him, but he accepted it, whatever that was.

She turned back to Makleor but hesitated before nodding. *I will learn.*

"Good. We've not much time."

Chapter 21
18.4 pc 937

Istaria awoke at dawn as gray clouds moved in.

The old mage had left in the night, after helping her to accept the magic pounding within her for release. He had shown her how to manage the forces of magic without fearing them. That much, he said, would aid her in any circumstances. He expected Darius to teach her to use the magic for specific tasks.

She sat up from her place around the ashes of their fire and realized Jayson was gone. His essence no more stirred the forces nearby as it had for the many days he had stayed with them. Although she preferred the presence of Darius, the absence of Jayson diminished her. He had helped to barter for food and clothes, and his presence had brought greater security.

Istaria looked down at the clothes she wore, the clothes of some boy she never knew. Despite her obstinate refusal to wear breeches and shirts, Darius and Jayson had insisted she try them. Never in her life had she conceived of wearing anything but the dresses befitting her status, but she had to admit the greater freedom of movement from the breeches.

Despite the convenience, she kept her dress for a change of clothes and to remind her that she was a noble woman.

"Good morning."

She looked up to the smile on Darius's face and returned it. *Where's Jayson?*

"He had to leave."

Will we see him again?

Darius shrugged and sat down beside her. "Unknown. He has other duties." He studied her face, but she could not bring herself to look him in the eyes. "You miss him."

Istaria nodded. *Not as I would someone close, but more in fear of losing his protection.*

"Of course."

She frowned. Darius seemed oddly relieved by her words. *What will we do now?*

"We'll continue on to the Second Realm of Eyr Droc as Makleor advised. As soon as you're ready, we'll be off."

What was Eyr Droc? Who was there?

The questions would wait, but she wished they would explain more about the white dragon and Lusiradrol, about why she was so important.

Only time would tell. Darius told her no more than what had already been said.

Chapter 22
26.4 pc 937

On foot with Baron's reins in his hand, Phelan led his group of weary soldiers through the streets of Setheadroc. His shoulders relaxed in the familiar confines, no longer rigid with defensiveness. Their trek had taken longer than expected after their encounter with the rebel band. At least they had avoided any further entanglements.

Phelan lifted his eyes to the great spires of the palace and sighed. When they reached the courtyard, he stopped and patted Baron's neck.

"M'lord!" The scrawny Jamison skidded to a halt.

Phelan handed over the reins for the boy to take Baron.

Jamison's gasp drew his attention from the normal activity about the courtyard.

"He's bleeding!" Jamison pointed to Baron's dappled neck. A line of blood beaded its way from beneath the thick, gray mane.

Phelan lifted the hair and found a matted, puffy patch of torn hide. "Not so easy was our escape then."

He pushed the red-stained mane to the other side of the horse's neck. It must have scabbed over during the race from the battle; and he had missed it in his haste and the rain that came soon after starting the pyre.

"Escape?" The boy blinked. "Were you captured?"

"Attacked by Tyrkam's army."

"Attacked?" Jamison gingerly touched the flap of hide cut a hand's length perpendicular to the crest of Baron's neck. The mane was matted where it had served as a wound covering. "Where?"

"Far from here." Phelan assured him with a faint smile. "Clean him up and feed him extra. He served me well."

"Of course, m'lord." Jamison led the stallion to the stable.

Phelan turned away, confident the boy would treat his friend with the utmost care.

Other concerns called for his attention. He had witnessed enough bloodshed to wish this war over and done, to wish Tyrkam himself dead and his army strung up for the crows.

Shaking his head, he climbed the steps. The guards on either side of the doors pushed them open for him. Behind him, his men parted to their own business. He would finish his, and he swore never again to allow such a massacre. He vowed to use everything in his power to hold Calli back, if he could.

First, he had to find her.

"Phelan!" The gentle voice rose over the bare murmur in the main hall. He smiled to the queen and bowed from the neck. She rushed from her company to embrace him.

"My son," Damaera said with her arms around him.

"My lady."

"You're late returning. I worried so much." She backed away, straightening into her proper poise once more. A hint of a smile played up at one corner of his mouth. His mother insisted on playing the perfect queen, though her mothering instincts interfered.

"I pray for good news."

"Lord Almont has agreed. He'll send his mares come spring. Derek encouraged it."

"Damned be those rumors!"

Phelan's lips curved up fully. Damned the rumors of his sister behind her veil, but it had saved the negotiations. The rumors had also led a different noble to cancel the betrothal of his son to Istaria, an arrangement made before she could walk. His mother had also been happy when that collapsed.

Damaera studied him up and down. "And what of you?" She gently touched his face. "You're pale and thin."

"We had trouble."

She frowned in deep concern. "What trouble?"

"None for your worries." Phelan started away and paused as deeper concerns rose to the forefront. "Is Calli here?"

"I never see her between sunrise and sunset, but she is here...somewhere."

Relief flowed over him. At least Calli had not yet sacrificed herself to the slaughter. If he had his way, she never would, or at least he would be sure she had what she needed to return safely. "Thank you."

He turned from the queen, weary from the journey, and walked away. He was ready for sleep.

First, he would rest. Later he would discuss his concerns with the king and speak to Calli alone.

Phelan climbed the stairs and strode through the lonely corridors to his room. Once there, he closed the door behind him and collapsed into sleep on his bed.

Chapter 23
26.4 pc 937

Calli lay on the dirt, beaten and sore. First Donaghy with the quarterstaff and mace; after midday, Morain had taken his share of beating her at sword fighting.

"Enough for today," Donaghy said from his place on a branch overlooking the unmerciful training.

Calli glared at him and pushed herself out of the dirt to sit. "Very thoughtful of you."

Morain chuckled, sheathing his sword. "Y'll rest this night. If ever yeh wish to quit, we'll grant yeh that."

"Kaillen never quit!" After they had expressed surprise at her fast learning, she had confessed to Kaillen's lessons. Since then, they had thrown every challenge they could at her without mercy.

"Very good!" Donaghy jumped from his perch and landed with a dull thud.

Calli rose to her feet, wincing with each new ache they had inflicted. She wiped a smudge of blood off her chin with her sleeve.

"We'll see yeh at the morn," Morain said. He joined Donaghy through the shadows of the evening light.

Calli let her breath out, focusing on making her muscles move her body. Though she had been working for more than a full moon cycle now, the days wore long, giving them more time to torture her. Never would she give in to their taunting.

She could turn to Lusiradrol.

Calli shivered and started forward. Lusiradrol made her shudder. That woman would not be her teacher. She would not sell her soul to defeat Tyrkam, but she would like to know what that woman knew of him. More than that, she wished to know how she had appeared without anyone seeing her come or go.

"How very interesting."

Calli whirled at the silken voice. The long shadows beneath the trees shimmered and budded off to form a woman. This time she wore the plain clothes of a squire, which fit snugly to reveal the curves of her figure. The black hair in a long, complex braid draped over one shoulder.

"Lusiradrol?"

A smile darkened on the woman's face. "You remember."

Calli searched around her, afraid of anyone watching them. "What purpose have you here?"

Lusiradrol stepped towards her and stopped two strides away. "I said I would come when you called."

"I've not requested you."

She smiled reproachfully. "Not with words you called, but in your heart you desire my help. Here I am."

Calli eyed her. How had she known? Perhaps she was a witch, or a demon. Had she not seen her materialize from the shadows, Calli would have thought it a trick of the sun. Now she worried that the woman spoke the truth about magic. What else could it have been? "I must soon leave. You may join me, if you wish."

She had cast her lot. No turning back.

"If you will promise to bring me Tyrkam's head, you'll have what you need when you need it."

The simple visualization of her words inspired a wave of nausea in Calli. She grimaced. "His head?"

Lusiradrol shrugged. "Any proof of his death will satisfy the contract. But his head is the best of it." Her eyes glowed with malice when she purred the last words.

"I'll do what I can."

"That's all I ask. Not so difficult."

"Not with the skills necessary to overcome him and his army."

Lusiradrol smiled her haunting way, black lips curving upward into her cold, white cheeks. Her eyes lifted briefly and she backed into the darkest shadows once more.

"Where do you retreat?" Calli watched as she melted into the same shadows from which she had emerged.

I'll join you when I am needed.

"But—" Too late; the woman vanished.

Calli stared at the spot for a while before blinking away the stupor. Was it an apparition?

She would find out too soon if Lusiradrol held to her pact. A shiver ran down her spine, making her hurry to the security of her chambers.

Chapter 24
1.5 pc 937

In the dawn of a new day, Phelan stood at the tall window overlooking the courtyard from the second-floor chamber. He listened for the footfalls of the soldier he had summoned. When the steady beat of a man's steps echoed to him, he turned to meet him.

"M'lord." The soldier handed him a sword wrapped in cloth. "This was delivered for you five days ago."

Phelan took the swordbelt. "Thank you." He excused the soldier with a nod and held the gift across both palms.

After so much time away, he longed to see Calli before arguing with his father on policy. At least he could present the gift he had commissioned specially made for her. The smithy had finished and delivered it in time for his return. He wished only that she would choose to stay and never need it.

Surely by now the men had her beaten. Donaghy particularly had a way of unnerving raw recruits with his confidence and skill, as well as a mouth of poison. However, if Phelan knew Calli, his plans had a fair chance of producing the opposite effect, the reason he had commissioned such a gift. He could not go with her, but he could do all possible in his means to ensure her survival.

Too much time had passed since he last saw Calli in her training. As he recalled, he had visited only one other time since he first introduced her to the two. Morain's rugged punishment must have stolen some of her attitude and determination.

He exited his room with the wrapped sword, finding his way to her room to prepare the gift. Once it lied in waiting, he hurried to the orchard.

Outside, he strode beneath the boughs of tiny fruit growing heavy on the branches.

The clack of staffs and spiteful words reached him through the trees. Images of her death bled from his hopes, draining them from his dreams. How could he stop her? What drove her to do this?

He had realized long ago that her spirit would not rest until she finished her task. He could only hope she accepted his gift for what it was.

As he drew closer, Phelan moved carefully among the trees to stay out of sight. He peered around a large trunk to watch, unable to keep from smiling. Donaghy landed on his rump with Calli standing over him.

She breathed heavily, strands of fiery hair plastered to her face with the sweat that beaded there. She stood triumphant with the end of her staff not a hand above Donaghy's throat, poised to strike if he should move. His scowl inspired a smirk on Phelan's face. She had beaten him, one of the two best weapon masters of Cavatar's army.

"Y've learned much, milady." Donaghy fixed a mischievous gaze on her. "Kaillen taught you well."

"Enough!" Calli jabbed him in the gut, leaving him hunched over. Morain jumped behind her and raised his sword.

She twirled the staff and swung it in line with her right arm, leaving her left to balance. Her eyes scanned her enemy.

Intrigued, Phelan crept out from his hiding to watch unimpeded.

Morain faked, but Calli barely flinched. When he attacked, she swung the staff hard at his arm. He jerked away in time and backed away again. Calli advanced forward, her eyes fixed on him but her intentions clearly for the sword lying in the dirt.

Meanwhile, Donaghy crawled to his feet, still catching his breath. He watched her closely, his eyes sparking with ideas. With her complete attention on Morain, he was safe to retrieve his sword—he cheated. By all accounts, he should have been out, had she a sharp weapon rather than a staff. He dusted himself and crept behind Calli as her attention shifted from him.

Donaghy struck at that moment, but to Phelan's surprise, she jabbed the staff backwards into his shoulder. She whirled as Morain attacked, leaving him to stumble towards Donaghy, while she stepped away. She cracked the staff across his back, sending him off balance. By the time he recovered, she had dropped Donaghy with another few swings of the staff before tossing it aside to grab the sword from the ground and hold it in two hands.

Morain recovered and attacked.

Phelan stepped out into the open, completely lost in the art of her fighting. She blocked Morain's thrust. However, he seemed to have bested her.

Calli surprised them all with a flip backwards that left her a handful of strides away. Both had to face her together.

Phelan stood with his mouth agape. The men had no such agility. Somewhere in his memory, he recalled stories of Kaillen's advanced martial training that no one else could master. He must have taught her with more success than what he had tried to teach to the royal guard and failed.

The trainers glanced at each other, their head bobs the only indication of the silent communication. They then circled opposite sides of her.

Calli watched each, the sword poised ready in her hands. "You fight without fairness to trap me."

"No one said Tyrkam was fair." Donaghy teased her with his sword, swinging it in various positions.

She watched each for that crucial moment.

They encroached on her with methodical slowness. Without taking his eyes from the battle, Phelan sat down to watch.

Her eyes flashed to him.

At that moment they attacked.

Delayed by the distraction, Calli lagged a step behind. Donaghy drew a line of blood across her shoulder while Morain stepped out of the way of her swing. She whirled on her attacker and slammed the flat side of the sword hard into his gut. He fell with a thump and lied still on the ground, his body rising and falling with each hard breath.

In her triumph, she glanced again to Phelan and found Morain's sword at her back.

"You be dead, milady," Morain said with steely calm.

Calli dropped her sword, cursing under her breath. She glared at Phelan. "Damn you!" She forcefully swiped a sweaty red strand from her face. "I almost had them."

He shrugged and stood up. "You cannot afford distractions in battle."

She curled her lip in a snarl.

Morain stumbled away in exhaustion, then fell back onto the slope to rest. He groaned with the effort of sitting.

Calli turned and retrieved her sword. Phelan stepped forward but stopped as she raised the blade to him. "Is it now your turn?"

He raised his hands, palms forward. "I've no intention of a duel."

She lowered the sword. "What *do* you intend?"

Phelan looked to both men and gave a flick of his eyes away. Each nodded in turn and rose.

"Good luck, m'lord." When he passed Phelan, Donaghy patted his shoulder. "Y'll need it with that one."

"Thank you, both." Phelan fixed his eyes on the warrior poised before him. She hunched like a viper ready to strike. "I'll take over from here."

Calli straightened, watching both with a frown. "What of my training? Is that the end?"

"What more can they teach?" He winced at the glare she shot him. "What is it that leads you to this end?"

She turned away and unbuckled the mail jerkin she wore. Grimacing, she slipped her injured arm out with care not to touch the wound.

Phelan came up behind her and offered to help. Calli whirled and held the blade to his throat, her eyes cold with suspicion.

"Tell me," he said.

"Why?"

"Whatever pushes you to death is not worth the trouble."

Her eyes narrowed, the tip of the blade pinching his throat. "Is not friendship worth the trouble?" Without his help, she managed to slide her arm out of the mail shirt. The links rustled and clinked when it fell to the dirt.

"Nothing is great enough to risk what I've seen."

Confusion played across her face for dominance and succumbed to defeat. She backed away. "What good will it do you?"

"At least help me understand why." He frowned, wishing she would trust him with whatever secret she hid. "I'll tell no one."

Calli eyed him cautiously. After a few seconds, her face drooped with sadness.

His heart dropped to witness such a dramatic change.

"I could not protect her, Phelan," she murmured without meeting his eyes. "With all my father's training I could not keep their hands off her."

Phelan stepped toward her to offer his comfort. "You were one person. Not even the guards could keep them away."

"But it was my duty, if not as a guard, then as a friend."

She pulled away from his touch, but he moved quick and caught her by the shoulders. Never had he heard such ridiculous guilt. "Look at me Calli."

She lifted her eyes.

He held her firmly in his gaze, his hands locked on her shoulders, and allowed her no chance to avoid the truth. "Nothing you would have done could have changed matters. Nothing you did or did not caused this. Let go of this guilt."

Tears welled up within her eyes and she looked away. He softened his grip so she could wipe her eyes and regain her composure.

"I must do this." She choked on her whisper. "I'll not abandon my friend."

Phelan sighed and dropped his hands. She would never change her mind, he realized. Nothing he said would convince her otherwise. He had only one option left. "If you must go...follow me."

When he heard nothing behind him, he stopped and turned. "If you'll not stay, at least I can provide some assurance that you'll return."

Calli watched him with a questioning look. When he started toward the palace, she followed.

He led her through the palace's less used corridors to Istaria's chambers to avoid the indignation of her red, swollen eyes and tear-streaked cheeks. He held the door open for her to enter.

She hesitated before slipping past him. Phelan let the door close quietly behind them.

After scanning the room, Calli fixed her eyes on the glint of metal from the bed. She reached for the gift and traced her fingers along the intricate pattern of curves and twists etched along the crossbar. By the look on her face, she recognized them as the writing of Loringale.

The smithy had sworn to know the language.

A few seconds later, she withdrew the long, perfect blade from the equally decorated scabbard. Green flecks throughout the narrow blade glittered in the sunlight spilling through the window.

"It's beautiful." Calli turned to face him, replacing the sword in the scabbard before smiling her gratitude. "Thank you."

"Some insurance that you'll return. The man claimed to use a special ingredient in the metal to resist breaking."

As he hoped, she leaned forward to kiss his cheek. He turned his head to catch her on the lips. She startled momentarily, but quickly relaxed. When she pulled away, the defiance in her eyes had faded.

"I wish I could join you."

She smiled weakly and nodded. "You're needed here."

"But you'll need more."

"I'll return with Istaria; have no doubts or worries."

Phelan smiled and reached inside his shirt. He could only wish that fate was on her side. He pulled out his royal seal on its fine chain and lifted it from his neck.

Calli accepted the pendant without a word.

"A way to remember your promise," he said.

When tears glazed her eyes, he took her in his arms and held her tight. Calli buried her sniffles in his shoulder. For the first time, he realized how afraid she was.

Chapter 25
1.5 pc 937

After leaving Calli to her new gift, Phelan's heart sank to the bottom. She intended to leave, and he could not stop her from her quest. For the sake of her finding peace of spirit, he would allow her this. Whether it meant her death or not, he could not say, but he had done what he could to prepare her, even if he could not join her.

Phelan strode through the corridors of the palace, deep in his thoughts. He intended to confront the king—again—about Tyrkam's use of his army as raiders along the roads. However, another matter festered on his mind, something from his visit with Lord Almont.

The ruler of the province of Doncran had said something that bothered him. Cathmor's behavior emphasized the point. Lord Almont said the baron had been pushing for open war with Tyrkam.

However, Cathmor had said nothing to him of it. Why would Cathmor not discuss building the army with the ambassador of his king? Though Cathmor held no ruling power, his power came in his influence on those who ruled.

The look on Cathmor's face when Almont had renewed his allegiance to the Isolders could have toppled a mountain. Phelan was sure the man hated him. For what, he knew not. Cathmor had given no other indication of his unrest.

Perhaps he had imagined the incident.

Phelan doubted it. Cathmor had trained the elite forces of Cavatar's army, including some of General Hammel's forces. His power depended on the support of the nobles who paid him for the services of his training.

Such contracts provided the base of the baron's power. Of late, Cavatar had requested no more. Phelan wondered if the king suspected any duplicity within the man and had purposely held back. If Cathmor decided to lash out in revenge because of any hardship to him, how much could they trust the loyalty of those soldiers?

Before he realized, Phelan stood before the doors of the study where he expected to find his father that time of day.

The guard standing sentry outside the door gave a simple nod as Phelan stepped forward. Though at one time the royal guard had played their part as honor guards only, in the present situation, their skills might be called on at any time.

Phelan pushed the heavy door open. Inside the room, Isolder hunched over the table with a stack of scrolls and papers piled high around him.

Sunlight slanted across the sparse room from the tall, open windows, spilling across the table and its stack, and the shelves of scrolls and bound volumes. It caught the multitude of documents and cast an orange glow over them.

Isolder never looked up at the echo of approaching steps, his nose buried in his scrolls.

Phelan stopped across the table from him and waited. Whatever engrossed the king stole his complete attention.

After a long minute of patience, Phelan said, "You bury yourself in work, my lord."

"As you will someday."

The grumbled response made Phelan shake his head. When would his father see what was before him and quit hiding? "You cannot hide behind parchment and pen forever."

Isolder peered over the paper he held. "I hide not, Phelan, but plan the future."

Phelan shook his head, the purpose behind this confrontation rising to the surface once more. "We've no time to sit around. Have you no care that, as we speak, raiding groups kill and destroy? They are supported by Tyrkam."

The only response was a grunt of acknowledgement.

Anger simmered to the surface. Always his father ignored his warnings. He never saw the truth, or wished not to acknowledge it.

Phelan slammed his fists on the table. "Damn you! Have you no care for the people?"

Isolder lowered the parchment to glare at the boy. "You know nothing." The threat in his voice chilled the room. "This war is not won by brute force, Phelan, but by understanding and strategy."

"What strategy?"

"The strategy that keeps Tyrkam coming."

Lost in the words, Phelan frowned. "What? Has my father gone mad?"

"Never, but I have not shared it all with you."

Phelan crossed his arms and waited for an explanation.

The king ruffled through the scrolls and books on the table before him. When the object of his search failed to turn up, he rose from his chair.

The scrape of the wooden chair on the stone floor rang in the room.

His father searched the rows of parallel shelves along the opposite end of the room. What could he possibly be looking for? What could a book or scroll have to answer his question about Tyrkam?

When Isolder found a tome bound and latched with intricate metal pieces, he pulled it from the shelf and blew a coat of dust from it. The cloud dispersed around him as he walked through it.

With no further comment, he let the volume drop with a heavy thud onto the table before Phelan.

"What is this?"

"Read it."

Isolder took his place at the opposite end and continued where he had left off in his work.

Phelan eyed the book suspiciously. Was this a jest?

Carved into the leather of the front cover was a dragon. Symbols—etchings resembling vines and leaves—encircled the dragon. The latch and spine braces showed as much skill and craftsmanship in their intertwining knots and creatures.

He ran his hands over the markings on the cover in curiosity. They reminded him of the designs the swordsmith had engraved on Calli's sword.

Slowly, he unlatched the book and opened the volume with the creak of something ancient and unused.

"It is what Tyrkam is after," Isolder quietly said. "An old legend I never believed. A story my father read to me once. I doubt he believed as well. It is the Legend of the White Dragon."

Phelan glanced up, but his father's eyes were fixed on the parchment. What was the Legend of the White Dragon?

Unlike the cover design, he could read the text within the volume. Written in his native tongue but in a dialect that took time to interpret, the book was readable.

It took only a few lines to draw him into the old legend. It reminded him of something.

As the story of the ancient dragons and immortal beings called Majera formed pictures within his mind, he realized this meeting would take longer than he expected. Phelan pulled a chair to the table and continued reading.

When servants entered to light candles, Phelan looked up. He had not realized how fast time passed. In his mind, he saw the Great Darkness, the coming of Light and its creations. He watched the first one, the Majera, split into three earthly forms and create dragons to aid them in the war against the Lord of Darkness. As they fought battles for control of the world, he thrilled with the victories and grew chill with each defeat. While the Majera, the dragons, and a First Race of men were immortal, the Second Race of humans they created were short-lived. However, a select few, the magi, could extend their lives for centuries.

He gasped when evil took on its own form and tricked those fighting against it. The history of the world unfolded in a tale of deceit and lies, until the Majera were able to focus their power in one dragon, the white dragon. The Dragon of the Light, the book said, was the culmination of their powers and the equal and opposite of the enemy, who had merged with a dragon embryo of its own creation and forgotten who he was. The Darklord had created a clan of dragons that lived on beyond his supposed demise, but he had been discovered in the rare black dragon.

The white dragon was the only one who could banish the black dragon for all time.

At that point, Phelan glanced up through the flickering of the candles. He sat alone in the room. Having been so engrossed in the ancient book, he had not noticed when the king left.

Forgetting his previous bitterness for this new interest, he continued his reading. If the king knew something about this legend and Tyrkam, he wished to know for himself what it was.

Towards the end of the long history, he read what mattered most. The white dragon had banished the black to human form, afraid to destroy her, lest she take on another form before he understood how to fully eliminate the darkness.

In retribution, the woman tricked humans into killing the white dragon. However, his power was said to live on for eternity, guarded by his spirit until a mortal of righteous heart and innocence of spirit was found worthy to continue his work and aid his return to corporeal form.

Was this the key? Was Tyrkam after the legendary power?

"But he cannot claim it."

The answer flashed through his mind. "Istaria!" He had found his sister in a cave, her hair white and no voice but able to speak only through what could best be described as magic. Had she found the power?

Could it be true? He sat in his chair, staring at the words on the page. What of the dragon horrors she had reported to him and the queen?

Another thought made him cringe. Did Tyrkam know? Was that why he had arranged her abduction?

Unlikely. They thought she was ugly behind the veil. No more than that, if Tyrkam believed rumors.

Phelan shut the book with a thud and latched the cover. "Such a power would allow Tyrkam, or any man, to rule the world."

At the revelation, he stiffened. There was the answer. Tyrkam wanted not only Cavatar, but also the power to rule the world. He would turn the power of light to darkness and destroy the hope of banishing the Darklord forever.

If the story was real, then the black dragon existed. He shuddered at the thought, feeling his world shrink a little more. Who was this woman, this black dragon exiled to human form?

Phelan opened the book to the end, reading the last page, a prophecy of the white dragon's return. On one page were lines of the strange symbols matching those on the cover. The facing page he guessed was the translation. It was a prophecy of the dragon's return for a final battle against the Darklord.

If Istaria was the chosen one, was she strong enough to fulfill the prophecy?

Chapter 26
8.5 pc 937

For what seemed an eternity, they traveled alone. Darius had led her through the forest of Wynmere into rockier terrain cut by streams and waterfalls. Many times they had had to find alternative routes to cross the endless streams and rivers flowing from the Northern Mountains.

This one was no exception.

Istaria studied the rocky path crossing the swift-flowing river and cringed. They had tried to find another route but encountered nothing within a short trek that appeared any easier.

Darius stood next to her in silent contemplation.

She looked up to the worried frown on his face. "We've no other way to cross that will not take us days off our course. The way is dangerous, but we've no other choice in our race with her."

He had purposely not said the name they feared, as if its utterance would draw her to them. It had been that way since Istaria awoke after the attack.

She swallowed.

"Rowen may not ford this channel easily. The current is strong. I would not dare to swim him across with both of us, but he can carry one of us—you." He lifted her up into the saddle.

Istaria gripped the pommel in her fingers.

Rowen hesitated, but moved on with some encouragement from Darius. With Darius leading him, the gelding placed each large hoof with great care on the stones spaced to let the water flow between them while forming a natural bridge. The spray of the river caught them on one side, the waters pouring into the pool down the other side.

Istaria clutched the saddle for security and hoped that Rowen kept his footing. Each step he took jerked her in the saddle.

A couple times she thought she would slip from the saddle, but she managed to keep her seat.

Midway across the river, Rowen nearly leaped forward.

Istaria lost her grip, her balance tipped sideways too far, and fell. She caught the stirrup, but her feet dangled in the churning pool. Rowen trembled with the effort to keep from slipping in while supporting her.

"My lady! Hang on!"

Istaria struggled for a better grip, the river spray blinding her. Her hands slipped on the stirrup.

She plunged into the chilling waters and struggled to reach the surface for a breath of air.

However, the current carried her away. The roar of the river filled her ears. She bobbed to the surface briefly and was pulled under before she could catch her breath.

"Istaria!"

The fear in the voice encouraged her to try harder. She burst to the surface, gasping for a breath. For a moment, she opened her eyes and spied Rowen already on the opposite bank. Darius was nowhere to be found.

She reached out for a handhold on one of the many stones that bumped against her, but her fingers slipped.

The current pulled her under again. She choked on the cold water and flailed her arms to right herself.

The surface came briefly before the water claimed her again.

※

Darius caught his heart in his throat. He could not lose her, not now. What use would he be as a guardian if he could not protect the chosen one from the elements of the world?

He struggled against the current to reach her.

The river widened and slowed, and she dipped below the surface again.

He took a deep breath.

In the cold, rushing water, he swam beyond her last position, following the flow of magic.

He caught hold of a limb and pulled her to the surface with him, where he held her head above the water. "My lady!"

She lay still.

Although the current had slowed, he struggled with what strength was left in him to reach the shore. He had to make it. She must survive, or they were all dead.

And her loss would drive him mad with sorrow.

Hanging on tight, he pulled her to the rocky shore and out of the water. She never moved.

"My lady!" Darius held her in his arms, the burning pain of loss threatening to overcome him more than the cool air.

"Not again. I'll not lose another." He had lost his dear Julaina in childbirth. He would not let this woman go for all that remained in his heart to love again.

He embraced her tight, rocking back and forth as tears formed in his eyes. He used all the magic he knew to pull the water from her lungs and revive her but she laid still. "Please come back."

She coughed.

Shocked, he released his hold. She pushed away and hunched over. Istaria coughed and heaved.

When she finished, she looked up to him through red, swollen eyes and sniffed. In an instant, she wrapped her arms around him, her body trembling.

Darius held her tight. Relief poured into him, washing away the grief with tears of joy. "I'm so sorry."

He held her until they both calmed enough to notice the bite of the air on their wet skin.

When she backed away, he smiled in reassurance and smoothed the silvery wet strands of hair from her face. "I'm so sorry for making you cross like that. It was my fault."

I lost my grip.

"But I could have—"

She quieted him with a finger on his lips. *No more. I want to forget it happened.*

He sighed, calming the shakes that lingered. He would never let any harm come to her. All day he had searched for a better way across but had found none. The various waterfalls added speed to the mountain runoff. His impatience had nearly cost her life. Never again would he take that chance.

Rowen put in his own apology and nudged Istaria in the back.

She chuckled silently, turning to rub his cheek. *I forgive you, too.*

Her words reached Darius, who smiled and rose to his feet. She could have directed her statement to the horse, but he suspected she meant it for him more than Rowen.

When Darius reached down to help her, she accepted his hands but stumbled into him on unsteady legs.

"Easy." He wrapped an arm around her waist to steady her.

What would they do now, he wondered. The rocky terrain would be difficult to cross in their weakened states. They needed rest, and time to dry. The chill of the air sent a shiver down his body. She pressed against him, shivering from the cold as well.

Both of them were dripping wet and needed dry clothes. He let go of her to search through the bags on Rowen's saddle. The horse had been the only one who hadn't dove in. Darius found their changes of clothes and the blanket that he had packed from his cabin.

Darius handed Istaria her dress, which she held out away from her wet clothes. "I'll be over here if you want to change behind that rock."

She looked from him to the dress to the large boulder behind them and headed toward it.

Although he dared not take his eyes off her, Darius turned away from Istaria and led Rowen to the sparse grass meeting the rocky shoreline. While the horse grazed, he busied himself changing into a dry shirt, his only change of clothes, and unsaddled the gelding. On the branches of the trees, he hung his wet cloak, shirt, and coat.

At one point, he risked a glance to Istaria. Though her back was turned, he caught a glimpse of a long braid of hair hanging between the shoulder blades of her slender body. In the next second, the dress slipped over her. He turned away immediately, realizing the lure of his attraction for her.

When her steps crunched over the gravelly beach with her approach, he turned.

Istaria handed him her wet clothes, while shivering in the chill air. *Thank you.*

"You're welcome."

He took the bundle from her in one arm. With his other he took her hand and lifted it to his lips. Her cheeks blushed.

When he released her hand, she rubbed her arms.

"Here." He pulled the blanket from the bag and wrapped it around her shoulders. She smiled and pulled it tight around her. "Rest. As soon as I can, I'll build us a fire to warm away the chill."

She smiled and moved to a place on the grass beneath one of the larger trees.

Darius worked quickly to find branches and kindling. Soon, he had a small fire crackling but had to find more wood to last them until after dark. When he had enough of a pile, he cooked a light soup to warm them.

Although he had made sure to keep the fire going, she snuggled next to him after eating. He smiled and held her, enjoying her nearness as much as the warmth. Perhaps she shared the same feelings he had.

Darius clamped his jaw, uncertain what to say or do. Dared he risk losing love a second time by assuming too much?

What is it?

"What?"

Istaria sat up and studied his face. *The colors changed. Your mood has changed. That much I know of you, Darius.*

His eyes soaked up the watery blue gazing back at him. Unsure what to say, he ran his fingers along the line of her jaw. "I was thinking."

Feeling, she corrected.

He smiled. "Thinking inspires emotion."

Or emotions inspire thoughts. What is it?

Perhaps she would understand. What had he left to lose, when he had almost lost her, his honor, and his own life?

He swallowed the discord within his mind and pushed all thought aside. "You."

What about me? She gazed at him expectantly, or so he thought.

Holding her face within his palm, he leaned forward and gently kissed her lips.

When they parted, a soft smile glowed from her face. *I wondered when you would do that.*

He blinked. "You knew?"

Laying her head against his chest, she said, *I hoped.*

A new sense of freedom burst from his soul. He embraced her tightly, vowing to never let anything harm her, neither nature nor Lusiradrol. He would not lose her.

Chapter 27
11.5 pc 937

The stars twinkled in the western sky, while in the east, the colors merged from midnight blue to violet. Dawn approached.

A gentle breeze carried with it the freshness of a new day, while the song of the night still played across the open land. That song faded as violet gave way to topaz. The steady chirrup of insects faded, replaced by the melody of birds.

Calli adjusted the weighty satchel slung over her shoulder. While standing on the terrace overlooking the courtyard and the town beyond the palace gates, she reconsidered staying.

She grieved for her friends, but Phelan grieved for her. She understood his feelings over her leaving. Nevertheless, she had to try. He did nothing. They all did nothing. She must do something! Istaria's suffering would mean nothing if they continued like this.

She had risen early, after spending all night with jumbled thoughts. With nothing else to keep her, she decided to rise and dress in the moments before dawn arrived.

Last night, she had instructed Jamison to saddle the gray gelding Phelan had offered her to be ready before dawn. As the boy roused Duke in the barn now, she smiled in relief.

Soon, she told herself. Her heart split in these last moments, afraid to carry out her task while knowing it was the only way for her to calm her spirit.

Before she could change her mind, she forced her feet to move. She had to leave before anyone awakened. Saying farewell would be too hard.

She entered the stable, where Jamison finished saddling Duke. He looked up in the process of grabbing the bridle from a peg in the corner.

"Calli."

"Mornin', Trouble."

He smiled a lopsided grin and proceeded to bridle the gelding. Duke dropped his head for the bit and chewed it while the boy slipped the headstall over his ears.

After straightening the dark forelock with unusual care, Jamison handed the reins to her. "Take it easy with him this morn. Nothing but a soft landin' from his spirit y'll get otherwise."

"I'll be careful."

"Just you be takin' care o' that one for me. Special he be; one o' Baron's get."

"I will."

After an awkward moment of silence, Calli tied her bundle behind the cantle. She led Duke outside, where she mounted with ease. All those years riding Black, her father's horse, had taught her about horses.

"I'll wait for your return with the Lady Istaria."

"I'll look forward to it."

Duke sidestepped beneath Calli as she gathered her reins. After settling him, she signaled to the guards to open the gates. She fought to contain the gelding's energy—they would have many days journey and she needed him to stay strong.

The queen had supplied her with a purse of money to add to the supply of food she took from the bakehouse. It should be enough, provided she was not robbed along the way. If that was the case, then she truly was not ready.

The portcullis ground open, roaring in the silence of the dawn. After a moment to take a last look of the palace, she turned away and rode into the quiet streets of Setheadroc. Duke's hooves clopped on the stone, until they reached the outer gate, which the guards had already opened. With a look to the men in their towers, she rode through to the beginning of her journey.

She rode from Setheadroc until the first rays of dawn gleamed from the slice of sun over the horizon. Calli stopped and turned Duke—

She caught her breath in awe. The palace sparkled and shimmered in the morning light. She had forgotten what it looked like from the outside. Its tall spires reached for the heavens, glinting as if the Creators had lit their tips. The detailed carvings of the finest artisans reflected the rays that caressed the stone. She stared for long seconds, etching the image into her memory.

After tearing her eyes away, she set off from her home at a canter. Somewhere in the world waited her friend. She would rescue her and bring her home. Then her spirit would find peace.

*

Phelan stood at his window, gazing out at the soft red of Calli's hair bobbing with the horse's movements. She started into a canter, hastening away from him, away from the future he had envisioned together. He watched until she vanished in the distance.

He knew she purposely left without saying good-bye, thinking it would be easier on both of them. Perhaps she was right, but he had hoped for one last chance to convince her to stay. He could have forced her to stay, but she would have found a way to escape. Had he ordered an escort, she would have considered it an insult. She had to do this on her own, for good or ill.

She disappeared, likely not to return.

Chapter 28
11.5 pc 937

His fingers clenched into fists, white-knuckled beneath the leather gloves that squeaked with the tension in his hand. The guards withered beneath his dark glower.

Tyrkam made no effort to hide his fury with the men and himself, that he had allowed the women to exit the castle in the first place. Something about the princess had appealed to his mercy. With his jaw clamped, the temper inside smoldered hotter without any sign of cooling. The soldiers had not reported back in a full moon cycle, although one could reach Thealon by foot in half a day. How dare they hide and pretend to have chased the princess, then lie to him of their failure!

However, they had reported an interesting surprise—the dragon spirit emerged from her.

Despite her possession of what he desired, he would continue his plans. He would overthrow Cavatar and establish himself as king over all the lands of Ayrule, with or without the power of the white dragon. In less than a cycle of the moon, the palace would fall; and in spite of the power taken by the princess, his goals would not falter. They would conquer Cavatar, and in time, Rivonia.

Only his methods had changed. He would need Lord Cathmor's alliance more than ever. The baron had pledged the loyalty of many of the soldiers within the palace and the city. He swore they would be ready to open the gates to let in the invaders. Tyrkam counted on that, though not completely. He never trusted anyone but himself and his second in command, Dorjan. Together they would ensure the victory over the leadership of Cavatar.

The first of his soldiers were already in place, thanks to the spells of the old wizard, which hid them in the nearby plains. He would leave soon to join them, bringing another regiment. Nothing less than a full legion of his army would sack Setheadroc.

The creak of leather brought his thoughts back to the failure of his men. His eyes narrowed. "Get out of my sight!"

The young soldiers spun on their heels and disappeared from the chamber in a flurry of tromping boots.

Tyrkam turned from the door to the fireplace. The flames fed his loose temper into a conflagration. They burned upon his front, boiling his blood into a rage.

An abrupt, chilling cloud cooled his mind several degrees. He turned to face her.

The sinister smirk on her face mocked his pride. "My, my. What a mess you have. No princess, no powers. No hope."

"You wish your death, demon."

"If only to avail yourself of such power." Lusiradrol moved towards him. Her flowing strides accentuated the curves of the feminine form of her exile. The gown she wore clung to her body beneath it like a second skin, her hair decorated in a complex series of braids and curls.

He liked seeing her in that fashion, sensuous and feminine. However, he knew the truth of her figure that lied beneath the surface, cold and reptilian.

"What have you to do with this?"

Lusiradrol shrugged, stopping before him with a haughty smirk. Her eyes probed his reaction. "Nothing, but to see your face in this moment."

"Bring her back!" Tyrkam barely contained the rage inside. She must have aided the princess to undermine his plans.

"If I could, what benefit might I gain?" She sighed. "But I've not the power, nor the will; so what good have I to fulfill your wish?" Her black lips curled up in a leering smile. "Never cancel an arrangement unless you intend to pay, generously."

"What have you done!"

Lusiradrol glided around him towards the fire. "When you start a fire, you will be burned." She walked into the flames and disappeared.

Tyrkam stared into the fire, imagining her destruction. Time had passed since their last encounter. Why might she appear then—was this not the ends to her means?

One answer came to him—she had set other plans, other activities in motion to delay him.

One other question remained—what plans had she made?

Chapter 29
15.5 pc 937

The chill more than his absence woke her. Istaria pulled the blanket tighter around her and rolled over to confirm what she already knew. Darius had left her sometime before she had awakened. Now she was glad she had put all her clothes back on after giving in to his gentle caress.

The crackle of a fire drew her eyes to the figure next to the flame. He turned a smile to her and stirred the contents of a small kettle amid the flames. "Good morning."

Holding the blanket around her for added warmth, she crawled toward him and sat down. The heat of the fire warmed her front. *Will we be there soon?*

His lip twitched. She knew the answer by his reaction. They had traveled more than a moon cycle since their first encounter with Lusiradrol. Like him, she feared another attack and knew time worked against them before the dark woman tracked them down.

Istaria pressed close to Darius.

"Look."

She turned to where he pointed at the horizon, where a sliver of sunlight emerged. She gasped in awe as the sky blazed bright.

"That's you."

What?

He met her eyes and smiled. "As long as he resides in you, he will not allow us to fail. As long as each day arrives, we have beaten the darkness once again. You must continue to practice using his powers as the mage instructed."

His words lifted her mood and she kissed him. *Thank you.*

The sun's light warmed her enough to remove the blanket. The breeches and waistcoat kept her more comfortable in the chilly mountain air than any dress. She had come to appreciate the insistence of Darius and Jayson on wearing the boy's clothes.

"Now, my lady, eat and we'll be off."

Needing no prompting to satisfy the growl of her stomach, Istaria eagerly served herself. They ate quickly and packed up Rowen for the day's journey.

Higher in the rugged terrain of the mountains, the grass grew sparser, as did the water. Their food ran low, but Darius rationed it. Wherever this Eyr Droc was, Istaria prayed they found it soon, and that the inhabitants had plenty of food.

No longer could they find adequate shelter, but were forced to rest in the open. The exposure set off a warning in Istaria's mind but, using magic, she searched the area and felt nothing to worry her. No one tracked them.

Darius stopped next to her, his eyes a comforting blue that eased her tension. "Worry not. We are no more than three days' journey from our destination."

His words energized her to continue. They would make it yet, it seemed.

As the thought passed, a sudden void opened in the magic and threatened to pull her in. Istaria gasped, her heart racing, and she turned the magic away.

Firm hands held her from falling. "Istaria!"

She blinked away the blur before her and focused on the source of the voice. Darius's concerned face grew more distinct with each deep breath she took. *It's Lusiradrol.*

"I thought as much." He peered around them at their surroundings—a steep bluff on one side and rocky terrain beside them.

A deep rumble shook the ground. The vibrations rattled upwards from Istaria's feet through her legs. When she looked to Darius for an answer, he turned to the mountain.

Boulders bore down on them at a ferocious speed, the thunder of falling rocks growing with each second.

In the flash of the moment it took for the situation to register, Istaria followed her instinctive desire to run. In seconds the mountainside would crush them beneath its weight.

Within three steps, Darius grabbed her arm and stopped her.

We must hurry!

He shook his head. "No. Use your magic. Use it now!"

Understanding what he meant, she reached inside for the magic guarded by the dragon. It swirled and shifted, its colors enveloping her. She knew what must be done but not how to make it happen.

The boulders careened toward them.

A flash of insight led her to the one right direction. A moment before they were buried, she pictured a barricade to block the avalanche of rock and debris. The stones crashed against the invisible shield, crunching and grinding against each other.

"Too close. Run!" Darius grabbed her arm and pulled her forward. The debris formed a canopy nearly touching the top of his head.

Istaria scrambled over the rocky path, while Darius led Rowen beneath the overhang of rocks.

They emerged into a clear valley snuggled between the mountains, but Darius insisted they continue well into it before she relinquished the shield.

When she released her hold, the rocks crashed behind them and blocked the pass completely. They could not go back.

Darius breathed a sigh of relief and took a seat on a tuft of grass. "That was close." He looked up with sparkling eyes and a smile that invited her to join him. "Now you see the reason that you must learn."

Istaria sat next to him and laid her head on his shoulder. She closed her eyes and breathed deeply, the panic easing away to leave a new weariness in its place.

As her eyes grew heavy, the void returned. With greater pull than before, it drew her into its depths, threatening to lose her forever. Darkness enveloped her.

In the distance, a voice cried out to her. It sounded familiar but she could not identify it.

"Istaria!"

Who are you?

"My lady. Focus! Come back to me!"

The voice—

She could almost place it. *Darius?* The name flashed through her mind without a thought, stirring up memories, recent memories and feelings. *Darius, is that you?*

"Focus on my voice. This is a trick of that demon. You must not succumb!"

Darius? She followed his voice and the void retreated behind her. Istaria blinked, regaining consciousness. She realized she lay on her back, held close to his warmth.

"My lady." The relief poured from his voice.

Istaria gazed up at his smile and reached a hand to his neck to pull herself upright. She held tight to him as he pulled her to sit up.

"It was Lusiradrol. When her direct attack failed, she must have formed a more subtle plan." He searched around them as if expecting something. "She's near."

"Very perceptive."

Both whirled at the voice. Lusiradrol stood three strides away in black armor reminiscent of the scales of a dragon, a dark scowl on her face. Before they could react, the ground shook.

Darius held Istaria close.

The colors of magic swirled about them, and Istaria realized he had started one of his spells. Curious about what Lusiradrol would stir up but aware a defense was needed, her attention split between the two.

Let loose the power within you, Darius said. *Let it flow.*

Istaria closed her eyes and buried her face against him, focusing on the magic within her. It ran between them like a living current, flowing back and forth and strengthening each other. *What I have is yours,* she told him.

The power surged forth from him.

The shriek from Lusiradrol pierced the air around her, as if she stood in multiple places.

Istaria pressed her hands over her ears, but the sound came not from without. It rattled through her like a gale wind, until it exhausted itself and faded away.

When all was silent, she gasped for a breath and opened her eyes. She searched around her but saw nothing of Lusiradrol or her magic. *She's gone. Darius—*

She turned.

His eyes rolled back and he collapsed.

Darius? Istaria leaned over him. Using what Darius had taught her, she reached into the magic. It gave her nothing. She had used all she had, although it had not physically drained her as much as the last time. Either she had exhausted her powers too much or he was dead. She refused to accept his death. The idea choked her.

Darius!

Laying down beside him, she let the tears flow. He could not die. She needed him to guide her. She needed him.

She cried until the fatigue of her sorrow covered her with sleep.

In a blink she opened her eyes. Shadows drew long lines across the valley and its rocky terrain. She had not noticed the time pass, but what had been midday had drained into evening. The chill in the air billowed her cloak and shivered down her spine. She instinctively pressed closer to the warmth next to her.

Better senses took hold. They would need a fire, she realized. In the next second of awareness, relief filled her that Darius was warm with life and Lusiradrol was nowhere to be found. At least the dragon woman had not returned to finish the task. Perhaps she was dead.

Not likely. Darius had told her that none but the white dragon could fully defeat the power of the black dragon, except the Majera. However, they would only provide direct help in a battle with the Darklord himself.

The white dragon knew the secret that would remove Lusiradrol from the world. That was why he must be allowed to carry out his prophecy. That was why Darius had taken this journey upon himself.

Istaria bent over and kissed his lips. The heat and softness calmed her fears of his condition. She could only pray he recovered.

For a fire, I'd give my right arm, she thought, scanning the few scrub brush and sparse trees. Leaving Rowen to stand over Darius, she gathered what she could for a fire.

With kindling and some dead branches, she followed the steps Darius had taken many times in building a fire. Without magic, she created a spark that ignited the dry kindling. Perhaps she could do this.

The fire grew with each twig and branch she placed on it. Although she struggled, she pulled Darius close to the heat. She sat next to him and placed his head in her lap, where she could reassure herself with a touch that he lived. Gently, she smoothed his hair until her fingers combed through it.

She gazed into the fire and recalled the few battles in which she had used her magic. Twice already she had fought the dark woman and twice had narrowly defeated her. She had used magic, but the spirit of the white dragon helped.

Only the gurgling and burning of her empty stomach distracted her from her thoughts. With gentle care, she moved Darius's head to the ground so she could stand.

After a quick search of the saddle bags, she found a little food left and picked some stale bread to nibble. It calmed her middle.

Firelight danced across the shadows of Darius' face

Istaria hoped he awoke before Lusiradrol attacked again. He was her only hope in repelling the woman's magic.

Chapter 30
21.5 pc 937

The living sounds of the forest harmonized their familiar tune.

Calli's mind wandered as she rode amid the natural symphony, unconcerned for the moment of any dangers.

Lusiradrol had taught her to listen to the world around her and plan. For the few days the strange woman had walked with her, Calli had absorbed much about tactics. When a small band of raiders followed, Lusiradrol helped her set up traps. All five went down with ease, too easy by Calli's thoughts. Lusiradrol left her soon after.

A couple days later, Calli had visited a village for supplies and was followed out by Tyrkam's spies. Although they had put up a good fight, she had succeeded in injuring or killing four of seven. The one death she knew of lingered in her mind and haunted her dreams. She would rather leave the killing to the soldiers but realized that on some occasions it would be necessary to defend herself.

Nearing midday, a multitude of voices reached her through the trees. Calli recognized the familiar chatter of a busy village and directed Duke towards it.

Of small size, it spread over the open land. Cattle and sheep grazed beyond the outskirts.

Her supplies ran low, and the cakes had gone stale. She needed fresh food. Her tongue rejoiced at the thought with her stomach in agreement.

Aware of her intrusion as a stranger, she pulled the hood of her cloak over her red braid of hair. Any man, woman, or child of sound mind could distinguish her as a woman with a look at her face, but she had seen few people with red hair.

Her emergence from the forest turned a few heads within the village. However, they quickly lost interest and turned away again. As she expected, a rider in a traveling cloak was not unusual.

The village boasted a small tavern with the finest ale. Calli shook her head in disdain but found no other place to eat. Eating within the tavern meant standing out from whatever local crowd gathered. Had she found an inn, she might have mixed with other weary travelers.

The village buildings stood sturdy upon their foundations of timber from the forest. The citizens of Cavatar made well with the resources available to them. She had observed it in the few other villages she had encountered. The king had made sure the provincial governments shared resources equally with the poor as with the wealthy landowners.

Like those of other villages, the people greeted her as a harmless stranger. She had observed on one occasion the people's suspicion of a man whose only hint of his loyalty to Hadeon had been the smugness on his face. She could only guess what she did to assure them that she meant no harm.

At the tavern, she slid off Duke and tied his reins to a hitching post. A few people watched in curiosity, but Calli ignored them. More urgent matters called for her attention.

She gave Duke a friendly pat before turning to the propped-open door. With a deep breath, she entered.

A table of men boasted loudly to each other across the room. The pompous drunkenness filled the air. The outline of a dragon on the bracers of two of the men confirmed what she suspected.

She caught her voice on a whisper. "Tyrkam!"

When she realized that she stared at the group, Calli forced her eyes away. She passed her gaze over the room before fixing on the small, surly man behind his counter. He eyed the five men, scowling in contempt. The few other patrons gave the group a wide berth.

None wished to jump into the middle of the war.

Calli ground her teeth on the thought. That they would not risk life and limb for their neighbor disturbed her morals. For that reason she had left the security of Cavatar to rescue her friend. In her travels she found another cause—to disrupt Tyrkam's invasive raider groups. If they caused trouble, this would be no different.

"What'll you have?" the owner asked her with his eyes on the noisy pack.

"Have you food for a traveler?"

The small man blinked and studied her profile. His round face betrayed the surprise she had come to expect.

Calli frowned at him and shook her head with an unspoken request to say nothing about her.

"Aye, ma—stranger. We've a fine cook."

"Bring me a plate."

The man gave a nod and, after a quick glance to the now subdued bunch, exited through his side door.

Calli sighed. At least he had not given her away. How many others would have jumped at the chance to hassle her?

She refused to entertain the thought.

While waiting for her food, she took in a more detailed sweep of the room. This time she noticed a lone stranger seated across from her. She could have sworn he had not been there a moment ago. He dropped his eyes to his mug when her eyes passed over him. Except for his timing, she'd have ignored him. Something about him stirred up curiosity within her. Why did he give her any attention?

He could have been anyone, but something—maybe the way he looked at her—said he was anything but ordinary. His black hair brushed his shoulders while black stubble lined his jaw. A brown cloak covered an average build, like that of a cavalry soldier. Above the beard, his blue eyes sparkled with curiosity and charm.

With a minute shake of her head, Calli looked away. Whether the stranger planned for trouble or not, she could not judge. She had taken it upon herself to defeat Tyrkam. The business of others was not hers.

The drunken group roared with laughter.

While she waited for food, Calli finished her study of the room's layout. A boar's head guarded the doorway from above, its fierce expression foreboding. The large crosshatched window spilled dusty light across the interior. A stone fireplace lay cold at one wall with a display of weapons next to it.

The stranger sat before the weapons, a sly grin on his face when her eyes passed him again. She shook the thought away.

The place could have used a little less attention at the moment.

The server returned to her with a clay bowl of stew, a perfect late-morning meal to her churning stomach. Calli scooped out the bites of meat and vegetables with the round loaf he set beside her. Grateful for the food, she set out more coins than he might have asked.

"You're too kind, stranger."

With her mouth full of the bland stew, Calli waved away his gratitude. When he set a mug of cider before her, she smiled. The scent of cinnamon and nutmeg tickled her nose without the nauseating effects of liquor.

Calli ate quickly, her ears alert to the group and their quiet mutterings.

Wood screeched on wood.

She stiffened.

The stomp of heavy boots approached until she detected the nearness of another by the rasp of his breath and ominous presence. Behind her the group whispered and chuckled.

"Hey," a gruff voice said. "Stranger."

She continued to eat her meal with no intention of entertaining his arrogance.

His hand gripped her shoulder. "I'ms speakin' to yeh. Y' deaf or just lookin' fer trouble?"

Calli tensed, her instincts ready for the one move he might try. With a timing she could not have planned better, he shoved her shoulder back to spin her around. She moved with his momentum and jabbed her elbow back.

It made contact with his hard gut. He grunted and stepped away.

When she turned, she suppressed a grin from seeing his hands holding his middle. Not bad against the size of this man; her head barely reached his shoulders.

"Oh!" She pretended to be sorry. Anger blended into surprise on his face. "Forgive me. I'm so clumsy." She moved to assist him to his seat and dug the heel of her boot into his toe.

The oaf growled through his teeth and hunched over.

"Let me help with that." Calli helped him limp to his table and lifted his half empty mug out of his way. In doing so, she slammed it hard against his jaw.

"Oh!" she said. "I'm so sorry. Here—"

She set the mug down, this time slamming it on his hand flat on the table.

He howled in pain while his friends watched in silence.

"Stupid woman!" He cursed her and reached to take the mug from her hand. Instead, he bumped her arm, sending ale spattering over his face and chest in a perfect, if unpredictable, end to her clumsy guise. "Get away!"

Calli's heart hammered against her chest as she backed away. She wanted no more trouble from this bunch and hoped to escape in one piece. However, the damage had been done. She prepared for the worst.

Her eyes passed over the others beyond the group and they turned away. The lone stranger met her eyes and smirked behind his mug. He understood. An ally? Perhaps.

She reached her bowl without incident. The group of men laughed at their companion. The object of her torment cursed and swore his anger.

She managed two more bites before multiple benches scraped behind her. It seemed the whole table of men stomped her way.

They stopped behind her, pressing in to corner her. Calli swallowed. A hard poke on her shoulder alerted her to their imminent threat.

"We've no likin' o' yeh," one of them said. "Yeh do not belong here."

"I'll soon leave." Calli took a small breath. She turned slowly, tensing for the expected fight.

"Y'll not leave until y' pay."

"Pay?" She cowered back against the counter. "I've no way to pay for your trouble."

The ale-drenched individual stepped forward through the others. He glared at her as she shrank away. "Then y'll pay in other ways." He eyed her figure exposed through the front of the cloak and grinned.

"I beg you reconsider." She glanced about, planning her opening against the brutes. "I meant no harm."

There. The one nearest to her. He left a space between him and the bar.

The leader flexed his sore hand. "Really?"

"Leave the lady alone!"

As one, they turned their attention to the black-haired stranger.

Calli looked up, surprised by the man's boldness.

He stood a stride away, leaning on a spear, which was missing from the display.

She let out her breath in a sigh of relief but hoped he had the ability to back up his confidence.

This was her battle. She intended no harm to anyone else, but his life was his own to do as he pleased. If coming to her rescue pleased him, who was she to argue? Besides, he carried an air of capability about him, or pretended very well.

"Your mother must have dropped you a few too many times," the stranger said. "Or you'd realize the odds against you."

The gang chuckled. "Five are we against one o' you," the biggest said. He stood a head taller than the stranger. "I've not seen better." His hand fell to the hilt of his sword and pulled it from the sheath belted to his side.

On an unknown cue from their leader, the two soldiers nearest to Calli stepped to her side and secured her arms. She looked up to each. Just as Phelan's distraction with Donaghy and Morain, the stranger here had distracted her and cost her an opportunity. She had to find another.

The stranger lifted his spear and took a step away, while the other patrons cleared from the tavern in a rush to the door. When the final pounding of their steps faded, Calli acted.

Using the two holding her for support, she kicked out at the drenched brute with his back to her, sending him falling toward the stranger.

The stranger reacted with a sidestep away and whacked his spear across the soldier's back.

The brute tumbled into the table.

Calli slipped away from the men holding her and whirled on her attackers. Too quick to catch, she dodged their moves in the confined space of the tavern and returned the punches.

Not without her faults, she took a hit. One of the three caught her across the shoulder, sending her sprawling into the benches of their table. The wood clattered and scraped. She groaned from the stinging of her left shoulder and the sharpness of the table edge into her back.

They came at her like a pack of wolves and circled her warily. Of skill enough to impress them, she had earned that respect.

"Now we've a prey worth catching." A hint of anger frosted the scruffy man's voice. "Rumors passed I've heard. A rider of fiery hair." He pointed to the braided red hair hanging over her shoulder.

"True," another said. His dark hair fell into his face, adding to his wild appearance. "I've a mind to wonder on truth."

"I think we've the mystery rider," the third said with a malicious grin.

Calli climbed backward over the tabletop and rose to her feet. "I think y've no chance of catching your mystery rider with poor skills as yours."

When they rushed her together, Calli leaped over their heads and rolled across a table behind them. She landed unsteadily on her feet behind the table. They turned and rushed her again, this time from opposite sides.

Calli ducked away from the first to swing at her. When one caught her waist, she swung her arm around to catch him across his neck. He released his hold as another grabbed her shoulder with the third. Her heart gave way in the moment she realized she could not escape.

"Is that any way to treat a lady?"

She could not have planned better timing. Realizing again that she fought with company, Calli looked up to the confidence on the stranger's face. She spotted the two lumps along the wall with the weapons display tumbled down around them. That was fast. Gratitude cleared away the despair. So busy had she been with her three that she had failed to realize the stranger had defeated two others.

He winked knowingly to her before one of the brutes holding her charged ahead. Left with one holding her arms, she kicked back at his shin. His grip loosened in reaction to the pain of her boot heel ramming against his bone.

Calli whirled, her elbow punching into his ribs. His fist flew at her but hit empty air. With a few moves of her own, she sent him sprawling head first into the wall. He collapsed into a lump.

"Not bad."

Startled, Calli whirled. When she realized who had spoken, she took a deep breath and dropped her hands. The other two bullies lied groaning on the hard floor behind him. She blinked at the speed with which her ally had disposed of them. Never had she imagined anyone capable of such action. "Who are you?"

With a charming smile he bowed low before her, exaggerating in humor, she would swear. "Your servant, milady. An admirer of your work." He reached for her hand.

With a puzzled frown wrinkling her forehead, Calli let him lift her hand to his face. His facial hair tickled with the lightness of his kiss.

"An honor I bear of your presence."

She stared at the gentle quality of his face and the watery blue of his eyes; eyes like Phelan's but aged by hardship. The memory shattered her heart and she looked away.

Now, one thought overcame her regrets of leaving—had she stayed, many would have suffered at the hands of those she had defeated.

Rousing herself from the memories, Calli looked away from her "servant" to search for her cloak. The owner of the tavern held it out to her, his eyes wide with wonder.

"Thank you," she said.

He gave a nod to both of them with a neutral expression. "Will yeh be finishin' your meal?"

She looked around them at the upturned benches and the five listless bodies strewn about the floor. They might awaken soon. With that, they would likely seek vengeance.

"I'll not be needing it. I suggest you tie them before they wake." She knelt beside one. After digging in his jacket, she found a purse with plenty of change. Though she cared not for thieves, taking from these brutes gave her no conflicts. It would make up for her troubles.

With a second glance, the sword hilt caught her eyes, the dragon crossbar alerting her to what she had suspected. Phelan had described the swords to her with a word of caution and a plea to remain within the security of the palace walls.

Since leaving, she had encountered at least three small groups like this, though not all carried the swords. She wondered if she had crossed the border into Hadeon.

The tavern owner looked to the mess in disdain. "Not much o' her left, but we are grateful o' their silence." He looked first at Calli, then to the stranger, who handed the spear to him. "I'll be more if y'd alert the village."

"Alert the king, man!" Calli looked him in the eye. Did no one understand? "These are Tyrkam's army. We have no rest until they are all defeated."

The stranger frowned. "What source have you to prove this?"

Calli pointed to the sword. "See the crossbar of the sword? It bears the seal of the dragon—Tyrkam's crest."

The stranger looked down and nodded. "A fool and his followers."

"What better than dead best be all them?" Their host grumbled on his way to clean up the mess.

Calli and the stranger looked to each other. He smiled. "Nothing less than human is the red angel chasing away the evil raiders."

The sparkle in his blue eyes matched the enchantment of his smile. Calli winked in return. "Have you a name?"

"Call me what you wish, beautiful warrior." He bowed low, an air of playfulness in his actions. This time she knew he exaggerated. "Though friends refer to me as Jayson, other names have been used."

"I'd not doubt that of such wit. I thank you for your services, Jayson."

"All my pleasure to serve, lady warrior."

Calli's cheeks flushed warmly. Never had she the intent of gaining a servant, or the admiration of any other man but Phelan. Jayson's attention flustered her. She looked away from him to hide the blush warming her cheeks and made her way to the thugs. "Help me serve our friend by cleaning our mess."

Together they managed to tie each of the thugs before they awoke to their predicament. By the time they secured them, others from the village returned to the tavern with the local magistrate and a crowd of onlookers. By the praises of the innkeeper, Calli and Jayson left with a few gifts.

Calli thanked them, anxious to escape the attention. With new rations filling her saddlebags, she climbed aboard Duke. He pranced within the tight crowd. Although he took his bit in his eagerness to run, Calli held him to a dancing, collected trot as they departed.

Jayson followed on foot with his bag of rations over his shoulder.

Beyond the sounds of the village, Calli stopped in the forest with Jayson close behind.

Duke pawed at the ground impatiently. "Easy, boy." He tossed his head but stood still for the moment.

Jayson took a step forward and put a hand to Duke's dappled neck, his eyes on Calli. "Have you need for a good warrior?"

"You may join me, if you wish. I've no other way to thank you for your services."

"I am honored, my lady."

"Then I welcome your skills at my service, Jayson." Her voice dropped at the disturbance in the forest's symphony. The song changed and quieted, the air tense about her. "We've no distance yet from trouble."

With an arm to Jayson, Calli helped him swing up onto Duke's back behind her. "Hang on," she said over her shoulder. His arms gripped tightly around her a breath ahead of her giving Duke his head. The horse burst forth on a bolt of speed. Jayson's arms squeezed her middle in response.

An arrow hummed past her.

She had wondered about the small group in the tavern. Tyrkam's raiding parties were all but stupid, if arrogant. She had suspected them of not comprising the whole group.

Amid the rain of thinning arrows, one thought arose. Had it been a trap?

The idea shot through her as if an arrow had struck her. She stiffened, her breath coming in gasps in her panic and their mad dash through the maze of trees. Had they known she would arrive and set themselves in place to fish her out of the crowd?

It could only be. What had the man said in the tavern? The soldier had known of her, if not by face but by reputation. She should have realized it then but in the midst of their fight, had not the capacity of thought to spare. Now, nearly too late she came to understand. As luck held out, she had taken the forest's warning and avoided the trap.

The hidden riders thundered through the trees around her. Calli glanced aside and caught the flash of movement.

She knew Duke's muscles worked hard beneath them, but he carried two people on his strong back without slowing. She wove a crooked path, climbing to the top of a steep hill away from those who followed.

The shouts and curses of the raiders faded behind them into the forest. She continued their race for a while, weaving a difficult path that none could follow. With enough distance, they would never find her. Few horses could navigate wooded areas with the same agility as Duke.

When only the sounds of the forest reached her, Calli reined in Duke to a slower canter and continued through the trees with ease. His high steps crossed branches without a snag.

With only the forest's busy cacophony to accompany them, Calli decided they had reached a safe point away from the raiders. Part of her wished to return and finish the fight, to reclaim for the people what they had lost with each attack by Tyrkam's army.

When she figured she had lost their pursuers, she slowed Duke to a fast walk. Jayson released her middle from his viselike grip and held, instead, the high cantle of her saddle between them. Beneath them, Duke breathed hard from his efforts with two people on his back, particularly the heavier man over his hindquarters. Calli pitied the horse but dared not let him rest yet.

They wound their way in silence from the forest to the river. At the river they rode a ways down the shallow waters, occasionally crossing from one bank to another, leaving tracks to confuse any pursuers. When they splashed through deeper waters, they rode out of the river for the rolling green hills of the eastern Hadeon border with Cavatar. There, they dismounted and walked.

"You're a good rider, my lady." Jayson's voice hinted of curiosity.

"Calli."

"This mystery rider has a name."

Calli glanced aside to him. With the midday sun on him, Jayson's features stood out. A trim beard covered his chiseled jawline beneath thin lips outlined by a short mustache. Following those features up, she took in the straight, perfect nose that led her to those amazingly blue eyes of his.

When he turned and caught her eyes on him, she looked away with an abashed shyness she had not expected.

He was handsome, she would admit.

She stumbled for the right words to answer his question, drawing attention away from her scrutiny of him. "My father was the king's best warrior. When he was not at war, he'd ask me to care for his horse. I rode many hours to return to my mother's wrath; I'd not done a chore as she asked." Calli smiled fondly at the memories of her mother's fury at her having gone off for a couple hours at a time on Black.

Her father's horse. Her father.

The more she thought of her father, the more her heart ached with the pain of losing him. She wished he was alive to advise her on what to do.

"I'd expect as much. You are no normal lady."

Her cheeks warmed from his flattering tone. Calli turned to Duke and patted his neck to hide her blush. "No true lady but of warrior blood. No less shall I prove than to defeat Tyrkam and rescue my friend from his treachery."

"May I ask who this 'friend' is to deserve such a valiant attendant?"

After a deep breath to calm her sorrows, Calli said, "None less than the Lady Istaria, princess of Cavatar." Not until she had taken several steps did she realize he had fallen into a contemplative silence. She looked over her shoulder. What bothered him? What had she said? "My words upset you?"

"No." He shook his head but the tension in his voice said otherwise. "I— Your words took me by surprise, though I should have expected your service to such a noble woman."

She forced a smile but it dropped to a frown, dragged by her grief.

Calli sighed away the regrets and continued on. They talked about other subjects. For short periods, they rode in a sometimes backtracking path that Jayson suggested—to throw off any trackers.

At sunset, they found a place within a grove of trees to camp for the night. They said nothing except to change watches.

Calli slept more at ease than she had since leaving the palace. She trusted Jayson. Nevertheless, her worries about Lusiradrol haunted her dreams.

Chapter 31
23.5 pc 937

Istaria searched the horizon above her. Although she suspected Lusiradrol would not attack directly from such a vantage, the rockslide made her wary of her surroundings.

She knelt at a small pool and filled the waterskin. Rowen grazed on the tufts of grass scattered among the rocks.

With a sigh, she dipped the skin into the cold mountain spring. Air bubbled out of the mouth until it was full. When it finished, she tied it closed and pulled hard to lift it from the water. For Darius the task would be easy.

She glanced back to his still form lying near the embers of her fire.

After four days, Darius had not awakened. She worried he never would.

While he lay unconscious, she had recovered her full strength and felt ready to defend herself. However, the food would soon run out, and she knew not how to find more in this desolate location. Whether directly or not, Lusiradrol might have her wish.

When she peered into the small pool, Istaria barely recognized the girl staring back. Her soft white hair fell across her shoulders, dull and dirty and tangled. This journey had stolen the dignity that had been hers. How she wished for a bath, finished by fragrant perfumes and the stroke of a brush through her hair!

Damn this existence! The girl in the pool pouted, her eyes swelling with tears. At least in Hadeon, she retained her dignity. What would she do now?

Tears burned in her eyes. She sniffed, trying to hold back the sobbing that choked her. With a glance back, she hoped for the countless time that Darius had awakened. However, he remained unconscious.

Frustrated and miserable, she let loose her tears. Istaria splashed away her reflection and fell aside onto a cool tuft of grass. Hope drained from her like a bucket with no bottom. The little that she had clung to flowed away with her tears.

At the edge of her awareness magic lapped in gentle waves. Only when it probed her with a purpose did she notice the presence of another. She tensed, fearing Lusiradrol had returned.

However, the disturbance shone bright and familiar, and welcome.

Istaria turned her blurry eyes to the sky and the bird circling high above. The scream of a hawk pierced the air. She smiled and remembered the shape-changing woman she had met so long ago. At least she hoped it was. How could anyone else have found them?

When the bird caught her in its gaze, a great wisdom passed between them. This was Gaispar.

Istaria wiped her eyes.

The hawk glided down to land and transformed into the slender woman she had met early in their journey. Relief poured into Istaria's soul.

Gaispar bowed her head. "They sent me to your aid, my lady."

She turned to where Darius lay on the ground. "It then is true, the words of Sethirngal."

Istaria followed Gaispar's eyes. *Lusiradrol did this.*

Saying nothing, Gaispar started toward Darius. Istaria carried the heavy waterskin a few steps behind.

Gaispar knelt next to Darius and passed her hands over his body. Istaria watched from his other side. What was she doing? Could she heal him?

After a few long seconds, Gaispar looked up. "I've not the knowledge to wake him. Only their magic can cure his sleep. We must get him through the gateway of Eyr Droc, if it's not too late."

Too late? Istaria's eyes burned with the threat of more tears. How could Gaispar say such a thing? There had to be a way to wake him.

"I will do all I can to help you reach the portal safely, but I'm no more than a shapeshifter. I cannot heal him."

Wishing she had not heard the truth, Istaria bit her lip and looked away. Her heart yearned for the past, before she knew anything about the white dragon. However, she would suffer it again if it meant Darius loved her just as much.

Istaria wondered about the future and what would happen to him. Before she realized, Gaispar had tacked Rowen and stood waiting. They were ready to go.

What of Darius?

Gaispar stood next to the horse and looked from the saddle to the man in careful consideration. "How confident are you in your abilities?"

Understanding what the woman intended, Istaria nodded. She focused on the magic and the task of lifting Darius into the saddle. With less effort than she expected, she set him astride the horse with his head lying against Rowen's neck.

She took a deep breath and smiled at her accomplishment.

Gaispar shared her triumph. "Y've learned to control it since last we met. He taught you well."

Pride swelled within Istaria and deflated just as quickly. *But I've not the ability to heal him either.*

The gentle smile on Gaispar's face said enough. Istaria pressed her lips together and took a few steps forward.

"They will teach you much more." Gaispar turned and led Rowen forward.

Istaria walked on the other side of the horse to catch Darius if he should fall.

Chapter 32
25.5 pc 937

Evening fell on the second day since Gaispar had found Istaria, who relaxed her watch of Darius. He had not yet fallen from the saddle, and she had come to doubt that Rowen would allow it.

Shadows stretched long across the rocky terrain. Istaria never saw the cave until they almost stumbled in. It masqueraded as the shade of a towering boulder.

Gaispar stepped toward the dark maw, but Istaria hesitated, uncertain about entering. The forces of magic swirled inside.

Gaispar halted and turned. "Is something wrong?"

The sun vanished below the horizon behind them, casting them in shadow. Istaria shivered as much from the chill as from her fears of the darkness. It reminded her of the cave in which she had wandered as a child.

She took a couple steps closer, stopping beside Gaispar with a frown.

"Fear not, my lady. The cave is not our final destination."

She hoped not. But where would it lead?

With Gaispar leading Rowen, Istaria followed into the darkness, her heart pounding

A few steps inside, she spied a light ahead. Magic twisted and swirled with a power she had not experienced except when it escaped from inside her.

"There."

Istaria continued over the smooth, well-worn floor toward the light. Gaispar led her through the passage until they approached a large opening. After crossing the dark of the cave, the light of a bright day on the other side nearly blinded her.

They stepped through into sunlight, where Istaria recognized nothing. Her jaw dropped.

Where are we? The land shone green with verdant beauty, thick with flora in a rainbow of colors. The fresh air inspired a drink of its purity with each breath.

A castle floating above them sparkled with crystalline elegance.

Istaria gasped from the spectrum of colors that burst from every facet of the castle. Upon the towers perched creatures whose scales shimmered in the sun's rays of shades from the deepest green to blue and gold, though no colors of the red hues. They stood poised in magnificent splendor, noble yet frightening in the same instant.

Gaispar turned to her. "Feel it. The magic flows freely in this land, where these creatures have for generations hidden from mankind. This is the land untouched by mortals and full o' life. Here you are free to use your powers without consequence.

"This is Eyr Droc, realm o' the dragons, also known to men as the Second Realm." She started down a slight embankment through a grove of trees without further comment.

Istaria followed Gaispar, walking beside Rowen to keep her eyes on Darius. At the bottom of the slope, they crossed the open land. A flurry of winged creatures zipped through the air. *What is our destination?*

"Long have they waited, milady, and with magic and others prepared a place. No grander a home of simplicity might another have built."

They came up over the hill to spy a strange house at the edge of a forest. It could have been a tree with its thick, twisting trunks, however, it lacked branches and leaves. From a bridge over the narrow creek meandering through the valley a neat path of flat stones led to the front door of the home. Flowers decorated the front of the building and the edge of the path.

Istaria stood in awe. Compared to anything she had encountered, this was the most beautiful in its simplicity and natural beauty. Also, after their journey in the wilds, she welcomed any solid shelter over her head.

She smiled her appreciation to Gaispar, who led Rowen over the wooden bridge to the front door of the two-level home.

Istaria stopped next to Rowen with Darius bent over his withers. *What of Darius?*

Before Gaispar could reply, a blur of motion flew before her. It circled around. The winged creature swooped down. Gaispar ducked in time to avoid it.

However, the small, green reptile circled around and settled on her shoulder.

"Jaren." Gaispar all but growled the name.

It blinked large dark eyes.

Istaria studied the foot-high creature. It gripped Gaispar's shoulders with tiny claws on its hind legs and steadied its balance with tiny claws on the joints of its wings.

I was bad? I only intended to welcome you home. I have not seen you for many days and was afraid you would not come. I was not allowed to look for you—

"Hush!"

Much apologies.

"Be careful next time." Gaispar looked to Istaria. "My lady, meet Jaren, our contact with the drakin, in a manner of speaking. Jaren, this is Istaria."

Pleased to meet you, Lady Istaria.

And you, Jaren, Istaria replied.

"Jaren, we need Sethirngal," Gaispar said. "Please hurry back with him."

As you wish, Lady Gaispar. It is my honor to serve you. If I can—

"Now."

In an instant, he dropped from her shoulder and flapped to the crystal palace.

Gaispar wasted no time and helped Istaria lower Darius to the ground. While they waited, Gaispar untacked Rowen and turned him loose on the ankle-deep grass.

Istaria sat on the grass in front of the tree house and held Darius's head in her lap. She smoothed away the hair from his gentle face, noting the brown stubble now covering his entire chin. She leaned over him and kissed his cheek, finding reassurance in the warmth of his breath.

A few minutes passed before she detected a large disturbance in the magic. Power resonated in a pattern of colors that stole her breath. An equally large shadow passed by overhead, drawing her eyes to the sky.

Istaria stared at the mountain of a dragon, which glided to a gentle landing on four clawed feet. With its snake-like body and gigantic wings, she held no doubts this was one of the dragons Gaispar served. Its green body started with a head full of rough scales crested by short spikes and ended in a tapered tail. The mouth full of jagged teeth made her shudder.

The dragon looked at her as the white spirit had, with a wisdom and confidence from ages of learning. Its nostrils flared, sending up puffs of smoke with each breath.

When it stretched its nose over Darius, she held tight to him, afraid the great beast might decide to swallow him in one gulp. Instead it let out a gentle rumble from deep in its throat and inhaled.

Not she nor other of her kind did this,
but another magic is here amiss.

Istaria blinked and loosened her grip on Darius. *What?*

The dragon gazed at her, his amusement changing the colors of the magic around him.

I see in you
the source of power true.
In you lies the cure

from your love pure.

Leaning close, he said, *Touch my face with your hand and set the other on this man.*

Istaria hesitated and looked up. Gaispar knelt beside her. "Trust him, my lady."

Unsure of trusting a creature from her nightmares, Istaria hesitated.

"Please, or he'll not recover. Sethirngal is the oldest and wisest of the dragons."

Swallowing her fear of the beast, Istaria set her hand on its face. The warmth surprised her, although the roughness of the scales did not.

Before she noticed anything further, a shock of magic coursed through her. It froze her in her place until the dragon pulled away. She blinked away the disorientation and searched those around her. *What was that?*

As great a source your powers may be,
but he not prepared will find difficulty.
Where he tried to direct your force
trapped him between without remorse.

Istaria frowned and turned to Gaispar. The dragon spoke in riddles.

"He had not the strength to channel your powers and was caught in the moment between life and death."

Stroking the hair from the face she loved, Istaria gazed at the peace she found there. She, or more correctly the white dragon, had caused this. *Now what happens?*

"We wait for him to awaken. Then they—" Gaispar indicated the dragon with a flick of her eyes. "—will teach you how to control your powers."

In a quieter voice, she added, "You must know how to defend yourself when next you meet Lusiradrol, or her minions."

Chapter 33
26.5 pc 937

Her wounds would heal. However, a heart blacker than the night swore revenge for the defeat. The white dragon would die.

Lusiradrol growled and limped toward the charred remains of the cabin. Magic emanated yet from the old residence of the man who had thwarted her attempts to banish the white dragon from existence. He had channeled the power of her nemesis to attack her. No ordinary man was capable of such a skill.

Perhaps the coals of his home hid some secret about him, and how to defeat him. She had been wrong in thinking no mortals knew the ways of magic except the Lumathir. She would not make that mistake again.

Lusiradrol focused the remains of her powers on the coals, sifting through them for any concentrations of magic. Tiny points remained, but she managed to separate them from the rest.

Her powers faltered with her strength but she piled the ashes together. One blackened item caught her eyes above the others, a metal brooch bearing a familiar emblem. The coiled, winged serpent slept, or so it appeared.

What is this?

She lifted the brooch to her face to study it closer. The dragon resembled hers, the ones the Ancients slandered as wyverns. *Are they not dead but sleep, as this image? What sorcery entraps them? What does he know?*

She scanned her surroundings amid evening shadows and scowled. The man who had possessed this graven image knew what she desired.

However, he had entered Eyr Droc by now. She could not pass through the portal's magic.

"He had another." A sly smile crept up as she recalled the first battle and the crossfire from the black-haired man. He had also wielded magic. Could they be connected? What knew he of this Darius, the woodsman who was not?

Lusiradrol sat back with a sigh from the weariness that drained her strength. *When I recover... They will reveal their secrets.*

Chapter 34
2.6 pc 937

Despite the sweat pouring into his eyes, Phelan never hesitated. He swiped at the drops with his sleeve but never removed his eyes from the swords before him. Donaghy fought with greater skill than last he recalled.

"Who taught you these new moves?" Phelan parried a downward swing and feinted.

The trainer never fell for the trick. Instead, he struck again in nearly the same place, not where Phelan expected.

They thrust and parried, but in the end, the trainer stood with his sword at Phelan's throat. Gasps arose from the faces around them in the city street. They had gathered an audience of several children from the city who stared in wide-eyed fascination.

Both breathed heavily, soaked in sweat from the intense practice in the heat of the day. After several long seconds, Donaghy dropped his sword and stood upright. Phelan straightened and sheathed his sword.

"Yeh be a long ways from practice." Donaghy swiped away damp, black hair from his face.

Phelan nodded. "I'd not say the same of you."

"Leave it to your lady friend." A wry smile crooked up Donaghy's cheeks into the black beard. "She's a spry one—the offspring o' Kaillen."

Phelan smiled. He had seen Calli's talents at work and harbored no doubts of what she could do and what she had taught these men. He always suspected Kaillen had taught his daughter to fight but had never seen it. "I'll wager you'll not allow another woman to best you."

"That's a wager y'll win."

With a light chuckle, Donaghy crossed through the open gates to the palace courtyard, where the day's activities wound down with the lengthening shadows.

Phelan followed the trainer through the group of kids. The evening meal would soon be served, if it had not already. More than he could count, he had missed meals in defiance of his parents' etiquette and routine as much as simply losing track of the day.

However, his stomach always grabbed his attention with full force when he dropped that attention from his other activities. At the moment, it screamed for food.

He hurried to reach the dining area to satisfy his hunger. He started up the steps at the front of the palace. At the top, a young servant raced to him.

"Milord." The blonde-haired boy gasped and hesitated before bowing with a gangly body. "His majesty requests your presence—" He swallowed and lowered his voice. "Some time ago."

Phelan continued to the door, the boy jogging to keep up. "I looked, I did, but found no one to tell me your place. I tried."

Phelan stopped and looked at the boy, whose eyes begged mercy as if he had done something wrong. Quite the opposite. "Thank you for not finding me sooner," he said with a crooked grin. He had insisted on practicing in the city to hide from interruptions.

The boy frowned and hurried away.

Phelan's steps echoed through the passages on his way to the dining area to find the king. Thoughts of what his father might want, a reprimand, most likely, made him grimace. He should not care, but the man was still king.

When he reached the dining chambers, the servants hurried to clean up what remained on the tables. Most guests visited in their groups, paying little mind at the moment to the king and queen, who sat at the head table in their own quiet discussion.

Amid the many servants clearing the tables, Phelan entered. He wove his way through the moving bodies, dodging precarious burdens in the process. En route, he managed to steal a loaf from one tray.

When he reached the head table, he stopped in a line with his father. "You called, my lord?"

King Isolder's eyes narrowed and he ceased his conversation with the queen. His beard had increased in the amount of white hairs among the brown, or so Phelan could have sworn. The lines of stress deepened on his father's aging visage. "Where have you been? When you're not of proper turnout, I've a mind that you care little for this land and its rule."

Phelan suppressed a scowl and stood up. "I've not the time nor the desire to argue petty details. We have a war on our lands and you've done no more to stop it."

The king's face hardened. "Tie that tongue in here!" Isolder spoke through clenched teeth. "We will provide a good impression to these visitors."

"You would rather lie, father, than permit these humble folks to protect themselves against demons?" His father had not listened to him in their confrontation, but had avoided a full-blown argument with his book. Phelan still longed for that argument, if only to relieve his frustrations.

His mother eyed him to say no more. Reluctant but obedient to her, Phelan obliged. "But of falsehoods or not, such a choice have you made. What wish you of my duty this time?" The words came out hanging with exasperation.

"See me in the visiting room." Isolder rose from the table and, with a quick nod to his wife, strode from the room.

Phelan pursed his lips and shook his head.

"Do as he says." Damaera spoke with a soft but stern voice. "I beg you stay your temper with him on this."

He gazed into her dark, tired eyes and sighed. With a light nod, he agreed. For his mother, he would do almost anything. "As you wish, my lady."

≈

In the late hours of the night, after most visitors had taken to their beds, Phelan pushed open the door to the visiting room. It creaked an announcement into the silent shadows flickering from the table-top candelabra. Without the oil lamps lit, darkness saturated the corners and crevasses of the room.

At the edge of the light, in the outline of the open balcony doors, stood an old man of creeping years, his eyes glazed over in thought. King Isolder suddenly aged decades ahead in Phelan's vision.

Humbled by the image, Phelan entered without a word.

The king remained focused on the three candles held upright in the silver candelabra on the table. "Come." His tone left no room for argument.

Setting his jaw in an automatic defiant reaction, Phelan stepped to the table.

They stood opposite each other as if frozen in time, unmoving and silent. The sounds from outside filtered into the emptiness between them.

The king stepped to the table. His eyes fixed on Phelan, who gazed back with unwavering confidence. "I've no desire to turn you away."

Isolder paused, the light of the candles flickering a reflection in his eyes. "I too resisted the advice of my elders as a young man, but have since come to understand their wisdom and foresight. Not many are meant to lead a great land as this. The Isolder blood runs strong in Cavatar, from the first of our line to you. We nourish and keep her. It is our duty. One day it will be yours, and your descendents'."

Phelan opened his mouth to object but bit his tongue. As much as he wanted to object, no good would come of arguing with his father, and he had promised his mother.

After a momentary pause, his father continued. "That is why I regret that you must leave. I've made arrangements for you to visit the sovereign of Rivonia in search of a suitable bride. He vowed his loyalty to you in the past."

The idea repulsed Phelan to choose a woman for convenience rather than marry whom his heart desired. However, he reined in his objections. One day the king might see the folly of his ways.

He grew older each day lost. Phelan slumped slightly with the burden of his heritage on his shoulders. Who else would rule Cavatar when he passed? What would come of Cavatar if he did not assume his birthright and lead their land?

The obvious answer drifted up from his thoughts. If he assumed the throne, he would command the armies of Cavatar and, therefore, plan the defeat of the dreadful warlord and his army of brigands. He could direct the outcome of the war and save Cavatar. He would rescue his people.

Or had he considered it but rejected the idea? Would Cavatar exist at that time?

He had to try. "I am ready."

Isolder raised a gray eyebrow.

"My time has arrived and I cannot deny fate. You're right, my lord."

"What brings this sudden change?" Suspicion leaked from Isolder's voice.

Phelan walked around the table to the open balcony doors letting in the cool evening breeze of late summer. "I've realized time not used is lost. I've lost enough time."

He turned to face his father. "My time is at hand and I must use it or forever lose it."

Isolder gave a nod. "You will leave at next morn on your journey to the shore, where a ship waits to cross the sea. On the other side, Farolkavin awaits you." Isolder paused and lowered his voice. "Travel safely."

"I will." Without further comment, Phelan strode out the door. Its thud echoed down the corridor.

Outside the room, he took a deep breath. His mind raced with ideas of what he would do to change the direction of this war with Hadeon.

Only one fault cracked the foundation of his ideas—by the time he came to power, it would be too late.

Chapter 35
17.6 pc 937

Fire rained down on familiar carvings, setting ablaze a vibrant courtyard and structures. People screamed, running in chaos. A bolt of white lightening struck the keep, shearing a hole in the masonry.

A gigantic blue-scaled head blew fire on a swarm of soldiers in ordinary clothes and armor. They lit up like candles.

Istaria opened her eyes with a start and gulped for a breath.

Relax, Lady. Come back slowly from the vision.

Istaria caught her breath and looked up to the dark green dragon. Sethirngal's large, reptilian eyes blinked at her in perfect calm from a face of rough scales. A crown of horns crested the edge of his head, while wispy smoke billowed up in clouds from both nostrils. Despite his fierce appearance, he no longer frightened her. She had grown accustomed to the sight of dragons.

Since Gaispar had brought her to this world with her dearest Darius, she had no choice but to live with them. She was not safe in her own realm. They honored her for carrying the magic untainted with the guardian spirit of the white dragon.

She lived in peace with the woodsman who had rescued her from Hadeon. However, a thread of guilt wove its way through her emotions, threatening to strangle her joy. She had abandoned her family and Calli at the directions of the dragons, but wished to bring them to share her blessings and free them of the terrible war. What had happened to them?

Images reared up from the ashes of the vision, unhindered by the fond memories. Her hands trembled on her lap. *I saw the palace...in flames.* Was that the fate awaiting the people she loved?

What you saw may yet be,
or maybe not it seems.
Where future tells and visions run,
not all motions have begun.

Istaria dropped her eyes. How could they set her home on fire? Her heart stirred in protest, but the other part of the vision cooled the burning anger threatening to rise. Her exhaustion also helped to cloud her mind.

Was it Tyrkam's army?

Her eyes jumped to Sethirngal. *I saw Tyrkam's men. They defended the palace against dragons.*

A deep sigh rumbled from the depths of the dragon's green body.

If truth it comes,
consider this, young one:
that Tyrkam defends the land of light,
he will with relish fight.
Unto mortals he brings this plight,
but will be crushed by dragon's flight.

Istaria frowned and blinked to keep her eyes open. The dragons had spoken in nothing less than riddles. Though she understood them better, she wished they would speak plainly.

The vision worried her. The idea of her home in flames ripped through her emotions. That the dragons would cause the destruction tore her apart. She had grown to trust them. How could they betray her?

She wished the dragons had left the power of prophecy alone. She wished they had not taught her to focus that gift. She wished she had not seen Setheadroc in flames.

Istaria closed her eyes tight, but it could not remove the images of death and destruction branded on her mind, despite the pull of sleep. The images coalesced into detail.

She opened her eyes, determined to banish the horrible vision. With a look up, she traced the tall ceiling that curved to the walls in an unbroken line. Like vines climbing the edges and columns, the crystal curved in organic patterns within the throne room of the floating castle. As if grown from living plants that had crystallized, the lines of the fortress curved softly, clouded in walls and various objects, but otherwise clear.

For the moment, the beauty of the fortress charmed away the horror of her vision.

Istaria took a deep breath. Her nerves calmed.

You learn well
to use magic without spells.

Not lightly nor with enthusiasm I accept this, Istaria replied. She had feared magic for most of her life, but Makleor had insisted she accept the power. She reveled in the connection to the world around her and had learned to make use of magic. Nevertheless, losing control of the forces within her held her back from drawing on the full power.

Her stomach stirred with nausea, churning up an objection. She frowned and put her hands to her middle. *Oh, blight. Why must I feel sick now?*

This is illness not,
for we know what. Sethirngal lifted his long head. The warmth of his joy washed against Istaria, pouring over her in currents that settled her stomach with the distraction of her mind.

She smiled at the dragon. *Thank you, my friend. But I fear it will not banish this illness long.*

Not an illness as you think,
but a baby on the brink.

Istaria caught her breath in her lungs. She stared at the unblinking gaze of her teacher. Had he said what she thought? Was this another riddle?

No. A part of her had known from the beginning, but had not faced the fact. Darius had loved her, and loved her deeper than any person ever would. But could she tell him of this? How would he react?

Sooner or later he must know,
since that belly will obviously grow.

Istaria grimaced, as much from the nausea as from the dragon's statement. She could not hide a pregnancy for long.

She lifted her eyes to the two cloudy blue pillars equal distance from the throne. Their sole purpose was to add decoration to this simple but breathtaking castle. Clear crystal vines curled and climbed them.

I will tell him when he is ready. She sighed and closed the connection with Sethirngal to keep her thoughts to herself. All this time with Darius. What thoughts had he of what would be?

Istaria winced at the rhyming that came without thought. All her time with the dragons had influenced her way of thinking, and speaking.

Had he considered raising a family? Darius had lost his first wife during childbirth and he feared losing her. Only after they arrived had he told her the story that Hlynn had touched with her comments.

When her stomach churned, Istaria winced. She feared losing Darius more than her home. She could not bear the same emptiness she endured when Thain and his gang stole her from the carriage and deposited her before Tyrkam in Hadeon. She would tell Darius when the time was right, when she was sure he would not leave her.

Sethirngal blew curls of smoke from his nostrils in quiet meditation.

Istaria gazed into the possibilities conjured by worries, until Sethirngal rose on all four legs and turned away in the great hall. His heavy steps sent the crystal ringing in a unique music.

The movement snapped her from the myriad paths sending shots of angst through her heart.

Come, Lady.

She blinked away the questions and images of blood and fire and rose from the elaborate throne.

Istaria sighed and followed the dragon out of the hall.

When she caught up to the swift beast, she strolled next to him in the wide corridors. She had plenty of room, at least on her side, while Sethirngal strolled on her other side. Someone had planned to share the castle with the dragons.

Where are we going? she asked.

What once was great to this land,
came from not a common man.
He shared his magic for the best,
though he fell with Lusiradrol's test.

Istaria dropped her eyes, gazing at the shimmering floor. They had mentioned Lusiradrol before in a way that emphasized her already bad experiences. The woman tempted men, including Tyrkam, to their doom. At least, she hoped it would lead the man to his destruction.

Makleor had fallen to her enchantments three thousand years ago. Lusiradrol had lured him to promises of grand rewards. His price was the slaying of the white dragon and his curse of immortality. Like all magi, he lived longer because of the presence of the Light in him, but was not fully immortal until the white dragon cursed him.

Istaria shuddered. The story of the black dragon sent a chill through her body. She looked up to the back of the green dragon's head. *Who was this man?*

A mage of gifts this world bestowed
from the tales and legends old.
He brought the sacred power of life
and from this realm chased all strife.
When the white one of legend rose,
he with the others thus proposed.
The white one of all hope was born,
but not long she had the world torn.

Sethirngal paused a moment and took a deep breath.

Jealousy and temptation and hate,
these were her tools to destroy men's fate.

Istaria considered his words, fighting the tiredness that had come with the nausea. Darius had told her the white dragon had been blessed by the Majera with all their power, but had used wisdom to prevent its abuse. She knew he had left his spirit to guard his heart, in which he had left his magic. For that Tyrkam planned to defeat Cavatar.

But the dragon spirit had claimed her first. As a child, she had wandered into the cave left by the dragon's body.

Now you, with your temper soft and mild,
shall possess both, as your child.

The dragon's hope shone through the magic with pulsing warmth.

Istaria smiled and put her hand to her belly. When another wave of nausea threatened to take her lunch from her, she grimaced.

Sethirngal stopped and turned his head around to her. Deep green reptilian eyes regarded her thoughtfully. *Wish you here to halt?*

She shook her head and looked at the gentle eyes of the green dragon. Wisdom and intelligence swelled in the depths of his spirit. It reached out to her, touching her in a way that had no explanation. In that brief instant, she understood the limitless bounds the creature had explored and the joys and pain he had reached.

When she realized her stomach settled again, Istaria smiled. His distraction had worked. *I'll be all right, for a while.*

Sethirngal continued forward. When they neared an opening to the balcony overlooking the land below, light splattered in reflections from wall to wall, filling the corridor with its glory.

Every day since she had arrived, Istaria had walked these halls with one dragon or another. However, Sethirngal taught her more often than the others. As the oldest, he had seen it as his duty. He remembered the white dragon, who had hatched almost five thousand years after him.

Istaria sighed. The images of her vision returned and threatened to tear her apart. She suppressed the tears by forcing her thoughts back to the present. What could a mage, as Makleor, have taught the white dragon?

Sethirngal stopped at a tall clouded door decorated with ornate curls and curves of sparkling gold vines. It opened at his bidding without a sound.

Istaria followed the dragon into an empty room with crystalline benches lining its rounded walls, which arched around the perimeter. No benches lined the straight side opposite them.

His feet sent echoes of tinkling music through the room with each step he took toward the flat wall.

A shiver of a different magic than the rest of the floating fortress resonated from it, barely noticeable. When Sethirngal passed through without stopping, she understood and followed.

She emerged into a chamber of immeasurable proportions. Like many of the other rooms she had seen, its proportions defied logic. It should not have fit in the castle, but it did.

A tall window arched at the top cast the light of the day across the room and its contents. Books stacked high above on shelves. No dust touched any objects.

Istaria walked around the dragon to the opposite side of the room. Near the window, she found an old wooden chair. Upon its seat and armrests it bore the scars of use.

In this room he sat and pondered,
while of his place others wondered.
In here sleeps the knowledge of his mind,
and vast explorations of dragon kind.

Istaria took in the books with a fresh sense of awareness. Each sent tiny ripples into the magic. She gazed in awe at the vast resources at her disposal, the mage's knowledge and some of his power.

Her insides jumped in excitement. Where she once feared the magic within her, she now sought as much information as possible to control it in finer detail. With greater control, she could use the powers given her without fearing harm to others.

Without warning, nausea swept over her. Her queasy stomach sent her looking for a container. Before she could find one, she heaved her lunch.

The dragon let out a deep sigh, sending smoke swirling upwards.

When you feel it ease,
climb on my back, if you please.
I will return you to your mate
to leave you to your destined fate.

With her throat burning, Istaria spat out the last bits that had stuck in her teeth. Her stomach burned but settled for the moment. How long it would last, she could not say. However, if she could return to the manor before it happened again, she might find something to settle it.

While her stomach quieted its protests, she hurried out with the dragon to the balcony and climbed onto his back. Sethirngal carried her on swift wings, soaring with the wind currents to the manor house at the edge of the old forest.

In the back of her mind, Istaria wondered about the mage who taught the white dragon. Who was he? Sethirngal had not answered her simple question, not that she would recognize the name. Curiosity flared up inside her to learn more. Perhaps understanding the white dragon lay with understanding his teacher.

At least the mystery kept her worries away.

Chapter 36
17.6 pc 937

Calli wondered about the region in which they traveled. They had met no raiders so far and so deep into Hadeon. She desired no battle yet almost wanted it simply to assure herself no men hid in ambush. "I would prefer a straight fight."

Jayson turned to her, one black eyebrow raised higher than the other in question.

She shrugged and stepped over the underbrush and rocks. The crunching of their passage marked their path, combating her desire for stealth in the woods of Wynmere.

In silence, they walked. Her ears grew more attuned to the sounds of the forest waning. The instincts honed by her encounters blared a warning that set all her muscles rigid with expectation. When Duke stopped with his ears pricked, Calli trusted his senses and halted with him.

Jayson stopped and gazed about as quiet pervaded the forest. His hand dropped to the hilt of his sword sheathed at his waist but made no move to pull it out.

Duke jerked his head aside at a sound only he heard or a motion he saw. Calli studied the bush on which his eyes had fixed but saw nothing. To Jayson, she mouthed, *Raiders*.

Calli signaled for him to move on ahead. In the meantime, she swung into the saddle. At sudden attention, Duke clanged the bit against his teeth; until Calli dropped her reins, the cue for him to relax. She could not risk the noise he made and was glad he listened to her.

He moved forward when she touched her heels to his sides.

As they moved in the direction of the intrusion, she flipped her hair under her cloak. She pulled the hood low over her face and close around her body.

Confident in her abilities and Jayson's support, she would walk into their path.

Duke's steps crunched over a bed of dried leaves and needles. Intermittent voices alerted her to the intruders' location. The fools knew nothing of their prey.

Though not particularly loud, they lacked the hunting stealth other groups had demonstrated. Something reached into her and planted a seed of doubt. She frowned but continued forward.

Tyrkam had trained his armies better. Was it foolish confidence or a trap?

At the moment she breathed relief that Jayson had gone around them. They would not corner her.

The indiscernible voices grew clear with their approach. She waited behind a ledge of rock and brush until their words became distinct and she could see the group—seven all told.

They hushed their voices. "I still have no liking," one of them said.

"Quiet."

They said nothing for a while, a good cue for her appearance.

Calli rode out into their direct path. Though they could not make out her expression, the surprise on their faces boosted her ego. At least her cloak and riding gloves hid her obvious feminine features from their scrutiny.

"Hey now." The burly man scrutinized her. "What's this? Where'd you come from?"

Calli pointed off into the forest but said nothing. Her voice would give her away, and she failed miserably at trying to hide the feminine richness.

"Whence came you, stranger?" a slender, fair-haired man asked. His intelligent eyes scanned her as he took a step forward. "What are you about—fellow traveler or robber?"

She dropped her right hand to her waist and drew her sword. In her left hand she gathered her reins tighter. Duke lifted his head and arched his neck, anticipating her next move.

"We've no intention of a fight," the burly man said with his hands raised before him, palms forward. "We are weary travelers in search of a comrade. Have you seen anyone?"

She waited for an explanation.

"Leave him." A younger man with shoulder-length brown hair spoke in a tone frosted by fear. "Any man bold enough to challenge seven knows his strength and wit."

"Overconfidence, you mean."

Calli studied them. Their clothes and words indicated not the cold precision of soldiers, but the ignorance of the untrained who labored in fields or forges.

Only two wore swords, the plain hilt design not of Tyrkam's army.

Either they played dumb very well as any acting troupe could not, or else they were as they portrayed and could not fake such.

The young man moved up to her.

Calli pointed the sword at his neck to caution him from coming too close. He stopped a full three strides from Duke's shoulder.

"Pardon me, but have you seen a rebel known as the Red Rider? We've heard o' sightings that lead this way."

Calli blinked. Could they mean her?

How did this come so far? She had never intended to gain fame for her small victories, yet it seemed the villages had spread word of her single-handed defeat of Tyrkam's raiders. What about Jayson's help? How big had the tales grown?

"We've come to find this warrior." He stared up at her as if to see beneath the hood, but she gave a nod and dropped her head. From the corners of her eyes, she spied Jayson peeking around a trunk behind them.

"Point us in the direction and we'll not bother you."

"What business have you with the one you call the 'Red Rider?'" Calli asked.

The men gazed in astonishment.

"I—Who are you?" the young man asked.

"Why d'you seek the Red Rider?" Calli tensed. What would they say? To kill her or to capture her?

"We wish to join in the efforts of this warrior," the burly man replied. His glance aside hinted that he was more amused by the others' reactions than the truth of her identity.

Calli lifted her head slightly, her eyes catching the wry smile he wore. A couple of them shook their heads, while the rest wore expressions similar to their apparent leader.

She whistled for Jayson, who would have heard the exchange from his near location. When his steps crunched an announcement of his appearance, they turned. She sheathed her sword and dropped her shoulders with a deep breath of relief.

"Greetings, gentlemen." Jayson bowed with a smile. "I welcome you in the name of the one you call the 'Red Rider'."

The young man's eyes lit up. "You know him?"

"Of course."

Calli loved the glowing smile on Jayson's face when his eyes fixed on her. He gave her all the confidence in the world with that look.

"Where is he?"

The burly man stepped forward and patted the boy's shoulder with a knowing expression. Without a word, he pointed towards Calli as she threw back her hood. "The lass, Cedric."

"You claim to want to join me." Calli studied their reactions. "What reason have you?"

"To join you in defeating these men who burn our homes and kill our families," the burly, older man stated. A deep sadness tinged with hatred hardened his voice and the soft lines of his face.

At his remarks, Jayson met her eyes with a smirk. Calli held his gaze for several long seconds before meeting each new set of eyes in turn. How many others sought her?

In a moment of insight, she realized she could not refuse their help. From the moment of the princess' abduction, she had begged and pleaded with the king and prince of Cavatar to send their men to rescue her. When she left, she had wanted no one to join her. This was her penance for failing Istaria and hers alone.

However, these men had their own reasons for wanting to join her—wrongs to right. She could not deny them their taste of justice.

"I pledge my service." The words of the stranger broke the silence. Each followed in their vow, while Jayson mouthed the same from where he stood fixed in his place.

"Any lass who serves defeat to that warlord's soldiers is worth followin'." The burly man patted the shoulder of the young man next to him. "An army we'll raise to cleanse our lands o' shadows."

Calli cringed at the thought. She owed Tyrkam's head to Lusiradrol.

However, with more support she stood a better chance of making that happen and fulfilling her pact. But how long would the dark woman wait?

※

From the cover of distance, black eyes glimmered. Black lips curled up in a malicious grin. Two with one trick.

From her hiding in the ruins of the old fortress, Lusiradrol watched the scene with magic. She counted the days until Tyrkam fell in battle.

Not only that, but one of her targets had set himself up with the girl. How easy to use Calli to pull information from this man!

Her rumors had grown with each village, spreading dissent among the men. They wished to join the army of a great warrior and destroy the enemy that burned and pillaged their homes.

With that would come the need for more power. The noble would become the corrupt and thus tangle in her web of deceit.

She would spread anarchy and deceit among the humans. Those the white dragon sought to help would suffer for his indignity.

Perhaps this one with the magic would reveal the source of that power. He had aided the princess and her woodsman, the same woodsman with ties to her clan. She would watch him for clues. Though she knew they were not dead, she could not locate her clan by any means.

She could wait. She had waited thousands of years. She could wait longer, but hoped for sooner.

Chapter 37
17.6 pc 937

Damaera stood in the entrance area of the Council chambers with several of the king's advisors and the escorts of the provincial representatives. The pillars separated them from the main council area. A long table filled the center of the room from one fireplace to another, around which the representatives sat.

Twining patterns painted along the top of all the walls circled the room. The design was of older, nobler days.

In his stately robes, Alric Isolder paced the room. He glanced her way on occasion, as if to seek escape from the tangle of bickering amongst the men. The shadows on his face played in the deep lines of concern accentuated by the lamplight. The council grew restless with worries of defeat by Tyrkam's army. All the leaders of the various villages had been alerted to the raiders crossing into what remained of Cavatar.

Isolder had warned the representatives to say nothing to the people of their provinces. The question remained to be seen whether they would hold up the advice or not. His advisors had warned about the possibility of unrest.

The recent news from his army only hindered his efforts. The army fighting for Cavatar thinned, or seemed to.

Damaera sighed at the arguments over the use of the different regiments and their best defense against Tyrkam. Each sought a full legion of soldiers to protect their lands, yet none wished to conscribe the men to build those forces.

Tired of the useless debate, Damaera quietly exited the hall. Voices rose in anger, echoing through the room. The closing of the door relieved her of the same old discussion.

The meeting would not last much longer. They had begun to repeat the same opinions several times. Soon, the king would tire of the head-butting and end the session for another day.

Damaera strolled the halls, realizing from her tiredness that her grief and lack of appetite had weakened her. She would rest until the evening meal. Though she doubted any food would appeal to her, she would make her appearance. Her heart dragged behind her from the torment of losses inflicted by circumstances of the last few moon cycles.

A movement in the corridor ahead caught her eye. The stout, short Baron Graelyn Cathmor hurried down the stairs to the second floor below. Both Phelan and Alric had mentioned a distrust of the man and his dislike of them. Why had he come to the palace if he so disliked his king?

Alric had stated a desire to keep a close watch on his activities for any sign of treachery.

Curious, Damaera followed him down the stairs to the Grand Hall. She stopped briefly to chat with a couple of wives of the provincial representatives, while keeping one eye on the baron.

He glanced aside before leaning closer to one of the guards, who nodded in response to something the baron said. One of those trained by him, she realized and excused herself from the women.

When the baron looked up at her approach, he motioned the guard away and presented a polished smile. "My lady, you look well."

Damaera responded with a rueful smile. Most of her serving maidens, and her husband, had expressed concern for her lack of color and flesh. "An opinion most would not share."

The cunning of his false charm broke the otherwise perfect image of nobility. "Always a woman of eloquence in her harshest truth."

Refraining from a sigh, Damaera clamped her jaw. "May I ask what has brought you all this way?"

"Re-establishing ties with the king." His ingratiating manner overindulged. She recognized the look on his face; he wished her to leave him to his business. "Will he be out of Council soon?"

"I know not, but guess before the meal."

Cathmor bowed with sharp precision. "A pleasure as always, my lady." In an obvious hurry to be somewhere else, he rushed off.

Damaera watched him. Something of his manner had not fit.

When a servant passed by, Damaera grabbed the girl's arm and pulled her close.

"Milady?" Surprise stole the girl's composure.

"I want you to keep watch on the baron. Tell me later his words and deeds."

The girl curtsied. "As you wish, milady."

Damaera watched the girl search out the retreating man. When she found him, the girl wove through the crowd and stayed too close behind. Damaera let out the sigh she had been holding back and shook her head. At least the girl could have made it less obvious.

Damaera knew he planned something. His manner was not the usual polite chatter for show that most nobles had perfected. Something bothered her about Cathmor's abruptness and slyness.

But she wearied of mind and body. Until the maiden returned with news, she would rest.

≈≋

Tyrkam scowled beneath his helm. He waited in the trees, hidden by the wizard's cloak, and barely held back from storming the city.

After giving orders to his men to infiltrate Cavatar and regroup just a few nights ago, he had discovered what Lusiradrol had planned. Reports had come back with many of them of a warrior of fiery hair who had bested many. Some claimed it was a woman while others denied the possibility. Others stated two such warriors had interfered with their movements into the lands of Cavatar.

Lusiradrol! Only she could have set someone loose to interrupt his plans. His anger burned his soul, flaring up on occasion. Not only had the woodsman taken away his chance of claiming immortality and the power to rule the world, but Lusiradrol toyed with him.

Damn them all! He gazed across the clearing at the enclosed city. He would rule the world, if only to spite all those who dared oppose him. They would fear him.

The horse beneath him clanged its bit.

Somewhere to Tyrkam's right, a horse coughed.

Though he had waited and planned for this night for more than a year, his sour mood about the loss of the power he hoped to obtain and the threat of rain pushed his patience to the limits. *Hurry it already,* he silently demanded. The sun had set ages ago it seemed. He would wait a while longer for the signal from Cathmor, but not much more.

≈≋

From the peace of her candlelit chambers, something disturbed Damaera. Though she knew not the meaning, the cause came clear to her. She had spent a few of her younger years with the Lumathir, enough to recognize magic, to sense its presence.

The shadows had lingered at the edge of her awareness for many days now. But she had not noticed until her mind quieted. A blanket of power lay beyond the city wall. Someone had cast a spell over much of the land around Setheadroc.

From where she stood before her mirror, she looked up through the tall windows at the raindrops splattering on the glass and running down in jagged streaks. Only one purpose came to mind after all that had transpired.

Tyrkam had brought the war to their front gates. What else could it mean?

She had to find the king.

Damaera rushed from her chambers into the corridor beyond. The guards at her doors made no move to follow. She raced down the stairs. *Undignified*, the noble-trained side of her accused. *Necessary*, her instincts argued.

The hurried tromp of boots echoed through the arched entrance at the opposite side of the reading hall. The first of the soldiers rushed through. She grabbed the banister in her abrupt halt to keep her balance.

A horde of guards in their pristine armor thundered past on their way to the main entrance.

Had the king discovered?

Voices shouted orders over the noisy din. She waited for the men to pass before following them to the Grand Hall. Most likely she would find the king there at this late hour.

When all had passed, she ran after them, her steps hidden amid the clamor of the soldiers. She had to tell the king, if he had not discovered—whoever invaded used magic.

They passed through the corridor behind the Grand Hall, where visitors mingled.

She hesitated at one of the doorways. A group nearby questioned one another about the situation. They knew of the attack but fooled themselves into believing they were safe. Under ordinary circumstances she would feel the same confidence. However, even with her limited Lumathir training, she knew otherwise.

Damaera glanced left and right, searching for Isolder's face amongst the crowd. When she could not find him nearby, she smoothed her dress and stepped into the crowd. People deferred to her as she passed them, bowing in respect. Damaera rushed by without a word, her heart heavy with the fear of what might come.

Finally, her eyes caught the familiar dark green robes with gold trim Isolder favored. He climbed the steps to the next level, the baron at his side.

"Is it not remarkable?"

Damaera turned to the source of the voice, a young cousin of the king named Sorin. His dark hair was smoothed back. Not a crease dared blemish his clothes.

"That this Tyrkam would dare attack so deep into Cavatar astounds me. He possesses quite the fortitude."

If only she could believe his words. "Excuse me," Damaera replied and rushed by him. She had no time for polite conversation, although decorum screamed for her to humor him. She set her eyes on Isolder and Cathmor and made a line straight to them.

They reached the top of the steps as she started up. Holding her hem from her feet, she ran up. She had to warn him, to tell him what she knew.

He had accepted her mysterious insights when she had revealed in secret her heritage, not as a Brethin noble as he had been told, but as a descendant of a line to the ancient magic-users known as the Lumathir, or magi to others. Mysterious to outsiders, many considered them witches with evil purposes and refused to believe the truth. Rumors from long ago had shaped the beliefs of many.

Alric Isolder had accepted but had not said any more about it. She had been warned as a child to say nothing of her untrained abilities. Men had come to think of magic as evil or sought to use it for evil purposes. Damaera had won over the king, however.

At the top of the stairs, Damaera glanced down the corridor. Muffled voices came from somewhere. She followed the sounds to a door.

"Milady."

Damaera jumped, her hand on the door steadying her nerves. Her other hand went to her chest to keep her heart from leaping out. She turned to the girl who stepped from the shadows nearby.

The servant dropped her eyes in shame. "Forgive me, milady. I meant not to startle you."

With a deep breath, Damaera smiled. So focused on the strength of magic outside had she been that she missed seeing the approach of the maiden. "What news have you?"

The girl glanced down both sides of the corridor and leaned closer. She spoke in a low voice. "Milady, you'd best keep an eye on the baron. His words spoke treason."

Damaera arched an eyebrow, her curiosity piqued. "Oh?"

"He said something to one o' the guards to open the gates this night."

Damaera stiffened. A powerful magic, and Baron Cathmor arranging to have the gates open. She had to warn Isolder. Cathmor would betray them.

"Send the guards to arrest Cathmor."

"As you wish, milady." The girl rushed off down the corridor and disappeared.

Damaera eyed the door. Should she interrupt, pretending she knew nothing? Should she leave the situation to the guards?

Or should she perhaps try to lure her husband away from Cathmor? What might the man do if confronted?

Her head lightened with the threat of fainting as she struggled to make up her mind. She needed to rest, but she had to warn him. *Great Goddess, be with us,* she prayed.

A wave of dizziness swept over her. Damaeara stumbled back against the wall as spots clouded her vision. The corridor fell away down a long dark tunnel and disappeared completely.

Chapter 38
17.6 PC 937

Horses chewed their bits, eager to race into the tide of battle. A portion of the king's army had engaged the first wave of Tyrkam's forces, while those who had infiltrated the city secured the area around the palace. The palace guards loyal to Cathmor worked from the inside.

Tyrkam waited. He could afford patience. With Cathmor and his well-trained soldiers on the inside, their siege of the palace would be expeditious.

He would wait.

In the void of the dark night, more than six thousand foot-soldiers and cavalry waited for action. The wizard's cloaking spell hid them within the shadows. The cloudy sky hid all celestial light; he could not have asked for darker skies. But he would have asked for less rain.

The nearby creak of leather and clank of metal occasionally broke over the distant cacophony of other entanglements.

Tyrkam's eyes focused on the entire battle. His lips stretched into a malicious grin. Another tide of the king's army emerged from the valley behind the palace. They numbered half of Tyrkam's total army. Nevertheless, they would pose a challenge.

You've something learned, oh, great ruler of Cavatar, he mocked. The thunder of horses rose above the clamor of the battle. A wry smile curved up his face.

"UNIT TWO!" With the preplanned signal, Tyrkam sent two thousand of his army into the foray. The rain hammered on their armor, repeating its earlier assault.

He had sent Dorjan with more than a thousand men to flank the soldiers around the back of the city and palace. His lieutenant would know when the best opportunity to emerge from hiding presented itself. Once they engaged the king's forces, it would occupy those forces enough to keep them out of the main melee.

The battle cry of Tyrkam's men rose into the heavens like the roar of a dragon.

He risked a glance upwards at the thought, his eyes piercing the blackness for a hint of their shape.

Whether they observed from high above or not, he could not discern. They had flown over his affairs at other times. He would not allow them to interfere more than they had already.

He forced the thoughts from his mind, focusing on the siege of the palace. If they watched, the dragons would not stop him; they only observed.

Tyrkam watched the onslaught of his men over the army of Cavatar. The king's army fell before them.

His forces outnumbered those of the king, and they fought like savages.

When the pace of their advance slowed, Tyrkam signaled for the next group of reserves to charge. They surged forth through the rain and the trees, a tidal wave of conquest. The rest of the cavalry stayed behind.

Tyrkam reined in the excitement of his horse as the men rushed past. He watched from a safe distance and waited for his army to conquer Setheadroc.

Small fires rose up into the night as if daring the rain to douse them. Flame rained through the air from the bows of his archers.

Setheadroc would fall, at last.

He watched the battle that rang through the night, following the clanking of metal and shouts of men. His eyes traced outlines in the light from the flames scattered among the combatants, who poured into the city.

The rain lightened to a steady drizzle after coating everything and making footing slippery at best.

The chill of the water flowing off his helm into his shirt cooled the excitement of victory seething beneath the surface. Tyrkam watched the battle rage on with relative calm, calculating his next move.

Another wave of Cavatar's army tore through the combatants. The trick amused him, at best, if it was a trick. General Hammel must have expected an attack from the rear to group many of his forces in the valley on the far side of the palace. The city did not extend into the steep valley, leaving a direct route to the palace, which was protected by a high wall. Tyrkam had no intention of sending men to scale that wall.

With a whistle, he sent in the last wave of soldiers. The last six hundred men fresh and eager for battle surged forth. They met the army of Cavatar with vicious determination.

A smile played on Tyrkam's lips. The army of Cavatar fell before his men. No more of the king's men would come, however. His cavalry should reach them soon, taking the palace from behind. If he overestimated Hammel, then he would flank the forces of Cavatar that much sooner.

When the fighting dwindled, he would ride into the palace in victory. All would soon be his.

Chapter 39
17.6 pc 937

For most of the night, fires flared on the plains around the wall protecting the palace. They also blazed within the walls, highlighting the soldiers along the battlements. They fought like savages amid the streaming rain and clamor of battle.

Tyrkam watched the battle from a distance, eager to claim the palace without risk to his own life.

The loud bang of a battering ram thundered through the dark predawn hours. They had reached the palace doors already.

Satisfaction crawled across his face. *Soon,* he calmed himself and wiped the rain from his eyes. Soon the king would be his.

The baron had better let them in. Most of the guards had likely converged in the courtyard to defend the palace proper. The baron could have overtaken those inside to unblock the door.

Another thought crossed Tyrkam's mind. Would Cathmor take out his vengeance on the king himself, not bothering to wait? Tyrkam scowled at the thought. Cathmor had agreed to hold the king for him, not to take his anger to action before the battle was won.

Tyrkam wanted the king alive. He had several questions the old man might answer.

When the bang of the battering ram thundered over the tumult, it resounded with the splintering of wood.

He took the cue and rode through the dwindling soldiers with almost no opposition. Those who dared fell before him.

The fighting outside the palace wall fell to the might of his men. By dawn the palace would be his, the fastest siege for many hundreds of years and the only successful siege of Setheadroc Palace.

The men fought before him, clearing a path that allowed him to enter unbidden. With Cathmor's soldiers joining his ranks, they entered the palace. Those who dared oppose them fell to their strength.

Once inside the palace, Tyrkam demanded an audience with the king. Only on the threat of killing every person present did one come forward. The girl led him up the stairs and through a corridor. The thunder of his soldiers echoed around him.

"I- I- In there." The girl pointed at one of the doors.

He motioned to one of his soldiers to open it. When the man thrust the door aside, he stormed in with several others behind him.

Tyrkam followed and caught sight of Cathmor with a knife to the king's throat. He eyed the baron with contempt.

Upon meeting his eyes, Cathmor withdrew, a deep scowl on his face. The knife vanished in a flick of his wrist. Had he arrived any later, Tyrkam was certain he would be executing the baron then and there.

"How dare you!" Isolder's icy tone chilled the room, the fire of challenge blazing in his eyes.

It amused Tyrkam, but he had to admire the man for his boldness. Isolder stood proud and noble even in his moment of defeat. "The palace is mine, as well as the lands. You are no more."

Isolder locked eyes with Tyrkam, whose scowl sent many cowering away. But this man showed no fear.

Isolder waited several long seconds before speaking, holding Tyrkam silent with his gaze. "You defile this place." His harsh whisper stilled the air. The rain halted its pattering and the fire ceased its crackling in the cold threat of Isolder's tone. "By me shall come your defeat before a new Cavatar rises from the ashes of your treachery."

"We shall see, old man." Tyrkam motioned to the dripping wet soldiers surrounding the king. "Chain him."

Two soldiers grabbed Isolder's arms and dragged him out. He shook them off and tugged his robes straight before he strode out with his head held high.

After Isolder disappeared, Tyrkam turned to Cathmor. "For holding back, you shall live." *For now,* he silently thought. Had Cathmor slit Isolder's throat before he had caught him, Tyrkam would have ordered his death then and there.

However, Tyrkam considered himself a fair man. He would reward the baron for his restraint. When it suited him, he would order the Baron's death. In the meantime, he could find other ways to make use of the man.

Chapter 40
25.6 pc 937

Calli grunted with the exertion. The sun glinted off her sword, which she swung two-handed at Jayson's side. He parried and struck back.

Sweat dripped into her eyes. She whirled a couple steps away and afforded a quick swipe of her brow. Jayson advanced, his blade before him ready to defend against her. When he attacked, she easily blocked each strike.

Calli varied her defense and offense, changing her stance for each maneuver. Since their meeting, they had practiced often. As with her trainers, she had learned his style. He played tricks like Donaghy, but thought through the situation like Morain. He challenged her, but she could defeat him.

At times it was too easy, almost as if he held back. She let the thought slip as he struck at her.

The sharp swords clanged with each strike.

"My lady!"

Startled by the call, she and Jayson froze and turned to the voice.

"Calli! Jayson!" Fenwar rushed across the clearing, his dark cloak billowing behind him. From somewhere behind, the creak of a wagon groaned through the trees. He halted before them, trying to catch his breath.

Amid gasps, he tried to speak. "Cavatar— We heard in the village— Setheadroc— Tyrkam laid siege not eight days ago. It fell in one night!"

Calli gasped. "Impossible!"

"Unless the soldiers lied—" He fought to catch his breath. The others with them stood eerily quiet. "—Tyrkam now rules all of Cavatar and most of Ayrule."

Calli faltered. When Jayson put a hand on her shoulder to steady her, she looked up at the pity on his face. He swallowed but said nothing. Her eyes burned with the emptiness in her heart. His face blurred in her vision. Her home was gone. What of Phelan, the queen, her friends?

She forced down the lump in her throat and lifted her sword before her. Phelan had commissioned it special for her. The swordsmith had included on the crossguard a blessing in the language of Loringale, her father's native land. Now, it was her last hope of defeating the wretched tyrant and reclaiming her home for the people of Cavatar.

"My lady."

She turned at Jayson's gentle voice and lowered her sword.

"Leave me." The words came out as a whisper. Anything more would have revealed the tremor of restrained tears.

She hurried to the tree near the river. She could not face them, not like this. These men looked to her as a means to defeat Tyrkam. She could not let some silly tears mar that image.

Yet, she had to let it out, to cry away the pain ripping through her from the news. Worse than the disappearance of her best friend, the downfall of her home to the evil of a merciless dictator stole her core. Only her father's death had hurt more.

She ignored the creaking of the approaching wagon. Instead, she watched Duke grazing without concern along the longer grass growing from the banks of the river. His dappled coat shone in the sunlight filtering through overhead boughs heavy with leaves. When she approached, he lifted his head, chewing a mouthful of grass.

His attention shifted a second later.

Calli caught the soft steps when she realized the horse looked beyond her. "I said leave me." Her voice trembled in spite of her efforts to steady it.

"This is not the time to be alone." The voice washed down her pride, and Jayson stepped around before her. "You'd fare better to share your grief."

She looked up, trying to smile at the kindness in his voice, but could not bring his face into focus. Instead, the tears blinded her as they poured forth.

Before she realized, he wrapped his arms around her. She took full advantage of it and buried her face in his shoulder. All that she had hoped for had torn apart in one moment. No longer could she return home, nor could she return to Phelan, if he still lived.

What of the princess? What purpose was to rescue her friend to live a life of hardship?

The comforting warmth of Jayson's body slowly overpowered the tears. She was embarrassed to show her emotions, but grateful that he offered his support.

Her mind cleared with the release of the tears. A new purpose grew within her, taking root where the other goals uprooted. She would build an army to rival Tyrkam.

If he could do it, so could she. The good men and women of Cavatar would never settle for rule under Tyrkam. How many more would join her for the chance to fight?

Better yet, how many of the army of Cavatar would love the chance to avenge their land?

The new ideas gave her goals to follow. Better than just the rescue of her mistress, she would defeat Hadeon once and for all.

When Calli looked up, she found Jayson's eyes studying her. "I cannot stand by and let this happen."

He smiled and smoothed away the red hairs sticking to her cheeks. "That's the voice of a patriot speaking."

"So be it." If she was to be this figure that they admired, she would not disappoint. "I'll lead them against the tyranny, if they'll follow me."

Ideas flew through her head, plans to raise and support an army capable of overthrowing Tyrkam. "First, we need a place to train, a home where we can be safe."

Jayson nodded. "The mountains. If we can cross before the snows fall, we may find security in the unknown regions to the north. Tyrkam would not dare cross the mountains."

"Crossing will be difficult for the same reasons he has not crossed."

"True. If you've other ideas, I'll listen."

Calli shook her head. She had no other ideas. Although she feared crossing the terrain this late in the season, she knew no other options. Such decisions were not in her experience. "I've none. We will be safer—if we can make it through—than to hide in the villages. But we know not what lies on the other side. And we'll need supplies if we're to hide for the whole season."

"Then we should leave immediately. The sooner we find a place, the sooner we can fill it with supplies."

"Agreed." At least Eldred had guaranteed what was available of his crops for these men. It would help.

Calli turned to where the men chatted with the burly old farmer and some new faces. He stood near a bay horse attached to a loaded wagon.

Her jaw dropped at the sight. How could he have brought so much?

"I think we shall be saved from starvation for a while."

She smiled at Jayson's comment, her mood lightened by the prospects, despite the cloud of grief over her heart. He patted her shoulder and left her for the gathering. Calli watched for a few moments as hope cast a ray of light into her gloom.

Perhaps they could make it happen.

Chapter 41
25.6 pc 937

Tyrkam smirked at the disheveled figure hanging against the stone wall. Lines of blood caked the old man's back. Purple marks blotched his face where the guards had beaten him.

The two guards took a perverse pleasure in their torture of the deposed king.

Tyrkam sat back in his chair. He ignored the dreary light that cast into the cold, lower room from the window. The palace had no prison towers. His attention focused on Alric Isolder hanging against the wall from the shackles on his wrists.

The guards stood back, recoiling their whips.

Tyrkam lifted a hand to stay their next lash. He leaned forward in his chair and studied Isolder in his unconscious state. He had waited too long for this moment not to enjoy it. After the beating, Isolder's body would burn on the pyre, which had lit the last few nights. The old man would burn last as his conquered people watched.

For the last day, the old man had shown no signs of giving in with news of the Red Rider, his son, or his alliance with Rivonia. His only words had begged mercy on the queen.

Tyrkam wanted to know about the person or persons who had attacked his soldiers. More than a hundred men had been reported gone—presumed dead—and over two hundred had reported attacks by the mysterious rogues. How much of that was exaggeration he could not say, but he wanted to know.

At the least, he tried to force something from the king. Isolder had denied any knowledge. Did he lie or speak the truth?

And what of his son? Isolder refused to say when Phelan would return. Tyrkam knew where the boy had gone. Only one place was possible. He had to be in Rivonia. Cavatar had no other allies left, or at least none of consequence.

"Old fool." Tyrkam stood and pulled his cold dagger from his belt. The guards straightened. He leaned over the filthy body of Isolder and set the dagger to the old man's throat. With his other hand, he grasped a clump of gray hair and tilted the head back. The man stank of death.

Isolder groaned.

"I give you one last chance to tell me what you know."

Isolder pressed his cracked and bloody lips together and spat.

Enraged, Tyrkam slashed the old king's throat. When he dropped the head, it thudded against the stones. Fresh lines of crimson ran down the body.

He waved to the guards, who rushed to the body and unshackled it. The chains clinked against the stone, echoing in the small room.

"Take him to the pyre. His people can watch him burn. Make sure they all see."

Tyrkam watched them carry the body away, one with the feet and the other with the shoulders. He followed them out, wiping his dagger clean on a piece of cloth from Isolder's torn shirt before replacing it.

Cleaning up after his siege left him a few more chores. He had tended to the biggest, but the others might prove as useful.

First of those was the queen. He knew from his spies that she was descended from the Lumathir. The women of the Light had the power to shape the world. He knew not whether the queen possessed the training of the mystics, however, but would take the risk to find out what she did know.

His discovery in the caves had told him what he needed about their ancient order. Lusiradrol had provided the rest of the information. As the mother of the princess, Damaera should also know something about Istaria's powers. The king had admitted nothing.

Tyrkam's heavy steps echoed through the corridors. Patrolling the palace in pairs, his guards straightened when he passed.

When he reached the tall, decorated doors of the royal chambers, his guards pushed them open for him to enter.

Someone had tied the curtains aside from the tall windows, allowing the light of day to spill across the room. On the nearest of the two beds lied the queen, where she had remained since the night of the siege. A serving maid sat near the bed, while two others stood on the opposite side.

All eyes looked up when he entered. Horror washed over them, draining their faces of color.

Ignoring their reactions, Tyrkam crossed the room. He marched to the foot of the bed and stopped. With his arms crossed, he peered down at the ashen face of the queen above the level of the bed covers. The skin hung on a face lean of flesh. Dead?

She sighed deeply, her eyes fluttering open for a second before falling still.

A slight smile crept up his lips. He caught the eyes of each servant and waved them out. They hurried away, but lingered a few seconds at the door before exiting the room.

After the doors echoed shut behind the servants, Tyrkam moved around the bed to the chair where the servant had sat. It creaked with his weight on it.

His eyes fixed on the gaunt woman in the bed. Her brown-gold hair hung off the top of her pillow, loose and neat. He remembered the beauty he had once seen from a distance. She had struck him as one of the fairest women anywhere.

Now, frailty took her. It almost planted a seed of pity within him.

"You did this." Her whisper was barely audible.

Tyrkam leaned closer, his interest in what she had to say piqued by the fact she had spoken. Perhaps she had something worthwhile to say.

"You caused this sickness," she said, her voice stronger.

"No more." He frowned. What use would the truth be than to turn her against them? "She's gone."

Damaera's eyes fluttered open. She stared into nothingness. "My daughter—"

"Taken by a woodsman."

Damaera turned her head slowly to look at him. Her blue eyes sparked with light. "A woodsman?" She closed her eyes again, a smile on her face. "Her woodsman." Her whisper faded with a sigh.

"Is this not a concern?" Did she not care that a strange man had taken her daughter away in hiding?

Damaera took a deep breath. A tear drew a fresh line from the corner of her eye. She muttered to herself. "What is his name?"

Tyrkam clenched his fist. She had known about Istaria's powers. What more could she tell him, *would* she tell him? He saw no harm in telling her the name, and perhaps it would lure her to revealing more. She knew not the man. "He is called Darius."

"Darius?" She frowned, but it slid away into the weak smile.

Her reaction bothered him. Perhaps telling her a name had proven unwise.

She sank with the exhalation of a deep breath. Her breathing steadied.

Tyrkam watched her in curiosity, considering the possible outcomes. Though she might affect his future, she could do little in her current state. In the time she had left, she might provide useful information. He would keep her alive for a while, or at least until she no longer suited his needs.

"My lady, tell me of the Lumathir."

Her eyes opened again, gazing into the distance. "I know so little."

He clamped his jaw in frustration. "What do you know?"

Damaera turned to him, a thin smile playing on her lips. "Nothing."

Rage boiled up inside him at the denial. How could she know nothing? "Impossible!"

With a deep sigh, she closed her eyes. "I was not intended as a priestess."

He clenched his teeth on an outburst, realizing he would not get anymore out of her while she laid ill. However, he would press her for information when she was more alert. The powers of the Lumathir could prove valuable.

In the stead, he had Vahrik and Cathmor to contend with. Both posed threats to his authority but could be used to his advantage. How to make use of them would prove interesting. At least with Cathmor, he had taken his greatest use, though he could still use his army.

Vahrik was another matter.

❧

Gaispar soared high above the pyres, but the stench of rotting corpses and burned flesh sickened her. She had witnessed up close as one of the hounds what had happened here.

Tyrkam had overthrown the king and taken Cavatar as his. Now, the princess had no home to which to return, even if she wished it.

One hope remained. If the Lumathir united with the Sh'lahmar, an army as none other would be formed, an army of Light to fight the darkness descending.

Every bone in her feathered body shuddered at the thought of what would happen if they failed. Lusiradrol would destroy the world in her endless search for power, a drive borne from the spirit of the Darklord within her.

Tyrkam had played his part as her puppet long enough to realize it, else she would gloat over this victory. Instead, Lusiradrol made no appearance but had found a new obsession with destroying the princess. With any harm to the princess would go their greatest hope of defeating the Darklord within Lusiradrol.

Gaispar found relief in knowing the black dragon could not reach Istaria in the Second Realm. A spell on the gateway prevented her from stepping through.

Gaispar left the gruesome site of the battle to return to Eyr Droc and the dragons. Unfortunately, the princess would also learn of the deaths of those she loved.

Chapter 42
13.7 pc 937

Gayleana stood quietly at the door to the inner chamber, respectful of her mistress's privacy. High Priestess Tahronen had called for her, her message carried by magic across the Ancient city. Gayleana had rushed through the old streets of Euramai to Tahronen's meditation chamber.

Despite the urge to rest her legs, she stood upright and correct. Tahronen would keep her standing if she showed any sign of impatience.

She studied the room to distract her mind but it contained only a couple of candelabra whose flames chased away the cold of night, a curtained window at one wall, and two columns on either side of the door to the inner chamber. Green banners hung limp along the columns.

Resisting the urge to let out her breath in a sigh, Gayleana focused on the magic flowing around her like a sea of water. The Lumathir had raised her and taught her from the beginning to be aware of every change in the magic, the power of the Light that had created the world.

The essence changed. Gayleana listened closely and recognized Tahronen's beckon.

Immediately, she turned to the large door and pushed on it. The hinges made no sound as she slipped into the dimly lit room.

Gayleana hesitated inside, peering through the drapes dividing the room. From behind a sheer curtain, tiered candles outlined the shadow of the woman.

"Join me, child." The strong, clear voice rang through the room on a whisper.

Gayleana approached the curtain and slipped her hands through the part. She pushed the silken fabric aside as the woman lifted her head.

She had visited with the high priestess many times in her thirty years. Tahronen's eternal youth always surprised her, despite knowing she was one of the immortal Majera. In spite of that youthful appearance, Tahronen spoke with wisdom beyond a lifetime of learning and carried a sadness

Gayleana suspected no one would ever fully comprehend.

She met the eyes of the high priestess. The fire of life reflected in Tahronen's eyes as the light of the world chased shadows from her face. Gayleana sat down before the inexplicable woman.

"The time fast approaches. Our daughter and sister will soon need us more than she knows."

Which student did she speak of? Several had been sent out with little training to learn the ways of the world, Gayleana recalled. In her life with the order, she had said farewell to a few sisters and apprentices. Though the numbers of women in the Lumathir dwindled through the years to the current total of forty-two, Tahronen had sent out others. No one could guess her reasons.

A thoughtful expression passed across the woman's face. Gayleana waited in silence.

"What do you remember when you were brought here?"

Gayleana hesitated, but knew better than to question the ways of the Majera. "I was very young. I've only shapes and impressions in my memory."

Tahronen raised her hand and outlined a circle in the air. Within the circle moving images coalesced, a scene of long ago. In the scene, the high priestess, with no difference from her current appearance, welcomed home a young acolyte.

The acolyte stepped off a horse-drawn cart bearing a curious toddler. At her feet, clinging to her dress, stood a wiry girl no more than four years. The older child peered about with wide eyes. The rough beauty of her features already shone apparent at that tender age.

"You had the advantage, coming to us so young. Your sister had already passed the tender stage when learning to use magic would have come easily to her. After a few years, we sent her to a noble family to foster."

Tahronen let the images dissolve into nothing and sat facing Gayleana. "The queen of Cavatar has played her part and needs us now."

Gayleana caught her breath. Queen? Her blood sister was a queen? Why had she not been told? How could her teacher never tell her she had a sister of royal upbringing? "Damaera?" The name flowed off her tongue with no effort, as natural as if she had known all her life.

She had known that the queen of Cavatar had been of the Lumathir, but had never realized she was a blood sister.

"Why did you not tell me sooner?"

"What would you have done?"

Gayleana hesitated. What could she have done? Nothing. "A more wicked truth I'd never conjure."

Tahronen smiled. "You have grown. That's why you are ready to join me to visit our sister and daughter. Go now and make ready. We leave at first light."

Gayleana nodded and rose to her feet. She started toward the drapes and hesitated. "Why now?"

A gentle smile rose on the face of the priestess. "In time it will reveal itself."

Realizing she would have to wait for an answer, Gayleana left the Majera to carry out her orders.

Chapter 43
13.7 pc 937

Calli led Duke on her right, their steps clicking and crunching on the rocky terrain. Jayson had taken two recruits to scout ahead or he would have walked beside her.

Behind her, Eldred rode the loaded wagon he had brought from his supply run with Fenwar.

Calli glanced back at him driving the heavy bay mare forward into the harness. The horse leaned into it, setting her legs for the difficult pull up hill with each step. The wagon creaked and groaned, rolling on behind her.

Behind the wagon walked the rest of their recruits. They had talked for a while, but after midday they ceased their chatter. Their energy had dulled in the endless gray light.

Hers had also dulled.

Calli turned her eyes to the road ascending into the mountains, taking care not to stumble on the rocks littering the road. High before them rose the Northern Mountains, the border between what had once been Cavatar and the Unknown Lands. Few travelers had challenged those pinnacles. Less had ever returned.

The thought sent a shudder through her body. She pulled her cloak over her shoulders. She hoped Jayson knew what he was doing leading them into the mountains. He had disappeared over the jagged rise no more than a furlong away. Beyond it loomed the dark shapes of the mountains, their peaks vanishing into the low clouds.

The clouds threatened rain, or snow. Calli shivered from a cool breeze and realized the dreary gray could as well drop snow on them. Her group would need to hurry to find shelter large enough for their uses.

"How far will we travel?"

Calli looked aside to the source of the question, Eldred's oldest son, Ellead. The tall, lanky young man looked nothing like his father, unlike his younger brother Siannon. Ellead's blonde hair brushed his shoulders, where

Siannon had Eldred's shorter, darker hair and stout build. While showing the results of working long days in the fields, Ellead was leaner. His longer face added to the impression of height.

"At least a few days." She could give no more, unsure of how long it would take to find suitable shelter.

With a nod, he fell back.

Eldred had brought his sons with the wagon when he returned to them. The raiders had burned their home before he left. While Eldred went ahead to find her, his sons stayed behind to finish the harvest and load all they could to catch up later.

The supplies had answered her prayers, but she worried how long they would last, especially since they had picked up a few others along the way.

Calli pulled out the pendant on the chain around her neck and studied it. What would have happened if she had stayed?

While playing with the royal seal, she continued up the rise.

They reached the summit of the hill.

The scene before her stole her breath. She dropped the pendant, forgetting her thoughts in an instant. "Great Goddess!"

Returned from his scouting, Jayson stopped next to her. "Apparently, part of the king's army decided to hide here, or at least what remains of this legion. That may help."

"How many?" Was this the chance she had hoped for? Or would the commander deny her?

The camp covered acres across the valley and over a small knoll to the other side. Herds grazed upon the lush summer grass away from the main camp of men.

A chilly wind blew against her. Calli shivered and pulled her hood over her head. She leaned against Duke's warm hide. He clanged his bit and ducked his head as far as the length of rein allowed. He wanted to eat.

Her stomach growled from the thought. They had not stopped in more than half a day. They could all use a meal and a break. The road they traveled would be long and difficult, or at least more so than it had been.

Without turning, she said, "We'll rest here."

"Wonderful! I've already sent word that we wish to meet with the general."

Calli swallowed and pulled her hood over her face. The brevity of leading her small group against Tyrkam scurried away in the face of meeting with one of the king's highest officers. She would have to reclaim it. The men would not respect her if she could not look them in the eyes and hold her own.

She took a deep breath and continued.

Eyes turned to them, but no one made a move to stop them. Calli led her group through the camp with false pride, hoping they could not see the cowering girl hiding inside. At least the hood would hide part of her identity.

Most took in their small group with some interest.

Calli tried not to meet any of their eyes but could not help noticing the bedraggled men who had once supported the most powerful kingdom on the continent of Ayrule. These were men trained to fight who no longer had a place to call home. Now, they were lucky to hide from Tyrkam's army.

She had not endured the same defeat these men had. How would she feel if she had failed in defending Cavatar?

Calli shivered in the cool breeze, wishing she could huddle around one of the many fires scattered throughout the camp.

In a way she had failed Cavatar, by not accomplishing her goal. However, by not rescuing the princess already, she had not made matters worse for her friend and had escaped the cruelty of Tyrkam's men for herself. In that she found some comfort, what little it was.

But what of the king's army? As the only woman—that she knew of—who could fight, would she be treated better?

As her uneasiness grew, she failed to notice the following they attracted.

When a robust young soldier stepped before them in polished armor, Calli halted. The group quieted behind her. The soldier stood at rigid attention, strict in posture.

"You will follow me to General Marjan," he said with no emotion in his voice. He turned sharply and marched ahead.

Calli looked to Jayson. He shrugged but indicated with an outstretched hand that she should follow the man. She took the cue, glad he walked next to her. If this was the reception they received from the soldiers, how would their leader react?

From behind the guard, she made out a tent flapping in the breeze ahead. The king's banner waved proudly outside the entrance. A sense of pride welled up within Calli to behold the symbol of Cavatar. At least this regiment had not lost their purpose with their defeat.

She allowed a hint of a smile but found a new anxiety creeping up her spine. If this Marjan adhered to ceremony in light of the circumstances, how would he view her? Would he respect her?

Would she end up talking through Jayson?

The guard halted and took up a post outside the tent opening. "You may enter."

She handed Duke's reins to one of the men behind her and stepped through the opening with Jayson.

Daylight from outside filtered through the tent fabric, aided by the flickering candles around the inside. The entrance flap closed behind them. She focused her attention on the man sitting in the chair, flanked by two guards rigid at their posts. The burly officer wore basic armor and a crimson cloak identifying him as the commander. His eyes, hardened from years of battle, peered at her from under bushy brows.

"I hear you seek our company and our loyalty." Marjan fixed his eyes on Jayson.

"I do, General," Jayson replied and turned to Calli. She dropped her hood, exposing the flaming red hair tied back into a braid. "But on behalf of the lady."

Marjan leaned forward in his chair, studying Calli with new interest. "Rumors have reached even me of such a bandit fitting your appearance. I doubted the descriptions as a woman. What say you to this, lass?"

"My name is Calli, not 'lass.'" Calli matched the confidence of his gaze. No man would talk to her like that. She had fought hard for the respect of her trainers, two of the king's best. To be called a lass irritated her spirit the way Phelan had in calling her a lady. "I am no bandit."

He watched her in silence, holding her in his gaze for several long seconds. Without any further indication of an answer, he sat back in his chair, his hand on his chin. "I've no intention of stirring trouble. My men have spoken of two people, one standing out in particular with hair of fire. Until now, the stories of one of them possibly being a woman have been ignored. I cannot say I trust you, but I see a look in your eyes."

What look? Calli said nothing but waited for an explanation. When he said nothing more of it, she dared not push the matter further.

The corners of Marjan's hard face softened, whether exhaustion or amusement, Calli could not identify. "What wish you of this weary army? We cannot provide much, but will not stand by while Cavatar falls to ruin."

"I agree, General." Calli glanced aside at Jayson. The hint of a smile and a barely perceptible nod encouraged her to continue.

"I ask only for alliance. I have little to offer than our loyalty to the same cause. We can support ourselves but would do better to build an army to rival Hadeon when we're ready. For that, we need allies."

As she spoke, his attention to her words boosted her confidence. He granted her that much respect. "To live, we need supplies and shelter. My group plans to cross the Northern Mountains before the first snows. Our hope is to find security on the other side, to give us time to train and to grow our supplies."

Marjan took a deep breath. Calli waited for him to respond, but it came after a moment of contemplation.

"Crossing the mountains not a cycle before first frost is foolish, lass."

"A lady no less," Jayson muttered.

With an amused smile tugging at his lips, Marjan glanced to him. "I'd not call a woman rumored to have killed a hundred o' Tyrkam's soldiers a *lady* either."

"Twelve," she said. "The rest are exaggeration."

He grinned. "So be it…rumors. I'll not deny you passage, but neither will I join you."

That was all she could ask, except for one thing. "If I may ask—how long do you plan to camp here?"

A suspicious frown hardened his face.

"If we find trouble, may we retreat to this position and seek shelter with your men? I've not the intention of failing, but seek assurance of an alliance."

He nodded, his posture melting into his chair. "What assurance have we that you'll not speak of our position to those who might give you trouble?"

"Only the same that you give me."

"I see."

Calli swallowed, realizing at that moment she had one means left to prove her loyalty and her sincerity. "And this."

She lifted off the necklace holding the pendant and held it out to him. Hopefully the man would not assume the worst—that it was stolen—but would believe her story. "A gift and a marriage vow from Lord Phelan Isolder."

The general snatched it away from her and examined the seal in the light of the candles.

Calli peered aside at Jayson, who dropped his eyes a moment. Though she was not certain, a part of her believed in his affection for her. Perhaps that was her imagination, formed from her desire for companionship and her uncertainty about returning to Phelan.

"You say a gift from the heir?" Marjan held the pendant up, peering at her across the etched surface. "I've to wonder…"

Her cheeks warmed in anger at the accusation in his tone. "I served the Lady Istaria as her personal servant, and her closest friend."

The memories choked her but she swallowed the pain and continued. "When she was taken from our carriage, I swore to bring her home. Phelan set two of his best soldiers to train me, hoping I would be discouraged. Instead, I fought, and I beat Donaghy and Morain. The daughter of Kaillen was too much for them together to take." The last part came out with the fire of her victories and her determination in proving herself. The general could think as he pleased, but she knew the truth. She would not allow anyone to doubt her.

"Morain, eh? And Donaghy." He grunted acknowledgement of the names. "Fine warriors. None more cunning." A slow smile crept to his lips and he stretched out his hand with the pendant.

Calli opened her palm and received it. "You know of them."

"Aye, lass." He sat back, his eyes fixed on her. "Either a good lie or truth, I cannot say, but I'll take your word, as the daughter of Kaillen."

He sat back again, at ease once more. "Your men may rest in this camp if you wish. I cannot say that my men will be as forgiving as I of who you are. Some may say a traitor, others the most loyal of servants, but your story will raise tensions. Tarry not but stay as few days as possible."

Unexpected relief washed over Calli. He had accepted her story and at least showed a willingness to help. Though she had not achieved an alliance, at least she had convinced him she could be trusted. "Thank you, General." Taking his words as an excuse from his presence, Calli bowed in respect and looked to Jayson, who had already moved to the entrance.

Before leaving, Calli turned back to the general. "One or two days is all we require to prepare for our long journey, and all we can afford to wait."

"I wish you luck in your crossing."

She flashed a quick smile at the sincerity of his tone and exited the tent with Jayson close behind. At least they would find peace for a day or two. The horses could rest and receive some care, especially the services of a good farrier. After that, they were on their own again.

Perhaps when the time came, however, Marjan and his troops would join her in the difficult struggle to reclaim the land.

Chapter 44
14.7 pc 937

Istaria watched Darius with interest. Since arriving in the Second Realm, as Gaispar preferred to call it, she had been too busy with learning from the dragons to think about her lover's past. Now, with the illness caused by the life within her, she could not bear their flight to the crystal palace.

Instead, she had settled into the routine Darius had taken. She watched his morning rituals and the simple magic he practiced to defend himself, learning more than she had in their flight across the territories of Ayrule. Every day she pondered where he had learned such skills. When they arrived and the world of magic opened wide to her, she assumed he had learned in this place.

Since then she had come to understand that he was no more familiar with this realm than she. Where had he learned his skills?

Darius cast his spell, vanishing before her eyes with no more than a shimmer to indicate what had happened.

She reached out through the magic that flowed thick in this land and found a faint disturbance she recognized as him. It moved around behind her in the blink of an eye.

Without warning, warm hands settled on her shoulders. She jumped in spite of knowing but relaxed as his hands kneaded her taut muscles.

When she turned, he smiled and bent down to kiss her. "My apologies."

Istaria stood, a faint curiosity about her slim figure flitting across her mind and out. The baby would show in time. Without thinking, she folded her hands across her middle.

Darius studied her a moment before inviting her to walk with him by a firm hand on her back. "Join me?"

She gladly took his hand in hers. However, something about his expression troubled her.

"I know you have been ill of late and I've not worried, but I must share something." He took a deep breath and let it out, turning his gaze to the puffy clouds floating like islands in the sky. "Though I know you are safe, as he would not allow harm to come, I cannot remove the doubts from my mind. I lost Julaina in childbirth. It was to be our first year of marriage."

He bowed his head a moment before looking up to meet her eyes. "I would never wish that on you, as I would not wish the burden you bear. But we cannot undo what is done."

In silence, he walked on through the trees. The drakin flitted in and out, playing their games.

She caught the conflicting emotions within him through the magic. *More weighs on your mind.*

"I wish not to worry you, but have a confession. I am not who you think I am."

Istaria smiled in relief that he said no more about his grief.

She had known all along he was more than a mere woodsman. In that she had found her courage to go on through the harshness of their travels. She had trusted him then, regardless of any secret, and still trusted him. Besides, none could have topped hers. *Am I not also a master of secrets? What harder a road could you travel that I have not?*

He lifted her hand to his lips and kissed it. "Forgive me, but I had to keep my secret from Lusiradrol."

She frowned, puzzled by this admission. *Have you not wished to tell me?*

"More than anything." Sucking in a deep breath, Darius stopped and placed his hand on her cheek. In that action, he opened his mind to her. The images he sent pulled her into a dark pit. Within it dwelled the presence of dragons. Faint but real, foul and cold, the magic twisted from each core. She counted more than a hundred such disturbances. Swallowing her uncertainty, she searched through the darkness as if standing within the vault. The groans of sleeping dragons echoed faintly around her, stretching into the distance of the large cavern.

Before she could see more, she found herself pulled out backwards, through caverns in rock. She stood before an entrance where two guards stood poised. The elaborate etchings along the archway behind them glimmered in the moonlight.

The image faded before she could see more, but she thought one of the guards looked familiar. The helm hid the details of his face, except for a black mustache, and the moonlight played tricks on her eyes.

"That is what I hide." Darius's eyes pleaded with her. "Lusiradrol must never find out. If she knew the existence of this place, the world would suffer."

Was that the Red Clan of the Darklord? Were they the ones cursed to sleep by Makleor? This was the story told by the dragons, but— She sighed and gently stroked his face. *I never realized.*

"I must never speak of it, but you are a part of this. Your role is vital to defeating them. Please forgive me for saying nothing."

She smiled. *There is nothing to forgive.*

In the distance, a familiar presence tugged at the threads of magic. Istaria lifted her head and searched their surroundings.

Almost immediately, Gaispar materialized from the trees. "Milady." She paused when she saw Darius, her face grim. "We must talk. I've...bad news."

Chapter 45
20.7 pc 937

Mountains towered high above, conquering the clouds floating by on the chilling winds. Below them ranged fertile valleys and deep trenches.

Calli wondered how long the wagon would last on the ancient roads, which sediment from the rocky landscape had covered.

At the moment, it refused to budge up the ledge they had met. Though no more than a hand in height, the uneven ledge hindered the wheels of the heavy wagon.

After two uneventful days with the army at the foothills, they had parted with a few more supplies to aid their crossing of the mountains. Marjan had seen to that. However, it meant more work for Eldred's mare, Danny.

"Push!" Fenwar said.

The four men able to fit behind the wagon while the others pushing from its sides grunted and groaned with the joint effort. When the wagon made slow progress, they pushed harder. The boards beneath the wheels—torn from the sides of the wagon—made a ramp for the wheels to climb.

Danny pulled with all her strength. Sweat soaked the bay mare and lather formed around the collar and straps of her harness. She planted her large hooves and strained against the weight of the wagon. Her muscles gleamed under the layer of sweat.

Eldred coaxed her forward one step at a time with his voice. Calli led Duke before them, ready to catch the mare if she surged ahead.

Leather creaked, stretched taut from all the pulling.

Stay together, Calli silently begged. *We're too deep to lose it all now.* They carried little on their backs, and not what they would need to sustain them on a return trek to Marjan's camp.

She glanced at the gaping ravine two strides to her right. Trees climbed the steep sides of the mountain base. She closed her eyes to the dizzying height and glanced back.

Danny surged forward a few steps before slowing. Eldred caught her reins as she stopped with her hooves planted.

"Keep going!" The voice rose in warning from behind.

Eldred led her forward, past the danger of rolling back down the crack. When they crested the mount of the road, they halted.

Calli led Duke back to the wagon. Danny dropped her head to her shaking knees, her sides expanding and contracting rapidly.

"Okay!" someone called from behind the wagon.

Eldred dropped the reins.

Calli glanced back and noticed the rocks planted around each of the four wheels. At least they could rest for a little while without worrying too much for the supplies.

She turned her attention to the tired mare and frowned. "Will she make it down?"

She lifted the black, sweat-drenched mane from the mare's neck and fanned it in the air. Duke put in his sympathy by sniffing his companion's muzzle.

Danny responded with no more than a flick of an ear and heaving breaths.

Calli frowned across the mare's neck to Eldred. "I guess she's done for the day."

"We cannot stay here, but she'll not make it down without a break."

Calli looked around them, at the wide valley to their right and the steep peak rising on their left. They could rest there, but he was right about the wagon—they could not risk it rolling backwards in the dark of night. Danny would have to find the strength to descend the road, but at least the men could help.

"I think they all need it," Calli said, looking back at the men, who had found seats on some of the rocks. She caught Jayson's eyes and suppressed a chuckle. His hair stuck to his face and he breathed as hard as the others. When he noticed her eyes on him, he stood and approached.

"How about next time—" Jayson took a deep breath, struggling to catch it in the thin air, "—I lead the horse."

Calli arched one eyebrow. "How about next time you let me help?" He had insisted she let the men do the work. She would gladly have dug her heels in and helped.

"Fair enough." Without warning, he fell back against a large stone and slid down, fighting to catch his breath.

Eldred looked at him with a light smile. "You did it to yourself. The air is light here. Y'll not recover as fast from your labor as in the lowlands."

"*Now*...you tell me." Jayson tried to smile but his need for air swept it away with each breath. Despite his labored breathing, a spark of mischief glimmered from the smile struggling to his lips. "Had I known that, I'd have stayed home."

Calli shook her head. "You would not."

Jayson frowned as if hurt, but the upside-down smile righted itself again. "I'd have missed following the Red Rider."

"Red Rider?"

All heads turned in the direction of the silky voice. A black-haired woman dressed in the pants and tunic of a man approached from the direction that they were headed.

Jayson jumped to his feet. His glare sent a shiver down Calli's spine. He stepped between her and the woman.

How had Lusiradrol found them? What did she want all the way out there? Calli had thought her gone. She had not heard from or seen the woman since she added to her training after leaving the palace.

Black-red lips curved into a chilling smile. In spite of the malevolent aura around Lusiradrol, Calli stepped out from behind Jayson.

When he turned, she put a hand on his shoulder. She needed no protector. He knew as much, but his posture here prepared for an attack.

Duke pinned his ears back and stuck his nose forward, baring his teeth. When she made no movement, he looked back at Calli with his ears up before pinning his ears at the stranger again, as he had the first time meeting her on the road.

"I see you've begun to form an army." Lusiradrol passed her dark eyes over the small group and a cold, hard glare at Jayson matching the look he gave her, before returning her gaze to Calli. "Impressive. It's more than I expected."

Calli caught the recognition in those dark eyes when Lusiradrol passed her gaze over Jayson. How?

The thin smile Lusiradrol wore stretched into a look of amusement. "What fighting skills have they? Have you taught them well?"

Calli glanced aside at Jayson and the others, who looked from her to the stranger. Hopefully no one would ask questions.

Catching Jayson's frown, Calli swallowed. She could not deny her association with this dark stranger. "They learn fast with dedication to avenge their loved ones."

"Excellent. Others wait to join this army. You will return to the foothills to guide them?"

Marjan, Calli thought. He had no wish to join her in crossing the mountains. In fact he had thought it folly.

A shadow passed over her mind. She ignored it, determined to stay focused on excusing the woman without trouble. "We first must find a place to stay for the winter. We hope to cross to safer territory."

The look from Lusiradrol sent a shudder down Calli's spine to her legs.

Before they gave out, the feeling left her. Calli gripped the reins tight in her hand and took deep breaths to steady the quaking. At least Duke could support her if her legs gave way.

"This road crosses the mountains to the wild lands in the north." Lusiradrol's frown darkened the sky when she said, "I'll not wait long."

Calli swallowed. Fear coursed through her veins to freeze her in her place.

"The wagon!"

Calli whirled as the creak of the harness answered the call. All hands rushed to the wagon rolling back despite Danny's efforts. The men caught it before it rolled too far. Danny strained to make headway.

When she turned back to Lusiradrol, only the lonely road met Calli's eyes. The darkness had lifted. The woman had disappeared, but by what magic? Calli hoped never to find out, lest it be turned on her. She would kill Tyrkam, and present his head to the dark woman, as promised, if that was what it took to rid her of Lusiradrol.

When the men stabilized the wagon, Calli took a seat on the rock to relax with the others. Meanwhile most of the men sat down and closed their eyes for a midday nap in the sun and cool air.

The light wind hushed through the valley below, bringing silence to the men. Calli looked around, seeing many heads nodding forward, except Jayson. He watched her with a frown.

He wanted an answer to the question of how she knew Lusiradrol. It played across his expression.

Calli motioned down the hill in the direction they traveled. Hopefully she could satisfy him without going into details.

Jayson met her a few strides from the resting group. His stern look prompted her words.

"I know that look, Jayson."

He said nothing.

With a sigh, Calli held her arms up. "What might I say that would ease your suspicion?"

"The truth."

A gust of wind blew loose strands of hair into her face, and she brushed it away. "She came to me to teach me more than my trainers. I'd not manage without the little instruction she gave."

"At what price?"

He knew a demon when he saw it. Lusiradrol created no less of an impression. "Tyrkam's head."

His eyebrows lifted in curiosity, or sarcasm. "You're to bring his head in exchange for her instruction. I see...You could have said nothing sooner?"

He put a finger to his lips in thought, then acted out the part as if a third person stood with them. "Lord Tyrkam. Splendid day is it? I hope you're not too attached to your head. You see, I need to borrow it to satisfy a pact." He set his hand on the pommel of his sword and fixed his eyes on her. "That simple, is it?"

How dare he mock her! Calli peered at him through narrowed eyes. He had no right to preach. "Y've no idea what I've gained from her."

"I've not, have I? Have you considered that she's using you to her ends, with the same plan for you as Tyrkam? Has that crossed your mind?"

Calli growled, knowing he was right but unwilling to admit it. "Leave me alone."

"Leave you alone?" He took a step toward her, the lines of his frown deepening. "To what? To watch you meet your death in that woman? That's exactly what will happen."

"I needed to learn all I could to save Istaria. I was desperate." When she glanced aside, Calli caught the stares of the others. Could he not speak to her in private or lower his voice? What did they think of all this?

Why did he feel the need to dictate how to live her life? She needed no one else running it. Her mother had tried that, but had failed miserably. "Leave it be. What's done is done."

He opened his mouth to object, but closed it as fast. Jayson dropped his head and gave a nod. "Correct you are—what is done is done. I've no choice."

"Like it or not."

When he looked up, she detected a sadness in his face that materialized from nowhere. What was this about?

"I've no trust of her." His tone had dropped to match the expression of his face. At least he knew when to drop the matter. The tension between them melted away with his concession.

"I agree." She glanced down the road they would travel, the road that had brought Lusiradrol to them. Had Lusiradrol the intention Jayson suggested—to do the same to her after she carried out the woman's plans against Tyrkam?

When the warmth of his hand landed on her shoulder, Calli turned. His touch soothed the frustration a fraction.

"Not all the warriors of Hadeon would face her as you."

Calli allowed a faint smile from the compliment, too aware of what she had come to know about Lusiradrol. She feared the woman as anyone, more so since sealing the pact for Tyrkam's head.

"Be careful." Jayson patted her shoulder and looked back to the others. When he glanced aside at her and headed for a place to sit, Calli followed.

She could use the rest as much as anyone, though she doubted it would come. Lusiradrol had returned from nowhere to warn her of her duties. Calli wanted to know what the woman intended.

Chapter 46
26.7 pc 937

They continued through six uneventful days, trudging deeper into the mountains, but staying to the road. Calli silently thanked whoever had built the narrow road that it continued so deep into the mountains. She prayed it continued all the way to the other side.

The mountains towered over all sides now. She could swear they had left the lowlands years ago, but in truth no more than half the moon's cycle had passed.

The long hours of walking had drowned out the days. Talk had quieted, but tended to rise on occasion if someone picked up an idea and tossed it around.

Her thoughts centered on their goal. The justice of leading an army against Tyrkam filled her with pride. She savored the idea. It sweetened more than the idea of trying to take him through subterfuge. As he had grown in power, so would she, to one day retake what belonged to the family she served.

Calli tipped her face up to the sun, basking in its warmth. It rose over the snow-capped spires reaching up to catch it. That same sun would shine on a new Cavatar one day, and she would do all she could to make it happen.

In the meantime, she worried about Duke. He had started the journey in perfect condition. Now he had slimmed so his ribs showed. They had not stopped as often as they should, but they raced against the seasons changing.

They marched through the afternoon before finding a place to halt. Rocky outcrops near the edge of a deep canyon reminded her of the balustrade in the palace's upper levels. On the other side rose a mountain. Between the barriers, they braced the wagon and let the horses rest. Eldred served a hasty lunch while the men separated for space to stretch out and nap. The journey had taken a lot out of them, but it had also toughened their bodies and minds.

Calli found a place near the mountainside where the smooth-worn rocks provided a good backrest.

The fair-complexioned Kirin leaned against the mountain two strides away. "We'll be lucky to finish the crossing before snow falls." He watched the clouds not far above them and let out a sigh.

Calli shook her head at the disheartening thought, ready to respond. In that instant, he vanished from her peripheral vision.

Fenwar drained of color and rushed to where Kirin had vanished. "Kirin! Brother!" He ran his hands over the stone, studying it closely for a minute before turning to her.

A puzzled frown deepened into grooves along his forehead. Seeing the worry, Calli stood on weary legs. What else would happen to them on this journey?

"How could this be?" Could Lusiradrol have set a trap for them? Why?

"This is not her magic."

She turned to the source of the voice. Jayson gazed back with unwavering confidence.

The others turned to him with suspicion, but his easy smile relieved some of the tension.

"It could not be."

Whispers swept through the group. Calli shivered. She hoped Lusiradrol had not decided to tear apart her army in spite before it was an army. What would happen to her if the woman decided she had failed?

She turned to the rock face and examined the striations and long grooves of age. How had a man disappeared into that? Had the mountain swallowed him alive?

She lifted her hand to set it against the rock and hesitated inches away. Would it take her?

Calli shook her head, sending the thoughts away. Neither rock nor wind could steal a man.

She set her palm against the cool rock face. Sharp edges pressed against the tender flesh of her hand.

Nothing happened to her. How had he vanished?

Calli looked up at the snow-capped cliff rising above the clouds. Behind her rose other majestic pinnacles swept away by the lazy clouds drifting overhead. "He could not disappear."

"Not without magic."

This time Jayson's voice startled her. Calli looked up to him beside her and caught something in his eyes. "What is it?"

"Legends."

"Legends?"

"The legend of Arronfel, the ageless land bound by mortal, dragon, and Majera. The stories I've heard speak of a hidden door that will open only when the key is found."

"Nonsense."

He cocked an eyebrow. "Is it? Would you not wish to prevent your enemy from entering your domain?"

Calli sighed in exasperation, recognizing the faint sparkle in his eyes. What choice had she now? Although she had caught only a glimpse from the corner of her eye, she could not deny that Kirin had fallen through the mountainside.

She looked aside as Ellead stepped up next to Jayson.

The young man swept a strand of blonde hair from his eyes and gazed up at the sheer cliff. "Passin' through would be easier than climbing. I've no likin' o' magic, though."

She glanced up and caught the quizzical but amused crook to Jayson's grin. What did that mean? His expressions baffled her at times, giving something away but nothing at all. "What thoughts dance in your head?"

He shook his head and returned his attention to the mountains. "The key is here."

Hesitant, Fenwar extended his hands to the face of the mountain and pushed against it. "He leaned against the rock to rest, but he passed through. How is it we cannot?"

He turn around and back against the steep wall. He had seen his brother fall through solid rock, or at least the illusion of it. When Fenwar allowed his weight to lean into it, nothing happened. With more confidence, he pressed back against the sharp lines of the rock, his feet braced outward. The wall held. "How is this possible?"

"I wonder..." Jayson excused Fenwar from the wall and took his place. He closed his eyes and took a deep breath.

Needles danced in Calli's stomach. Why did Jayson feel it necessary to test this magic? Why could he not leave it alone? Perhaps Kirin played tricks after all. Perhaps he was the one possessing magic to fool them.

When nothing happened, she let her breath out, not realizing until then that she held it. "Step away from the rock."

"Worried?"

Calli crossed her arms, fixing him with a cold glare. "Why must you argue?"

Jayson grinned and came up close beside her. With his mouth close to her ear, he said, "It amuses me."

She twisted around as he walked away from her. Unable to respond, she turned back to the solid wall mocking her better senses. How did magic make a sudden appearance in a mountainside?

The prospect pressed its worries through the tangle of other concerns. Calli grimaced, her eyes fixed on the place where Kirin had disappeared. "Why now?"

She leaned against the stone, her eyes closed to forget the others and clear her mind.

She welcomed the calm that took over. In the few seconds before her baggage returned, a faint glimmer of hope lit within her. They would find a way through this. They would find a shelter for the winter safe from Tyrkam's army. Somehow they would find Kirin.

When the calm took over her mind, she fell. Her shoulder cushioned her fall. Calli pushed herself up to her feet and rubbed the bruise.

What met her eyes made her jaw drop. Two parallel ruts wound through a thick carpet of grass broken by immense boulders jutting from the ground. The overgrown road passed through a narrow stream and vanished over a grassy knoll.

She turned around. The men had gathered behind a gray haze. They knocked on air, though in a second she realized it was the mountain she had leaned against.

"What is this place?"

She should go back, if she could. How had she passed through the barrier? Could she return to explore this new land? It could not have fit inside the mountain. Blue sky spread wide overhead with mountains rising at the far edges of the valley.

Hesitant to make either choice, she took in the view in a quick scan and turned to the haze.

When she stepped into it, the gray shimmered and parted away from her. In two steps she emerged from the mountain.

"Milady!" Multiple voices rose in surprise.

"Praise Goddess, you came back."

Calli smiled to Eldred in gratitude for his concern.

"Where'd you go?"

"How'd you pass through?" Fenwar asked.

Calli took in all the shocked and curious expressions. Jayson's wry grin took her by surprise. He knew something.

"Where's Kirin?"

She turned to Fenwar's hopeful face. "I saw no one." She paused and looked to the others. "But there is a valley with a stream and lush grass on the other side. I saw nothing else but a hill. Beyond that, I know not what may be."

Jayson stepped forward. "Had to have all the glory, I see."

Calli caught the mischievous look but had no time to entertain him.

"As sure as winter coming, you tell me not to go near the mountain, and you do just that."

She shook her head. The others paid no mind to his exaggerations.

"What?" He looked around him innocently with his arms out in question.

She had no time for his jests.

He dropped his arms and took on a more serious nature. "So, how'd you do it?"

That was more like it. At least he could bring the subject back to the forefront. "I—" How did she do it?

Calli moved into position where she had been before leaning through the mountain. Could she do it again? "I stood here and—"

She sighed as she had before. The memory of the calming effect returned. "That was it! I was trying to bring calm to my mind. I remember letting go and feeling a light and I fell."

"A light..." Jayson's voice trailed off.

"Yes! Though nothing like a candle flame or the sun, but an inner light when all the worries are gone." Calli closed her eyes and pushed aside the questions, clearing her mind to make room for the light she recalled. When she caught it, she reached forward.

Nothing blocked her and she walked forward into the green valley.

"It's true."

At Jayson's muttered words, she looked up. He had figured that out quick enough.

Before he could speak, two more joined them. They gasped in awe. "What wonders be!"

When all but Eldred materialized, Calli remembered the horses. "Oh, blight!" She raised her voice and said, "I'll return in a moment."

Without waiting for a reply, since they paid no attention to her, she turned into the gray haze. She joined Eldred, who tried to lead Danny forward with the wagon while Duke followed behind.

"You returned. I'd thought to be stranded with these two. Help me cover her eyes; she'll not step near the mountain. Looks like a wall to her."

Calli held the mare's bridle while he tied a scarf over her eyes. Danny flared her nostrils at the blindness.

"Easy, girl." Eldred's voice failed to soothe the nervousness from her, but she followed with small steps.

"You understand how to pass through?"

"Aye, milady. I've an idea."

She watched as he backed through the mountain, leading the mare and wagon forward. When Danny had vanished halfway, Duke lifted his head and snorted.

Calli tried to soothe him with her voice and a touch on his shoulder. Only when the wagon vanished completely did he lower his head and nudge her. "Lost interest already?"

He rubbed his head against her shoulder in reply. With a smile, she pushed him off. "None o' that. We have to move on now too. There's grass aplenty through that way." Hopefully it was not already claimed.

When she led him to the mountain, he sniffed at the rock face. However, he would not walk into what would have seemed a barrier to him, as it had to her and the others until they understood. She removed her cloak and covered his eyes. He lifted his head but followed her with little hesitation.

On the other side, Calli pulled the blindfold off. Immediately, his head shot up with ears pricked forward. "See now?"

Duke let out a high-pitched call and posed in expectation, his nostrils quivering. All voices hushed. If anyone lived in this valley, they would know strangers had arrived.

The wind whispered across the tall grass. After what seemed an eternity, a faint call replied.

Horses? Calli looked at Duke in wonderment, her cloak hanging on her arm. His head could have risen no higher or the dark tips of his ears been no closer to touching. The gray horse stood frozen, the unexpected answer claiming all his attention.

When she moved up beside him and stroked his neck, the spell broke. He lowered his head and chewed his bit, sniffing the cloak as if nothing had happened.

"Did you hear that?" one of the others asked.

"But if there be horses, why not men to ride them?"

"Be it so, we're not in the advantage."

The distant thunder grew louder. A gradual vibration reached their feet from the pounding of the hooves of many horses.

Calli clutched her reins in reassurance and rested her hand on Duke's neck. The least she needed was for Duke to take off, though she doubted he would. He had stayed by her in far more tempting situations.

She was right. When a line of colorful horses appeared over the crest of the hill, he never moved.

His piercing whinny was enough.

Calli gazed at the shining coats of various colors on all different ages. Suckling foals strong and ready for weaning, long-legged yearlings, plump mares, and a few scraped and rough-looking stallions. Though the horses were small, they appeared hardy.

"Horses!" The stunned words whispered off the lips of many of the men, who stared in disbelief.

Jayson joined Calli at the back of the group. "That's a lot of horseflesh."

The horses stopped at the stream to drink and stare at the strangers. None dared to cross.

Duke dropped his head a moment and chewed the bit impatiently. "Easy, boy. We know not how they'll receive us. Better to chase them away than rush into a fight."

At an unseen cue from one of the mares, the herd whirled and raced away over the hill. As quick as they had materialized, they vanished into the distance. The thunder of their hooves died away and only the wind rushed past.

A smile crept to Calli's lips at the image of beauty that had come and gone as a fleeting dream.

"Amazing." She led Duke forward, glad the herd had left them without trouble. "Horses to train for an army."

The others looked at her with a mixture of smiles and grimaces. Those with grimaces she supposed had little experience with horses. They would not be required to handle animals. Foot soldiers would be needed as well as cavalry. Her father had taught her that much.

Calli stopped at the stream. Duke dropped his head before she could take a step forward, tugging her arm down. She let him drink. The men took advantage of the clear, cool water also and filled their waterskins.

She silently thanked the Creators for their fortune. Water had been scarce along the high pass, but for the rushing waterfalls. Now, the horses could drink to their fill and more. At last, she could cease her worries about finding a suitable place to live. This valley would provide for their needs.

One oddity stood out, however. Calli needed no cloak. The chill air outside the hidden door did not pass through. As if summer had decided to linger, the warmth of the sun chased away the cold.

After everyone drank their fill, they splashed through the stream and followed the road curving around the hill.

From the top of the hill, Calli beheld the truth. She halted and studied the immense valley. It stretched a few miles ahead and at least a couple to either side at its widest. In the distance, a rainbow arched in the spray of a waterfall. It poured into a small lake feeding the stream.

"I must be dreaming," Calli said.

"Magic."

She glanced aside at Jayson.

He shrugged but said nothing.

She led them to the waterfall. If the valley was as long as she estimated, they could use some of the land for crops with plenty to spare for animals. The trees growing up the mountainsides would provide wood as well.

One question drove her forward. Where was Kirin? Had he followed the road?

Beneath her feet, the soft grass cushioned each step, alleviating the sores and stiffness from the hard mountain road. Calli inhaled, welcoming the scent of blossoms with each breath. The land could not have been more pure.

"Surely someone lives here." She recognized Eldred's rough voice.

"Or we've passed into a dream," one of the others replied.

They spoke in low voices of the one fear plaguing her mind as well, that someone inhabited the valley and would not welcome strangers.

Halfway across the valley, Calli thought she made out unnatural formations tiered to take advantage of a natural slope. A pile of rubble lay before a wall and what appeared to be openings. Could it be caves or the shelter of the ancient men who had dwelt in this place?

Rejuvenated with hope for shelter, she hurried toward the image. It grew before them as they neared it. Distinct shapes took form along the cliff face.

To their left the herd grazed, paying the humans no notice. At a few nickers that drifted over the breeze, Calli turned her head. A smile crept to her lips. The foals playing while their dams dozed or grazed lifted her mood. She watched them for a few seconds before turning back to the rubble.

The formation in the valley wall grew more definitive. It rose high above the valley floor. Sheets of stone curving outward had broken in places and crumbled. Before she realized, Calli pictured a fortress of stone carved from the mountain. Rounded tiers spread out as they descended. Homes of stone filled each layer while the pinnacle boasted the elegance befitting a ruler.

Like a vision it passed before her eyes. Children played in the streets while women watched. Men and some of the women practiced moves like those her father had taught her while others worked the fields. Life carried on with a serenity she had never imagined, hidden and unconcerned with the outside world.

When she blinked, the images faded, along with the giggle of young children. It had all been so real for a flicker of time, as if she had been here before.

Calli shrugged the disorientation away, shifting her thoughts to why no one had come to greet them.

After crossing the few miles, they stopped at the base of the rubble.

Calli tilted her head back and counted five tiers, the first three bearing holes of crumbled stone into the next lower level. At the top rose a stone peak richly decorated with broken carvings and pillars glistening in the sun.

"My eyes deceive me."

She paid no attention to the speaker, though she shared the sentiment. Indeed, her eyes must have deceived her. This place should not be possible.

As if reading her mind to answer her question, Jayson lifted his voice for all to hear

"On Snowtop's valley arranged in clouds,
where river starts in Norilas,
there lies the dwelling, strong and proud,
of men who bore the ancient past.

Linfrathâr they called their home
a name of honor wielded grand
written in the mage's tome,
there to make a final stand."

Calli turned to him. Where had he learned those words? What did it mean?

He strode forward through the crowd around her and stopped at her side. "The Song of Llyra."

"Never heard of it."

"Not surprising. No bard has sung it in over a hundred years."

"How do you know it?"

Jayson shrugged. "I studied much of ancient lore."

Although she wished to ask him about his studies and how he knew about this and the secret entrance, she decided they could talk in private later. "Be that as it may, we've no time for pleasure."

Calli cleared her throat and raised her voice for all to hear. "We will make camp here. We'll need a corral for the horses and a camp for the night. I also need volunteers to explore the fortress."

Jayson leaned over to speak closer to her ear. "Linfrathâr."

Calli ignored him. "Let us find what may be found, though demons I'd rather not, and if all is well, we shall call this our home."

Voices of consent muttered in reply with nodding heads. Volunteers stepped forward for the primary tasks while only three held back. Calli assigned them to duties and joined the majority who scaled the ancient fortress.

Only Eldred was allowed to avoid the hard labor. As the oldest of their group, he had not the strength of his youth. Instead, he had taken the role of cook and set to work on preparing the next meal.

Already visions of the restored prominence of this fortress rose in her mind. She imagined a kingdom in this small valley, where she could live in peace.

After clambering over the rubble, she stopped and gazed upward at the overwhelming height, which blended into the mountainside. The snow-capped pinnacle of the towering rock loomed above the drifting clouds, no longer ominous but standing sentinel.

Calli welcomed the freedom this valley brought. It chased away many of her worries as she had wished, as if the Creators had heard her prayers. Here she could be free to consider more important matters.

Here she could contemplate her plans for an army to defeat Tyrkam.

Here she could worry more about the increasing loneliness burdening her heart. Though she wished to remain distracted, it grew in her mind to overpower other concerns.

Calli clutched at her shirt and the pendant beneath it. If only she knew what had become of Phelan.

Without thinking, she looked down at the men who had grabbed what they could to try to break up the pile of stones. Most were small enough to carry and they piled the pieces in a wide circle below.

Calli's eyes found Jayson among the eight men. An easy smile formed on her lips. None of this would have happened without his help. She was glad he stayed with her. It felt right to have him at her side.

However, she wondered what he knew. His expressions more often than not hinted at some deeper understanding. She wished he would tell her, although she could be wrong.

Perhaps she read too much into it.

With a sigh, she returned to the task of exploring the fortress. They had a good portion of daylight before dusk fell. She would take advantage of that. If this would be their home, they would need to rebuild it.

Resigned to her task, Calli started up the flight of stairs to the second tier.

Chapter 47
26.7 pc 937

Phelan stood at the parapet overlooking the cliff, gazing out over the waves washing on the rocks and sand below. The sea rushed in and withdrew with a steady wash of foam he despised. Despite the monotony, the Darnasian Sea had mesmerized him in his endless hours looking to the north, toward his home. Now the sun sank into the ocean to his left.

He had adjusted to the sea air blowing along the coast, but he had not adjusted to being away for so long. Already his journey had stretched over more than a moon cycle. He expected to stay another before heading back.

However, he would not be returning for Calli but for the land he would inherit, with a wife he was expected to choose.

A deep sigh escaped him. Phelan lifted his eyes to the orange-tinged waves ridden by the setting sun.

Calli would love the sea, he mused with a hint of a smile.

The rush of the waves crashing over the rocks and sand had not soothed his troubled thoughts as he expected. Instead, it cleared his mind for other concerns.

The ruler of Rivonia, Sovereign Kassar Farolkavin, had promised any of his twenty-one daughters as a suitable bride. Since Phelan's arrival, each had taken turns serving him. One a day for the past eleven days had served his needs. They had all blurred together. He knew not what choice to make, but wished to return to his dearest Calli and claim her as a wife. Instead, he suffered through the rituals of Rivonia's customs to satisfy his own.

He knew his choice, but for the sake of Cavatar, he would choose another. The sovereign had twelve wives, eleven more than he would ever desire. He would never know how to handle twelve women at a time, not when he could barely handle one of strong will.

"My lord," a soft voice said from behind. The accented Ayrulean brought a smile to his lips. Although they spoke his native tongue well enough, he had learned enough Rivon to impress his hosts.

Which daughter was this? He rummaged his memory to match the voice to a name. When it would not come, he turned to the patient woman.

The generous black hair cascaded over her delicate, brown shoulders to a straight edge at her waist. Black make-up highlighted her dark eyes in the fashion typical of her people. Dressed in light garments exposing her shoulders, she stood before him aglow in the last light of day. The simple headdress of spun gold and faceted gems glittered with an ethereal fire amid the charcoal hair.

Phelan caught his breath on a moment. These women showed none of the conservative approach to clothes that those of his home held sacred. His Goddess frowned on the lust of men's eyes. As a consequence, most women revealed little skin, which had only tempted him more.

"Naiyel."

The corners of her lips twitched into a hesitant smile. "Your mind works now."

A full smile spread across his face. With all the names and faces, he had rarely used the correct name.

"The evening meal is nearly set, my lord."

After a last look over the distant horizon of water, Phelan turned toward the doorway and its intricate curves and pillars. She led him between the spiraled pillars and into the guest hall.

They stopped at the balcony circling the columned hall. A wide, grand staircase descended from the balcony to the floor at his right and another across the room to his left. In elegant maroon and green with gold accents on the tiled floor, spiraled columns, and banisters, the room radiated the wealth of Rivonia, the only land he had ever visited with greater beauty than Ayrule.

The noise of conversations buzzed through the hall as courtiers and guests mingled below. He had seen it every night he stayed in the care of the sovereign—ornate banquets to honor those in attendance, great feasts that could feed a full village. He could never imagine Cook letting as much go to waste. Even in the best of times, his father had never ordered such lavish feasts except on special occasions.

"Lord Isolder."

Phelan turned to the source of the familiar voice. Farolkavin approached with four of his wives around him, each as beautiful as the next with charcoal hair, dark eyes, and the slender form typical of the Rivon people. The crimson fabric of the sovereign's clothes shimmered with each movement, catching the light of the oil lamps massed amid the room. The fabrics of the land had taken the markets across the kingdoms of Ayrule, including Cavatar. His sister had been gifted a dress of the finest Rivon materials, only to pass it on to Calli.

Phelan fondly recalled the way the red-head glowed in the sun in the shimmering green.

Sovereign Farolkavin stopped before him with his wives.

Phelan pushed aside the memory and offered a slight bow to his hosts.

"I see Naiyel has claimed you from your longings."

He glanced behind him at the calm demeanor of the princess. "Please accept my apologies for any offense."

"Long have I watched you, and always you are distracted," the sovereign said. "Are not my daughters worthy of your attention?"

Phelan shook his head. "If only to resist their charms." What else could he say? Neither the truth nor a lie would pacify the sovereign. Only one answer came to him, along with the somber reality of what he expected. "I long for home. For a few years Cavatar has defended its people from a rising warlord. I fear what will be when I return."

Farolkavin waved his words away. "Fear not, Lord Isolder. My alliance you have. Long have our lands traded. Though I worry also the outcome of this war, I'll not let it defeat me before it has."

Phelan smiled his gratitude. A weight he had not noticed until then lifted from his mind. At least Farolkavin found no offense in his distraction, but had interpreted it for the lesser meaning.

Without a word, the women dispersed, leaving them alone to speak. What did Farolkavin wish to say that had not been said, unless he had news of the war? Or did he see through Phelan's words into his reluctance to choose a bride?

In a low voice, Farolkavin said, "This war you mention goes not well."

Could the sovereign have said it any clearer, it would have rung like a bell.

Phelan shuddered and leaned over the banister. "You are perceptive, Lord."

"I have seen trade diminish." With a sigh, Farolkavin leaned on the banister next to him. His dignified presence commanded attention. Phelan found himself caught as if in a spell, awaiting every word to issue from the man's mouth.

As a boy in the land of Rivonia, the first son of the sovereign led the armies. After a lifetime of conquest over his enemies, Kassar Farolkavin had taken his father's place. His leadership and authority carried Rivonia into greater wealth and power.

Phelan glanced aside at the dark-haired sovereign with the trim beard. Although Farolkavin wore the robes of a ruler, his presence was that of a military leader, rigid and cunning. He set the air about him on alert from the thoughts always working in his mind.

"My ancestors first crossed the sea in search of greater territory. The people of Ayrule resisted. The kingdoms united to defeat us." Farolkavin turned to Phelan with a smile gleaming through his beard. "You have since conquered us with trade. We now depend on Cavatar and the other lands of Ayrule for profit."

The smile melted and Phelan caught the glint of malice in his dark eyes. "This 'Lord' that threatens you also threatens our way of life." Unexpected bitterness snapped in the sovereign's tone.

Before Phelan could ask, the sovereign reached inside his cloak and pulled out a scroll. "You should read this."

Phelan took the parchment and unrolled it. The words he read made his heart sink.

Images flitted across his mind. He recalled the palace in its grandeur and the laughter of maidens playing in the sun. In the next glimpse, his mind filled in the rest. Fire consumed what it could and soldiers beat down the doors. How could this have happened so soon?

"A messenger brought it this evening. He demands I send you back, or face open warfare."

The tone of Farolkavin's voice drew Phelan from his visions. Heat rose to his face at the sovereign's words. "He dares threaten you?"

"He does, but he'll not have you. You are the rightful heir, not this Tyrkam. I shall honor your father's request. And I shall honor our treaty. This affects Rivonia and its neighbors as well as Cavatar."

A smile tugged at the corners of Phelan's mouth. Farolkavin had been the strongest overseas ally of Cavatar and had proven his worth once again. Tyrkam would not last long as ruler of Ayrule.

"Will you accept my allegiance, Lord Isolder, and the aid of all the forces I can spare?"

"Of course." The smile that sought escape mixed with despair into a grimace. How could Rivonia defeat the armies of Hadeon? They would need to plan carefully to make the most of an attack. Tyrkam could have forces waiting on the coastlines, and winter would soon arrive to his homeland.

Ideas blossomed before him, blending with his rage and emptiness. They depended on Farolkavin's vow. "I accept your allegiance, but request asylum, my lord. I cannot return until the time is right."

With a nod Farolkavin stood back. "You are welcome. When the time comes, we will erase this traitorous exile from the world. He will threaten us no longer." He offered his hand in friendship.

Phelan clasped the hand offered to him. Relief soothed the fury threatening to boil over. The promise of aid was more than he could have asked. He was grateful for all he received.

Only one problem nagged at him. What had become of Calli? Would he ever see her again?

Chapter 48
26.7 pc 937

Tyrkam lifted the chalice to his lips and guzzled the bitter drink before its taste lingered on his palate. With his thirst satisfied, he set the empty chalice on the table.

Three men sat opposite him. Dorjan with his calm demeanor said little, but said as much as needed. Cathmor, however, said much but little worthwhile. Vahrik brooded over his ale.

Tyrkam studied the baron, unsure what to make of his loyalties. Cathmor had betrayed the king, but that meant little of his loyalty to Hadeon.

Tyrkam trusted no one, except Dorjan, who had for years stood by him without question. The rare red hair stood out wherever he went. People identified him and gave him the respect he deserved, which he had more than earned.

"I will consider your pledge." Tyrkam watched Cathmor but the old warrior never flinched. If he attempted deceit, it was far from obvious in his manners.

"My lord, I am honored to serve you."

Vahrik snorted and rubbed his bandaged right shoulder, his eyes burning Tyrkam.

Tyrkam ignored the boy, having planned his end after he turned up alive but injured in the siege of the palace.

Of any young men to worry about, Tyrkam feared Prince Phelan Isolder more than Vahrik. The king's heir was not to be found. Darius had taken the princess, but Phelan had vanished of his own accord.

One of the servants had confirmed that the boy traveled overseas to Rivonia to seek a bride. He was out of reach, but still posed a threat, particularly with a strong ally behind him.

Tyrkam gnashed his teeth on the news. Once he secured all of Ayrule, Rivonia was next. The sovereign would feel his wrath to the fullest.

However, Tyrkam had more important matters in the present. He had dispatched units of soldiers to the coastal towns to watch for the prince, though he doubted the boy would be alone. Tyrkam could subdue the last threat, to worry about more important issues.

Lusiradrol had warned him she had other plans. Certainty set in his mind that she had some connection to the rebels who thwarted his men. Only she could train such worthy opponents.

Tyrkam scowled at the thought. Neither Vahrik nor Cathmor nor other Lords possessed the power to defeat him. However, Lusiradrol did. Anyone linked to her was a threat to him.

"Prove your pledge through deeds, not words, Lord Cathmor." The threat in Tyrkam's voice brought a slight frown to the older man. "Bring me the body of this one they call 'Red Rider' and his companion." He leaned forward on the table as the thought took hold. "Better than dead, bring them alive. I've a few questions on my mind."

"That one—" Cathmor leaned back, dropping his eyes to the table in thought. "That one I've heard no reports for a while. Have not your soldiers killed him?"

"Not if he is a woman."

Cathmor's eyebrows lifted with his eyes. "A woman? How might a woman carry on the deeds reported of this criminal?"

"It matters not. I seek truth."

"And vengeance?"

Tyrkam turned to Dorjan. Had the man not been his lieutenant, he would have cut him down for the revelation before the others. He would admit no weakness such as this person exposed. "My business is my concern."

"I'd worry more the return of Isolder's son," Cathmor said. "When he hears of the fall of Cavatar, he will surely ask Rivonia for allegiance to lead an invasion against us."

Us? Tyrkam smirked. "And have your head on a platter for your treachery."

Cathmor shrugged, a cold menace falling over his features. "I'd as soon have his for the disgrace his family has caused me."

Tyrkam studied the warrior for a moment but the seasoned veteran displayed no hint of what he spoke. "I'll give you that if you capture the rebels."

Cathmor's eyes flickered with anger. "You'll have your wench."

Tyrkam allowed a faint smile. The search for the elusive rebel should keep the baron busy, at least for a while. It would give him time to plan his demise. He had taken his use of the man. Disposing of him now would not hurt his plans, and Shadow needed work.

"Tell me what you know of this...person."

Tyrkam described to Cathmor all he knew from the reports of his soldiers in the villages. The most recent reported her to have gained a companion as skilled a fighter as she. Two skilled warriors posed a greater threat than one.

After the meeting, Tyrkam excused the baron to prepare for his return to the castle on the lake.

That left Vahrik sitting with his arms crossed and a scowl on his face. He distracted himself by picking at the bandages on his injured shoulder, where a well-aimed thrust of a spear had almost severed his arm. Unfortunately, it did little more than stop at the bone.

"Someone must return to Wynmere to take over for Gilcress. Vahrik, I want you there."

Vahrik ceased his restless activity and studied the warlord, suspicion crossing his face.

"Dorjan will accompany you."

"I figured as much."

"You will listen to him." Menace chilled the room several degrees when Tyrkam spoke. Vahrik sat up at attention.

"Yes, milord."

"Now, leave us. Prepare to leave at daybreak."

With the scrape of wood on stone, Vahrik pushed his chair from the table. He departed without a word, the door thudding closed behind him.

"You've no trust in the boy," Dorjan said.

"I trust no one, but him the least. He would be useful if he had not the arrogance to listen to no one." Tyrkam let out a breath and sat back in his chair. He had never trusted the boy, but had hoped he might submit. Too much of his father's blood seared through those veins and not enough of his mother. That could be fixed.

Ehtashe mi, Nayavi. He could not keep his promise to protect someone who would rather slash his throat than obey. Farolkavin would one day suffer for his deceit and the dishonor it had brought him.

"You know my mind," Tyrkam said.

Dorjan gave a nod. "When."

"When you can corner him with any allies."

"I've not seen him with anyone, but I know they await him."

"Be sure they are all taken."

A chilling smile curved up into the bearded face. Dorjan would not fail him. They would root out Vahrik's companions and cut off any rebellion at the head.

❧ ☙

Damaera gazed down from the balcony overlooking the reading hall. Soldiers stomped through without regard for the quiet, their steps echoing to the heights of her room. A deep frown crossed her face.

"Milady."

Damaera sighed and turned to the servant girl. She could go nowhere without them harassing her to return to her quarters. Her grief for her family and the kingdom had stolen her health, but she had recovered from her fever and had strength to walk short distances.

"Please, milady. You're not well. I should not like to see you collapse here, for *them*—" She spat the word like a curse on the conquering soldiers. "To carry you back."

"You speak wisely. I should not like to be carried by any of them." Conceding to the servant's pleas, she turned to the tall doors at the end of the hall.

The loud clomp of approaching steps sent a chill down her spine.

"My lady." Cold confidence carried the words and drew her head around.

She frowned and held her chin up. "My lord, Tyrkam."

He stopped next to her, a farce of worry on his face. "Why do you risk your health this way?"

"This is my home. I will come and go as I please."

A moment of anger flashed and was gone from his face, but Damaera realized she had pressed him to the edge of his tolerance. It gave her some satisfaction.

"I would rather you rest to build your strength."

"You're right." She turned away. "I have seen enough of your fools." She would never forgive him for the murder of her husband, a ruler dedicated to his people and herself. Also, he would learn nothing of the Lumathir from her. She had nothing to tell him.

With dignified poise, she strolled away, the servant at her side.

≈

Tyrkam watched her go. She could be a problem, but he had not yet learned from her what he wished. Even after recovering from her fever, the queen had said little about Istaria, but for the story of how Phelan had found the young princess in a cave. The girl's hair had changed from brown-gold to white. Though he had never heard the story, it was useless. The queen knew not what he required.

However, her presence would serve him well if Phelan returned to reclaim what should have been his.

He had one other use for her. What of the Lumathir? What knowledge did she have? What skills did they have to combat the dragons?

In a flash of insight, he whirled and sought the guards who would accompany Dorjan and Vahrik.

When he found them, he gave them orders to bring Makleor to the palace. Perhaps the wizard knew something of the Lumathir.

One way or another, he would defeat Lusiradrol and whatever weapon she brought against him. He would have his revenge against Rivonia.

Chapter 49
26.7 pc 937

Calli peered through the gloom. Wispy spider webs floated on the breeze of her passing. Debris lined the corridors, though only in small pieces. The inner halls had withstood whatever had knocked holes through the outer barrier walls.

Dust stirred under her feet and insects scurried away. The film of ages coated various objects in the dim corridors, from shreds of tapestries to scattered dishes on benches. The place had been deserted in haste and everything dropped in its place.

She crept through the labyrinth of corridors, curious of what else the legends said. She would have to ask Jayson when she returned to him. He possessed a curious knowledge of these things.

From the intricate dust-coated painted designs and etched scenes of life over archways she realized this fortress had been home to hundreds of people, perhaps thousands. Only a massive team of stone masons could have finished this place in as much detail.

In the dim light of the sun from the windows, she made out empty sconces along the walls ahead and some holding blocks of crystal.

Calli continued past rotted wooden doors to various rooms. Her heart quickened at the gloom and the musty smell hinting of death. However, the faint echo of running water calmed her nerves with its soothing rush.

She pulled her cloak around her from the chill of the shadows and followed the sound around another corner.

A wide entrance opened onto a large hall. Sunlight poured in through the upper windows. She halted at the top of the steps at the entrance to the high-ceilinged room.

Memories flooded back of the reading hall with its reflecting pool in the section of the palace of Cavatar housing the royal bedchambers.

Though with slight differences, the simple but elegant design reminded her of home. Water shimmered in the running fountain in the center of the room. Large empty planters sat in each corner, the etchings and colors on them dulled by a thick layer of dust. Though dark soil sat in each, the plants, which had long ago grown in them, were gone, decomposed most likely.

In the loneliness of the room, her steps echoed louder than they had in the corridors. Calli circled the flowing fountain and the bottom pool thick with algae. The splash of cool mountain water inspired a shiver.

She reached into the water flowing down from a cracked stone lily into two progressively larger basins until it trickled noisily into the bottom pool.

Unconsciously licking her lips, she cupped her hand and caught a swallow of the icy water. Hesitant but aware of her thirst, she sipped.

The taste refreshed her, reviving her spirits. Calli reached out both hands to catch water and drank until she sated her thirst. At least she could spare her pouch.

Once she satisfied herself, she sat in the quiet of the room. It could have been a part of the palace in some respects.

She pulled out the pendant and held it in the light of the room. The edges shimmered in the streak of sunlight piercing the gloom from one of the windows. "Where are you? What mind have you of me?"

Before she could answer her question, the weight of her journey crashed over her.

She remembered. She remembered the palace and its impressive halls and elegant décor. She remembered waking next to a moody head cook who also was her mother. She remembered the delicate sophistication of the queen and the authority of the king. She remembered the snow of apple blossoms in the spring. She remembered sharing the joy of living with Istaria.

What had happened since she left? How could the palace have fallen so quickly? How could it have fallen at all? She should have been there, should have stood beside the family in their time of need.

Before any tears could fall, Calli rose to her feet. She swallowed the emotions rising from her heart. She had a job to do in the present. Lingering in the past would hold her back.

Resigning to the task, she hurried from the room. With all luck, she would never have a need to enter the sitting room again. She would not fall to her regrets.

The other rooms and corridors resembled those she had already passed through. However, the memories lingered at the edge of her mind.

She refused them entrance into her conscious. Once again, she was the woman who would've made her father proud.

She also had new friends.

A smile crept through the sorrow and regrets freshly sprouted. She had Jayson, Eldred, and the others. They had helped her confidence and proven they could work as a team and would make fine soldiers to lead the fight against Tyrkam's army. They would succeed, whether it took a year or ten.

Distracted by her thoughts, she stumbled over the rubble strewn through the corridor. Calli gasped and plunged forward into the floor. She dove into the wall of a cross corridor ahead.

Her head smacked against with enough force to jar her teeth. Like a spear, pain flashed through her head. Calli pushed herself onto her hands and knees, coughing amid the cloud of dust surrounding her.

"Milady!"

The shuffle of feet hurried closer.

Calli opened her eyes and looked up to Kirin's worried face. She blinked away the pain. "When no less than inept I am, you appear."

"I meant to return sooner." He reached a hand down, which she accepted.

The blacksmith pulled her to her feet as if she weighed nothing. Before she could thank him, a sharp ache stabbed through her head. Calli blinked and lifted a hand to her head.

"Are you injured?"

She groaned as the pain slowly faded. "Paying for my lack of eyes."

"I'll say nothing."

Calli fixed her eyes on him, studying his expression. If he jested, it would show. However, only concern touched by amusement lingered in his grin.

"I appreciate it, to be sure." She looked around but only they occupied the room. Sighing, she dropped her shoulders and asked, "Why'd you not return to us?"

Kirin's eyes lit up like stars. "This place is—I've no words to describe it!"

The excitement in his tone distracted her from the throb of pain lingering in her head. "We were worried."

He bowed his head and attempted to contain his energy. "Forgive me, milady."

While holding her head with one hand, Calli waved away his apology. "Already done. Just—" She took a deep breath to clear away the last of the pain. "—Tell me what you found."

He gesticulated wildly while describing his walk-through of the fortress. Kirin had never been one to hide his emotions.

Calli listened to him tell of running across the valley to this place. Being unable to resist exploring, he entered the lower level. He passed a few homes and found the doorway to the inner halls. They went on forever, as he described, connected tenements and vast courtyards. He passed through at least one kitchen strewn with pots and pans and jars and plates and all matter of cooking and eating utensil made of clay or metal. A dozen ovens lined one wall while basins and kettles lined another. He had never seen as large of a facility.

After the kitchen, he found a stairway rising to the next level and the next. At the top, he found what must have been the royal domain. Though detailed etchings seemed to be everywhere, nothing compared to the craftsmanship of the upper level.

Kirin proceeded down from the top level to study the others until he found Calli.

"You know the rest," he said in conclusion.

She nodded. "We've now others in this fortress, and less than a few arcs of the sun yet today."

"I've seen enough to know this place is what we need; a blessing from Goddess."

"That's yet to prove. I'd rather not stay here this night, lest it be otherwise." She frowned. If indeed someone lingered, she certainly would not want to be caught in there at night, especially without a torch. "Show me these stairs you found."

Kirin guided her through a maze of corridors until they reached a dark archway at the end of one. Inside the gloomy passage, he led her down the steps. She counted seven for every landing, spiraling down, and a floor after three landings.

At the bottom, she beheld the enormous kitchen. Sunlight slanted across the room from the windows. No glass blocked the mountain air from entering, but a few contained the grooves to prove that glass had been used, or at least shutters. Fragments lay scattered about the floor.

As she crossed the long room, Calli scanned around her. The familiar setting inspired visions of cooks and servers bustling in a frenzy to feed the numerous people this fortress must have housed. It reminded her of home.

She blinked, dissolving the forms back to the quiet.

She had left a cold and heartless mother to search for the friendship that had stayed her sanity and brought her joy. Cook could have her bakehouse.

Calli never regretted leaving her.

After crossing the length of the room, she never looked back. That life was over for her.

Kirin showed her to the door out of the fortress and away from the memories.

Chapter 50
5.8 pc 937

In a few days, they managed to construct a large pen using piled rocks as a fence in which to contain Duke and Danny. Though the herd had visited them in their confinement, only the stallions had challenged the newcomers, when the mares took too much interest.

Most of the men set to cleaning the first level of the mountain fortress in shifts while others searched the higher levels.

Calli opted for work outside, cleaning up the rubble of the walls. She could not face the memories haunting her, nor the strange visions. Though the tedious nature of removing the rubble allowed her mind to wander, the struggle to carry each piece and the company of those around her provided adequate distractions. For that she was grateful, but the ache of her body after each day questioned her judgment.

By nightfall of the sixth day since their arrival in the valley of Arronfel, everyone ate in silence around the fire. The stars sparkled overhead while the crescent moon shone upon the valley.

When Calli finished her ration, she sat back against a hill of rubble she used as a backrest. With her blanket covering her to deter the chill of the night, she gazed into the dancing flames. She tried to ignore the aching of every muscle in her body, but it returned with each movement.

Not since Donaghy and Morain had she been so sore. The trainers Phelan assigned to teach her to fight had started with a simple but arduous task to build her strength. She never expected she might appreciate their harsh training, but now she understood.

She missed her life at the palace as much as she missed her best friend. Part of her found comfort in her current independence, and Jayson's attention eased some of the pain.

When she looked to the men settling down to rest for the night, she caught two sets of eyes on her. Jayson and Eldred had ceased their discussion.

She dropped her eyes and pulled her blanket to her chest. Though Eldred turned away, Jayson's shadowed face still watched her. She wished she could read his expression among the shadows. What was he thinking?

He said something brief to Eldred and rose.

Calli frowned, wondering what he intended. More often than not, he tried to humor her. Tonight she wanted only to rest.

He made his way to her and sat down.

"Is the sky not to your liking, or shall I command the stars to go out?"

Calli shook her head and turned to him. "I've not the mood tonight for jests."

"There! See? I told him I could get a reaction." He waved to Eldred, who smiled in return. When Jayson looked to her, his smile beamed from ear to ear. "He said you've not said much the last few days. I bet him I could get you to say more than two words." He shrugged. "I guess I won."

She pressed her face into the blanket and growled in the back of her throat. Could he not see she wanted no company? She had too much on her mind.

She debated sending him away to inform Marjan of their hidden fortress. However, the idea sent her into confusion. What if she needed him while he was away? The journey would take a full moon cycle before he returned. The prospect of him being gone for so long stole away her security and filled it with loneliness. She needed him.

Calli hid her face and the warmth that rose to it at the thought. To further hide it, she rolled onto her side away from him. This could not happen. Not now. What of Phelan?

When she regained her better senses, she swore she could feel Jayson's eyes burning a hole in her back. Somewhat annoyed by his persistence, she rolled over and looked up into the blue eyes shadowed by the firelight.

"After all this time, I would think you could trust me."

She sighed and dropped her eyes. Perhaps by sending him away, she could sort through her emotions and clear her mind. "I've had much on my mind recently."

"Has it grown too heavy to bear alone?"

She took a deep breath, her patience at wits end after the long days behind them. "I need you to return to Marjan and invite him to join us, if he will. I know he'll trust you." She paused but he never replied. "I worry only about the issue of power, though I'd best leave such to him."

The look on his face could have been the result of shadows, but she doubted that. The doubts running across Jayson's expression could not hide in shadows. "He seems not a man to allow you charge of his men, nor that his men will allow you charge of them."

Calli nodded, realizing he spoke the truth and tired of the debate, which had lingered at the back of her mind. "I know, but we cannot leave them to be found by Tyrkam, and we can use the help rebuilding the fortress."

Jayson looked to the looming structure before them. "He would turn you into a lady once more."

"That I must not allow. Will you help me?" She looked up, meeting his eyes.

Jayson lifted her hand to his lips and kissed it gently. "Your servant always, my lady."

"Then the matter is settled. Y'll leave at dawn." She hoped he could not see in the dark the warmth flushing her cheeks.

Jayson stood and walked to his place near the fire to lie down. She watched him until he stretched out, before doing the same herself.

She laid down with the warmth of the fire at her back, thinking back to the beginning. Since she had met him, Jayson had stood by her without question. What would happen with a general like Marjan around?

Would she continue to lead? She had grown accustomed to the respect of those with her. Did she want to lose what she had worked so hard to gain?

If she hoped to build an army, what other option had she?

Calli yawned with fatigue. The questions could wait until the morning light. She needed rest.

꿈꿈

The next morning, Calli awoke refreshed. When she stretched, her arms ached less. She stood up and inhaled the crisp, clean air. Cool blades of grass greeted her bare feet, until she pulled her boots on.

Several figures moved about the small camp. They had packed away their gear and helped prepare the meal. Two men returned with filled water jugs they had found intact in the fortress. Though the clay jars were old, they withstood the rigors of their purpose.

"Good morning, milady."

Calli turned and caught the cheerful smile on Kirin's face. "That it is."

He gave a nod and wandered off to the pot over the crackling fire. Eldred stirred its contents and looked up. When he caught her watching him, he waved in a quick motion and returned his attention to the pot.

After rolling up her blanket and setting her things aside, Calli wandered to the paddock where the horses grazed. They had already eaten the grass to its roots and put on a few pounds. She hoped Duke continued to bloom into good condition. When he saw her, his ears pricked up and he nickered a quiet greeting.

"Same to you, old friend." She stroked the dark muzzle, welcoming the tickle of his whiskers on her hand. "Feeling better? Y've a long trek ahead. Just be sure to bring him back to us."

He nuzzled her cheek as Danny joined him.

"Looking for treats too, are you now?" Calli chuckled as the mare pressed her muzzle into her chest. "Sorry but I've none."

"Too bad."

Calli whirled at the sound of the voice that sent her nerves sparking. Her heart caught in her throat.

In the shade of the paddock wall, Jayson sharpened his sword. She swore he had not been there a moment before.

"Never do that to me!"

He paused his work and looked up. "Better to be on your toes than grow stagnant."

Regaining her composure, Calli crossed her arms. "Hiding now? I thought you better than that."

"Yes." He rose to his feet and looked down on her. "But you walked into my space."

Jayson lifted the shining blade before him and examined its perfectly clean edge in the sunlight. "As a sword should be."

"You're ready to leave?"

"As soon as I've a mount." He paused, frowning at a miniscule nick in the blade. "By your words to Duke here, I gather you'll be lending him to me."

Calli swallowed, realizing the full ramifications of what she had said. She hated giving up the gelding to anyone, but she trusted Jayson. How had he interpreted her confession to Duke?

"Marjan's farriers will be a good addition with horses to care for," Calli said. They had found him at a crucial time—the horses required work when they encountered the camp in the foothills. Duke and Danny had trod easier after the good care.

"We need a few skills if we plan to stay a while." He held up a fist and counted out his fingers. "A farrier for one, and a few more cooks, horse trainers, smiths—though Kirin will suffice for now—healers. We're sure to bring back wounded men after each encounter."

Calli sighed, seeing the scope of what she had begun spread out before her. The task seemed insurmountable without Marjan. "We need contacts in the villages."

Jayson snapped his fingers. "Excellent idea!"

She blinked in surprise.

"We've need of rangers to scout the land and report of movements of the armies."

Catching the intent of his idea, she nodded. "That to be sure, we need. A source of information, a web like a spider, connected but invisible."

His eyes sparkled in the sunlight. "Yes!"

"I'll speak to Marjan of that when he arrives."

"As my lady requests." He sheathed his sword and bowed with exaggerated flair.

While Jayson packed supplies for the trip, Calli led Duke from his paddock. He stood calmly as she saddled him and took the bit with an eagerness he had not shown before. By the time she finished, Jayson started tying the bags behind the cantle.

She stroked Duke's soft muzzle, tracing the edge of his nostrils to his lips, which twitched to take her fingers. "I'll miss you," she said to the horse, though part of her spoke to his rider. Phelan's other gift, Duke, had carried her through danger and depression. He had boosted her confidence with his companionship.

Until Jayson.

Calli glanced aside at the man as he tightened the girth another notch. Without noticing her eyes on him, he walked around behind Duke to make adjustments on the off side.

Now she would lose both for a while. The impact of the thought rattled her emotions. Had she come to depend on Jayson that much?

Not dependence, she realized, but something more.

He returned to her side of the horse and caught her eyes on him. His warm smile slipped as he studied her face. "Worry not, my lady. I'll return in good time."

At least he had mistaken her expression. Calli smiled her gratitude, but his wink warmed her cheeks.

She held Duke while Jayson jumped into the saddle with the grace of a cat.

When he picked up the reins to turn Duke away, Calli grabbed the nearest rein. Duke tossed his head in protest and Jayson looked down.

Unable to let go, Calli hesitated. Like tearing off her arm, seeing them go took a part of her she was unwilling to part with. It had to be done, but she wished otherwise. The two individuals who meant the most to her left together. "Be careful."

He gave a nod. She could have sworn a cloud passed over his face. However, the light of his spirit shone through. "I will."

His gaze lifted above her as warm hands settled on Calli's shoulders. She twisted around to catch Eldred's supportive smile. His presence filled part of the emptiness. She released the rein and lifted her hand to wave farewell.

"All will be well," The old famer said.

Eldred had taken to her as his own daughter, a role she appreciated more than he would ever know. Although she wished for Kaillen to stand at her side, Eldred's support encouraged her to continue.

She let him turn her away. Only the fading creak of leather told her of Jayson's and Duke's departure.

Chapter 51
8.8 pc 937

After an initial portal to take them within a short trek to the palace, they traveled indiscreet, their heads covered with hoods.

Gayleana knew better than to question the High Priestess about the wisdom of traveling in these perilous times. Bandits roamed the woodlands and open roads, ready to turn their greed on any traveler. Although she knew the woman guiding her was powerful, Gayleana wondered about the road travel. Why could they not have created a portal to transport them directly to the palace?

Half a moon cycle had passed since they left the remote, hidden city of Euramai, the dwelling place of the Lumathir. Each step took them closer to the dangers of Hadeon.

Worse than the warlord, Gayleana feared running into Lusiradrol. Although she had never met the dark woman, the stories of legend had fed her imagination since her youth. She would not expect to live to speak of an encounter with the demon.

However, Tahronen showed no signs of worry. On the contrary, she seemed at peace, radiating it like a wave of warm water from her core. Whether intentional or not, it helped to calm Gayleana's apprehension.

She sighed and tried to enjoy the beauty of autumn. The trees stood mighty and tall but barren of leaves, statements of the conquest of nature, never to be defeated.

After the many days on foot, Gayleana tired of travel and wished for her bed back home, the only home she remembered.

What would her sister think of that, she mused. The queen had known mostly riches and the comforts of such wealth. Though the lifestyle of the Lumathir was not lacking for amenities, it fell far from attaining the level to which Damaera had known.

Tahronen halted, her hand on Gayleana's arm.

The clash of swords and voices of men alerted them that they were close to their destination. The squeal of a horse rose above the noise of the battle not far from them.

Gayleana reached out with the magic and found the entanglement of a few dozen men beyond the rise to their right.

She followed Tahronen away from the noise, stepping over twig and leaf without a sound as she had been taught. They had hoped to avoid the armies of either side until reaching their destination.

When the noises faded, Gayleana breathed easier. However, the flow of magic twisted.

Tahronen halted again. *Calm yourself. We are not safe.*

Gayleana fought off the desire to look around. Instead, she used her higher senses to feel for them. Three men approached from in front and two others from behind. They could easily escape, but Tahronen stood her ground.

In a few seconds, the waiting ended.

The crunching of leaves and twigs announced the presence of the riders who reached the top of the hill before them. At the same sounds from behind, Gayleana turned her head slightly to see them. They wore no uniforms, only armor and weaponry.

The middle of the three in their path rode forward and halted several strides away. "You do better not to travel alone, ladies."

Gayleana peered up from beneath her hood. The rider wore the posture of a nobleman. The clean line of his jaw exposed beneath the decorated helm showed the breeding of this man. Could he be of the king's army?

"Who are you, good sir?" Tahronen asked, raising her face.

He faltered a moment. "I- I am—was—the commander of a unit of the king's army."

"And these men?"

"All that remain of my unit, my lady."

Gayleana realized that Tahronen had used some spell on him, something subtle to bring out his better qualities.

"I see. Was the palace taken so easily?"

He summarized the battle and how many of the soldiers fled from defeat. He spoke of the rumors of deceit allowing the hasty victory of Tyrkam's forces. Gayleana listened intently to the end.

When he finished, the soldier blinked as if from a daze. He stared at the two women. "If you know what's best, you'll leave this land, before you become toys for his men."

Gayleana cringed at the suggestion, but Tahronen nodded. "I appreciate the warning, but we've business with the queen."

"She is no better than the king for her position now. She has no influence over Tyrkam."

"But she lives," Tahronen calmly stated.

"Perhaps. Last I heard. The king is dead and the army scattered." His horse shifted beneath him, eager to go. "Be you mad or not, the palace is not the place you wish to be in these times."

"That is where we are needed." Tahronen gave the statement a calm finality that he could not rebuke. Instead, the soldier gave a nod and turned his mount.

With a signal to the others, they raced off.

Gayleana waited until the creatures of the forest raised their voices over the dying hoofbeats. "Should we not heed his words?"

"That we shall, but our mission remains." Without further comment, Tahronen continued in the direction she had been traveling.

Several days passed before the palace spires, some blackened by fires, peeked into view.

They paused just out of sight of Tyrkam's soldiers, who patrolled the area like ants around their colony.

Gayleana studied the organization of the armed men, as well as the large, smoking pit between them and the city. The twisting of magic confirmed what her enhanced vision told her. Tyrkam had burned bodies in that pit.

"We must be cautious."

Gayleana turned at the coarseness of Tahronen's voice. The Majera hunched over like an old woman. Gayleana realized then the illusionary magic she used.

She followed the old woman into the open.

Near the city wall, she made out the damages. Pity for her sister dimmed her spirit. What had Damaera endured in the struggle? How had she survived since?

Following in quiet contemplation, Gayleana strode through subdued streets. The people took little interest in them, giving more attention to the soldiers on patrol.

At the palace gates, Gayleana let her breath out. At least the soldiers had been few and left them alone.

"Halt, wench!" one of the sentries barked. "What business have you here?"

The voice of the Majera was not hers. However, it seemed to fit her age, Gayleana marveled. In the creak of an old woman, Tahronen said, "I am a healer. The queen sent for me."

He eyed her warily and passed his gaze over Gayleana. Self-conscious, she pulled her cloak close about her.

"This is my apprentice."

Gayleana swallowed, aware of the eyes studying her. She wished for less attention—the gazes of these rough-looking brutes made her shudder.

The guard frowned but waved them past. "Go on."

When Tahronen turned her head slightly, Gayleana caught the glint in her eyes, and the momentary disappearance of the false wrinkles lining her face.

They passed through a courtyard of men in armor. Some joked about the old woman while making lewd comments about her companion.

Gayleana tried to ignore them, avoiding eye contact. Only a couple of them wore the sad expressions of the oppressed. Two stable boys paused in their work to view them. One shook his head and turned away.

They climbed the steps to the main hall. When the sentries opened the doors on creaking hinges, Gayleana caught her breath. They entered a spectacular hall lined by two high balconies supported by smooth, round columns.

At the opposite end, one man stood out from the few others around him; partly because of the void around him that let no magic penetrate, but also because he wore the mantle of power and the cloak of menace. He turned to them, the ring of black about his mouth matching the darkness of his eyes. His darker skintone was not of any of the natives of Ayrule.

She had heard of such a man. This was Tyrkam.

He finished with those around him and excused them all. Like roaches, they scurried into the darker recesses of the hall.

Tyrkam strode toward her, a malevolent smile on his lips.

"My ladies." He halted a stride away and mocked them with a bow. "Have you business in this palace?"

When Tahronen spoke, the crack of age broke her voice. "Long ago they sent for a healer to cure the queen's illness. We have traveled far to answer the summons."

His smile grew. He signaled and a guard rushed forward. "Take them to the royal chambers."

With his attention focused on the two women, he said, "You may attempt to cure her ills, healer, but I fear her condition is an ill of the heart, not the body. As you may or may not know, the king is dead, his son vanished, and the daughter..." He shrugged, taking too much pleasure in the anguish he described. "She is gone. It is true I wish the queen alive, but it matters not."

Gayleana seethed to hear his words. She wished to cut him down then and there. However, she dared not expose her magic yet, and killing without remorse was not the way of the Majera. Tahronen had taught her that much restraint.

"I must try. I have not traveled this far to turn back."

"As you wish." He moved aside and indicated for them to follow the guard. "Do what you will."

A slim smile touched Gayleana's lips. Indeed they would do as they wished, and he could not stop them.

They followed the guard up the steps and through the corridors. After another set of steps, they emerged into a corridor overlooking a simple, elegant sitting area with a shallow pool in the center. A hint of jealousy colored her heart, but Gayleana pushed it aside. This was not the time to discuss lifestyles granted to each of them, but to pity the misfortune her sister had suffered as a result.

At the end of the hall stood two large doors carved with a man and woman walking a path. She recognized it and longed for the same bond her sister had found. But it was not her fate. Hers was the way of a mage, the Lumathir.

The guard pushed one door open for them, allowing them to slip into the queen's chambers.

After they were both in, the door echoed closed behind them. Gayleana jumped slightly at the unexpected thud and fixed her eyes on the shadow in the sunlight.

Two large windows spilled light into the room. Within the beams stood a lone figure, wasted and frail. She turned to them, deep shadows accentuating her features.

With each step she took toward the woman, Tahronen transformed to her normal self. Gayleana followed a step behind.

"What wish you of me?" The weak voice fell with exhaustion.

When they stopped within arms reach, Gayleana fought back a gasp at the gauntness of the beautiful girl Tahronen had shown her in the vision. "Sister."

Damaera frowned. "Who are you?"

"Gayleana, your younger sister."

Damaera's eyes focused on her, a touch of recognition lighting within them. "Gayle. Little Gayle? Can it be?"

With relief coursing through her, Gayleana let go all formalities and wrapped her arms around her sister. "I never realized..."

"Gayle." Damaera embraced her with hesitation, as if still unsure. "You were but a babe."

"Yes."

Damaera's arms tightened. "My little sister. Has it been so long?"

When they parted, tears dripped from Damaera's eyes and glinted from her cheek where the sun kissed it. "I had forgotten."

"I never knew, until recently." Gayleana turned to Tahronen, who threw back her hood from her youthful beauty and looked from one to the other.

"We have much to discuss, child," the Majera said. "And very little time."

Chapter 52
11.8 pc 937

Jayson traveled much faster alone than with the others. However, he was not alone.

The cold void left by *her* presence made him shiver. Lusiradrol was the Darklord, though she understood none or little of what that meant. They could not allow her to learn her true name, nor to release the clan of her dragon half. Either was as much a threat to the world as the other.

Jayson stretched out with the magic, always cautious of an attack. However, since following him, she had not risked an open confrontation. That meant nothing for his safety, since she might decide to attack at any time.

When he stopped to rest, he slept lightly, unable to take his mind from the possibility of confrontation.

The next morning he awoke to a chill. Had winter come early to the mountains?

Jayson shivered and opened his eyes. His breath crystallized out of his mouth. Then he saw her standing over him.

"So, he wakes." Her mocking tone grated on his nerves.

He cursed himself for sleeping too heavily. What could he do now? She was too powerful and too close for him to avoid her magic. Only one thing came to mind. "I wondered when you'd show yourself."

Lusiradrol squatted over him, her dark eyes menacing, and clamped her fingers around his throat. "Do not toy with me, mage."

He arched an eyebrow, slightly amused by her position. "If you were any other, I might find this interesting."

Lusiradrol looked down at her posture and snarled. She stood and stepped aside, her face livid.

Invisible forces lifted Jayson to his feet.

Lusiradrol stood with her arms crossed, showing no strain of the power she used to hold him in the air. "Tell me who you are."

He stretched his toes to reach the ground. "Jayson."

Her eyes blazed at the mockery in his voice. She stepped close and held something to his face. "What is this? What does it mean?"

Jayson recognized the brooch given to all Sh'lahmar. He carried his with him. Where had she obtained the talisman?

Hoping his expression gave nothing away, he frowned. "Looks like a sleeping dragon. A very odd piece."

"Tell me the truth!"

Magic swirled about them, the forces too powerful for him to control with even his advanced training. Nevertheless, he held his ground. "What truth? That which you wish or that which I know? Be it what you wish, I can say little. I know no more."

In a fit of rage, she sent out a blast that knocked him back against a boulder. "Fool!"

Jayson caught nothing else; his head hit the rock hard and the world disappeared. His last thought focused on Calli. He hoped she would not fall into the demon's trap.

~

"Jayson!" Calli woke with a start, searching the room sprayed with moonlight. Many days had passed since Jayson left and every night she woke to nightmares about him.

Since his leaving, she had become cautious. No one in the camp had gained her trust as he, except Eldred and his sons. However, they could not ease her fears.

The men grew restless. Although she did what she could, they had changed since Jayson left. Something was missing. As tangible as the hard bed beneath her, it stirred among them, despite the improved conditions of the fortress.

Seeing nothing to arouse her suspicions, Calli laid back down. A deep sigh carried away the fear pounding in her chest. It had been her imagination, or a dream. Tomorrow they would continue their work on rebuilding the fortress. Already, they had cleared out sleeping quarters for everyone. As the only woman, she was given her own room, although the loneliness sent shivers down her spine when night fell.

Calli rolled onto her side and pulled the thin covers over her. Closing her eyes, she thought of Jayson and wished he would return quickly. Only then would she feel at ease.

~

Jayson groaned at the throbbing in his head. It pounded for his attention, until he heard the voices. They spoke quietly around him, various discourses mostly concerning his well-being.

"He's comin' to, General."

Risking a look, Jayson opened his eyes. A nearby campfire flickered in the starless night. He tested his mouth, moistening it with each movement. In spite of his best efforts, his voice came as a whisper. "What ha—" He tried again with better success. "What happened?"

"We found you against the mountain. Looked like you been beaten."

He looked up at a man with trim hair and a sword belted at his waist. "Who are you?"

"I might ask the same, but we've seen you before, along with your companions."

Jayson searched around him. A handful of men sat near the fire. One of them looked familiar, his posture upright and proud. Marjan? The general had sworn not to cross the mountains this time of year. What had changed his mind?

At least it made his job easier.

The younger man who had stood above the one by the fire whispered something in the general's ear. Calculating eyes turned to Jayson.

"So, you're awake." Marjan stood from his chair and approached. "Thought you might well be dying."

"I ran into trouble." Jayson frowned, his memories catching up to the situation. Why had Lusiradrol left him? The rumors of her malice left no one alive, or had she other plans for him?

Focusing on the general, he thought of another question. "I thought you wished to avoid the mountains?"

The frown on the man's face said more than he needed.

Tyrkam.

"Our scouts reported a legion of Tyrkam's forces approaching our position. We are no match for their numbers but had nowhere else to hide."

"Funny you should say that." Jayson swallowed and tried to sit up. The movements sent his head reeling with pain. He winced but blinked away the spots. Next time he met Lusiradrol, he would hold his tongue.

"We found a place in the mountains. She sent me to extend an invitation."

Marjan waved one of his men over with a cup and directed him to offer it to Jayson.

"Thank you." Jayson gratefully took the cup and lifted it to his lips. The chill of the water slipped down his throat and cooled his empty stomach, reviving him.

"Interesting coincidence."

Jayson swallowed another mouthful, a hint of a grin tugging at the corners of his lips. "I'll agree. That you stopped for me, I wish to thank you."

"Thank me when it matters." Marjan wore his hard face, the distrust apparent. "My men had not rested in two days when we found you and the horse. Not care was it but an excuse to rest. We must move deep into the mountains with haste. Tyrkam is set on extinguishing all opposition."

Jayson dropped his eyes and lowered the cup. "I see." Marjan had made good time for moving such a massive force. How fast could Hadeon's armies move?

At least Arronfel was secure. If they could reach the valley without trouble, the enemy would never find them.

"What is this place you found?"

One thing that impressed him about Marjan was the man's pragmatism. Jayson questioned how he would accept magic, particularly since the others had found it difficult. "A hidden fortress deep within the mountain. We stumbled upon it by accident."

Shadows danced across the harsh lines of Marjan's face. Jayson read the question before the general could ask. "An ancient city thought legend but real. The lady awaits us there."

"I've no patience for games." The words came out in a growl. At that, Jayson realized how hard these men had traveled and fought to survive. Marjan thought he joked.

"I speak truth, General. I swear if I am wrong my soul is yours."

A smirk crept to Marjan's lips, surprising Jayson at the suddenness. "Keep your soul. If your word is true, I'll follow you to this fortress."

Jayson let out an inaudible sigh. "You'll not be disappointed."

With a nod, Marjan rose and turned to reclaim his seat near the fire. Jayson wondered how he had assumed so much about the general. At least Marjan proved he was as human as the rest.

That was the problem. Many men desired power. Would Marjan be willing to share that power as others joined their ranks?

Jayson laid down again, his eyes to the fire. Calli would be on her own to prove herself, as she had with the others. With the fire that burned inside her, he doubted she would back down.

He took some comfort in that. However, as much as he wished to see the day she proved her worth as a warrior, he would have to leave her. Lusiradrol knew too much. He had to warn the Sh'lahmar.

He wished he knew why had she allowed him to live.

Chapter 53
18.8 pc 937

Jayson recognized the aura of leadership radiating from General Marjan. The general's poise and confidence carried the respect of his men; his fairness and reason sealed it. Calli could never achieve the same.

They rode together ahead of the remaining regiment through the mountains. At the crags that had hindered Calli's group, Marjan's soldiers quickly filled them in. They moved with purpose and efficiency pushed on by the hope of finding rest at the end of their journey and the fear of what followed their trail.

With that motivation, they would reach the gate much quicker than he had imagined possible for such a large group.

Jayson glanced back at the triple columns of weary soldiers. They had traveled fast and far, and soon they would be rewarded with rest. Part of their work involved herding goats, sheep, and cattle as part of their supplies, oxen to pull the wagons half empty of crates and barrels, and a couple hundred cavalry horses. All the animals walked with low heads, their sides as shallow as the men's.

The valley would fatten the animals and revive the men. However, they would have a good deal of work to make the fortress a home.

He turned forward again in the saddle.

What would they think of magic? Many mortals had heard dark tales of magic beings, mostly to scare children into behaving. Few had heard the truth, of the good things magic could do. Would they accept living in a place shrouded by magic and sustained by it?

He could only hope.

The sun hung low over the mountains when Jayson spied the landmarks around the hidden passage not far ahead. They continued forward, shadows stretching long fingers across their path.

As the sun touched the western peaks, they reached the rock face.

"Halt your men, general." Jayson reined Duke to a stand.

With a frown, Marjan called back for the columns to halt and rest. "Rest here is not the answer."

Jayson met the steady gaze of the veteran leader. With that look, they dismounted. Marjan followed him to the rock face.

"If you will trust me, close your eyes and calm your mind."

For a second, Jayson thought the task too great for the man, but Marjan humored him. "Now, the key lies within you. It is an act of faith and hope. Let it grow."

"You toy with me."

"Not so. Trust me, General."

Marjan took a deep breath. When the stern lines of his face softened, Jayson placed his hands on the general's shoulders and led him to the wall. They passed through without incident to the lush lands of Arronfel.

"Now, open your eyes."

Marjan obeyed, his eyes immediately widening in wonder. "What devilry is this?" He turned on Jayson. "Dark magic!"

"Not at all." Jayson had expected as much. "You may return at any time, if you wish." He stretched his arm toward the gray haze behind them, where dark figures had gathered. Their muffled voices called for their leader.

Although suspicion poisoned his tone, the spark in the general's eye hinted of his interest in the valley. "Where are we?"

"The hidden lands of Arronfel, abandoned long ago by the Ancients."

Marjan scanned the clear, trickling stream and the hill on the opposite bank. His face revealed nothing about his mood. "I should return to my men."

Jayson bowed slightly and followed behind the general. They stepped from the mountain to a sea of curious faces.

On the other side, questions rose from the men who had witnessed the spectacle. Marjan lifted his hands to his face as if unsure he had survived.

Jayson led Duke to the mountain, meeting the curiosity in the general's gaze. To the others, he said, "Follow, if you will, but only those with peace in their hearts shall pass."

Whispers carried among the men. They could do as they wished, but he had carried out his task. Marjan had to make his own decisions.

In the meantime, shadows filled the valley with the coming of night. His heart yearned to see Calli again, though he ached to tell her he had to leave once more. He wished he had more time, but Lusiradrol's discovery of the brooch had cut their time short. He had to warn the others before it was too late to stop her.

He should never have joined Calli when he saw her, but he had to know why the colors of magic were different around her than other people. More than that, however, that first look had stirred feelings in him he had never known. He could not leave her without learning more, nor could he have left her in danger.

Eager to return to her, Jayson mounted Duke, who perked up at the sight of the valley. "We're home, boy." He patted the gelding's neck and started forward.

"Will you so quickly dismiss us?" a gruff voice questioned.

Jayson twisted with the creak of leather behind him. A smile crept up his face. Perhaps magic would not deter them. As it should be.

Marjan mounted and rode up to him. Behind him filed men who scanned the scene with wonderment. They hurried forward. "I must admit to some hesitation," Marjan said, "but I'll not deprive my men and animals of the resources here."

With a wry smile, Jayson met his gaze. "I promise you'll not be disappointed."

Both of them rode through the shallow river, splashing cool water up with the horses' steps.

They climbed the hill on the opposite bank and stopped at the top. While Marjan turned to check his men, Jayson reached out through the magic toward the fortress at the other end of the valley. Although her presence created only a small disturbance in the magic, he found Calli.

Jayson turned to the general. "If you'll excuse me—"

Marjan turned.

"—I'll ride on and announce your coming." At least it gave him an excuse to rush off to the fortress.

The general nodded but said nothing, his eyes on the men trickling through the passage and the many who stopped at the stream to drink and fill their waterskins.

With no mind to wait, Jayson touched his heels to Duke's sides. The gelding needed no motivation and surged forward.

Jayson leaned forward in the saddle, the horse's long, dark mane slapping his arms with each stride.

In minutes, they reached the fortress of Linfrathâr. Duke breathed hard beneath him and slowed to a walk amid the cheers of the men.

"You made good time." Eldred smiled and patted Duke's neck, walking beside him. "And to think she worried."

Jayson smiled down at the old farmer and briefly clasped his hand. When he looked forward again, Calli strode toward him, nearly running from the door of the lowest level of the fortress.

He jumped from the saddle and led Duke the rest of the way to meet her. His feet welcomed the soft grass cushioning each step after the hard road.

When she was half the short distance from them, Duke nickered. The greeting set her feet hurrying faster. Jayson stopped, expecting her to reach him in seconds. Her loose, fiery waves of hair bounced from her shoulders with each step, blazing within the red light of dusk.

When she reached him, she flung her arms around the gelding's neck. "How I missed you, my old friend." Duke lowered his head and nickered softly.

The scene both lightened his mood and hurt his pride, though less the latter. He should have expected as much. Jayson shook his head, fighting against a smirk. "That's gratitude for you."

Calli stood back as if realizing for the first time that he stood there. Something in her eyes and the sudden flush of her cheeks told him she could not express what she wished at that moment. "Of course, I'm glad to have you back as well, Jayson."

At the thunder of racing hooves, she looked past him. Jayson turned, aware that she stepped close to him at the approaching rider.

Marjan reined his bay to a hard stop and acknowledged her with a nod. "My lady." He glanced to Jayson but focused his words on her.

"General. I see Jayson brought you as I asked."

"Indeed." Marjan dismounted and handed his reins to one of the men standing nearby. "We've matters to discuss, I hear."

His quick glance was all Jayson needed to excuse himself. He had plans to make, and needed to rest his weary body for the long journey ahead. "If you'll excuse me. General. Calli."

After a nod to each and a lingering gaze of Calli, he mouthed, *Good luck,* and led Duke away.

❧

Calli watched Jayson leave, wishing they had more time to talk. He was unusually tense, or perhaps she saw the result of his hard, fast travels of the last twelve days. Whatever it was, he needed rest to clear his head. Then, she might steal a moment.

"You've a good man there." Marjan's words broke her thoughts.

She allowed a faint smile and fixed her attention on the rough-looking general. "I know."

The moment she had dreaded and hoped for had come, much sooner than she expected. "Join me inside?"

After a look back, he started toward the fortress.

Calli followed his gaze, impressed by the numbers swelling over the hill at the other end of the valley. Returning her attention to the general, she strode through the rubble into the fortress.

She led Marjan through the corridors now familiar to her, up one of the stairways, to one of the many large rooms. The one they entered overlooked the second level courtyards below. Though the wood had long ago rotted too much to sit on, the chairs had lasted as most of the doors—ready to crumble in one's hands. She and the others had erected candelabra in some of the rooms, using the remaining wax as little as possible. As soon as she had seen the men approach, she ordered the room lit for this meeting.

Marjan took easy strides, circling the room and examining the elaborate designs carved into the stone. "Impressive. He said you found it by accident?"

"Yes. Nothing but dumb luck that one of my own stumbled through the mountain wall."

He gave a nod, his only indication of the thought processes in his head.

"Makes me wonder why it was abandoned." This time he met her eyes, the shadows from the candles flickering coldly from his gaze.

"I'd not wish to find out while we reside here." Calli stood near one of the tall, glassless windows looking over the valley and inhaled the clean, cool breeze. "If y've no desire to stay, I'll not force you."

"Mistake not my words, Lady Calli," he said with a hint of surprise in his voice. "I've as much need to hide as you, and I'll not refuse shared resources."

Shared... Good word. Hope rose within her. "So, you intend not to take my authority."

A grim smile fell across his rough features. "That you are a woman of great skill, I'll not deny. You know the looks my men gave. I cannot say they respect you the same. I'll not lie to you o' that."

He stopped before her. "Most men know women for nothing but keeping a home. However, I knew the king. I knew the men who trained you. Was many a time in my ranks they outwitted the enemy."

Calli stared, her eyes widening. He had commanded Donaghy and Morain?

Marjan turned to the window. "Men of a skill few possessed, which was why I recommended them to the king to train his guards. He had need for them after his last was killed."

He paused and frowned, his eyes studying her in thought. Calli wondered if he had ever met her father.

Shrugging away whatever thoughts he had pondered in those few seconds, he continued, "If they trained you, I trust you know how to fight. I'll not question it, but my men are restless to taste vengeance for the loss of comrades. They'll respect no less than the leadership they know."

When he turned to face her again, Calli recognized in his countenance the same level of respect Phelan had granted her in the end. It occurred to her that, as in her previous encounter with the general, he had never spoken in a condescending tone, although his choice of words had sometimes bothered her. If he treated all his men with the same courtesy, she understood why they would stand by him without question.

"I'll not hand over this place to anyone."

"You mistake my words, Lady Calli," Marjan said. He let out a sigh, dropping his shoulders in an unexpected expression of fatigue. She suspected he would never allow it to show in front of his men. "Though they follow me, they'll recognize your authority here. I will see to that. I ask that you leave the king's army in my care and challenge not my authority over them. In that you will lose."

"However, in return I'll counsel the lady of this land as she wishes." He bowed with all the grace and dignity of a nobleman. "I recognize your claim to this place and respect the work you've done. As a woman, that is no modest feat."

Calli could think of nothing to say. "Thank you," was all that came to mind, though seemed less than what Marjan deserved. "I accept your agreement."

"Alliance."

She smiled and offered her hand. "I accept your alliance, General. I hereby agree that all matters of building a new army are yours to command."

"I yield to your authority as the bearer of the seal of Cavatar, Lady of Arronfel."

A small shudder rippled through her, but she ignored it. At least he had not called her queen. She hoped with all her heart that the rightful queen of Cavatar still lived. The title felt wrong in regards to herself. "It is agreed then. My men will show you and yours where to rest for the night."

"Beneath the stars will be enough. We've much work to do before settling into this place."

"As you wish. Rest your men and animals. We've a long winter ahead to make ready for spring campaigns you might plan." Though he seemed genuinely relieved, Calli wondered how much of this encounter weighed on his mind. Perhaps the travel had worn him out.

A great weight lifted from her shoulders with his reassuring words.

All able bodies were needed to fix the deserted fortress city of Linfrathâr. With a couple thousand more, that task would move fast, though growing pains were inevitable.

At least Jayson had returned.

She smiled and exited the room behind the general. At least she had that.

Chapter 54
22.8 pc 937

His steps echoed softly in the dark passages. Jayson made no attempt to hide them. In the moonlit corridors, he discerned the outlines of the stone benches left by their makers, now cleared of the dust of ages like those in the other passages in the fortress.

Calli and the others had managed to clean up most of the bottom two levels and part of the third before he had returned. Four days had passed since Marjan's men arrived with him. Most of the fortress's endless passages had been cleared with the help of all the men working together.

For the first time since he could remember, he had slept on something other than the ground. The rest had done him wonders in recovering.

The memory of his confrontation with Lusiradrol made him wince. Why had she allowed him to live? What game did she play? Had she plans to use him in the hopes he would expose the answer to the riddle that plagued her? She must have realized he would never betray his secret.

A frown crept over his face before he realized. He passed his hands over the beard he had trimmed to stubble since returning to Arronfel. Though the black hair on his head had grown a little, it had spilled to his shoulders for many years. His master's words criticized him for his preference as a danger in battle, but he had long ago learned to heed his own judgment.

He would hear those words again soon enough.

He shook his head and continued through the quiet corridors. His mind returned to the issue concerning him most. Since he had returned with Marjan, he had found no time to talk with Calli. Finally, with the newcomers settling into their new home, everyone relaxed into a state of acceptance. Routines started to form, which the men worked into their days. With routines came a comfort level that lent to a calm predictability.

Now was the best time to break from the work. He had stayed too long. Hopefully Lusiradrol had not learned more, but she would try.

Before he left, he had to say farewell to Calli. He could not leave with her wondering whether she would see him again. The friendship between them had grown strong. More than likely he would not return, but instead would be called to serve the Sh'lahmar to protect it against the now inevitable invasion by the black dragon.

Saying farewell to Calli would be difficult. Already, she held his heart within her hands. He had not hidden his feelings but had not taken them further than he dared. If she asked, he would not deny the truth. That much he could reveal to her without regret, but he was afraid. She had given her heart to another. By never revealing his feelings, he might spare himself the hurt of learning she still loved the man who had pledged his love to her.

His breath quickened with each step to her door. This should not be a difficult task. Why did it make him so uneasy? He took a deep breath to calm himself and knocked twice. When no one answered, he knocked again, louder.

Still no answer. Could she be asleep?

It's too early for her to rest, he answered his question and put his hand to the door. He hesitated a moment, not wishing to interrupt her sleep. However, the desire to speak with her overrode formality and he pushed the door open. "My lady," he said in a hushed voice.

Moonlight spilled through the open window onto an empty bed. A quick scan turned up a barren room. Where was she?

Puzzled, Jayson closed the door with only a faint squeak of old hinges. Through the magic, he reached out for her unique presence. He should have done so sooner, but had expected her to be here.

He found her near, much closer than he expected. She stood outside near the wall on this upper level, which was still whole. Whatever had damaged the lower levels had not climbed further than the third tier.

Jayson smiled and followed her presence through the corridors to the nearest exit into the air.

On silent feet he approached the doorway. She stood with her back to him on a rail-lined terrace looking out over the third tier of the fortress and facing out over the valley. Loose red waves glistened with silver under the moonlight. Her robe and gown billowed in the breeze about her.

He stood a moment, frozen in the enchantment of the image. Not the skilled fighter he had come to know, but a lady in all her delicate charms stood alone.

She held something before her. When moonlight glinted off a slim chain, he realized she held the royal seal aloft. Her words to Marjan drifted back from his memories. The seal had represented a promise to another man.

Part of him died at the thought, but the other part of him reasoned that he cared no less for her. That was why it had hurt, and why he had released it from his mind. She had never brought it up before or since. He had chosen to ignore it as much as he could, telling himself he had a duty to perform.

Until now.

After a deep breath, he stepped outside the doorway.

Calli dropped her eyes and turned her head slightly. "I wondered when we would have a moment."

Jayson blinked, his thoughts catching up only when she turned her smile to him.

"Come now, Jayson. I know you better. Never have you been one to show surprise. Have I caught you in your own thoughts this once?"

He walked forward with a sheepish grin and stopped at the chest high wall next to her. "You caught me."

She turned to him, the moonlight dancing over the soft lines of her face. "Liar."

He looked down at her, admiring the view, and shrugged. "What would you have me say?"

"You've said so little since you returned but your eyes say so much. I've seen the likes before. Something is on your mind."

Without a word, he took the pendant she held. She dropped her hands and watched as he turned it over to study the seal.

"A gift, as you know," she said quietly. Her voice faded. "Now I've no way to know what happened. I have no home but this. Marjan agreed that as long as I bear the seal, I bear the authority it brings. He has kept his word to provide counsel. Though he calls me the Lady of Arronfel, I'll not give up my desire for vengeance."

A smile tugged at the corners of his lips. The Lady of Arronfel. He could not have given her a more appropriate title. "A warrior or a lady suits you. Which is more accurate I cannot say."

Jayson set the pendant gently to her chest as it had been, noting how it laid above her breasts.

"A lady, as you warned." She sighed and looked out over the valley. "I must again prove myself or risk the life I ran from. The daughter of Kaillen was not meant to stay locked within walls."

When she looked up at him, he met her eyes and swallowed. He could fight demons and dragons but could not face the truth before him.

"A more worthy truth I've not heard." Such a truth had drawn him to her in the first place and kept him at her side for this long.

She smiled and patted his chest. "You know me too well."

"Admire is more like it."

Calli quickly looked away without a reply. Seeing how the compliment affected her, he took the opportunity to put his hand on her shoulder in support.

"Thank you, Jayson, for all you've done." When she laid her head against his shoulder, he smiled and wrapped his arms around her. The warmth of her body calmed the worries at the back of his mind.

"Stay here," she whispered.

He buried his face in her soft locks, unsure what to say. She had read him too well.

"You plan to leave again," she quietly said. "I recognized the look on your face when you returned. It was as my parting with Phelan."

"I was never meant to stay as long as I have. Now—" He sighed, trying to let go of the jealousy that tightened in his chest. "Now, I've stayed too long."

She looked up to meet his eyes. Moonlight washed her face in sorrow and regrets. He wished he could make her smile again, but when he could not touch the humor in himself, he knew not what to do or say.

Instead of words, he brushed the red hair from her face, memorizing it for future reference.

She tried to smile but failed.

Before either broke the spell with words, he turned and strode away, almost running to get away before he could change his mind. He had to leave now if he was going to leave at all.

Although he knew it was for the best, part of him regretted that she made no effort to follow. No steps or words trailed behind him.

❧❧

Calli watched him go, her heart grieving over the loss. Despite their time spent together, she could not help feeling that he hid something from her. She wanted to understand him better.

She turned to the valley again, hoping to catch a glimpse as he rode to the gateway. Despite the demands on her, she would never forget him.

After a time, she saw him below, taking the reins of one of Marjan's warhorses. He swung up in the saddle and briefly turned his face up to her. A moment later, he turned the horse and rode for the gateway.

Chapter 55
22.8 pc 937

Makleor watched the happenings from the privacy of his tower in Wynmere, where no one dared disturb him. Amid the stacks of books floated the images that most interested him.

At last the Sh'lahmar guards would know of the threat to them. However, the circumstances fell into the guidance of the prophecy. As it was foretold by the white dragon, so it would happen. Lusiradrol was closer than she realized to the truth.

Soon, he consoled himself. All would fall into place as realized by Gilthiel.

In the seeing orb, the images changed. Three women stood facing each other, each a reflection of the other. A thin smile crept to his lips. Tahronen had claimed her lost child. The Lumathir prepared for the coming.

When the prophecy arrived, he would find rest. In the meantime, Tyrkam had requested his presence. He would not disappoint the warlord, nor miss the opportunity to add his support to Tahronen.

However, Makleor refused to travel the miles. Instead, he called forth a portal. The magic called to him, connecting to a chamber at the palace. Leaning on his staff, Makleor stepped through and into a dim room. The portal carried him instantly to his destination, though it tired him to use so much power.

⁂

"He is here." Tahronen opened her eyes and turned her head in a listening posture.

Damaera frowned. "Who is it?"

A knowing smile spread over Tahronen's face.

Gayleana turned. "He is the beginning and the end."

"Who?" Damaera looked from one to the other, hoping for more of an answer. She grew frustrated with their riddles.

Then she caught it, a powerful magic. It reminded her of the night Tyrkam invaded. Colors twisted over one another in an orderly dance.

Tahronen turned to her, her eyes sad but her voice firm. "He is called Makleor. Because of his mistake we are here."

They had told her the story of the death of the beast haunting her daughter and about the mage involved. Not until she heard the full story had she ever believed Istaria. Now, she realized what the girl had been telling her all those years and why her nightmares had focused on dragons.

Although Damaera hated the dragon for what it had cost her daughter, she understood it was necessary.

However, part of her loathed the old mage who had started the prophecy in action. The other part of her hated him for working with Tyrkam, the man who had broken her family apart.

Damaera silently seethed at the thought of working with him.

Despite her feelings, she trusted Tahronen's judgment that he was necessary to the resolution of the prophecy. As she had learned throughout her life, one need not like the person required to complete a task.

"He is on his way now," Gayleana said.

Damaera fought away a scowl at the thought but continued to focus as Tahronen had been trying to teach her. Unlike her sister, who had grown up training to use magic, she had little training. Her purpose to this point had been to continue the line of magic users.

Now, however, they needed her for more. She tried to learn, but the abilities bred into her came with difficulty. Using magic was not as easy for her as for her sister. Sensing it had come easy, almost effortlessly.

When the door opened, the magic spiked with her emotions. A ball of lightening materialized around the old man who entered. His long gray beard contrasted the midnight blue of his billowing cloak. The crystal held by the ivory dragon topping his staff glowed, absorbing the energy. In seconds, it dispelled everything.

All eyes turned to Damaera before she realized her anger had caused the attack. She let out a sigh, dropping her shoulders, and regained her composure. No good would come from losing her temper. "Forgive me. You must be Makleor."

He hobbled nearer to the three, his staff tapping on the stone floor.

An uneasy feeling crept up Damaera's spine at the power approaching, similar to Tahronen but not as pure as her radiance.

He stopped a stride away and looked up from under his hood. His good eye sparked with life, fixed on her. "So much anger, my dear. So much pain." He shook his head.

Damaera clamped her jaw. How could he know of her pain, the ache tearing her soul apart? They had just met.

"I see now, that which resides in you has strengthened her."

She straightened, fully comprehending what he spoke of—her daughter. Her emotions stirred her to full alert. "What do you know of Istaria?"

"Only the strongest spirit would contain his power. That came from you. That is why he chose her."

"What do you know of my daughter?"

A smile crept out from beneath the gray beard. "Beware a mother's wrath." His amusement lifted his voice. "Lest she attempt to burn you with lightening."

Stricken for her rudeness, Damaera closed her mouth on a rebuke and dropped her eyes. The gentle reprimand of his tone stole the fuel of her emotional outburst.

"She is well, my dear, but you've more training ahead if ever you wish to live to see the ones you love again."

Damaera nodded, submitting to the truth he spoke. Indeed, she would need the skills of magic from her birthright. If nothing else, they might at least save her when Tyrkam decided she was no longer useful.

The old mage looked on her with a whimsical smile before turning to Tahronen. To her, he granted a bow as low as he could. "It has been long since you honored me."

Tahronen granted him a nod as of royalty acknowledging a lesser noble. "You serve us well. What news have you?"

Makleor told them of Istaria and also of the Sh'lahmar. When she realized he also spoke of Calli, a great weight lifted from Damaera's shoulders. That she had joined forces with General Marjan and what remained of his regiment lifted Damaera's spirits. Although the general could be harsh on his men when necessary, he had always shown respect to those he served.

Who the Sh'lahmar guard was bothered her, however. From what Tahronen and Gayleana had described, these men learned as the Lumathir, but used their skills to maintain the sleep of the red dragons. Why had such a man teamed with Calli? Why had he left?

Tahronen showed no reaction to the news. Either she knew something of it already or her experience provided a cushion of wisdom.

Gayleana met her eyes when she glanced aside. *Worry not, sister.* The words whispered in Damaera's mind in the same way Istaria had spoken to her. *All will be revealed when the time is right. We cannot risk Lusiradrol learning.*

She wished to understand everything now and hated the wait. Nevertheless, her patience held fast, though it would not last long.

Chapter 56
1.9 pc 937

Lusiradrol followed him. That much he knew by the void lingering in the magic. Five days had passed since he rode from the valley, one less than when she had found him. Although she had not confronted him, he knew she would.

However, she might as well follow him back to the vault. If that happened, no one would be safe.

What could he do that she had not already considered?

Jayson puzzled over the question, limited in answers by his meager abilities. He could not teleport as a full mage could, nor could he disguise his presence from one as powerful as Lusiradrol.

Either option would be preferable to leading her to the Sh'lahmar.

The horse beneath him lifted its head, ears pricked, listening to something. Jayson took the warning and halted. If an animal with the experience of one of Marjan's warhorses sensed danger, he would not deny its instincts.

The horse lifted its head high and scanned around them. Its attention jerked from one focus to another. The tension in its body alerted Jayson to the seriousness of the matter. He stroked the red hide, trying to calm himself more than the horse. "Easy, boy."

The horse snorted but stood frozen in place.

Aware of the approaching void, Jayson pulled on the magic, gathering it within himself in preparation. His connection grew.

Her presence nearly consumed him.

Jayson gripped the reins and pulled his cloak tight about him to block out the wind blowing up the mountainside with winter's early chill. Perhaps she had not the patience to follow. *Pity,* he thought, *I had hoped to make the journey in peace. At least I've no more worry of your intentions.*

Despite the humor of his thoughts, the aura of the Darklord penetrated his soul, latching onto the instinct to fear it. He was ready, although if she chose, she could destroy him at any time.

He waited, the wind picking up and sending his cloak flapping behind him.

"What trickery have you fallen to?" he called to her, clutching his cloak in the cold air.

A cackle broke over the roar of the wind. With its fading, the wind died.

Jayson peered around him, wary of further assault. However, the calm of the mountains returned. He urged the horse forward, cautious yet of the dangers around him. She toyed with him. What could he do but continue on as fast as he dared? Whether she followed or not was less of a concern now.

Jayson reached out with magic but found nothing of Lusiradrol. Had she left him with plans to find him later? Or had she found other things to amuse herself?

He shuddered at the thought. Would Calli be safe in Arronfel? Lusiradrol knew where to find her, but would the ancient spells continue to hold against the dragonwoman's determination?

Why had Calli made such a pact? Had he the powers to go back in time, he would have arranged to meet Calli before Lusiradrol sank her claws in Calli's naiveté.

But he could not. Now, he had to trust Calli to fate's hand.

He had to trust that Lusiradrol would leave him to his mission and hoped the incident was nothing more than a reminder of her powers.

Chapter 57
14.9 pc 937

Half a moon cycle passed without confronting Lusiradrol. The chill of winter blew across the land. Jayson detected nothing more of her presence. Either she hid it well, or, as he feared, every day while he rode in peace, she decided to take out her amusements on Calli.

Every day he wished he had stayed with Calli, to protect her. Every day he wondered how she fared. He wished to stand at her side and help train the army, and serve her in whatever need she had. Despite his morning meditations, he had been unable to clear his heart of the feelings rooted there.

Every waking moment he longed to see her again. He could not banish it, but neither did he wish to. Where he once vowed his life to the Sh'lahmar, he now desired to give it to Calli.

As much as he tried to forget her, he could not. With only two days until he reached the entrance of the compound, he had not purified his mind and heart.

His master would be disappointed that he had allowed his feelings to interfere with his duty.

But he refused to give up the lightness of his heart every time he stood in her presence. *Master Haiberuk can take his code and—*

"Jayson."

He froze at the calm tone, his heart in his throat, and suppressed a grimace. He swallowed and halted the horse before turning to the source of the familiar voice.

A robed figure stood on a ledge of rock to his left; a hooded figure he recognized. The man looked up, his eyes sparkling with ancient powers. That face had not changed in the eight seasons since he had been sent to follow Darius, nor should it have on an immortal being.

"A long time have we awaited your return."

"Forgive me, Master." Jayson paused, his mind catching up to him that he had not noticed Haiberuk's presence in the magic sooner. Had he been that distracted? "I've had some trouble."

A wry smile crept up on the immortal's face. "You have been followed for some time."

He should have known the master would be aware of his actions, as well as those of the black dragon. He had also suspected her of following, though just out of range of his senses or masking her presence.

"Your mind is impure. You must cleanse it of these emotions before you can proceed. Join me." The figure faded and materialized on the ground by the horse's head.

A surge of power told Jayson what he expected. Haiberuk created a portal, which, while invisible to the eye, stirred the forces of magic into a vortex. He led the horse through without trouble with Jayson still in the saddle.

They emerged in the compound of the Sh'lahmar before Jayson could take a breath of relief. At least Lusiradrol could not follow him to the front door. The Majera's powers masked the area. They would have a few days more to prepare.

The few simple buildings around a square with a well in the center brought a sense of peace he had forgotten. For too many years he had been away. Home had never felt as welcome, nor as fragile. Although magic guarded it with the trees and jagged hills, it would pose very little challenge to a determined Lusiradrol.

For the moment, he found peace in the quiet living area.

Jayson dismounted as a young boy materialized and approached on foot. Although he knew such simple tricks as invisibility, they would never have hid him from Lusiradrol.

The acolyte bowed to Haiberuk and took the reins of the horse. With his eyes on the robed lad who led the horse away, the immortal said, "A fast learner, though a bit of a dreamer."

Jayson nodded. A smile crept to his lips with the awakening of memories. "Reminds you of someone?"

The look on Haiberuk's face told him the master caught on to the meaning of his words.

"But he grew in discipline. Young Aeric has far to go." His tone dropped and he turned to Jayson with a grave expression. "However, all will be needed in the days ahead if we are to defend the vault."

Jayson nodded, returning his attention to the matter at hand. He followed the master to one of the structures. Its simple design with few windows matched the other buildings around the square, each nearly identical to the other. Unlike the Lumathir in their ancient city behind high walls, the Sh'lahmar lived in simplicity behind a shield of magic. Few would think to look for the power of the guards within such simple living quarters.

Only the Son'tal lived with the master, although they rotated overseeing the other houses. The master reminded them every morning of the importance of their jobs.

At that thought, Jayson grimaced. Had he come all this way to face his death for leading their enemy to this area? What else could he have done?

"Worry not, child," Haiberuk said without turning from the doorway. Jayson had not been called a child in a long while, but the master referred to all his followers as children. In a way, Jayson supposed that they were as much Haiberuk's children as Tahronen's, although Haiberuk had not interfered as his sister had.

Jayson paused at the doorway, peering into the dim main room. In the center was a circular area a step down from the entrance floor. Panels of ancient languages surrounded the meditation chamber. Light other than the lone candle in the center of the room highlighted the histories written on them.

Haiberuk stopped in the center area and turned to face him before sitting. Jayson stepped down and sat on the opposite side of the candle.

"We've not much time, as you know, and need all those present to defend against her." Haiberuk slipped the hood from his head of golden blonde hair, his blue eyes sparkling in the flicker of the candlelight with the power restrained. A natural inner light deterred the shadows from his face. "Free your mind of this burden and release your heart of its guilt."

Jayson nodded and began his meditations with a few deep breaths. As his head cleared, he noticed the connection of power with his master. He allowed Haiberuk to probe his emotions and memories to aid in the purification.

Although his master succeeded in pushing aside his worry for Calli, he touched none of the other emotions connected to her. This surprised Jayson, but he let it fall aside as his whole being cleared with the help of the master.

The jumble lifted layer by layer, clearing his focus on the magic. It grew more distinct than it had since leaving the security of the grounds. In the shedding of his stresses and worries, he found a new peace within himself. With his cooperation, Haiberuk peeled away the layers weighing on his conscience.

With his soul balanced again, Jayson opened his eyes. The refreshing freedom within him tuned into the magic around them with a clarity he had forgotten existed.

Haiberuk smiled. The deep shadows of the room failed to penetrate his gaze. "You are closer. In the morning we will continue the purification."

With that dismissal, Jayson rose on stiff legs aching with each movement. Had he been sitting that long? He realized the answer when he glanced out at the starry sky through the window.

He bowed to his master and left the shelter. Outside in the cool of night, lights shimmered from a few square windows. On the steps of one of the shelters sat two men he recognized, both wearing the black cloaks of the elite guard. By the occasional nod or smile, he realized they conversed using mindspeech, their thoughts sent to each other. Master Haiberuk had always taught his pupils to respect the presence of others. In this way, they disturbed no one.

At Jayson's approached, they both turned. Astonishment stole across their countenances.

Jayson?

He grinned. *That's the name I was given, although others have called me worse.*

The speaker shook his head and stood. *Always the dragon tongue.* All of an imposing six and a half feet, Cadel reached out and embraced him. *Good to see you, old friend.*

When Cadel let him go, the average-sized Gavin offered a less vigorous embrace. Jayson accepted both with enthusiasm, the warmth of old friendships uniting him with the past more than Master Haiberuk could.

Where have you been all these years?

The drill from the beginning of his advanced training flowed easily into his mind. The elite guards knew nothing of the Son'tal, the chosen of Haiberuk who comprised his council. They knew only that if they broke their vow of silence, their lives would not be spared, nor would the lives of outsiders who learned of their secret.

My errands for Master Haiberuk have carried me on distant travels to learn what I could.

They nodded, watching him with an intensity that expected more. Jayson told them of the princess and Darius and the white dragon's spirit safe in the Second Realm, leaving out the detail about following Darius since he left. They had served with the banished guard and would ask too many questions. He also told them of the fall of Cavatar. However, he said nothing of Calli or Lusiradrol. That he would leave to Haiberuk.

In return, they told him of changes in the guard and the increased vigilance of Master Haiberuk in recent cycles.

None of them gave away much detail, trained to use discretion since they were young boys sent from their parents. When they finished, the moon shone its light on them.

The two guards showed Jayson where he could sleep in their single-room house rather than with the master. He gladly stretched out on the simple grass mat in the shelter, amid the other men already asleep near the fire in the center.

As the calm of sleep passed over him, he looked back once more. His thoughts passed over Calli before changing to his purpose for returning.

The worst was yet to come.

Chapter 58
16.9 pc 937

Having slept better than he had in a long time, Jayson woke after the others disappeared to their training and duties. He welcomed the time alone to sort through the memories floating back to his consciousness.

A bowl of food materialized near his sleeping mat. With a smile, he accepted the sweetened porridge, which satisfied his stomach, and enjoyed the warmth of the fire. The larger meal would come later.

When he finished, he left the empty bowl and wandered out into the square.

A couple of young boys swept away a light dusting of snow from the tightly fitted stones connecting the buildings to the well. On his way to Haiberuk's shelter, he passed the acolytes with their white garments under their heavy, winter robes. They paused in their work and bowed to him.

How long had it been since he had earned such respect? Thirty years? Forty? Age was irrelevant he had discovered. Most outsiders had assumed he was quite young, a fraction of the years he claimed. Magic had that affect.

Jayson sighed away the thoughts. Although it boosted his pride, Master Haiberuk would strike him down for such thinking. Pride in oneself overshadowed the purpose of the Sh'lahmar. However, pride in the service of others that came from the pure desire to serve enlightened the provider of the service.

After acknowledging each of the boys with a nod, he continued on his way to the shelter. When he looked up, Master Haiberuk stood at the top of the three steps to his door. With his hood off, the sun set him aglow. His smile chased away any doubts.

Jayson returned the smile, unable to resist the light mood of his master. Without a word, he followed Haiberuk into the dim room for another session of purification. He welcomed the touch of magic helping to free his spirit of disturbing thoughts.

When he emerged, the sun shone from its zenith in the sky, warming the air. Clouds floated idly by on the light winds. Many of the guards and trainees had returned from their chores. The mass of their power together flooded his connection to it.

The scent of a hot meal floated on the breeze. Jayson inhaled deeply, memories flooding back with the familiar smells. Not until then had he missed his home. The outside world had presented its own wonders and challenges, but nothing could compare to home.

How much longer would it remain? What destruction would Lusiradrol unleash?

He would do all he could to protect it.

"All is not as it seems."

Jayson turned to the frown on Haiberuk's face.

"They prepare for the greatest challenge of their training."

"What do they know of the threat?"

Haiberuk looked into the shelter. "That is what I wish to discuss. Come. The Council will meet soon."

While following the master into the meditation room, Jayson considered his words. The Sh'lahmar knew they faced a crisis.

Before his thoughts ran off, Jayson noticed the plates of hot food set out for him and Haiberuk. The students who had brought them practiced their invisibility, although he could find them easy enough through their effect on the flow of magic.

He sat and ate in silence. Haiberuk sat across from him with his own plate. The food drew out further memories of Jayson's childhood and training. More and more, the years peeled away with each passing moment in his home.

When they finished their midday meal, a handful of hooded figures entered wearing the crimson cloaks of the Council. Their brooches of sleeping dragons secured their cloaks.

The sight made him feel out of place without his. However, he had his brooch on him, a reminder of who he was. In that he found a connection with old faces.

Jayson recognized the shadowed visages of two of the men. He vaguely recalled the other three who had begun their special training when he was sent out. However, one of his old friends had not appeared.

That meant Galen, Breogh's charge, was still alive. The man had issues against Haiberuk that Jayson had questioned, but the master had insisted he would never betray them. Jayson had seen nothing of Galen or Breogh since leaving to follow Darius.

Rather than ask Haiberuk, he set his empty plate aside and took his place in the circle of the Council of Seven, the seven Son'tal chosen by

Haiberuk. Without Breogh, they should have been only six, but he counted seven of them including himself. The master had added another.

When Haiberuk took his place, all seven of them sat. The six robed figures removed their hoods, their eyes fixed on the master.

"We face a terrible crossroads." Haiberuk looked to each in turn before continuing. "The black dragon has discovered that her clan lives. How she learned, I can only guess, but that she has also learned of our existence in connection to her clan threatens the world."

"What of the Darklord?"

Jayson recognized the speaker as an old friend who had trained alongside him. The long jaw line and wiry frame only fit on Jerrod.

"We must not speak of that. She must not remember the truth." The tone in Haiberuk's voice silenced any objections. "If too much is revealed, she will remember the wretched power within her. Then no one will survive."

Jayson frowned at the sadness in the master's voice. Had he known something he wished not to share?

"What time have we before she finds us?"

"Days, perhaps minutes. We know not how close she was."

When Haiberuk's eyes fixed on him, Jayson swallowed. He had accepted that he led her to the hiding, but would she not have found them eventually?

"Jayson has returned to warn us and aid us in the coming war."

As fast as it crossed his face, Jayson banished the surprise. Master Haiberuk would not shame him for his accidental leading of Lusiradrol to the Sh'lahmar. Instead he turned their attention to the good of his intentions.

"I faced her in a few confrontations," Jayson said.

Surprise crossed the many faces watching him. He knew what they thought—he should not be living to tell of even one encounter. Their curiosity to know more held their tongues in check.

"The first was while aiding Darius and the chosen one when Lusiradrol had weakened them. She was also weak by the time I arrived. While defeating her was not easy, my presence helped."

He paused on a breath before continuing. "Sometime between then and my next encounter, she put more pieces together. She had what I can only guess was Darius's brooch. She demanded I tell her of it. When I didn't—" He shrugged. "—She threw me. I woke up some time later and she was gone."

"She let you live?" one of the younger members asked.

"She had her reasons." Haiberuk said.

Jayson nodded gravely. "She last confronted me as I rode here, though I'd doubt she saw it as no more than a game. Only a wind and laughter; no more."

They sat in silent contemplation. He saw the workings of their minds drawing the correct conclusion. He had told them what had happened. The rest was speculation but obvious.

"She used you." Cairdwyn's face twisted into revulsion. When he looked up at Jayson, he shook his head.

"He had no choice."

They turned to Haiberuk, who rose to his feet and proceeded to one of the sections of text on the walls. "The ancient forces cannot stay in balance forever, though they always come back to balance. We knew this day would come when the white dragon chose his day to return. Jayson acted in righteousness to protect his bearer. Lusiradrol has made the connections."

When he returned his gaze to the seven, he said, "We must strengthen the wards protecting the vault, or prophecy will reveal itself."

"What can we do against her?"

The scorn on Haiberuk's face when he turned to the speaker froze them. The room fell into a silence that would have startled any of the acolytes.

"Forgive me, Master, for my doubts." The young man dropped his head with the apology.

"We'll do what we can. If we fail, at least the white dragon is protected. We have hope."

"Then we have not failed but already have succeeded." Jayson breathed easier at the smile on the master's face from his statement. They had all vowed to give up their lives to protect the vault and aid the return of the white dragon.

"Is this no more than a distraction?" one of the others asked.

"This is quite serious," Haiberuk affirmed. "No less a threat is the Red Clan than the Darklord alone. We have sworn an oath to protect mankind from the threat they pose. We will uphold that."

Jayson rose to his feet, his purpose clear. "I am ready for whatever action you ask of us."

"I am also ready," Jerrod agreed with a smile to Jayson.

"I am ready," another said. The rest followed in turn until no one could sit aside.

When all seven of the men stood, Haiberuk bowed his head to them and led them from the meeting. He stepped out the door and stopped on the deck. With the others who lined up on either side of the master, Jayson took his place. A wave of power passed from Haiberuk. The call of the magic pulled him to this place.

The preparations would begin soon. One by one the elite guards and acolytes gathered in the square.

When a few dozen stood facing them, Haiberuk spoke. "What I ask of you is nothing less than what you have trained to do."

Although Haiberuk spoke as if holding an ordinary conversation, Jayson knew each of them heard him as if he stood next to them, no matter how far away.

"The time has come to gather at the vault. The black dragon has discovered our secret. We must secure it with our lives all parts of the day with as many as we can spare. Soon she will arrive." He paused and closed his eyes.

Jayson watched random individuals walk away. Soon a voice in his head said, *Join them at the vault. I will come later.* As commanded, he left the gathering.

Along the walk, a dark cloud crept over his mind. His heart grew heavy with the imminent battle. Despite his attempts to shake the feeling, the threat stayed at the edge of his thoughts, always reminding him of what lay ahead.

The path to the vault had been well groomed to blend into nature. To the untrained observer, it never existed. Through the trees and over a small hill, he followed the invisible trail.

At the peak, he stopped. Four guards stood watch before the height of the maw in the next hillside. Their uniforms matched those of his friends he had reacquainted with the night before, though the men on duty wore helms bearing a dragon's head over the nosepiece and dragon wings carved into the sides. Their black cloaks hung over their armor, keeping them warm in the chill of winter's approach.

Though they stood with spears at their sides, swords at their belts, and daggers hidden, they moved at blinding speeds if the need arose. No amount of weaponry would hinder their purpose—to keep out any intruders not authorized by Master Haiberuk.

Many others joined him on the hilltop, a mix of the older and younger, before he strode down. They gathered in an arc around the entrance. The guards made no motion as the others formed a protective barrier around them. Jayson could only guess that Haiberuk had contacted them.

Jayson noticed the flow of magic change when he took his position. It strengthened with each man who added his power to the ancient spells guarding the entrance. However, unlike the magic set in place by the magi of old, their powers could not hide the use of their combined magic. Their invisible barrier would call to her.

Chapter 59
16.9 pc 937

The shadow crawled through Jayson's being. Their efforts would send up a signal fire to the one they wished to protect against. Lusiradrol would find them soon enough without it, having followed him to the Sh'lahmar already. This way they fortified their defenses at the same time.

In spite of his internal reassurance, the shadow continued to creep through his mind.

Not until the forces around him twisted with a sickening menace did he realize she had traced their gathering to this. But she was not near.

Where was she?

Daring to break part of his concentration from the barrier they had erected, he reached out and discovered the truth. She had other plans. Haiberuk and the others battled her at the sanctuary.

Jayson focused on the barrier with increased intensity, unwilling to allow her to distract him. The barrier wavered as others made the discovery, most likely the younger members.

"Hold it steady!" Jayson called out. "She seeks to divide our attention."

The barrier strengthened again. He worried about the acolytes, however. Would they hold up to whatever words or magic she used to twist their thoughts?

He could only hope.

Sooner than he expected, a pillar of flame materialized on the top of the hill facing them. It vanished as quickly as it appeared, leaving her standing in its place.

She stood on the knoll, dressed in black from head to foot, an equally black cape billowing in the breeze like the wings she once possessed. The aura of nothing emanating from her left a void within the rainbow of magic. She stood as menacing as a dragon.

The barrier held when the others saw her for the first time. Jayson watched her closely, pouring forth all his effort into maintaining the barrier and setting an example for the younger members.

In a blink, Lusiradrol vanished and reappeared within feet of the invisible barrier. The smile on her black-red lips fixed on him. "So this is your secret." Her eyes scanned the arc of robed figures. "Your little friends cannot keep me out."

Jayson braced for the worst, prepared for any attack she might conjure. Instead, her smile crooked upwards with sinister mischief. "Just as the spells of Arronfel can not."

He faltered. *Calli!*

Before he could recover, she struck at their barrier. Despite the fear and worry sprouted in him, he kept his place and refocused his powers on the barrier.

It held.

Lusiradrol hissed. "If you keep me out, I will destroy them."

"You would destroy them anyway."

Her eyes narrowed and she organized the magic into something he had never felt before. It grew in scope, eating away the varied colors of magic and leaving only a void. Was this the Darklord in her?

Stand strong! he called to the others.

They increased their power to the barrier and stood their ground, although doubts sprang up in a few of the younger men. Lusiradrol could intimidate anyone who had heard only stories of her power. However, with Calli's life at stake, he fought harder to protect her from the horror the demon would unleash. He would not let the others fail.

When Lusiradrol struck, the force of her blast knocked several men to the ground. Only a few rose again on unsteady legs.

She laughed in mockery. In a flash, she attacked again, sending some of the weaker members bouncing away from the barrier.

Only a few standing held the line.

"Fools!" she cursed.

Jayson used what remained to him, but his own powers weakened with each spell she unleashed. He grew tired with the strain of holding against her.

Where was Master Haiberuk? What had she done to the others?

Lusiradrol formed another collection of power as he watched. In his heart, he knew they would fall with one more, unless reinforcements arrived in the next few seconds.

One did.

His confidence climbed at the sight of the master, who materialized behind her.

Lusiradrol whirled, her face hardening. "You! I thought you left this world." She searched around her. "Where are the others of your kind?"

Jayson knew the Majera were powerful beings created by the Light to protect the world, but the master had also taught them that the Darklord was equally powerful. One of the Majera would be no match for his complete powers. Only together could they hope to match him. but she was not yet her true self.

"They prepare for the prophecy."

"The prophecy will never be!" She let loose her final stroke at the barrier.

The force of her power shoved Jayson onto his back, the wind knocked from him. Through the spots in his vision, he made out Haiberuk's battle with her. As much as he wished to stand and help, he could not.

By the time Jayson regained sufficient alertness to rise, Lusiradrol knocked Haiberuk's containment attempts aside and strode for the opening of the vault. The four guards raised their spears. The magic of their powers surged forth in a new shield.

While she prepared to attack them, Jayson jumped at her. Together they rolled to the ground. Despite her struggles, he held fast. However, in his weakened state, she managed to escape his locking hold and throw him aside like a rag. The ground slammed against him when she flung him down.

He peered about him in a daze, noticing others recovering. Before anyone could react, Lusiradrol let loose a blow that rocked the ground beneath them. All four elite guards flew into the hillside with enough force to leave indentations in the rocky soil.

Unimpeded, she entered the vault.

Jayson crawled to his feet, determined to stop her. She had grown far more powerful since his first battle with her. He paused for a second, the spots in his vision dancing with the throbbing of his head.

When it faded, he stood straight. Haiberuk stood next to him. "Come. We've one last option."

Jayson nodded and followed his master into the dark maw, only a few others behind him. They ran through the descending passages of the old caverns, now filled with stalagmites and stalactites over their once smooth surfaces. Ancient writings covered the walls, but Jayson rushed past with a touch of magic from Haiberuk to light the way.

Through the twists and turns they followed the echoing footsteps of their attacker.

"Curse them all for this!" Her voice echoed back to them from somewhere ahead. "Awaken, my brothers and sisters!"

"Hurry!" Haiberuk sprinted ahead with no indication of tiring. "She calls them forth."

Jayson dipped into his last reserves of energy to keep pace. Ahead of them, threads of dark magic wove their way through the caverns. Would this nightmare not end?

When they reached the chamber of the sleeping dragons, he gasped. Never had he set foot inside the chamber. Over a hundred dragons must have filled the vault, red mounds of scales and wings.

Already a few of the red beasts stirred from their drowsiness. Their heads measured at least as long as a man stood tall, marked by various patterns of spikes and ridges. Reptilian eyes blinked away the millennia of slumber. The great mounds shifted and stretched weary limbs.

The Red Clan awakened before his eyes.

The others halted behind him, their presences disturbing the flow of magic barely enough to notice.

"Join me," Haiberuk said. He turned to Jayson and held out his hand.

Jayson placed his palm over the master's and turned to the next closest of the Sh'lahmar. Haiberuk pulled the power flowing through their connection to himself. What remained to him, Jayson gave up freely.

The beasts stirred further, their growls and groans reverberating in the underground chamber.

Whatever Haiberuk had planned, Jayson hoped he hurried.

As the nearest beast rose up using the claw joints of its wings, he realized the Red Clan differed from the other dragons. With powerful hind limbs and long tails, they resembled their brethren, but these were not like the other dragons.

Jayson gasped at the sight of the wyverns, the vicious creatures of nightmares, moving.

One army against another. The Majera had created dragons to defeat the Darklord, who in turn created wyverns to destroy the dragons.

The Red Clan screeched their anger.

"Rise, brothers and sisters!" Lusiradrol's triumphant voice rose over the clamor of their awakening. "Today you shall have your revenge!"

Haiberuk lifted his eyes to the roof of the cavern. A grim expression fixed on his face, his eyes focused on the stalactites, some as large as the dragons.

The cavern shook, breaking the enormous spears free. They rained down on the beasts, stabbing many in their vulnerable points on their heads and leaving them dead. However, the hardness of their scales deflected many of the missiles.

"NO!" Lusiradrol turned to them, her eyes ablaze with malice.

The cavern continued to shake beneath them. Jayson swallowed, realizing they would likely die in the attempt. He took small comfort in knowing they had diminished the population of the Darklord's servants.

Lusiradrol wobbled amid the pounding of rock collapsing around her. In a flash, one of the wyverns ducked down and she jumped aboard its neck.

Together they rushed the Sh'lahmar.

Jayson winced at the wave of red bodies racing at them. However, Haiberuk stood his ground, still focused on pulling down whatever he could to pummel the beasts.

The one racing bearing down on them with Lusiradrol roared its hatred and let loose with a breath of flame. Before they could duck away, Haiberuk deflected the fire upwards.

Screaming at the defeat, Lusiradrol drove the beast to attack.

At the last second, Jayson and the others let go and ducked away. He rolled into a pile of rocks, slamming his head into a boulder. His vision scattered, though he thought he caught sight of the dragon running through the master.

When they had passed, Haiberuk stood in the same place.

The last vision he caught as a dream. One by one the wyverns rushed out of their hibernation.

The fight drained from him with the realization that he had failed. The prophecy would not be fulfilled as it had been stated.

Somewhere in his dream Master Haiberuk stood over him and smiled. *Trust in yourself, child. You are the last.*

The image faded. As unconsciousness threatened him, Jayson reached out for reassurance. In a distant part of his mind, he made contact. Only when he knew she was safe did he give up the struggle.

Calli...

To be continued in Book 2: *Dragon Legends*

About the Author

Melanie Nilles grew up on a western North Dakota cattle ranch and farm. Along with her interest in horses, she always had a fascination with science fiction and fantasy. After high school, she continued her education and graduated from college with a bachelor's degree in Business Administration.

She currently resides in central North Dakota with her husband and kids. In her spare time, she enjoys training her horses for dressage and hunter or just riding for pleasure. Her published works include the Legend of the White Dragon series and Dark Angel. She continues to write with a passion for science fiction and fantasy. For updates and other information, visit her website at www.melanienilles.com.

Appendix A
Basics About Gairdra

Cavatar: Cavatar is divided into five provinces that form a confederation joined under one ruler, a king. However, the Advisory Council to the King of Cavatar is composed of provincial representatives, each with equal voice of the laws over their lands. Since the Isolders are the heirs to the leadership position and live in unrepresented territory, they have no binding loyalty to any one province. The white horse is the symbol of Rivonia. Aric Isolder adopted its use in the family crest when he formed an alliance with Rivonia, the enemy from across the Darnasian Sea. The five stars represent the five provinces of Cavatar.

Continents: Three of the five continents are in close proximity and are also the largest land masses. In order of size, from largest to smallest, they are Ayrule, Rivonia, and Voshtrau. The two smaller continents of Lotar and Caprion are more comparable to large islands. On Ayrule, the largest kingdom is Cavatar, which is actually a confederation of provincial governments under one central leader. Rivonia is named after the people who dominate in power—the Rivon—although the Caveshan Plains make up seventy percent of its territory and are named after the tribes that control the area. The majority of Voshtrau's territory is inhabitable as dry wastelands (Known as Amril Nos).

Dragon Wars: This is the time starting when the Red Clan was created to when they were put to sleep. The dragons were the first army formed by either side to defend the claims of their masters over control of Gairdra.

Linfrathâr: The name of the fortress means "mountain city". It was one of the domains of the Ancients before their Exodus to the three islands they now call home. The five-level city is located in the valley of Arronfel, which is hidden by an illusionary spell to keep out enemies. That magic does not extend beyond the mountain peaks around it.

Lumathir: The word Lumathir is a misspelled combination of the Gairdran words *lûmea*, meaning "light", and *m'athêrred*, meaning "children". Their order of priestesses began around the end of the dragon wars, a few hundred years before the founding of the Sh'lahmar. While Sh'lahmar guards are also considered *m'athêrred rî Lûmea*, or "children of the Light", they are generally not referred to by the word Lumathir.

Lusiradrol: The name Lusiradrol was given by the mage Makleor shortly after the black dragon was exiled to human form. It is derived from the words for black, *lusif*, and the word for heart, *drolasa*. She liked the new name, which was intended as a curse, and abandoned her self-given dragon name of Nefarthissen.

Moon cycle: The time it takes for the moon to make one full cycle of faces. It is equal to 26 days. A year, *annul* in Gairdran, consists of almost 14 full cycles. The new year starts on the spring equinox, which usually cuts the last cycle of the previous year short by one to two days. The new year does not always begin on the same moon phase but every cycle within that year will.

Setheadroc: Over 937 years before the start of the current timeline, in the days after peace was formed among the warring states of Ayrule, the Council of Laerenthal was formed. From the leaders of all the torn lands, they chose a new leader under which they could unite. His name was Isolder. His heirs would eventually claim his name to identify them as the heirs of the kingdom. Thus, the kingdom of Frîmor was formed. When Rivon forces invaded in pc (post confederation) 386 in ships full of men and horses, they were driven back by the forces of King Damien Isolder of Frîmor. After twenty-three years of various warfare and Damian's death, his son Aric formed an alliance with the sovereign of Rivonia. In light of that agreement, a new name was given to the kingdom. Cavatar is a combination of the Rivon words meaning "honor" and "peace". The palace was designed by Rivon architects in honor of the peace accord.

Sh'lahmar: Over the thousands of years since they were established, the Sh'lahmar have guarded the vault in which the Red Clan slept under Makleor's spell. The full title of *Shinna Lahamar* was slurred and condensed into its current form. The original meaning of "guardian of the secret" was rarely used in its full form of *shinna rî atlahamar* before becoming the shortened title of *Shinna Lahamar* (translated word for word as "Guard Secret" but meaning the same as the full description).

Son'Tal: A higher order of Sh'lahmar was established whose duties were kept secret from the others. The sontheniel talri or "protector elite" whose existence remained unknown, carried out the same duties as the ordinary guardians while living in the home of the Sh'lahmar. However, on the rare occasion that a Sh'lahmar could not morally carry out his duty or left the guard to pursue a new life, a Son'tal Sh'lahmar was secretly assigned by Master Haiberuk to the man for the rest of his days to be sure he never divulged a hint of the vault or its location.

Song of Llyra: In the early days after peace with Rivonia, Makleor had written much of the history of the world in the tome he left in the library of Cavatar. The stories were known to many of the people, rulers as well as commoners. Naturally, bards looked to the tales as ways to entertain people. The Song of Llyra was written around pc 237 for the princess Llyra Isolder as a gift for her thirteenth birthday. The full story recounts the exploits of a brave warrior of the First Race who lived in the time after the dragons disappeared but before Makleor defeated all the demons that roamed the world. Not until generations later did the politics change and access to the library was limited. By then, the bards had found newer stories to use for songs and plays.

Translations

Nâlasa fer enthander — From the tongue of the Majera meaning "my life in your service."

Ehtashe mi, Nayavi — Means "Forgive me, Nayavi." It is a thought stated in Tyrkam's native tongue.

Appendix B
Dragons

Dragons of Light

The true dragons were made by the Majera to aid in their battle against the Darklord and can be considered "Dragons of Light". Of these, two kinds developed, the firedrakes and the waterdrakes. Both were given potent magic and great wisdom and most often speak in rhyme and riddles.

All dragons have scales harder than diamonds that cannot be penetrated by any weapon. They shed their scales as new ones grow to replace smaller, older scales. Because these dragons grow throughout their entire lives, they shed various scales at different times. The First Race of humans discovered that the scales contain residual magic from the dragons and figured a method to grind them for use in the metal of their weapons and armor.

Some of the oldest dragons have grown to the size of large hills. Their scales would be large enough to use as shields.

Dragons are immortal, barring injury, and are immune to all illness. However, they can be killed. Like any being, breaking their neck will end their lives.

The only means to slay any dragon is to deliver a thrust into the brain. Only two ways to do this are known and one of those, by a spike through the back of the throat can only be carried out when a dragon open's its jaws. The only place on the outside of a dragon where the brain is vulnerable is a soft spot on each side of the head. These cover the hearing organs and catch the vibrations of sound in the air. Usually a dragon must be sleeping to get close enough to slay it by this method.

Dragons command the most powerful of any magic except the Majera. Because of this, they cannot be killed by magic.

They do not possess the organs to vocalize words. However, they are intelligent enough to understand speech. The first dragons quickly learned to communicate using a magical means that has come to be known as mindspeech, whereby one projects their thoughts so the intended recipient hears them.

Some differences do exist between the two types of dragons.

Firedrakes

Firedrakes were the first kind of dragon created. With fire as their main weapon, they need to consume certain ores on occasion to maintain the chemical reaction. For this reason they are fond of the mountains or rocky areas..

The high cliffs of the mountains also provided protection for the nesting matriarchs, or breeding females, before the Second Realm came to be.. They may have up to three matriarchs, usually two green or light blue and one gold. Although this can vary, at least one is always gold. Female firedrakes reach breeding age around a hundred years, males at around seventy. The other females help to incubate the eggs and guard them or bring food for the matriarchs and any new hatchlings.

Firedrakes range in color from gold to a deep blue. Any color in the blue spectrum ranging from less than deep blue to an almost yellow-green are a mix of the two primary colors and may be either male or female. True blue or dark blue dragons are always male, gold dragons are all female, and green or lighter blue dragons are of equal gender. Gold is a rare color as it can only mix with the others and gold dragons always have smooth scales. Green and blue are the most common dragon colors with the texture of their scales ranging from very rough and spiked to almost smooth.

Waterdrakes

Waterdrakes may also be known as sea dragons or the Water Clan. They are well adapted to life in the sea. Although they can stay underwater for long periods of time, they must return to the surface for air. They have no wings for flying, and claws of their feet are spaced wider than a firedrake with a thin membrane between the toes. Their bodies are long and sinuous with a fin that runs down their dorsal side starting at their head. Because they swim in an undulating motion, like giant eels, they have often been regarded as sea serpents.

Since they live in water, the water clan does not use fire as their primary weapon. Instead, they can let loose electrical discharges of varying strengths. However, outside of the water, they find that it is more effective to command the weather into a storm.

Waterdrakes are all the same color, a dark blue dorsal with a lighter belly as camouflage within deep water.

Before all the female waterdrakes were slain, they mated and incubated their eggs on dry land. Like the firedrakes, only certain matriarchs mated while other females provided support and the males provided protection.

All the seaports of the Ancients had a wide area of beach to allow the waterdrakes to come to land. When the females laid their eggs, a designated group of caretakers would help care for them until hatching.

Dragons of Darkness

The Red Clan

The dragons known as the Red Clan are related to the firedrakes and are also classified as firedrakes but are not usually referred tocalled by that name.

The Red Clan was created by the Darklord. He commanded his demons to steal eight eggs from the firedrakes. He then took the eggs and immersed them in the dark forces, which mutated the embryos inside. They hatched red, and forelimbs that were separate from the wings on the Dragons of Light, or true dragons, had merged with the wings so that a three-fingered claw appeared on the fore of the wings. The only separate limbs are the hind limbs, which had grown thicker in the mutation.

Because the true dragons consider the Red Clan an abomination, they are not called "dragons" by anyone except their master and his minions. Others refer to them as the Red Clan or as wyverns, which is a slur they will not tolerate.

The Red Clan are as immortal as the true dragons. However, the Darklord took away a level of intelligence and lessened their magic. Fearing the possibility that the Red Clan would not stay loyal to him, he wished to insure ensure that they could not overpower him as the true dragons had shown they could do in several confrontations.

The Red Clan mature faster than true dragons but reach a peak size around fifteen to seventeen years of age that is smaller than the true dragons. By two years of age, they can take down a horse with ease. By twelve years, they can breed, although only one female breeds. That female becomes known as the queen. Normally the queen lays a clutch of eggs once every eight to twelve moon cycles. Eggs in a clutch usually number five to eight.

Due to the violent nature of the Red Clan and the status of the queen, competition is fierce among breeding females for dominance. While the other females settle to serving their queen, occasional fights will arise when one wishes to challenge the current queen.

Most of the Red Clan are female. Males are rare and usually for breeding purposes only. The Red Clan has one breeding female, known as the queen. Normally the queen lays a clutch of eggs once every eight to twelve moon cycles. Eggs in a clutch usually number five to eight.

Drakin (Drake Kin)

The drakin are not dragons but winged reptiles. They reside in what is known as the Second Realm, or Eyr Droc by the dragons who took up residenceresiding there, to escape the Second Race of humans when they turned on them. That is the place of the drakins' origination.

Drakin earned their name because of how similar they appeartheir similarity to the dragons, or more accurately, the Red Clan. They look like they could be drake kin, thus the source of their name for their kind.. They have two hind limbs, long tails, and wings but no separate forelimbs and are all a shade of green that allows them to hide among the foliage of trees. Their scales are like those of reptiles, however, and almost more of a heavy skin.

That is where the similarity ends. Where Dragons have sharp, tearing teeth for ripping meat, Drakin have jaws full of flat, grinding teeth. Drakin primarily eat insects and berries and sometimes... Sometimes they eat but also enjoy occasional soft fruits. They also are not very intelligent and have a short lifespan of only about thirty years.

Drakin have none of the cares of the dragons. They would rather play all day, chasing each other through intricate acrobatics.

Ever since the Unnamed Majera gave them the ability of mindspeech, their only magical skill, they enjoy speaking. They can, however, talk non-stop for hours, which is likely because drakin easily get sidetracked when telling stories. Those who know them have learned that they must interrupt a drakin in order to keep it on the same subject.

Some of the dragons mentioned in the series

Anthârgal - green male; offspring of Sethirngal; oldest of younger drakes—those not on the council.
Darmentôs - green-blue male, moderately rough scales; offspring of Darmîndren.
Darmîndren* - dark blue male.
Dethanea* - gold female; gave up matriarchal duties to younger females.
Fessingal - green male, rough scales; offspring of Anthârgal.
Frendal* - topaz male, rough scales.
Gilthiel - white dragon.
Jêrafînas - blue female.
Rathenefîr* - dark blue male, brother of Darmîndren.
Sâremath - gold-green female.
Sethirngal* - green dragon; oldest of all dragons; Istaria's primary teacher.

Lusiradrol - black dragon in human form.
Fresthan - male red wyvern.

*indicates Elder Drakes

Printed in the United States
115720LV00002B/19-21/P